JILL SHELDON

REVENGE IS SWEET

Enquiries to:
Robinson Publishing Ltd
7 Kensington Church Court
London W8 4SP

First published in the UK by Scarlet, 1997

A copy of the British Library Cataloguing in
Publication data is available from the British Library

ISBN 1-85487-957-X

Printed and bound in the EC

10 9 8 7 6 5 4 3 2 1

To Sue Curran. Thanks for the kick start!

PROLOGUE

Chloe Walker slowed her steps. Oh, she'd be late for summer school again, but presented with a batch of her famous raisin oatmeal cookies Mr Duncan would forget all about detention. She hoped.

Almost there. She slowed even more. Her dawdling had nothing to do with laziness. She knew there wasn't a soul in the tiny mountain community of Heather Glen who would consider her lazy, no matter how chunky she was. Hadn't she just spent her entire free Sunday after church helping clean St Patrick's Retirement Home because they couldn't afford to hire someone? Even though it had been her fourteenth birthday?

She smiled, coming to a stop in front of *her* place. *Homebaked*. Okay, it wasn't hers. Not yet. But as her mouth watered over the delicious smell coming out of the window she promised herself that someday it would be.

She watched the hustle and bustle through the windows of the small café and sighed with pleasure, knowing that she looked right at her future. She loved this town, absolutely loved this place, and knew if she worked hard enough she could do it. She could make this place hers.

A shadow crossed behind her and she turned. Her gaze collided with a brilliant blue one. For an instant she could do nothing but blink in stunned surprise as the cold fury settled on her. But she recognized the boy, if not the reason for the chilling rage. Thomas McGuirre. Her older sister Deanna's latest conquest. The boy her father wanted out of town – badly.

Jet-black hair settled on his threadbare collar. Patrician features hardened on a beautiful face that belonged on an artist's canvas. Thin, gangly limbs on a body too long for itself. He couldn't have been more than two years her senior, yet the hard-earned knowledge in his gaze made him seem much older.

Chloe had known him all her life, and yet they'd never once exchanged words. As the town darling, and the daughter of the beloved mayor, everyone knew and liked her, but she couldn't say the same for Thomas McGuirre. He had a bad-boy reputation that made every parent of a teenage girl nervous, yet to Chloe's knowledge he'd done nothing to deserve his label of dangerous and uncooperative – except to be the son of a slippery, manipulative con man. Secretly, she thought her father unreasonable in his hatred of him, but didn't quite dare say so.

Her sister had slept with Thomas in the woods behind the hardware store, and Chloe could only wonder at what exactly that meant. Images, forbidden, wicked and unknown, flashed through her mind. Trees, wind and bare skin. A secret purling from deep within confused her, but became easy to shove aside. Still, she couldn't speak to him. Known for her chatterbox ways, it wasn't often she was rendered speechless, and yet Thomas seemed to do it easily enough with just a look. He had since they'd been kids. Impulsive as always, she made the rash decision to change that, starting this instant.

'Hi.' She made herself smile – the same smile that had turned Johnny Myers upside down just yesterday.

He didn't return it. In fact, he turned and walked away.

Chloe stared in surprise. No one had ever snubbed her so outright. Her popularity had not gone to her head in the slightest, yet it scraped at her blooming femininity that until now she hadn't even been able get him to so much as glance at her. 'I said, hi,' she called out to his quickly moving form.

He kept walking.

'Got a thing against being friendly?' She put her hands on her hips when he slowly turned back to her.

Her next retort died on her lips. For the first time she realized he shouldered a backpack. He carried a sleeping bag. And alongside his tight, angry jaw was a growing, ugly purplish bruise. Her heart constricted and a lump the size of the muffin she'd gobbled down earlier stuck in her throat as the rumors flew back.

His father beat him. Obviously Thomas had just had another run-in with his father's fists. Coming from a home where the harshest treatment she received was a stern word, it was hard for her to comprehend.

Taking a shaky breath, she let her hands drop to her sides. 'I'm sorry,' she said quietly into the face of his palatable wrath. 'I didn't mean to be anything but friendly.'

'Friendly.' He said the word as if it were foreign. He let out a short, cold laugh that for some reason tore at her and shook his head. 'Obviously your father doesn't know you're talking to me.' Without another word, he turned on his heel. His worn backpack hung between his wide but bony shoulders.

'You're leaving.' She knew it, could feel it. And it saddened her terribly. In a town of less than two thousand people, everyone knew everyone's business. And that collective everyone had decided, no matter what Thomas McGuirre said or did, that he was just like his no-good, gambling, conning father. It didn't make sense and it certainly wasn't fair, but it remained so. She felt an overwhelming shame at her father's part in his being run out of town.

She was a girl with a soft heart and a giving soul, and it made her ache for him. She couldn't let it go. He hadn't slowed and she had to run to catch up with those long legs of his. They kept moving, and in less than two minutes they were in the woods, surrounded by towering pines that masked the bright sun. Water from the creek crashed over rocks, hiding the noise of the town only several hundred yards away. 'Where are you going?' she asked, already breathless.

Still he didn't slow. 'Back off.'

Chloe rarely did as she was told. And, as always,

4

the need to right wrongs and fix problems overcame her, no matter what the cost.

'Don't run away.'

He scoffed, said nothing, and kept going.

'People will see the real you, Thomas, if you'll just give them a chance,' she huffed, still running along-side of him, dry twigs crunching beneath her feet.

He did stop then, and gave her a long, hard look. 'You know nothing about the real me.'

What was it about him that so struck at her heart? His beautiful face with the eyes hardened beyond their years? The bruises she couldn't see but could sense?

'You live in a dream world, so don't even try to understand this.' This time, when he walked, he tailored his steps to hers.

'If you'd just try a little harder to fit in, people would stop comparing you to your father. I know it.'

'Do you really think I give a damn what everyone else thinks?'

She took a good look at him. His eyes could have been ice as they bored into her. She'd never experienced such hatred. Or such blazing, stabbing, haunting pain.

'Do you?' he asked again, tilting his head. The sun glinted off his dark hair, shading his face. He looked mean, but, even as young as she was, she knew it was merely a defense.

'No,' she whispered, absorbing his hurt as her own. It was always that way for her; she always seemed to feel things deeper than others. And Thomas's agony nearly brought her to her knees.

'Good guess.' He walked away.

He had to. Thomas McGuirre didn't have time for dreams or pudgy little girls who looked at him with their hearts in their eyes. It took every second of his day and every ounce of strength he had just to survive. With his mother long gone and his father the local town scum, Thomas had long ago abandoned the hope of someone rescuing him from the pathetic squalor in which he lived. He'd learned the hard way that people expected him to be just like his old man.

Despite everything, for years Thomas had allowed himself to believe in fairy tales. Dreams do come true, he'd convince himself as he lay huddled beneath his bed, hoping to escape his father's notice. Someone would save him. Someone would love him.

By the time he'd been old enough to know not everyone had a father who gambled their every penny and beat the living daylights out of their kid for needing food, Thomas no longer believed in love or dreams. And he didn't want to be rescued by anyone in Heather Glen.

He'd do it himself. And when he'd accomplished that, he'd come back. He'd come back and get his revenge on a town that had looked the other way one too many times.

CHAPTER 1

Fifteen years later . . .

The little shiver of thrill never changed, and it was still just as strong now as it had been five years ago, when she'd bought the place. Unlocking the door to *Homebaked*, Chloe stepped in, and for a minute just stood there, ignoring the snow that blew in around her, ignoring, too, her icy hands since she'd lost her gloves again.

With more than a little satisfaction, and a silly grin that made her look sixteen instead of nearly thirty, she spun into the room. Dawn hadn't yet broken and her assistant cook hadn't arrived. Chairs were still tipped toward the tables. But in less than an hour the place would be brimming over with breakfast customers, the smell of coffee would fill the air, and so would the laughter, the quiet conversations, the occasional shout of greeting. For now, silence prevailed.

She took in a deep breath, but couldn't contain her small, triumphant laugh. All hers. Oh, she was mortgaged to the gills, and she had never faced so many challenges in her life. But she loved every second of it.

7

Moving forward, she flipped on the heater and the lights, hit the radio and put on an apron. She piled her hair on her head. Glamor, definitely not. And certainly not the life the mayor's daughter had been expected to lead. But it was the life she wanted.

'A bit early for you, girl, ain't it?'

Chloe turned at the crackling old voice, her smile still firmly in place. 'Have to keep you on your toes, now, don't I?'

Augustine smiled, showing the wide gap between her two front teeth. 'Good to see someone's still the same around this town, sassy or not.'

The comment put the first real cloud on Chloe's good mood. She knew exactly what Augustine referred to. The rumor that Sierra Rivers, a huge resort conglomerate, had just decided that Heather Glen was perfect for its next resort ran rampant. Instead of the expected dismay, the entire community of Heather Glen seemed ecstatic. Hoping to make a mint, many had started to gobble up the available land around town, planning to sell it at an escalated price to the corporation. Her father and her sister had invested alarming amounts of money, catching the greedy fever.

The entire business made Chloe nervous.

True, the dwindling economy in their small town made good business difficult. Too far off the highway, and too far from the neighboring Mammoth Lakes, they didn't pick up much tourist traffic. Everyone was hurting. A resort would revive the scenic old mining town. But Chloe hated to see

8

many of her friends and family, already hard pressed for cash, spending what they didn't have on land that would be worthless if the resort didn't come through. She wished she knew who was behind the rumors, and how she could find out if they were true.

Augustine slapped the daily newspaper on the counter, a look of disgust crossing her old wrinkled face. The bold headline blared up at them. HEATHER GLEN SELECTED LATEST SPOT FOR CLASSY SIERRA RIVERS RESORT. OUR TOWN IS SAVED! She snorted indelicately and slanted Chloe a narrow glance. 'You've got a head on those shoulders. You've kept out of it, I hope?'

'Yes.' Chloe sighed, tucking a long unruly strand of hair into place as she moved towards the kitchen. Usually cheerful to a fault, she couldn't explain her pessimism over this venture that would only be good for their economy. 'I've not had much choice.'

'Not much choice, huh? That's pretty funny, coming from you.' The older woman laughed heartily, which prompted a coughing fit. When she straightened and saw Chloe's irritation, she laughed again. 'Honey,' she managed in that rough voice, 'you know perfectly well you do exactly what you want, regardless of the choices. You define the words "single-minded" and "stubborn." You have since you could talk.'

Chloe had to smile. 'I meant money-wise. I couldn't possibly have managed to invest. Not when I'm still shelling out to Mr Thorton on the first of each month.'

'He still bothering you about making your rent?' Augustine scowled. 'Some nerve, that man. Especially since you've been giving every spare cent and minute you've got trying to keep the Teen Hood open. Without you those kids would have no place to go after school except to make trouble – including his own three hellions.'

'I think he'd rather I pay him on time.' In the kitchen she pulled out the ingredients for her famous blueberry muffins and popped her head over the counter. 'And I can't say I blame him for that. I never mean to be late; it just happens. I always seem to take from one pot to pay the other, thinking it'll all work out. One of these days I'll get better organized financially.'

Augustine laughed again. 'Organized? *You?* That I'll have to see.' She tied an apron over her reed-thin waist. 'Stay out of that dough, now.'

Chloe closed her mouth around a huge bite and smiled guiltily. *Delicious.* Augustine just shook her head. Chloe swallowed and just managed to resist popping another spoonful into her watering mouth.

In the past years she'd lost her baby fat, but even so she continuously struggled to be good. She combated her slow metabolism with rigid exercises, that she hated, and a will power enforced by the fact she simply refused to buy clothes in a bigger size. Thankfully, she had yet to go naked. But she still loved to eat. Busying her hands instead of her mouth, she let herself be soothed by her deep love of cooking and the joy it brought her.

Augustine might not believe it, but when she thought about her money situation too much it made her nervous. If something happened and she lost *Homebaked*, she'd . . . wither away. Yet she couldn't seem to help herself from becoming involved in all the other projects that took up her time. The troubled teens center, teaching illiterate women to read, saving the ocean. Facts were facts, and she had to face them.

Chloe loved a good cause. But it was breaking her.

Augustine's work-roughened hand settled on her shoulder, startling her. 'I wish I could help, honey. I know how much you worry about that second loan on *Homebaked*, and I hate like hell that you had to take it. You know I'd give you my last dollar to help pay it off. If I had one.'

'I'll be fine,' Chloe said with bright cheer, moving through to the dining room to prepare for opening. She looked around at her wonderful surroundings. Blue and white dominated the lovely room. Wooden tables and chairs matched the shelves along the walls, filled to brimming with assorted candles, books, and her personal collection of cookie jars. She loved this place beyond reason, and it didn't take a shrink to tell her why.

She'd gotten it all by herself, completely without the considerable influence of her father, the mayor. Her sister, the genius biochemist, hadn't had a say either. Even her mother, the city's only orthodontist, had managed to stay out of it, though she knew that none of them felt she'd quite lived up to their standards.

Homebaked was all hers. Except for her business loans and the new investor she'd been forced to take on. But unflagging hope had always been her strong point, and it stuck with her now. It would get her through.

She knew that her family had all wished for a more spectacular career path for her, knew too that they considered her nothing more than a glorified cook. But they loved her, and that was good enough for Chloe. She loved them too. But she also absolutely loved *Homebaked*, and she refused to lose it, no matter what. No matter that in three days she had a business meeting with her new investor, where she'd be expected to produce a five-year plan for getting herself out of the red and firmly into the black. She'd handle it.

Within a few short minutes she could no longer dwell on it. Her place had filled with her usual morning customers. The delicious aroma of breakfast wafted over them and the contented murmur of pleased voices lulled her. Lana, her assistant cook had called in sick, so Chloe hustled about to fill the void. On her way back to the kitchen she paused to ring up Mellie's bill. Mellie was her eighty-year-old neighbor, who never failed to show up for her bagel and coffee.

Slowly, meticulously, Mellie pulled out her coin purse and started counting pennies. Her hands shook faintly with age, making Chloe's heart twist. Gently she laid a hand on the other woman's. 'It's on me today, Mellie.'

One would have thought Chloe had given Mellie a pot of gold. Gratitude, disbelief. *Relief.* 'Bless you, Chloe.'

Chloe caught Augustine's eye. Resigned, her employee and friend shook her head and mouthed the words, 'You can't afford that either!'

Embarrassed to have been caught, Chloe lifted her shoulders and turned away, unable to face Mellie's sweet smile and Augustine's bittersweet one.

Then she froze.

Chloe hadn't been rendered speechless in so long she couldn't be blamed for getting a little annoyed at finding herself in that predicament now as she locked eyes with a piece of her past.

Thomas McGuirre.

Those mesmerizing baby blues of his hadn't changed one bit, though the man had. Jet-black hair still curled down nearly to his shoulders, but this time the collar looked as if it had come from the finest store in Italy, not the second-hand one down the street. So did his charcoal suit, which had obviously been made just for him. There were lines on that hauntingly beautiful face now, rendering him even more masculine if possible. And that body, the one that had once been too scrawny and awkward for its own good, had since filled out. Perfectly.

Thomas didn't so much as blink at her as he nodded curtly and held out his bill. Not one little nuance to tell her he recognized her as painfully as she recognized him. And, as it had so many years ago, his absolute indifference rankled. So he was gorgeous. So what? He also exuded a toughness, danger, an edge she didn't quite understand and never had. But her curiosity, the very same thing that her mother had repeatedly warned her would be the death of her yet, reared its eager head.

At least he waited until Mellie had wandered away before saying, 'Still a bleeding heart, Chloe? Or should I say, *Slim*?'

He did remember her.

'Maybe.' She took his money, annoyed that her fingers fumbled nervously on the register's keys. What was the matter with her? She'd seen lots of good-looking men before. *Millions*. 'You're back,' she said, then inwardly winced at the stupid comment.

'So it seems.' He reached for his change. Their fingers brushed together. An electrical current ran past her fingers up her arm, straight to her jittery stomach, but he didn't seem to notice.

'Thank you,' he said formally as he pocketed the coins. His voice hadn't changed. Deep, rough and slightly cynical. As if everything were the greatest joke. Only he didn't smile.

He lifted his cold, unforgiving gaze again and Chloe became uneasily aware of two things. One, his icy eyes didn't quite manage to hide that compelling mix of scorching anger and unbelievable pain, and two, he could still stop her heart with just a look.

'Are you just . . .?' Her tongue tripped inside her mouth. She'd been about to stick her foot in it and ask him if he was visiting. But he had no family left,

14

not since his father had gone to jail years ago over some scam that had robbed some of the town seniors of their savings. She doubted he had a single friend left in the entire town. 'Are you here on holiday?' she asked instead, awkwardly.

One dark brow raised. 'In Heather Glen?' His mouth quirked, but the humor didn't reach his eyes. 'No, I'm not on vacation. But I have to say I'm disappointed in the town gossip line if you haven't heard.'

'Heard what?'

Those lips curved slightly, ironically. 'I've moved back.' Negligently he leaned against the counter, crossing his leather-shod feet. *Casual*, said the stance. *Attitude* screamed the expression.

'Moved back?' she repeated.

'Not much has changed, I've found. You're still trying to save the world, and your father's still the mayor.'

She felt certain he considered the former to be a deep personality fault, and the latter a misfortune for the entire town. Her father wouldn't be thrilled to see Thomas McGuirre; that was certain. He had a nasty habit of holding a grudge.

'And your sister. She's on her third husband.'

Oh, yes. He'd slept with Deanna. Well, to be fair, so had just about every male within the city limits, and then some. Her sister seemed to have this promiscuous streak that everyone attributed to her genius. 'Last time I checked.'

A sound that might have been a laugh escaped him,

and it startled her. It sounded rusty, as if he wasn't used to finding amusement. She wondered what it would be like to see him let go, to hear him roar with genuine laughter. She bet it would soften that hard, dangerous-looking face, making it even more attractive. 'Why did you come back?' she asked, remembering how embittered he'd been when he'd left.

'Business.'

'Opening a shop?'

'No.'

Obviously he had no intentions of elaborating, but Chloe felt obligated to fill him in. 'Heather Glen isn't as prosperous as you might remember. Things have changed drastically. The lumber mill closed up after their last fight with the US Department of Forestry. Almost half the population had to leave to find work. I doubt you'll find any truly successful business here.'

He leaned close and those sharp eyes honed right in on her, all signs of merriment gone. 'Still giving free friendly advice? Or is that a not too subtle invitation to leave?'

It was a forcible reminder of the last time she'd seen him, the first and only time they'd spoken before. Back then she'd asked him to give people a chance. He hadn't listened then and she doubted he'd listen now, but she didn't take offense at his harsh tone. He'd probably deny it, but Thomas McGuirre seemed to sport a sensitive side, and, given how he'd grown up, it was no wonder. But one look at his hard face and she knew compassion would get her nowhere, though she was itching to give it. Poker-faced, she said, 'Are you kidding? I never kick out a paying customer.'

He stared at her, then slowly relaxed. 'Smart move. I tip good.'

'Well, then, please come back as often as you like.'

'You might be sorry you said that.'

That she could believe. The din around them started to dull, as the rush time came to a close. Still, she felt people staring at them. Or rather, *at him*. Chloe was sure he made quite a picture; all that cold, dangerous, hard attitude, dressed to the nines, leaning on her counter as if he didn't have a care in the world.

'It's been a long time,' she said. 'What have you been doing with yourself?'

'You mean since I ran out of here with my tail between my legs?' Again, that half-mocking stare. And the flicker of rage that simmered just beneath his surface – the one that for some reason made her want to reach for him.

The need to soothe, assuage his anger didn't surprise her; she felt it for every cause she took on. But the strong, pulling attraction did. She smiled at him, hoping he'd return it.

He didn't.

Stretching her hand out to pat his arm was second nature to her. She meant only to ease the hurt she could sense but not see. As her hand brushed against tensed, coiled muscles he jerked his arm back, as though she'd burned him.

17

Looking into those unforgiving eyes, she took a step back, mentally and physically. She neither saw nor sensed hurt now, just a carefully blank expression. No feelings, no emotions. Yet she knew she hadn't imagined it.

'You didn't run out of town with your tail between your legs. You went proudly and sure of yourself,' she said gently, remembering that part very well. 'I can't imagine you really feel that way.'

'Don't even try to imagine how I feel about anything,' he said in a low, controlled voice. 'We're not kids anymore.'

'No, we're not,' she said, the questions flying through her mind. Why did he hold onto his control like a trophy? Why did he hate to be touched? And why, oh, why, had he given up on the simple joy of life? 'You had your reasons for leaving, and I'm sure they seemed good to you at the time.'

When she smiled freely, a little hopefully, Thomas cleared his throat and looked away. What the hell was he doing? He'd come here with one purpose. To have his well-planned revenge against a town that had taken his happiness, his innocence. Already he'd penetrated many of the remaining struggling businesses and exploited their weaknesses to his advantage – all owned by people who had shunned him, ridiculed him, tried to mold him into being like his father.

They hadn't succeeded, but Thomas wanted retribution all the same. For years, especially in the lean times, he'd dreamed of little else. It had been pathetically easy to start that rumor about the resort moving in, especially since he happened to own the gigantic corporation known as Sierra Rivers. He'd come to *Homebaked* this morning to see for himself what he'd invested in just last week, when he'd given the owner a second loan on the place. He'd come to search for *Homebaked*'s weaknesses, so he could exploit them, then dive in for the kill.

One more business down.

But being face to face with his victim didn't give him the satisfaction he'd craved. In fact, it made him feel a little sick. He didn't know what he'd expected but it hadn't been Chloe Walker. Last time he'd seen her, she'd been a nosy fat kid who'd worn glasses thick enough to sink a ship. Well, she'd lost her excess weight and gained subtle curves in all the right places. The glasses were gone and he'd never seen eyes so green, nor hair so sensuously brunette.

He'd wanted to hurt her. He'd set out to do so. But now, staring at the woman whom he remembered as being only kind, it didn't seem quite so easy. Especially after witnessing her giving that old woman a free meal ticket. He remembered all too well what it was like to need, to be desperate, and watching her understand that need had nearly brought him to his knees with unwanted memories.

He wanted to destroy and conquer, dammit. Instead, he lounged here flirting with that painful reminder of his past, with no regard to the years of sweat and hard work it had taken him to get here.

Frowning, he straightened. Not once in all this

time, in all these years, had he let his concentration slip. To find it doing so now unsettled him. So close, he was so very close to executing his plan to bring down Heather Glen. Nothing would get in his way.

Not even this glowing green-eyed beauty, whose very smile could light up the darkest night.

Absolutely not.

Moving aside so one of her employees, an older waitress with a huge gap in her front teeth, could ring up a customer's bill, she asked him, 'So what do you do for fun?'

'Fun?' He blinked away the dark thoughts and the desperate, haunting need for revenge.

'Yeah, fun.' Chloe grinned a little impishly and tugged on his lapel, careful not to actually touch him. 'Don't tell me that since you've put on a tie you've forgotten what that is?'

She was teasing him, he realized with some surprise, even mocking his clothes – though she'd managed to do so while respecting his need for distance. Thomas had hundreds of employees – more if he counted all his subsidiaries – and many acquaintances. Not one of them would have dared.

'I'll have to assume you have forgotten,' she said with an exaggerated sigh, pushing back a strand of wayward hair with an impatient gesture that reminded him of the girl she'd once been.

'I'm perfectly capable of having fun,' he found himself saying in self-defense. 'I just doubt that anything Heather Glen has to offer could be called such.'

'Well, it might not exactly be what you're looking

for,' she admitted, 'but there is a town meeting tonight. You might find it interesting – especially if you're back for good.'

'No one said anything about being back for *good*.'

Her eyes narrowed speculatively, as if she couldn't figure out if he was kidding or not. Evidently she decided he was, because she gave him another one of those easy smiles that made it increasingly difficult to look her in the eyes.

'Well, if your mission here is business,' she quipped, 'you won't find a better place. Everyone will be there, snow or shine.'

'Including your father?' he asked with renewed interest. He couldn't wait until he could personally tell the mayor that not only did he, Thomas, own Sierra Rivers, but that the corporation would *not* be building a resort as rumored. That the money they had all spent gobbling up surrounding land at depressed prices had been wasted. Of course, out of generosity Thomas would offer to take that land off his hands. At an even more depressed price.

Everyone – except him, of course – would lose their shorts.

Then maybe, just maybe, he'd build that resort after all, and laugh all the way to the bank.

'Yes. My father will be there.' A twinge of unease crossed Chloe's face. 'You never did tell me what kind of business it is that you do.'

'No, I didn't.' And because he couldn't handle the questions in her sweet face, he turned and walked away.

'Some day, Thomas McGuirre,' she said to his retreating, cowardly back, surprising him with her insight, 'you'll stop running. It was just a question.'

That stopped him. 'It's bad genes,' he offered. 'Ask anyone. They'll be happy to tell you.'

'No.' She shook her head at that. 'You don't believe that either, or you wouldn't have come back.'

If she only knew. Slowly he turned back to face her. 'Okay, I'll play. Especially since you seem to know it all, Miss Walker. Why did I come back?'

'Maybe to save the town?' she asked hopefully, as always willing to give everyone the benefit of the doubt.

She didn't expect him to spin away again, this time heading straight for the door. 'Would that be so strange?' she called out.

'Yeah,' he shot back over his shoulder. 'It would. I'm not a white knight, Slim. You'd do best to remember that.'

Looking at those wide, tense shoulders of his as he retreated, she sighed. Pride ran hot and deep in a man like Thomas McGuirre. Oh, he wanted to be hard – mean. And certainly to everyone else he was. But she saw something different, something more.

Now all she had to do was get him to see it too.

CHAPTER 2

Chloe always looked forward to a town meeting, which was more like an entertainment event than anything else. It gave her a chance to see people she was regularly too busy to see, but, more than that, it gave her a real sense of home. Despite its financial woes, Heather Glen was a happy place. Everyone came to these meetings, no matter what the weather; mothers, babies, grandparents, kids – everyone.

Braving the storm, she stepped out of her car, her booted feet sinking a little into the fresh, unpacked snow. The night was incredibly clear and crisp, and a thousand stars lit the way to the lodge.

Once inside the old stone town hall, she stomped the snow from her feet, pushed back her hood and smiled. It seemed almost as noisy as *Homebaked*. Two young boys dodged by, chasing each other. A group of men laughed loudly. Augustine's mother sat in one of the back chairs, knitting. Chloe waved at her and moved further inside. The best seats were already filled, and just as she craned her neck to check for her father someone placed their hands over her eyes, blocking out all sights.

23

'Your wallet, your watch and all your jewelry, ma'am.'

The laugh gave him away. 'Conrad, you know perfectly well all you have to do is say please.' She pulled at his hands and turned to face one of her best friends since kindergarten. His laptop was in its case and slung over his shoulder. 'I see you've got your appendage. Do you ever get tired of being the town computer nerd?'

'Never.' He grinned, uninsulted. 'Someday, Chloe, someday you'll have to break down and learn how to work a computer. Or to type, for that matter.'

'Heaven forbid,' she said with a shudder. She wasn't interested in balancing her own checkbook; why would she want to tackle it on a computer? But she understood how Conrad felt.

He'd been working diligently at perfecting a children's reading program for several years now, and she knew he'd placed high hopes on it being picked up by a big-name company. When he wasn't working on that, he alternately bussed tables for her and volunteered for Heather Glen's Sheriff Department. He was a good man, and a great friend. More like the brother she'd never had. But not even for him did she want to learn how to create a file or use a function key.

'You can learn some pretty interesting things,' he said enticingly, raising his eyebrows until they disappeared into his sandy blond hair.

She knew that look. He had a secret. 'All right, Sherlock, what have you discovered?'

'What are you going to give me for it?' he asked knowingly, tucking those big hands of his into his pockets. 'And it'd better be good. This is a big one.'

'Conrad,' she laughed. 'We're not in grade school anymore.'

Patiently he studied the ceiling, completely unmoved, and she gave in. She loved secrets and he knew it. 'Name it, then.'

From his considerable height, he tipped his head down at her, the rest of him completely still. 'A kiss.'

She laughed. They'd been kissing since grade school too. In fact, he'd been the one to teach her to do it properly. 'That's easy. I'll owe you. Now tell me.'

'Thomas McGuirre's back in town.'

'How did you know that . . .?' She sighed. Conrad's hacking abilities never failed to amaze her. 'Never mind. I'm sure I don't want to know.'

'You already knew about Thomas,' he accused, shaking off his coat. 'Does Deanna know?'

'I doubt it. She's still on that extended honeymoon in the Greek Islands, remember?' At Conrad's long look, she caved. 'Yeah, I knew he was back. He came by *Homebaked* this morning.'

'After all this time, why would he come back?'

She knew it wasn't petty gossip that made him wonder. Conrad had been one of Thomas's few acquaintances. A more unlikely pair had never been made; the dangerous bad boy with eyes dark and full of secrets, and the school jock and star student who was kind and caring. When Thomas had disappeared, he'd probably never looked back, but Chloe knew Conrad had missed him. 'I don't know. Why don't you ask Thomas?'

'Ask me what?'

They both whirled around to face Thomas, who stood watching them with a sardonic half-smile twisting his lips.

'Nice to know some things never change,' he said evenly. 'I still give everyone something to talk about.'

After a slight hesitation, Conrad smiled genuinely. 'It's nice to see you, man. We were just wondering why you'd bother with Heather Glen after all this time.' He stuck out his hand.

Thomas stared at it for a millisecond before taking it, making Chloe wonder at the man beneath the cool, controlled exterior. She neither saw nor sensed any happiness or joy in him. The way he'd stared at Conrad's offered hand tugged at her.

He didn't expect friendship. Sadness welled for him. When he turned to her she hid her sympathy, knowing he'd hate it.

'You did say this would be interesting,' he said, glancing around at the utter chaos. 'You weren't kidding there.'

Wanting him to feel as if he belonged, she gave him her friendliest smile. Though he didn't return it, his intense eyes softened slightly. She took it as a great sign of encouragement.

People jostled them as everyone surged into the main room, looking for seats. Surprisingly, since she knew just about everyone, most did not even stop to say hello.

Aware of a strange sense of tension, Chloe turned and looked questioningly at Conrad. His mouth had tightened, and his eyes moved to Thomas.

Then Chloe realized. As many years as had gone by, people hadn't forgotten Thomas McGuirre, or where he'd come from. He stood there, as darkly handsome as ever, looking every bit the dangerous outsider they thought him to be. Shoulders wide and set, hands low on his hips, feet far apart, he surveyed the crowd with casual uninterest.

Even though his eyes were cool and impassive, Chloe imagined the snubs hurt. Anger came quick and unexpected, but she knew how to deal with that.

'Patricia,' she said with a bright smile, grabbing the first unfortunate person who happened by. Patricia Micos had been doing her mother's hair for twenty years, and could recite the town population by heart. 'I want to introduce you to someone.'

'I remember Thomas McGuirre,' Patricia said coolly, her friendly smile disappearing. Chloe's heart sank, but it was too late to stop the woman. 'You went to school with my niece. Michelle Feeney.' Even from her diminutive height, Patricia managed to dip her nose down to study the quiet Thomas. 'Ruined the girl's reputation on the first date, if I recollect correctly.'

Some emotion leaped in Thomas's eyes, something Chloe would have sworn was amusement, but she couldn't be sure.

'I'm sure you recollect correctly, Ms Feeney,' he said. 'After all, knowing everyone's business *is* your business.'

When she'd huffed and walked off, Chloe decided she'd give it one more chance. 'Mr Wilson,' she said as an older man passed then, plastering another happy smile on her face. 'How are you tonight?' She took his hand and willed him to look at Thomas.

Mr Wilson, the postmaster, peered over his bifocals at Thomas. 'McGuirre. Thought you'd be in jail by now.'

'Why would you think that?' Chloe asked desperately, afraid to glance at Thomas.

'Well, that's where his father is, isn't he?'

Chloe took a deep breath and forced herself to remember that old memories died hard. Patience was what was required here, and that was something she had an abundance of. Or so she told herself.

'Drop it, Chloe,' Thomas said in a low voice, when she eyed someone else and opened her mouth again.

Only with great reluctance did she give in, not quite daring to push him. Not when his eyes were so dark and fathomless, revealing nothing of his inner thoughts.

'I didn't expect a red carpet,' he murmured, watching her struggle.

'But – '

'Let's find a seat,' Conrad suggested quickly, taking Chloe's hand in an easy gesture that was as familiar as brushing her teeth. But somehow she didn't feel right. She wanted to demand that everyone stop the nonsense. She wanted to apologize to Thomas for the rejection of an entire town, for what she knew must have hurt his feelings.

But she didn't.

As Conrad led her down Thomas followed. Though they didn't touch in any way, she became intensely aware of him walking behind her. Her skin tingled, as if reacting to the touch of his eyes.

How silly, she thought. He's probably not even looking at me. But she risked a small peek over her shoulder, then whipped her head back forward so quickly her vision swam.

Oh, he was looking at her all right; that deep, inscrutable gaze was following her every movement. The tingling increased, so did the awareness, and if she closed her eyes she could see him as he'd been before he'd ever left Heather Glen. Alone against the world.

Just as he seemed now. Why would a man like that really come back to a town that had so mistreated him? To make peace? She wanted to think so.

Suddenly a small boy ran out in front of her, and as she stopped short her hand ripped out from Conrad's. Following too close on her heels, and unable to stop so quickly, Thomas plowed into the back of her, propelling her forward. Just as she would have fallen on her face, his arms encircled her waist and hauled her back against him.

'Sorry,' he murmured in her ear, his hands moving to her hips so that she could gain her balance. His body heat seeped through both his clothing and hers, searing her skin. 'You okay?'

Being snugged up against him as intimately as she was gave her a distinct disadvantage. She lost her ability to talk. But she could still feel, and what she felt had her heart drumming. Every inch of him was as solid as a rock.

Ahead of them, Conrad turned and frowned. Chloe straightened and smiled shakily. 'Almost fell.'

Conrad nodded, looked briefly at Thomas, and again moved forward. She followed, striving for the casual look, not daring to risk another peek at the man she knew remained directly behind her. Or at the twenty people at least who'd witnessed the whole thing.

It would most likely be in the headlines in the morning: MAYOR'S DAUGHTER FALLS INTO THE ARMS OF HEATHER GLEN'S RETURNING BLACK SHEEP. NEWS AT ELEVEN.

Glancing over her shoulder proved how ridiculous she'd been. Now Thomas wasn't even looking at her, but scanning the audience with a strange intensity that she could only wonder at. Already he'd completely forgotten her. Too bad she could still feel the hard imprint of the front of his body on the back of hers.

'As close to the front as you can,' she whispered to Conrad, determined to be more immune to Thomas's strange pull. Then the lights dimmed, signaling the start of the meeting. 'I plan to quiz the mayor on that new "no sleeping in the park ruling."'

A soft laugh escaped Conrad. 'I'm sure your father is well aware of your standing on the issue, Chloe.'

'I just want to be sure,' she said, raising her chin primly, purposely getting on her soap box. 'The recreation center is the only place some people have to go at night. We can't just let them freeze to death.'

'My daughter, the bleeding heart.'

'Dad!' Chloe stopped as her father stepped toward them in the aisle. 'Uh . . . you remember Thomas McGuirre.'

Robert Walker lifted his brows as Thomas stepped up, directly behind Chloe. 'Heard about our upcoming fortune, did you?'

'Dad,' Chloe corrected him softly, 'he's back in town for business. Not everyone's as interested in the resort as you are.'

But Thomas said nothing.

The mayor nodded, still studying the younger man. 'True enough. Heather Glen's a clean town, son. See that it stays that way.' He smiled at his daughter, who resisted the urge to roll her eyes, and walked on.

'I'm sorry,' she said, knowing her father still viewed them as children.

'It's not your fault,' Conrad said in her defense.

Thomas remained silent.

They found their seats in awkward quiet now, with Chloe wondering why her father couldn't have shown some of his famous charm to Thomas, as he would have any other newcomer.

As the town meeting started she realized it would be different from business as usual. The entire agenda had been tossed aside to discuss the expected

31

announcement from Sierra Rivers about the new resort. The mayor had received a phone call from their office saying the official announcement would come any day.

A rush of voices and hands all spoke and raised at once. Everyone wanted to discuss how much land they'd bought, what they wanted to buy, how much the value would go up when Sierra Rivers bought it from them.

Chloe sat and listened and shook her head, feeling inexplicably saddened. Greed, she thought. Pure and simple greed. Or maybe not so simple, if their hopes all fell through.

For, as she saw it, there was no guarantee of this resort. No promise had been made. The town's money would be so much better spent in other ways. Better daycare for the working parents. Free family counseling for marital problems, discipline problems, abuse. New and improved roads to avoid some of the nasty collisions that occurred each year on their narrow mountainous highway.

Buying and selling property for the sole purpose of making money from Sierra Rivers seemed wrong. But no one cared to hear it.

'You seem awfully quiet for the mayor's daughter.'

'Hmm?' Chloe turned and looked at Thomas as she shrugged into her coat. 'Oh. Just thinking.'

He wondered how anyone could think in the deafening din around them. The entire town seemed to be trying to fit through the door together, and as quickly as they left the snow and wind outside appeared to gobble them up.

Greed, he thought with disgust. Every last one of them was rushing home to gloat over their new land purchase, or to plan their next buy.

He told himself they deserved what they got. He'd spent his entire life planning this, and he was going to enjoy it. Especially the mayor's downfall.

'I hope you understand that my father didn't mean to insult you. He just takes his responsibility to this town very seriously.'

Thomas knew damn well that the man had meant to insult him, as well as warn him to stay away – something Thomas wouldn't do. He'd left this town a nobody and had a returned a millionaire a hundred times over. He made the rules now, and short of breaking the law, which he had no intentions of doing, Mr Mayor had no say.

Conrad moved closer in the hall, bumping up against Chloe in a way that irrationally irritated Thomas. Especially since he himself had done so earlier, and couldn't get the feel of holding her soft form against him out of his head.

'Sorry.' Conrad grinned very unapologetically and tipped Chloe's chin up. 'Remember? You promised me a kiss.'

To Thomas's further annoyance, Chloe grabbed Conrad's face in her hands and smacked him hard on the lips. 'There. We're even.'

'You call that a kiss?' Conrad shook his head. 'Try this, babe.' Bending her back over his arm, he covered her mouth with his, taking his damn sweet time. A pure green emotion rushed through Thomas as he watched Chloe's hand fist in Conrad's shirt.

When he finally lifted his head Chloe straightened, her mouth red and wet. 'Well,' she said, letting out a breath, looking a little dazed. 'Remind me not to promise *that* again lightly.'

Conrad laughed, looking very satisfied with himself.

Thomas wanted to strangle them both. But then Conrad slapped him on the shoulder and told him how great it was to see him again, leaving him further unsettled.

Conrad had once been the only person to bother with him, during a time when his very life had been a living nightmare.

Chloe chose that moment to turn to him and smile innocently. God, she was sweet. And open and caring. From somewhere deep within him, in the place where he'd sworn his heart had long ago shriveled and died, something stirred.

Something definitely better left alone.

Conrad moved away and Thomas followed Chloe out into the swirling, frigid snow. As luck would have it – or not – he'd parked near her.

'You do that often?' he found himself asking.

Tucking her gloveless hands into her pockets, she hunched over to keep warm. 'Do what?'

'Kiss whoever asks for it?' Why the hell he cared was beyond him. But he did. Asinine as it sounded, he'd hated watching her kiss another man.

To his further consternation, she laughed. *Laughed*. 'Just Conrad.'

His gut tightened. 'I see.'

'I doubt it,' she said easily. 'He's my oldest friend. I think of him as my brother.'

Thomas doubted like hell that Conrad felt the same, but he decided to leave that one alone. 'Didn't look like a brotherly sort of kiss to me.'

This time her laugh seemed . . . nervous. 'Well, maybe we disagree on what exactly a brotherly sort of kiss is. Besides,' she muttered, more to herself than anything else, yanking out her keys, 'that was a new one for me too.'

Moving to unlock her car, she suddenly let out a little cry and dropped to her knees.

'What?' he demanded, sinking to the cold snow and automatically reaching for her. Twisting out of his arms, she made a sound of distress.

'Goddammit, Chloe, what's the matter? Where are you hurt?'

She straightened, her face white and scared. His stomach clenched. She was in pain. He looked wildly around for help, but they were isolated by the nearly blinding snow as it fell around them.

Shit. *Why the hell had he come to this meeting?*

'Hear that?' she cried. 'Oh, the poor baby.' She stretched out on her stomach in the snow and dirt. 'Come on, sweetie, come here. It's okay now. Come on.'

Thomas stared in amazement and growing irritation as she wriggled her behind in the air, reaching

35

for something just out of his sight. Then she scooped up a small bundle of wet fur, sat up and cradled it to her chest.

She looked up at him, her face streaked with ice and mud. Her black jeans had turned white and were probably wet. Those eyes seemed huge and green. 'It's an abandoned kitten. Can you believe it?'

No, he couldn't. He eyed it suspiciously, having never owned a pet before. It looked incredibly pathetic and dirty. Much like the woman holding it. 'What are you going to do with it?'

Her look was reproachful, as if she couldn't believe he wasn't melting at the sight of the scrawny, mewling thing. 'I don't know. I'm not supposed to have pets in my apartment.'

'Well, let it go, then.'

'I can't just leave it here,' she said indignantly, obviously shocked he could even suggest such a thing.

He sighed. How had he known she would say that? 'Chloe, in case you haven't noticed, it's freezing out here.'

'Exactly.' She managed to balance the kitten, her notebook and her huge purse as she fumbled with her keys. Snow stuck to her hair, and she shivered when a gust of icy wind hit them, but she never lost her gentle hold on the tiny animal in her arms. 'I'll just take it home.'

She'd just take it home. Just like that. She was just as cold, wet and tired as he was, he could tell. Yet she would set her own needs aside to care for a kitten, of all things. Now why did that give him a strange lump in his throat he couldn't swallow away?

Chloe cursed under her breath when her keys fell into the snow. He retrieved them and unlocked her car for her, feeling unaccustomedly chivalrous and protective.

At the look of gratitude she shot him those feelings died away, and annoyance fell in. He forced the hardness back, wondering what it was about this woman that made him forget himself.

Suddenly eager to get as far away from Chloe Walker and her damn cat as possible, he waited for her car to start. Eagerness deserted him and so did any hope as her car sputtered and died. He took a deep breath and willed the engine to catch.

But, of course, because his night was predestined to be the night from hell, it never did.

'I really appreciate this,' Chloe told him, dripping snow and dirt all over the leather seat of his new Jaguar. She shivered.

Thomas sighed yet again, and reached forward to turn up his heater. His success in business had brought him plenty of monetary rewards. Large houses, exotic vacations, sleek sports cars. He took it as his just due, but couldn't help but notice how shocked she'd been to see what he drove. All his life he'd wanted to come back a somebody. It had been the motivation behind every move he made, including buying a brand-new car each year.

So why, then, didn't having it now give him the satisfaction he'd thought it would?

'Great car.' She wiped surreptitiously at a particularly nasty-looking spot of mud she'd left on the console and eyed him worriedly. 'I'm making a mess of it.'

'It'll clean up,' he told her, knowing it wouldn't.

She cuddled the sleeping kitten close, tucking it beneath her neck and rubbing her cheek to its fur. Her eyes closed and she made a little sound of contentment as the kitten started a rough purr and pushed closer against Chloe.

Thomas, finding himself in the uncomfortable position of actually envying a cat, jerked his gaze back to the window as his annoyance level rose considerably.

'You never did tell me what it is that you do,' she said after a silent minute, turning to him.

'No, I didn't.' *Keep your distance*, he had to remind himself, especially when he felt the full weight of those huge, trusting green eyes on him. *You're here in Heather Glen for a purpose. Remember it.*

'Turn left.'

He frowned as he did so. She was taking him into the roughest part of town, on the outskirts, past the railroad tracks.

'It's this apartment building on the right.'

He stopped the car, looking out with growing dread at the dump she'd indicated. The cleanest apartment building on the block, certainly, but a dump nevertheless. 'You live here?' he said flatly.

'Yes.'

'I thought you owned the café.'

38

'I do.' She didn't meet his gaze, but that chin of hers lifted several notches as she studied the stormy night. 'It's just not a huge money-maker, that's all. We can't all drive Jaguars, you know.'

'I didn't mean that.' The five-story building looked stark and in great need of repairs. 'Your father's wealthy.'

'I'm old enough to take care of myself,' she said quietly. 'I'd never ask my family for help.'

No, maybe not. Any knowledge of what a normal family did for each other was beyond him. But still, they could have offered, he thought with unreasonable anger for the undeniably pretty woman beside him. 'You shouldn't have to ask.'

Her shoulders stiffened slightly, proudly, as she gathered her things, still cradling the sleepy kitten. 'I like to do for myself,' she said evenly. 'Thank you for the ride. I'll insist on paying for any damage I've caused to the interior.'

He doubted she could pay to have the thing washed, but that didn't matter. He'd insulted her without meaning to. Why that should bother him, he had no idea. 'That's not necessary – Wait. Chloe, *would you wait a minute?*'

She was already out of the car and running up the slippery path by the time he got his seat belt off. He had no idea what he thought he was doing, but he followed her, right out into the stormy, miserable night.

Already he could barely make out her figure as she ran away from him. The night simply swallowed her up. It didn't help that her building was completely dark – no lights.

'Chloe! Wait!'

Did she even slow? No, the woman who Thomas was beginning to understand defined the word 'stubborn' just kept going. From what he could tell, she didn't even look back.

'Chloe!'

She lifted her hand and he squinted through the sleet, wondering if she was being friendly. No, she was waving him off. Telling him to go away. 'But – '

But nothing. She kept going.

'Well, at least slow down!' he called, picking his way carefully after her. 'You'll fall!'

She didn't slow or fall, and he swore as his own feet skidded a little on the ice posing as a sidewalk. This was dangerous. Very dangerous, he thought again as he made his clumsy way, nearly falling on his face. Locking his knees, stretching out his arms, he just managed to save himself.

And Chloe walked this path every morning and night. What was the matter with the owner? Why wasn't it shoveled? Where were the lights?

Her landlord was slime. Right there and then Thomas decided to lower her monthly payments on her *Homebaked* loan so she could have more money to get a better apartment. He'd just tell her . . . 'Chloe!'

Of course, she chose that exact moment to turn back, and it would forever be burned in his memory as his moment of humility. For, just as she looked at him, his feet slid out from beneath him.

He landed right on his butt in the wet, clingy snow.

Her voice came clearly to him, carried on the dark night. 'Oh! Thomas!'

He closed his eyes and contemplated the numbing dampness seeping into the seat of his pants.

'Thomas?'

He didn't want to, but he opened them again to Chloe, kneeling before him. He expected her to be laughing, or at the very least gloating.

But her eyes were serious, and more intent than he'd ever seen them. 'You okay?' she asked softly. 'Did you bruise anything?'

Yeah, his ass. Resisting the urge to rub it, he stood gingerly. 'Just my pride.'

A little smile touched her lips. 'Oh, that. It'll heal, trust me.' Her sparkling eyes rested on his and the funniest thing happened.

Time stood still.

Looking deep in her eyes, again he felt that unaccustomed something in the region inside his upper chest. That feeling that maybe his heart was stirring.

But he didn't have a heart, he reminded himself.

The snow came down around them. The wind blew. The kitten lifted his head and sneezed. But still Thomas and Chloe just stared at each other.

'I have to get inside,' Chloe said shakily as she pulled the kitten closer, still looking at him.

Thomas was abruptly reminded of that day so long ago in the woods, when she'd tried to convince him to stay in town. She'd looked at him with her heart in her eyes. Just, he realized with growing horror, as she looked at him now.

It had to stop.

He was used to women staring at him. With his status and money, they tended to be attracted to him like flies. And he'd been blessed – or cursed, depending on how you looked at it – with decent looks. The kind of dark, dangerous looks that made people look twice. He hated it.

But Chloe had no calculating speculation in her gaze, no starry, sick, crush-like adoration. Just honesty and . . . affection.

It unmanned him as nothing else could.

He had to get the hell out of there. But he couldn't do that until he'd seen her safely inside. Grabbing her elbow, he led her across the small, frozen courtyard, the seat of his pants uncomfortably wet. 'Which apartment?'

'Third floor.' She kissed the kitten's head and stuffed it down the front of her coat. 'Be quiet, sweetie,' she whispered.

'Mew.'

'*Please*,' Chloe added, with a quiet desperation Thomas didn't understand.

One of the bottom floor apartments had a sign on the door that read 'Manager.' It opened as they passed, revealing a short, bald-headed man of about forty, with a narrow, nervous-looking face.

He took one look at Thomas, then his eyes widened slightly. 'They said you were back in town. Didn't believe it.'

'Believe it.' Thomas tugged on Chloe again, but the man wasn't finished.

'Your pa owed my pa money.'

'Yeah?'

'Yeah. A lot of it. Pa's dead, so I figure that money should come to me.'

Thomas bit back a sigh. Would he ever stop paying for his old man's sins? 'Take it up with him.'

'Now, just – '

'Mr Thorton,' Chloe said, with a hasty glance at Thomas, 'Thomas can hardly be held responsible for his father's actions. Especially ones that took place so long ago. Now, if you'll just excuse us – '

'Heat's out again,' Thorton said gruffly, changing the subject. 'Don't turn it on.'

'Okay,' Chloe said quickly, grabbing Thomas's hand and tugging. 'Thanks.'

'What?' he called after their retreating backs. 'No complaints?'

'None at all, Mr Thorton.' She threw the man a smile over her shoulder, panicked that he'd see the kitten. There was a strict no pets rule, and if he found out she'd disobeyed it again, she just might be forced to find another place. And she couldn't afford that right now. 'Take care, Mr Thorton.' She tugged harder on Thomas's hand.

The kitten, completely unaware of her new owner's growing alarm, crawled up her chest, using its needle-like claws. It stuck its head out and wailed plaintively.

'What was that?' her landlord demanded, craning his neck to see over her shoulder.

43

Chloe faked a loud and obnoxious sneeze, shot Thomas a desperately wild look that she hoped told him to keep quiet, and said, 'Just my terrible cold. Nothing to worry about.'

The kitten sounded again, louder. Chloe sneezed again too, making it sound as much like her kitten as she dared.

'You're sick?' Mr Thorton looked at her disbelievingly. 'You never get sick.'

'Rotten cold,' she intoned, keeping her voice as nasal-sounding as she could.

'Sounded more like a cat than a sneeze,' the man muttered, giving her a hard look. 'You'd better not be sneaking any animals in here, Chloe. Not like last time. You know the rules.'

'I do,' she assured the man, with a smile she hoped looked honest. Her kitty dug its sharp claws into her neck and she gritted her teeth to keep from wincing.

Thomas's gaze dipped down to the area of her chest where the moving bulge of kitten nearly gave her away. *Please, please, don't expose me*, she prayed, hoping she was right about him.

He didn't disappoint her.

He took her hand. 'Excuse us,' he said curtly to Mr Thorton, without so much as looking at the man. He led her away.

As soon as they were on the third-floor landing she stopped him, sticking a hand inside her coat to disengage the claws poking painfully into her tender skin. 'Ouch!'

Thomas just backed up a step, looking at her as if

she had lost her marbles, which gave her an insane urge to giggle. Since Thomas looked so thoroughly annoyed, she didn't dare. Instead, she opened her door and flipped on the lights.

'Sorry it's so cold,' she said, dropping her things and pulling the kitten from her coat. 'Looks like it's going to stay that way a little bit longer.' She set the kitten down, dropped her coat and straightened her soggy, snagged sweater. She tried not to think about what she must look like, with her matted hair and dirt-streaked wet clothes. 'I'll start a fire in a second.'

'Why aren't you wearing gloves?' he demanded. 'Your fingers are blue.'

She glanced at Thomas, who still stood by the door. The shutter was back over his haunting eyes, making him look cool and distant again. Tall and lean as he was, he looked impossibly imposing – mean, even. His black jacket only added to his dark, sophisticated and dangerous air, and so did his wet mane of jet-black hair.

Was this the same man who'd just a moment before been sprawled out in the snow on his butt?

Hard to tell, since he was masterfully in control of his emotions. Yet, even so, she sensed a restlessness, a despair so deep he managed to hide it well. But Chloe, sensitive to such things, felt it, and took it on as her own.

'I keep losing them.' She rubbed her fingers. 'But they're fine.' *Frozen.*

'How are you going to keep that thing a secret?' He pointed to the cat as if it had grown wings. The kitten

45

looked at him and meowed pathetically. 'Why would you want to? And what did that man mean about the other animals you've sneaked in here?'

One look at his face told her he was absolutely not ready to hear about her other escapades in saving homeless animals. She scooped up the kitten in her hands and stepped closer to Thomas, wondering if he ever let down his guard for anyone. As she did so he actually backed up a step, which nearly made her smile. But she didn't, because what she wanted to do was suddenly so important.

Turning from her, he dropped to his knees before her fireplace. She waited patiently, because patience was one of her few true virtues. In less than three minutes he had a roaring fire going.

'Where did you learn to do that so good?' she asked, impressed.

He let out a sound that might have been a laugh. 'Boy Scouts.'

Right. This man had never been something so luxurious as a boy scout. They both knew he'd never been given a chance in those years to do anything other than survive.

He was staring at the wet bundle in her hands, his dark brows knitted tightly together. 'What are you going to do with that thing?'

'He needs a home.'

'Not from you, he doesn't.'

Holding the kitten up for him to look into its eyes, she said softly, 'Look close, Thomas. Real close. He's been abused. Abandoned. He's starving and neglected. Probably terrified, poor baby.' She thought of the boy he'd been so long ago, and knew that, although he'd buried that part of his past, it had still molded the man he'd become. 'Can you really tell me you don't understand what he's feeling?'

Thomas stared at the cat, his jaw tight, eyes cold and ungiving.

'Thomas,' she whispered, daring another step and trying not to give in to the terrible pain she could feel just beneath his surface.

Leave me alone, he seemed to say.

But she couldn't. She stroked the kitten. 'He's completely alone. And though he would probably prefer to not have any contact with humans, he has no choice. He needs help.'

'Let someone else give it.'

She shook her head. 'He would have died tonight. Of exposure, shock – whatever. If I hadn't taken him, it would be over.'

She saw him swallow, hard. The fire crackled loudly in the quiet room.

'I couldn't just leave him there, Thomas.'

'Anyone else would have.'

'Not me,' she said firmly. She gentled her voice, aching unbearably for this man, who used his coldness as a front to cover emotions he'd never given in to. All he needed was someone to show him, she thought. To show him how life could be. It didn't take money or fancy cars to make happiness. It came from within. 'I know you could understand, if you tried.'

His eyes, those cold, hard eyes, flashed to hers, and she allowed her unbearable sadness for him to show. Slowly the ice cracked, but it didn't dissolve.

Encouraged, she said, 'I couldn't let him die, Thomas.'

Nodding slowly, he stood tall, his hands in his pockets. 'No, I guess you couldn't. You're something, Chloe.'

She gave a little laugh. 'Is that good or bad?'

He only shook his head and took a deep, shuddering breath. 'I hate it that you can remember me before.'

'You mean when you were young?'

'I'm not that person anymore, Chloe. And I don't like thinking about it. You make me think about it.'

Yet he'd come back here, to the place of his pain. Why? she wondered again.

He turned to face the door, his hand on the handle. 'Don't forget to call the auto club about your car.'

'I don't belong to one.'

He mumbled an oath beneath his breath. '*Christ*. Fine. I'll call.'

Then he was gone.

CHAPTER 3

Thomas lay in bed. Nice and warm under his down comforter in his heated house, he couldn't help but wonder about Chloe. She no longer had any spare meat on her, and now she had no heater. What if she fell asleep and the fire burned too low to generate heat? Would she be able to get it going again? Or would she lie huddling under the meager blankets he imagined she had, too icy to move?

What the hell?

Sitting straight up in bed, he shook his head at himself. *Worried about Chloe Walker?* He plowed his hands into his hair and rested his elbows on his knees. Oh, he was losing it, definitely losing it. How long had it been since he had worried about someone? Had he ever? He'd always been too busy fending for himself to give much thought to others.

But he had given Chloe plenty of thought ever since he'd seen her again yesterday. Far too much.

Revenge. And then more revenge.

That was what he wanted. He mustn't forget that. Satisfied, he lay back down. But he slept uneasily, and dreamt of things he'd thought he'd long ago

49

forgotten. Warm arms and sweet-smelling hair that he knew had belonged to his mother, before she died. Hard, fast hands and demeaning words he remembered from his father. And last, wide green eyes filled with humor and affection. Chloe's eyes.

Only they turned reproachful and hard when she learned of his plan for ruining Heather Glen and everyone in it. The knowledge that he, and nothing else, had turned Chloe bitter didn't sit well, even in his dream. When he woke, the vague and haunting memories stuck with him.

He would have jogged them off, but the snow had fallen steadily throughout the night, making running impossible. *Great*. He looked out his huge bay window to find a white blanket covering everything. He was stuck in this house. Although it wasn't a bad house to be stuck in, he had to admit. Huge, airy and very expensive, it was nothing even close to the dump he'd grown up in, which was not too far from where he'd left Chloe last night.

He'd bought this three-story mountain cabin because it was not only on the top of the hill, overlooking a gorgeous valley, but because it was the best Heather Glen had to offer. After all, he had a statement to make.

But nothing changed the fact that for now he was very stuck, no matter how nice the house. So he went down to his basement, where he'd installed a gym with the latest and best workout equipment, and used his body until it could give no more.

Only when he was quivering and aching did he

climb back up the stairs, looking for a hot, soothing shower.

What he found instead had the impact of an icy bucket of water tossed in his face.

'Hello, son.' His father smiled from his comfortable perch on the couch. His scuffed dirty boots were on the oak coffee table, his arms outstretched with the air of a man completely at ease. Not bothering with a glass, he'd helped himself to the one and only bottle of wine Thomas had in the house.

Thomas's stomach clenched as his nightmares slammed back home. Hot sweat from his workout turned icy on his skin. He hadn't seen his father since the day he, Thomas, had walked out of Heather Glen all those years ago. That day he'd been sporting an aching jaw, cracked ribs and a bruised heart.

Now he had no heart. 'Get out.'

'*Get out*?' His father's eyebrows lifted in mock surprise. 'But I just got here.' He glanced around, eyes cold and appraising. 'And what a nice place you have.' His smile turned speculative. His eyes gleamed. 'Fancy that. You've actually made something of yourself.'

'How did you get in?' Thomas was meticulous about locking the house up. Not out of fear for anything material, no, it went far deeper than that. Growing up as he had, with dignity stripped daily, he'd never felt completely safe. Much to his shame, he still didn't.

James McGuirre grinned and cracked his broad, hard knuckles. 'It's a special talent of mine.'

Thomas frowned and kicked his father's feet off the coffee table. 'I thought you were in jail.'

'I'm out on good behavior.' James took a swill from the wine bottle and wiped his mouth with the back of his sleeve.

Thomas grabbed the bottle and set it aside. 'Well, take your special talent and vacate. I'm busy.'

'I'm not going anywhere, son. Not until we have a little chat.'

'About?' Again came that greedy smile that made every single one of Thomas's muscles tighten.

'What? You're not happy to see your old man?' He laughed. 'I can see not. But I've done some checking, Thomas. And you're rich, boy. *More* than rich.'

'Is there a point?' he asked coolly, knowing there was. His father was nothing if not sly, and he never allowed his confidence to lag. It defeated the competition, as he'd always said to a much younger Thomas.

'I've had a string of bad luck, that's all. I was hoping you'd help me out a bit.'

'You mean you scammed someone and are about to get caught, and now you need money to hide.'

James's face hardened, reminding Thomas sharply of his past. 'You're a cold man, son.'

'I learned from the master.'

'I thought you'd be happy to see me after all this time. And all I'm asking for is a little help to get me back on my feet.'

Thomas moved to the door, opened it. 'Not a chance in hell. Now get out.'

His father rose with surprising grace. He'd aged

remarkably well. As tall and well-built as his son, James McGuirre looked every bit as hard, cold and lethal. Maybe more. 'You'll change your mind,' he said quietly, in a threatening voice Thomas remembered well.

'I doubt it.'

James's cold blue eyes leveled in on his son's. 'I know about Sierra Rivers, Thomas. And to keep me quiet will cost you big.'

It took every bit of control Thomas had to keep his reaction to himself, to remain calm, when he wanted to wrap his hands around the man's neck and physically boot him out. Struggling, he just managed to find his own icy calm, the one he'd spent the past years perfecting. 'Sierra Rivers is no secret.'

James laughed, a vile and ugly sound. 'That you *own* it is. Do you really plan to build that resort, I wonder?' He studied Thomas, then smiled again, coldly. 'It doesn't take a genius to figure out that you're toying with this town, son.'

'Stop calling me that,' Thomas said through his teeth. 'You're no father to me.'

James put a hand to his heart and shook his head sadly. 'That hurts, really it does.' His eyes hardened. 'And every new insult will cost you thousands more.'

Thomas took a step toward his father, shocked at the violence that raced through his veins. He found himself shaking with it, and stopped to stare down at his clenched fists. Was he *that* like his father, then? Reduced to pounding any opponent who got to him, the weaker the better?

No. *No*. He wouldn't resort to that. Forcing his shoulders square and his body to relax, he lifted his gaze to his father's. 'I will not pay to keep you quiet.'

'No?' James seemed amused. He stood, walked to the fireplace and studied the marble in silence. Slowly he turned back to face Thomas. 'I can be a lot of trouble for you, son. A lot of trouble.' Again that superior grin. 'Just ask anyone in town.'

Thomas didn't have to. He already knew exactly how much trouble James McGuirre could cause. Visions of his well thought out plans went swirling down the toilet, making him even more furious. He hated feeling helpless against the man he'd sworn would never see him weak again.

'Pay me ten thousand right now and I'll go away,' James said, those bright eyes shining with rapaciousness. 'I'll just disappear back out of your life for good. I promise.'

'And if I don't?'

Once more those expressive brows lifted. 'I'll tell everyone, starting with the mayor, that Sierra Rivers is playing with Heather Glen. They'll stop buying up that property, Thomas. The rumors will cease.'

Damn him, but his father actually laughed in delight. Thomas tensed again.

'You'll lose your chance at your petty little payback, my boy. Nice as it was.'

The unbearable part of it all was that he would indeed lose his revenge. He couldn't let it happen. He'd worked too hard and too long at this. 'I pay you and you'll leave?'

'Yes. Today.'

'I want your word you'll not come back. Ever.'

A slight, cynical smile touched James McGuirre's lips. 'You trust my word?'

'Never mind.' Thomas jerked open a drawer of his rolltop desk and yanked out a check. It wasn't blackmail, he told himself. Ten thousand seemed cheap to keep the man out of his life. He slapped it in his father's eager, greedy palm. 'Now get the hell out.'

James McGuirre practically danced to the door. 'Pleasure doing business, son.' He waved the check over his shoulder, laughed, and left.

Thomas stood there, shaken to the very core. *He'd paid the man.* Backing to a chair, he sank into it and rubbed his aching head, feeling sick and disgusted. He'd given in to the very person he'd sworn would never manipulate him again.

It all slammed home. The overwhelming helplessness, the black desperation, the bone-eating hunger. The fear. Damn his father, but he felt sixteen all over again.

With nowhere and no one to turn to.

As usual, Chloe ignored her alarm. When it went off again she shoved the clock off her dresser, where it landed on her floor with a satisfactory crash.

She turned over and buried her head in the pillow. After less than a minute, the buzzing continued, this time near the region of her neck.

'*What?*' She tried to sit up, but something warm

55

and fuzzy sat on her head. Then a piece of sandpaper raked at her ear. And the buzzing went on.

'Mew.'

Chloe laughed and rolled over. The kitten put its purring face against hers and kneaded her chest with soft paws. 'Oh, you're cold, poor baby.' She opened her covers and the kitten climbed right in, as if he was used to such things. 'I know, I know, the fire died down. Brrr. Well, hopefully that mean old Mr Thorton will have our heater fixed today.'

The cat studied her intently, as if catching every word. Cleaner now than last night, thanks to a quick sponge bath, he sported a black spot off the right side of his nose, surrounded by a sea of orange fur. 'What am I going to call you?' she wondered aloud, watching the cat's serious face. 'You're too dignified for the usual "Fluffy" or "Whiskers." What do you think about . . . Red?'

The kitten didn't blink.

'Okay, too ordinary.' She stroked his chin, smiling at how the kitten's eyes closed in ecstasy. 'I had a red-headed uncle named Harold. How about that?' She laughed. 'Somehow you look like a Harold.'

The kitten closed its eyes and settled against the warm spot between Chloe's neck and shoulder. 'Mew.'

'You're probably hungry,' she mumbled, drifting back to sleep, thankful that the snow would have made getting to work impossible anyway. Besides, it was Augustine's turn to open *Homebaked*. 'We'll have to find you something.'

The kitten hummed its agreement and then mewled again. Chloe opened one eye. 'Oh! You need a kitty box, don't you?' She'd have to figure something out – quick. It wouldn't do to stain the carpet and annoy Mr Thorton more than necessary. She leaped out of bed, shivering a little in just her T-shirt and gray woolen socks. 'I'm sure I can figure out something, but we'll have to be careful to keep you hidden until I can decide what to do with you . . . Harold?'

The kitten lay still, stretched out in the bed, fast asleep.

Someone knocked at her door. Laughing a little at her sleepy, lazy kitten, she shivered again, wrapped herself up in her blanket and moved through her bedroom to the living room.

She opened the door a crack and peeked out, her eyes widening in surprise.

Thomas stood there, his arms loaded with bags, scowling at her. 'You didn't ask who it was.'

'I – '

'And why didn't you have the door chained?'

'Because – '

'The least you could have done was wait until you knew who I was. I could have been anyone.'

Like maybe a dark, dangerous-looking Thomas McGuirre? She bit back the smile she knew he wouldn't appreciate. 'Good morning to you, too. Are you always so chipper in the morning?'

He shouldered though the door and pushed past her, still frowning.

'Come on in,' she muttered, moving aside to shut the door.

'You don't just answer the door like that, Chloe. Not in this neighborhood . . . It's freezing in here.' He shifted the bags in his arms and looked at her. 'How are you keeping warm – '

His eyes narrowed in on the blanket that had slipped off her shoulders. 'Christ. You're not even dressed.'

She stooped down to work at the fireplace. 'It's early yet.' With fingers that were blue-tipped with cold, she had to strike three times before she managed to light a match.

'You always answer the door like . . . that?'

At the rough, strangled note in his voice, she glanced over at him, but his face, as his eyes roamed over her, remained impassive.

Did she only imagine the quick flash of heat in his eyes as the blanket slipped once again? 'Only when it's before seven and I haven't had any coffee.'

'I got you out of bed.' Now he seemed embarrassed. Hunkering down beside her, he took the poker from her hands, his expression carefully blank and his voice more chilled than the room. 'You've got goosebumps. Don't you have anything warmer than that?'

Amused, she padded through the tiny room to the even smaller kitchen. Actually, 'kitchen' was a kind word for what was little more than a hole in the wall. Wrapping the blanket more firmly around her, she put on coffee.

58

'I'm sorry I woke you,' he said a minute later from directly behind her.

He filled the small doorway. His face was shadowed and he hadn't bothered to shave off a night's worth of dark stubble. Those glacial eyes held fatigue and a banked fury she could only wonder at. Looking at his tense shoulders, his balled fists, she knew something had happened.

'I was up,' she said easily. 'Just trying to figure out what to do about Harold.'

'Harold?'

How was she going to get him to talk to her? To tell her why he seemed coiled for a fight? 'The kitten.'

'You named the kitten *Harold*?'

She smiled at his disbelief and offered him a cup of coffee, which he accepted gratefully. 'Yeah.' She shrugged, and again the blanket slipped.

This time there was no mistaking that flare of heat.

He took a step closer, his face hard and troubled, his eyes hungry with a need that tugged at her. She knew he hurt over something, but what she had no idea. She wanted to know, wanted to help, knowing instinctively that he yearned for more than his wealth and the material things his money had allowed him to buy. She wanted to assuage his needs, give him hope and laughter. She wanted to show him how life could be.

And, unladylike as it might be to admit it, she wanted Thomas McGuirre.

'I'll make you breakfast,' she offered. The heat from the fire he'd built worked its way into the kitchen. Her muscles began to relax from their stiff, cold state. 'You can tell me what got you up so early.'

'You don't want to know.'

'Yes, I do.' She reached for his hand. It was only to pull him further into the small, cramped kitchen, but he didn't allow it. Easily, she moved back, making space, and he came in on his own. Okay, she thought, he just doesn't like to be touched. A touchy person herself, she might not understand, but she could respect it.

'You can tell me about what you've been doing all these years,' she said, seeing his little start of surprise, and she was forced to wonder how many people had offered this man simple friendship.

'I'd bore you.'

'Well, then. You can tell me why you're upset,' she said softly.

Face grim, he said, 'Don't wonder about me, Slim.'

'I can't help it.'

Those eyes didn't shift from hers as he set down his coffee and reached out, fingering the blanket at her neck. 'You should get dressed,' he said quietly, his knuckles connecting with her skin, sliding down to one shoulder, bringing both her meager T-shirt and blanket with it.

With just that small connection, her every muscle went on alert, becoming instantly tight again. 'Then will you tell me why you came?'

'You're courting disaster, Chloe Walker.' His voice was silky. Those clever fingers trailed up, back over her neck to her throat, stroked her jaw. Her breath caught. 'Right here in your own kitchen,' he said, in that same voice that so hypnotized her. 'Do you know it?'

She did and didn't care. It wasn't promiscuity. It was Thomas. He did something to her insides, brought out something in her that made her throw caution to the wind. Turning her face into his palm, she sighed, loving the feel of his hands on her.

He tensed.

She tried to look at him, but he held her jaw in strong fingers. 'That damn cat got you good.' Lightly, he touched the four angry scratches she knew ran from her ear to her neck.

'He didn't like being shoved down my coat last night.'

'He'd better learn to behave.'

'He's just a baby.' With a sigh, she straightened her blanket. The strange and intimate mood was shattered. 'He was frightened half to death. And starving too. He drank nearly a quart of warm milk.'

Thomas shifted uneasily, uncomfortable with how she looked at him, as if she could see right down into his black soul. What the hell had brought him here like a shot after dealing with his father?

But he didn't question that too deeply, was afraid he knew -- afraid that maybe he had actually needed to see a friendly, unthreatening face.

Only how long would her face remain friendly once she learned the truth about his plans for her town?

61

Feeling stupid, he muttered, 'I brought you a few things for him.'

When her face lit up, he backed out of the kitchen that was beginning to stifle him. Too damn small, he thought. And Chloe was too damn close. Chloe, with her soft skin, sweet-smelling hair and light smile that made him want to believe things that were plain impossible.

Absolutely impossible, he reminded himself harshly.

He closed his eyes briefly, feeling incredibly out of place. Why had he come? He wanted, *needed*, his revenge. Getting close to Chloe would only make that more difficult.

'Here,' he said gruffly, nearly throwing the things he'd brought at her. 'I've got to go.'

'Right now?' She sounded surprised, disappointed.

For a man used to the people of Heather Glen either looking the other way or being out and out rude, her sweetness touched him. Yeah, definitely time to get out. 'I have to go –' Hell, what did he have to do? 'Work,' he muttered finally. He couldn't even talk right around her.

He got to the door.

'You got me a kitty litter box. And some food. How sweet, Thomas.'

Sweet. She thought him sweet. God knew what had possessed him to prowl the general store for supplies for her idiotic cat, but he had. Had even stood the contemptuous gaze of the clerk, who obviously remembered his father.

He heard the bags crinkle as she searched through them, but couldn't turn to look. He didn't want to see the gratitude he could hear in her voice.

He didn't want her to like him.

Or did he?

CHAPTER 4

Still angry at his father, and bewildered by how he'd reacted to Chloe, he tugged her door open so hard the cheap handle nearly came off in his hands. But before he could step through, she was there, laying a hand on his arm.

He stared at her thin, work-roughened fingers, struggling with himself. He couldn't continue to concentrate on what he had to do in this town if he stayed near her. And he wouldn't give up on his plan – not now, not after all this time.

'Thomas,' she said softly, looking at him with those heartbreaking eyes, 'won't you tell me what's the matter?'

It terrified him that she could see through him so clearly. For a second, he contemplated answering truthfully. *I just saw my father again for the first time in years and felt nothing but disgust. For him and myself. I came here because . . . Hell, I came because you're the first person to make me feel something, anything, that has nothing to do with business.*

She'd be shocked. She'd feel pity. He'd be able to see it in her face. It would kill him.

'Nothing's the matter,' he said gruffly. 'Can't a guy bring your damn cat stuff without getting the third degree?'

Uninsulted, she smiled. 'Not you, I don't think.'

'Why?' he demanded, uncomfortably aware that she found this whole situation amusing.

'It's not your style. Thomas, tell me what's the matter.'

'What's the matter is that you don't ever give up.' He felt something brush against his leg and glanced down. Red kitten hair stuck to his black jeans as the cat rubbed his face over his ankles. Then the kitten stretched out on his little back, gracefully studying Thomas from heavy-lidded eyes.

From well over six feet above, Thomas could hear the unsteady gravely purr. It was *purring* for God's sake. He felt the most ridiculous urge to bend down and touch that soft belly, but he bit it back. 'Move out of my way, cat.'

'*Harold*,' Chloe corrected mildly, smiling. 'His name is Harold.' She stooped down to pet the thing without a single regard to the blanket slipping off her shoulders. Couldn't she see that it drove him crazy? That he had some insane need to rip the rest of it away and . . .? He closed his eyes and sighed.

He needed out. Now.

'Thomas?'

Reluctantly, he looked at her. She was still kneeling before him, and her face came up to a very suggestive level. He could see flashes of bare leg sticking out the blanket. Erotic images floated

65

through his mind about what they could do in this position, or in any other.

'I think we have a problem.'

No kidding. He blinked her back into focus, furious with himself at having been caught gawking like a lust-crossed teenager. 'Problem?'

She looked horrified, and he had the ridiculous urge to cover up his erection with his hand.

But her eyes weren't on him. 'Harold can't be Harold,' she said in a funny voice.

He stared at the cat, then back at Chloe's reddening face. 'What are you talking about?'

She covered her mouth, seemed to choke back a laugh, then dropped her hand. 'Have you ever heard of the name Haroldina?'

Thomas dropped his confused gaze back to the cat, and despite himself broke out into a grin.

Harold was a girl.

Chloe looked so shocked, he actually felt that grin spread over his face.

'Chloe?' a voice called out. 'Is that you?'

From his perch in the doorway, Thomas saw him first, and all humor quickly faded. 'Thorton's coming up the stairs,' he murmured, gripping Chloe's elbow to lift her up while nudging Haroldina further inside with his foot. 'Go get dressed.'

When Chloe just stood, staring at him in horror, he pushed her none too gently toward her bedroom. She paused to grab Haroldina.

He waited until he heard her bedroom door shut before turning to the landlord. 'Chloe's . . . busy.'

Mr Thorton's lips tightened unattractively. 'We don't allow overnight guests here.'

'Don't you?' Thomas leaned against the doorjamb. 'Why not?'

He had the pleasure of watching the man sputter around that one for a moment before Chloe appeared, looking frazzled in a long sweater and leggings that hugged her long, graceful legs.

'Good morning, Mr Thorton.'

He glared at her. 'I was just telling your boyfriend here that we don't allow overnight guests.'

Chloe shot Thomas a startled look, and it nearly made him laugh. He was not a man given to spontaneous laughter, and it gave him a moment of pause that being with this woman seemed to change that.

'And,' Mr Thorton continued, 'I'm sure your parents would be disappointed. Especially seeing who the company is and all.'

'I'm of age,' Chloe said with quiet dignity, despite her obvious anger and embarrassment. 'What I do, and who I do it with, is no one's business but my own.' She took Thomas's hand and pulled him into the apartment.

'Heat's fixed,' Thorton grumbled, just before she shut her door, nearly catching his long, bony nose.

She leaned against the closed door and took a shaky, embarrassed breath, then looked up into Thomas's eyes and promptly let it out again. His eyes were smoldering like blue flame as they searched her face. For a long moment they settled on her lips.

'Mr Thorton likes to interfere,' she said, breathless. Unable to help herself, she dropped her gaze to his wide, sexy, unsmiling mouth.

He made a noise, deep in his throat. Taking a step closer, he set his hands on the door on either side of her head. Instead of feeling caged in, she felt deliciously framed.

'I warned you,' he said in a low voice, his lips a breath away from hers. 'Twice. Did you forget?'

She licked her lips, her heart hammering in her throat. He held his body a fraction of an inch from hers. 'Something about courting disaster?'

'Yeah. Something like that.'

'You suggested I get dressed,' she pointed out shakily. 'I did.'

'Hmm. Doesn't seem to matter much.' Those blue eyes never left hers as he slowly tilted his head and nibbled at the corner of her mouth.

Her stomach fluttered. She couldn't think. But she could move, and she did, coming into full contact with that dangerous, delectable body of his. That fully aroused, dangerous, delectable body.

Another sound escaped him, a low, deep growl. 'This isn't going to be some brotherly kiss, Chloe. Not by a long shot. So hold on tight.' Capturing her head in his wide hands, he held her steady and leaned in to take her mouth.

'Mew.'

Thomas stiffened, lifted his head and pierced her with a look. 'I'm going to kill that cat.'

She managed a weak smile before slithering out from between him and the door to scoop up her kitten. They hadn't even officially kissed, and already, she was far more dizzy than from any kiss of Conrad's. Her knees were so weak she could barely stand, but Thomas had that cold, superior look back on him, and she refused to let him see how much one little almost-kiss could affect her.

She had pride too. But, she thought with a flash of giddy glee, she'd caught that look in his eyes before he could mask it. That look of pure hunger. Need. She snuggled Haroldina close, watching Thomas stalk the room. She'd get that look back again. It surprised her how much she wanted that.

She realized she wanted to show Thomas McGuirre things. Things like friendship, happiness . . . fun. She had a feeling all that had been sorely missing from his life. But most shocking of all, she thought, with a little touch to her lips, she wanted Thomas McGuirre in her life. Not the Thomas he showed to the world, but the Thomas struggling beneath. The real Thomas McGuirre.

All she had to do was let him out.

'Mew.'

Thomas stopped pacing long enough to scowl fiercely. 'Feed it or something, would you? It's starving.'

'Meow.'

'Oh, Christ.' He strode to the bags he'd brought, dumped out a can of cat food and thrust it at her. 'Hurry up.'

He did care, whether he wanted to admit it or not. He couldn't stand the thought of Haroldina going hungry. General sympathy, she wondered, or first-hand knowledge of what it was like?

She moved through to the kitchen and opened the can, hating the image that thought projected – an abused, hungry Thomas. But he'd survived, she reminded herself. No matter how cold and unforgiving he'd become, he'd survived. And maybe, just maybe, she could help him with the rest.

Haroldina dived in with absolutely no ladylike grace, getting both her face and paws dirty. Chloe looked up to find Thomas studying the kitten with little-concealed distaste.

'You can't keep her,' he said flatly. 'You'll get kicked out.' The heat kicked on in that moment, with a loud cracking noise. It sounded as if the place was in the center of a hurricane. He shook his head. 'But whether getting kicked out is a bad thing or not, I can't tell.'

'We'll be fine.'

He pushed away from the wall and shook his head again. 'You're stubborn.' He walked to the front door and pulled it open, sparing her one last look. But he shouldn't have.

Her eyes were filled with an ill-disguised longing he couldn't take. Her lips, those red, still wet lips, begged for his attention, and he was surprised at how much he wanted to give it to them.

Which was exactly why he wouldn't. He had to learn to control himself around her, although why it was so difficult was beyond him.

Catching him staring, she smiled at him, a simple,

sweet smile that had him scowling. 'I called my auto club,' he said shortly. 'Battery needed changing. Your car will be delivered in an hour.' Then, in order to not give in to his incredible need to kiss her senseless, he shut the door on her. Hard.

Despite the frigid morning, he was sweating.

Inside, Chloe kept smiling. She even hugged herself. Yes, Thomas pretended not to like her much, and certainly he could hardly tolerate the kitten, yet he'd brought her home last night without complaint, gotten her car fixed and brought Haroldina supplies.

And he wanted her.

Smiling, she bent down to pet the kitten. 'Know what, baby? Thomas McGuirre is not as tough as he thinks.'

Haroldina merely purred her agreement and daintily licked her chops.

By the next day Thomas's mood had not improved. Standing in the center of the suite of offices he'd just purchased downtown, he seethed.

Someone had vandalized the inside, spray-painted obscenities throughout every room of the freshly painted place. Every light fixture had been smashed. Glass lay scattered across the carpet. It infuriated him because he knew it wasn't just a random act of crime. It couldn't be — it felt too personal.

Someone knew about him.

Much as he would have liked to pin this on his

father, he knew better. With money in his pocket, the man would be two sheets to the wind, living it up in Vegas.

There was simply no way he would have bothered to hang around a town where everyone knew him and no one wanted him.

Leaving the building, Thomas drove through town, checking on each and every business he'd purchased a part of over the past few months. Everything else *seemed* fine, but still he didn't breathe a sigh of relief.

He couldn't. He couldn't let his guard down, not even for one minute. Which meant he had to stay ten miles away from one Chloe Walker because she did strange things to him. Like making him forget what he was doing in Heather Glen.

He drove past *Homebaked* slowly, but didn't stop. Everything looked to be fine. The parking lot was filled. But he couldn't help but wonder what Chloe would say if she knew that Sierra River's subsidiary, Mountain Mortgage, was the one that had given her that loan she'd so desperately needed. That she was, in effect, indebted to him. That his original intentions had been to find her weakness and capitalize on it until her business was his.

She'd hate him.

It shouldn't have bothered him in the least. It certainly shouldn't have taken away from the satisfaction he'd waited so long to feel, but it did.

Deprived of his satisfaction, he sped past *Homebaked*, not ready to admit something else.

That he was filled with an irksome amount of dread for their scheduled meeting, only one day from now.

Dread was something he hadn't felt in far too long, and it didn't sit well. But he forced it from his mind with the ruthless determination of the successful business magnate he was, and concentrated on the here and now. He had lots of businesses he could destroy between now and then if he chose.

And lots more victims to his land deals.

Nothing worked. Frantically, Chloe yanked off the red dress and tossed it over her shoulder. Shoving hangar after hangar aside, she plopped down on her closet floor in frustration.

Thirty minutes before her meeting with that new investor, and absolutely nothing to wear. Not one thing in this pathetic closet even closely resembled what she needed. Not one stitch seemed . . . bankish enough.

With a loud, exasperated sigh, she settled on the only suit she owned. A bright teal number, with a fitted jacket and a short skirt. It didn't cover enough leg to suit her, but then again she hadn't bought it to cover what she considered her best assets. Yet at this point it was the best she could do.

It left her with only one worry, as a glance at the clock told her that in order to be on time she would have had to have left three minutes ago. Why, oh, why didn't she have a pair of pantyhose in her entire apartment?

By the time she literally tore into the parking lot at *Homebaked*, she was out of breath and more nervous than she'd been in a long time. What if the representative from Mountain Mortgage didn't like her? What, she worried frantically as she tugged at her creeping hemline, if she didn't look right? What if they decided to pull her loan?

Oh, God. They couldn't – wouldn't.

With a last, useless look at her wrist – she'd forgotten her watch – she tore in the backdoor . . . and plowed directly into a solid body.

'Whoa,' Conrad said, grabbing her close and swinging her around under the meager hallway light. When he got a good look at her face, he sobered. 'What's the matter? Are you all right?'

'Oh, Conrad.' She gripped his arms. 'Is he or she here yet? How late am I?'

He lifted shoulders still in his deputy sheriff's uniform. 'I don't know, honey. I just got here. Slow down and tell me what you're talking about. Is who here?'

'The investor – the one I told you about last week. I have to convince him – or hopefully her – that I'm definitely good for the loan. And that I can manage my business successfully despite my lack of a track record.'

Panic seized her again and she slapped two hands to her nervous stomach. 'I can't take this,' she muttered quietly. 'I'm not used to stress.'

'I told you,' Conrad said calmly, pulling her into the kitchen and smiling at Lana, who was flipping burgers. He opened the large steel refrigerator and reached for a huge chocolate brownie. 'I'll give you the money you need. No interest.'

'No,' she said firmly, watching him shove the entire brownie in his mouth in two big bites and wishing she had a metabolism like he did. 'I'm not borrowing from you, Conrad. It's your inheritance. We've discussed this.'

'Fine,' he said evenly. 'Don't borrow it. Take it.'

'Conrad – '

'You're in trouble, Chloe,' he said, more urgently than before, the affable expression gone. 'Don't expect me to sit by and watch you sink, not when I'm capable of helping you.'

She hated the lines of worry etched in his face, knowing she'd caused them, hated even more the sympathy and understanding she saw so clearly in his eyes. 'I'm not sinking.'

'Ask her if she charged Mellie for her breakfast today,' Lana said in a stage whisper as she moved by them to take down a box of napkins.

Conrad's mouth tightened even as his eyes softened with pity. 'Paid your rent yet?'

Okay, she was sinking. But just last week she'd given half of her rent money to the Martinez family on the second floor. Not that she could admit that to either Lana or Conrad, both of whom cared about her greatly. But the Martineze's had three young children and Thorton had wanted to kick them out into the cold. 'I want to do this by myself, dammit.'

Lana rolled her eyes and squeezed Chloe's arm as

she hurried past them yet again, this time back to the sizzling stove.

'Then stop supporting the world,' Conrad snapped. He straightened, dragged a hand over his face. 'God, I'm sorry. But I worry about you, Chloe. You take care of everyone but yourself. It scares me.'

Augustine flew in, started to smile in greeting, then took one look at their obviously taut faces and decided against it. Grabbing several plates that Lana handed her, she escaped quickly.

Chloe ran her hands through her hair, wishing she'd pinned it up for a more professional look. 'I'm fine.' She peeked into the dining room, looking for a banker-type wearing fangs. 'Besides,' she said over her shoulder, 'you should be more worried about the rest of this town, investing in that crazy real estate deal.'

'I am,' he said evenly. 'But you, Chloe, worry me most of all.'

'I really don't have the time for this,' she muttered, squinting to see all the way across the dining room. She was hopelessly nearsighted.

'Of course you don't,' he said with a shake of his head. 'You never do when it comes to worrying about you. What's the matter? Aren't you wearing your contacts?'

'Yeah, but they need to be stronger. I just haven't gotten a chance to get in to Dr Roberts yet.'

With a heavy sigh, he came up behind her, scanning the room for her. 'No, I don't see any cannibal bankers who like to gobble up people trying to run an honest business.'

Looking up into his worried, hurt eyes, Chloe sighed. 'I'm going to be fine.'

'Promise me,' he said softly, shutting the door on the pleasantly noisy dining area and cupping her face. 'Promise me you'll come to me if you're at rock bottom – before you do anything rash like take out another loan. Or hock something.'

She was able to laugh. 'I have nothing to hock.' At his frown, she relented. 'Yes, I'll come to you.'

Forcing a smile, he tugged a strand of her hair. 'Well, you'd better go out there and face the music, then. Late won't look good. I've got to go back out on patrol anyway. Just needed some chocolate – and there's no brownie like yours for fifty miles.' He grabbed another, stopping to look at her. 'Good luck, Chloe. I believe in you, you know.'

'Thanks,' she whispered, giving him a quick hug. She watched him close the back door behind him, fighting sudden ridiculous tears. As her best friend, he'd backed her more over the years than her own family ever had.

'Well, that looked cozy.'

Whirling, she faced the now opened kitchen door. Thomas McGuirre filled it, his arms crossed, his shoulder propped up against the jamb. No smile marred that mouth, but the heat in his gaze more than made up for it.

Which was no reason to make her heart trip, then race. No reason at all. 'Don't tell me you came for a brownie, too?' she quipped, forcing calm.

'Not a brownie, no.' Pushing away from the door,

he came forward. He had a way of walking, not a cocky strut or a carefree easy gait, but a long-legged stride that showed off all that tall, lean, dangerous grace. It was a crazy combination – that magnificent body and those icy eyes that said, *Go to hell*.

Once again she was struck by the need to bring humor to those features, to hear him laugh. To see him let go of that control. But then that intense gaze of his went on a trip, roaming from the top of her untamed hair down to her pumps, then back again, making curious parts of her body tingle with awareness.

'You dress up nice, Chloe. Real nice. Pretty fancy for serving tables.'

'I'm not – not today anyway.' She licked her nervous lips and his gaze shot to them. If she closed her eyes, she thought, she would be able to feel his mouth on hers. 'I'm late for a meeting.'

He nodded and said nothing.

In the silence, Lana sent Chloe a meaningful glance. 'You okay?' she asked, scooping up a heavy platter to take into the dining room.

Chloe was startled to realize that Lana didn't want to leave her alone with Thomas. Did the whole world think he was evil because he sported long hair, an attitude and had a jerk for a father? 'I'm fine. Really, I'm just fine,' she added at her employee's doubtful look.

Anger for Thomas, and at the injustice of it all seeped over her as Lana eagerly left the kitchen. Yet was it really the town's fault that they'd been sucked in by a con artist and felt bitter?

Chloe met Thomas's intense gaze, and for the life of her couldn't look away.

The silence seemed weighted . . . full of anticipation that Chloe didn't understand.

But Thomas did, and he hardened himself to his next move. Just because she looked like smoking dynamite in that suit, and just because her legs had to be five miles long and absolutely perfect, that was still no reason to give up what he'd wanted for so long.

Nor was the conversation he'd overheard between her and Conrad. 'Promise me you'll come to me . . . before you hock something,' Conrad had said. Chloe had laughed a little, but her eyes had been sad when she'd answered, 'I have nothing to hock.'

It wasn't his problem, Thomas reminded himself now. Not his problem she'd gotten herself in so deep that she was vulnerable to predators, like himself. 'You're late?' he asked.

'Yes.' She lifted a wrist and her green eyes smiled guilelessly into his. 'I always seem to forget to put on a watch. I've got to go, Thomas. I'm sorry. Did you want to see me about something?'

'You could say that. Is there some place we could talk?'

'I have a small office,' she said. 'But I'm waiting for someone.'

'Your wait's over, Slim.'

Her smile faltered. 'What do you mean?'

Purposefully he lifted a briefcase. 'I'm your meeting.'

'No, there's some mistake.' Again, she flashed that

smile, the one that was so bright it hurt to look at it. 'I'm waiting for a representative from my loan company. I had to take another loan, you see, and – '

He had to cut her off, had to stop her talking about the mess she was in or he'd lose his resolve. 'There's no mistake. I am the representative you're waiting for. Or rather, I've been waiting for you.'

Her chest didn't heave exactly, but the shallow way it rose and fell suggested that she was desperately trying to control herself. 'You've . . . been waiting for me?'

'That's right, Chloe.' He'd wondered, while he'd been waiting, if she was out in the snow saving another kitten. Or maybe a dog this time. But then he'd discovered the cozy little scene in the kitchen, and his irritation had risen so that he didn't care how fantastic she looked.

He'd gone to a lot of trouble to make sure she owed him a hell of a lot of money, and now she did.

Which meant only one thing to him at the moment: she, like just about everyone else in the town of Heather Glen, was vulnerable to him.

Lana rushed back into the kitchen, her arms full of empty plates. Augustine came through too, and started to prepare a salad. Both gave Thomas a long, sullen look he had no trouble reading, but at the moment he was more concerned with Chloe's next move.

'You've been waiting for me,' she repeated inanely. Both Lana and Augustine turned around at the strangeness of her voice and he came closer, speaking quickly and quietly.

'Let's go to your office, Chloe.'

'Thomas, you work for a bank?'

Dammit, he knew she wasn't as slow-witted as she was acting, but if she continued, both her very nosy employees would get a full, detailed report of her money troubles. 'No,' he said tersely. 'Not a bank. A mortgage company. I own it.'

'Mountain Mortgage is . . . *you*?'

He glanced at the avidly curious cook and waitress, hanging on each and every word. Well, if she didn't care, why should he? 'Yes. I am Mountain Mortgage.' He was also Sierra Rivers, the mega-conglomerate that owned the company, but he wasn't about to admit that.

It finally clicked into her befuddled brain what he was trying to tell her. And she'd believed him harmless. A little dark and mysterious, certainly attractive, but basically harmless. She would have laughed if she'd had the air in her lungs to do it. A fool was what she'd been. A complete fool.

His shoulders, in his crisp white dress shirt, were so wide she couldn't see anything but the man. But she could feel both Augustine's and Lana's intense interest. Tipping back her head to look at him was a mistake, but what the hell? She'd already made so many it didn't matter.

His eyes, full of dark and dangerous secrets, were right on her. If she had any last, lingering doubts, they fled. She knew right then that he was the furthest thing from harmless she'd ever seen.

And he owned her.

CHAPTER 5

Chloe managed to hold onto her anger – even after her meeting with Thomas was over. Normally she couldn't stay mad at anyone, especially someone who drew such an amazing sense of awareness out of her as he did, but, oh, was she good and furious.

Thomas had been low-key, even surprisingly friendly during their talk, despite her obvious hostility, offering her very fair terms and agreeing with her business plan.

Yet the man was up to something, and she knew by the simmering emotions in his eyes it had to be no good.

Thank God her car had started right up afterwards, in spite of the snow. And by the time she'd driven up to her apartment, she'd worked herself up so that she didn't feel the cold one little bit.

Storming past Thorton's door, she didn't bother wasting the breath to swear when she felt his beady little eyes watching her from the window. She had other slime to think about.

But her hands shook as she threw open her door, because of course she'd forgotten her gloves. Yet she didn't feel the numbness so much, not when fury was pumping her blood.

'Chloe. Wait.'

That low, rough voice was the last she wanted to hear, no matter what her fluttering stomach said. Without looking back, she slammed her door – hopefully right on that aristocratic nose of his.

It immediately slammed open again, and Thomas filled her vision – the snow swirling behind him, his long black trench coat billowing about his endless legs, his dark tie against that stark shirt emphasizing his tough, chiseled features. He gave her a grim look. 'Chloe, do you have any idea how fast you took that last turn?'

'Yeah. Pretty fast.'

That mouth tightened. 'Too fast. You were on two wheels when – '

' – Did you follow me all the way out here to discuss my driving?'

'I want to talk to you – '

'Well, I'm talked out.'

He yanked at his tie and stretched his shoulders as if they ached. Snow continued to fall down around him, dusting his long coat. 'Christ,' he muttered, getting a look at her blue fingers then turning his scowl on her. 'Where the hell are your gloves?'

No. She locked her wobbly knees, forced the thrill of the sight of him back. It just wasn't fair that her body reacted to him against her will. Especially when he stood between her and the only thing she'd ever wanted – *Homebaked.*

83

'Step over that threshold,' she warned, 'and I'll call the police.'

Without hesitation, he stepped in. Chloe took a giant step back, crossing her arms over her chest. 'I mean it. Don't tempt me.'

Slamming her door and crossing to her in three quick strides, he yanked her hands in his. 'You're going to get frostbite.'

Then he brought her frozen fingers to his mouth and blew.

Her stomach tightened, and various other parts of her body made themselves known in interesting ways. His eyes watched her over their hands so she lifted her chin, pretending that he *hadn't* just turned her insides to mush.

'I'm giving you to the count of three to get out, Thomas.'

'Oh, I'm going to get out,' he promised coldly, in complete contrast to his searing eyes. 'Just as soon as you tell me why owing me money is so disgusting for you.' As if he'd just realized he still held her hands, he abruptly dropped them.

Her jaw fell open as she stared at him. The answer on the tip of her tongue was a glib one, and as she watched him waiting stiffly for her answer she knew it would also be the wrong one.

'It's not you,' she said quietly, her anger gone as fast as it had come. 'Oh, Thomas, I'm sorry. I'm just being selfish. And too full of pride for my own good. It's not you. Really it's not.'

'It sure as hell seemed like it was me when you

stormed out of our meeting after I asked about your five-year plan. It was a legitimate question from a banker to client, and a relatively simple one, I'd think, for you, since you always seem to know your mind and aren't shy to speak it.'

'I didn't storm out. Not exactly.'

One dark brow quirked, disappearing into his wet black hair. 'The door hit the wall so hard Augustine dropped an entire tray.'

'Okay, I slammed out.' Turning from him, she faced her little apartment. Haroldina, fast asleep on the couch. The wild cherry chocolate cake she'd baked from scratch on a whim late last night on the counter. The adding machine Conrad had lent her in the high hopes she'd actually balance her books. 'But it's hard, Thomas, very hard to admit I need help.'

'Especially from me.'

Moving around to face him, she asked the question that had been bothering her for several hours now. 'Why didn't you tell me? Didn't you have the heart for it?'

'I don't have a heart.'

That stopped her for a second. And her own heart twisted at the fact that he thought he couldn't feel that way. 'Well, you have a brain.'

His eyes narrowed on her. 'Business is my job. I told you that.'

'Did you know who you were lending money to?'

'I saw your name on the application.'

'And you didn't think to tell me it was you?'

Agitated, he paced the room. 'Look, it's no big deal. I do this all the time.'

'Lend money? Or make fools of people?' she demanded, stepping directly into his path and meeting his stormy eyes. 'Because that's what you did, Thomas. You made a fool of me.'

A muscle in his jaw worked as he stared down at her. She could see the war within himself, could feel it. But she still had no idea what he was battling, only knew she couldn't stand to see him suffer. Gently she laid a hand on his chest. 'I'm going to assume you didn't mean to hurt me,' she said.

He went unnaturally still. 'That's quite an assumption.'

'Is it a wrong one?'

Dropping his chin to his chest, he studied the hand that still touched him.

'Is it, Thomas? Did you mean to hurt me?'

He closed his eyes, remaining motionless. 'You have a way, Chloe. A way that cuts right through me.'

Spreading her fingers wide, she let her hand move over his chest. 'At least you're feeling something.'

A low rumble came from deep in his chest; a laugh, a groan, she had no idea. 'Oh, yeah,' he said. 'I'm feeling something, all right.'

She'd never heard so much approval, so much emotion in his voice. Her heart pumped. Her breath quickened. All antagonism deserted the air, replaced by an unbearable tension, anticipation.

Suddenly, with a soft oath, he grabbed her hand, and Chloe thought he meant to fling it away from him. Instead, he backed her to the wall and drew both her hands in one of his, pinning them over her head. His warm, callused palm cupped her face. 'I don't like this, Slim. Not one bit.'

Stretched out the way she was, she felt open, vulnerable, and so needy she could have cried with it. 'It may grow on you.'

'Chloe . . .' His lips were almost on hers. 'You have no idea what you're getting into here.'

But she pressed her chest against his, leaving him no choice.

Her lips were so soft, so perfect, Thomas thought. No gloss, no added color, just pure Chloe. Nothing between them and absolutely everything between them. When he touched his tongue to the corner of her lip she opened her mouth beneath his, no hesitation, no resistance.

It undid him. Hot satisfaction rolled over him, and a surge of possessiveness at her simple acceptance. He'd expected her to pull back, to hold onto her anger. He'd never thought she'd give in.

And she was right. She *was* growing on him – in a way he hadn't thought possible. Hadn't wanted to believe possible. It had never happened before.

Her mouth, that sweet, hot mouth, was driving him half-mad.

Over his lifetime he'd had his share of hot, spicy kisses, but nothing like this one. Nothing that had stripped his soul bare, that had left him with no self-control. Certainly never had a kiss felt so special, so *just for him*.

But kissing Chloe brought all those feelings and a whole lot more. Right this minute, with her arched against him, helpless and moaning in her throat, he wanted to forget the secrets between them, forget that he could trust no one.

All he wanted to do was kiss her. Teasing, he nibbled at her bottom lip. She tipped her head back, offering him more. For pleasure, he did it again, and reveled in her answering shudder.

He moved closer, until her hands flexed in his. Her chest crushed to his, the hard points of her nipples branding him. Dropping her hands, he let his own slide down her neck to catch her shoulders. Then he streaked his arm between her back and the wall, yanking her closer to press his lower body to hers.

Chloe shifted her hips to accommodate him, letting his arousal stroke her intimately, and he couldn't believe how far gone he was after just a kiss. His lips slid to her shoulder, moving aside her suit jacket as he –

The phone rang, and when she stiffened in his arms, he swore. Blinking, Chloe lifted her head, and the mood was shattered. Slowly, he backed from her, watching her pick her way across the floor to the telephone.

'Hello, Dad,' she said into the phone, shrugging her teal jacket back into place. With a self-conscious gesture she smoothed her skirt down. Her lips were wet and red as she stared at Thomas wide-eyed.

Women didn't look at him like that, all unsophisticated and . . . innocent. Uncomfortable, he turned away and listened to her voice, still shaky and whispery.

'Yes, I know he's here to stay.'

She made a little sound that had him turning back around to look at her. She averted her eyes and he knew . . . They were discussing him.

'I can't do that. He's my friend.' She sighed, stroked Haroldina, who had crept onto her lap, and listened to her father go on about how he and her mother wished she'd moved into a more reliable neighborhood, how they wished she'd hire a cook so she wouldn't have to work so hard at *Homebaked*, how they wished she had a real job like her sister did, how they wished . . . *she was anyone but who she was.*

Oh, he didn't really say the last bit, but he didn't have to; it was just there. An unspoken incrimination. Blinking away the surprising hurt, Chloe straightened and spoke quickly, before she had to listen to more. 'I'm sorry you feel that way, but you're worried about nothing. No one's going to hurt me.'

She met Thomas's steady gaze and let out the breath she'd been holding. 'I've got to go, Dad. Please don't worry about me.'

When she'd hung up and just looked at him, Thomas had to take a deep breath. 'I take it you've been suitably warned about the big bad wolf who's in town.'

'He thinks you're here to cause trouble,' she said, laughing nervously. 'You know, huff and puff and blow down a few houses.'

He didn't need the reminder that of course he was. 'And why do *you* think I'm here?'

A pretty, open smile crossed her face, sweet enough to make his chest ache. Standing, she came close again, but didn't touch him. 'I think you're here to make peace with your past.'

Such blind faith, he thought, even as he backed away. Too bad he'd have to shatter that faith before he was through. Because, committed as he was to hurting Heather Glen, he was just human enough to almost regret how he was going to have to hurt her too. 'I told you before, I'm here for business.'

'You could have done your business anywhere. I can't imagine you'd come back to this town without a good reason.'

If she only knew . . . But how long had it been since someone had believed in him, or, if not believed exactly, had at least not thought the worst of him? Even his multitude of employees all kept their distance, working for him only because while he demanded the best he also paid better than anyone else.

Chloe was different, and he wasn't sure that was a good thing.

'I understand banking is your job,' she said, cocking her head to one side to study him with an unusually serious expression. 'But I still think you could have told me what you'd done. I applied for that loan months and months ago. You knew long before the time you moved to Heather Glen it was me who owned *Homebaked*.'

'You could have checked out the loan source better,' he pointed out.

She winced. 'To tell you the truth, I had no other options.'

He already knew that, knew how desperate she'd been when he'd come along. He'd counted on it. 'So you are still mad.'

'Mad?' She pondered that. 'No. Disappointed, maybe.'

'But you kissed me.'

Now she grinned, a little embarrassed. 'I can enjoy that,' she said, 'and still be disappointed in you.'

'Can you, now?' Growing hard just at the look on her face, he stepped closer, ideas flitting in his head about just how much she could enjoy.

'Meow.'

With another nervous light laugh, Chloe scooped up the kitten and rubbed noses with it. 'Hungry, baby?'

'You still have that thing?'

'This *thing* has a name. And feelings.' She held up the tiny red ball of fur. Baby blue eyes stared solemnly at him. Its little body was still pathetically scrawny, sharp ribs sticking from its sides, which rose and fell with its quick breathing. The creature clung to Chloe's hand, trying to back pedal rather than get closer to him, before it opened its little mouth and mewled again.

It was hungry, and Thomas knew that feeling all too well. The unbearable, mind-numbing hunger

91

that came from too long between meals. The fear that maybe food would never come again.

That funny thing happened inside his chest again – that uncomfortable sense of understanding. It was just a cat, for Christ's sake, he told himself. Not a little boy so desperate he stole to eat. Yet he still had the insane urge to dash into the kitchen and open every cupboard, dumping food into its bowl until her skinny stomach bulged with food.

'Feelings or not,' he said dryly, purposely taking his eyes off the cat so his own stomach could relax, 'you're not supposed to have it here.'

'*Her*,' she corrected, 'and since when did you get to be such a stickler for rules?'

'Rules are important.'

She snorted. 'When we were growing up, rules only existed for you so that you could break them.'

'That was then.'

'And you've changed so much?' She laughed and shook her head. 'I don't think so, Thomas. Deep down, you're still that boy you were then.'

That got him, and good. He'd buried that part of him, purposely, cruelly, and he never wanted to be reminded of it. Certainly he didn't want to be compared to the boy he was then. That boy had been weak, dependent on others. He'd changed all that, and he planned on never being dependent on anyone for his welfare ever again.

'You know nothing about me, Chloe,' he reminded her coldly. 'So don't pretend to understand me.'

'But I *do* understand you, Thomas,' she said simply, with a heartbreaking, solemn smile. 'You're just going to have to accept that.'

Thomas smacked a button on his computer, then waited for the financial statements to come up. While he did, he looked at the snow whitening the dark night outside his office.

Winter. Freezing cold, wet. High Sierras winter. Yet, just this afternoon, one of his new buildings had burned to the ground. All that was left of a perfectly usable warehouse was the lid to a toilet and some copper piping. His insurance company wouldn't be pleased, though it appeared to be a fluke of nature. An accident.

Right. *And pigs could fly.*

No matter what the fire department came up with, Thomas knew as surely as he knew his own name it was arson.

Yep, he'd pissed someone off, and good. It should bother him, but for some stupid reason he couldn't concentrate.

All he could see was Chloe, in that damned tight suit that showed off her every curve to perfection. Her luscious brown hair sparkling with snowflakes, her eyes bright, her cheeks red from the cold.

And her fingers blue. The damn woman. Couldn't she manage to take care of something as simple as gloves? Didn't she have any idea how quickly one could get seriously hurt in this cold?

What the hell . . .?

Was he listening to himself? Fretting over her gloves?

Christ, he was losing it. He'd set the woman up for a fall and now he couldn't stop worrying about her. It was ridiculous. It would have to stop.

He couldn't go soft now, not when he was so close. No matter how she kissed.

A glance down at his screen told him what he needed to know. More residents of Heather Glen had gobbled up land, and even more of them had borrowed deeply.

Before he could take a breath of satisfaction, he heard a knock at his office door and a uniformed sheriff entered.

As always, the sight of a badge made him stiffen. *Relax, you've done nothing wrong. And this time you're not a scared young punk who doesn't know he has rights.* But he'd spent so many years being harassed in this town, it was old habit.

'Just me,' Conrad said, giving him an easy smile as he moved, uninvited, into the office. 'Guess your secretary's gone. I hope you don't mind, I let myself in.'

Thomas let his eyes rise above the badge to see a smiling, friendly face, but it didn't matter. He *did* mind. He wanted to be alone. He didn't want any more reminders of his past. 'I'm busy.'

Conrad didn't take offense. 'I see your famous charm's firmly in place. Nice to see not too much has changed.'

'Plenty's changed. You're wearing a badge.'

'Nervous?' Now there was challenge in those kind eyes, as well as humor.

'Should I be?'

'Not for any reason I know about.' Conrad plopped his long body into the chair directly across from him and leaned back. 'Ah . . . it's been a long day. Heard it was for you, too.'

He'd underestimated Conrad. Those eyes might be friendly enough, but they were sharp as a tack and missed nothing. 'I don't know what you're talking about.'

'Don't you? Hmm.' Slipping a hand in his back pocket, Conrad pulled out a pad. 'Says here you had a building torched to the ground. Accidental, it says. Strange that, since it's so wet outside. Wouldn't you say?'

Just what he needed. A curious cop.

Thomas couldn't let him dig too deep. He knew Conrad was smart enough to put the pieces of the puzzle together and place Mountain Mortgage with Sierra Rivers. 'Arson happens.'

'Not here, it doesn't.'

'It happens to me.'

Conrad's brows lifted. 'Why's that? You have enemies?'

'You know I do. Did I mention I'm busy?' he asked, not very politely, watching a slow smile ease onto Conrad's face. 'What the hell is so funny?'

'You are.'

That smile spread, irritating Thomas. There was only one thing he hated more than uninvited guests and that was being laughed at, especially when he didn't get the joke. 'Look – '

'It's good to see you back in town, Thomas. Real good.'

The air whooshed out of him, and he studied his screen for a long moment. 'I don't know what the hell to say to you.'

'How about, It's good to see you, too?' Conrad laughed at the look on Thomas's face. 'Okay, maybe not. We'll start slow. I'm here to take a report from you on the fire.'

'I don't want or need your investigation.'

'Maybe not, but I'm going to do it anyway. It's required.' Whipping out his pen, he straightened, then looked right into Thomas's eyes. 'Would it be so awful to consider we're friends, Thomas?'

Dammit, he didn't want a friend – wouldn't know what the hell to do with one – but somehow he couldn't bring himself to hurt Conrad's feelings. Once upon a time, Conrad had been the only kind soul in a town full of hate. It was hard to forget something like that.

Except Chloe, he remembered suddenly. Chloe had been kind too. And Conrad looked at Chloe the way he knew he himself was beginning to look at Chloe.

With hunger.

'I don't have much need for a friend,' he said.

Conrad shrugged. 'We all need one, once in awhile. Just keep it in mind, then. Now, tell me about this building.'

* * *

Sleep refused to come. Too many thoughts and figures ran through his head for that. After how he'd been treated in and out of town for the past several weeks, Thomas knew he should have been pleased with how he'd entangled Sierra Rivers' many subsidiaries into Heather Glen's daily economics, without anyone the wiser as to what he'd done, but he wasn't. And he couldn't explain why.

More senseless vandalism bothered him. So did the phone call from the mayor – ostensibly to ask him if he planned on joining the local business association, though the real message had been clear enough. *Keep out of trouble and away from my daughter, or else.*

Since he had no intention of getting into any trouble that anyone could pin on him, or of hanging out with the mayor's precious daughter – no matter how damn sexy she was – Thomas had been doubly annoyed at the phone call.

Almost annoyed enough to get into trouble. With Chloe.

But that was a side luxury he couldn't afford right now. Not if he wanted to keep his wits about him. Because when he was with her, he just couldn't think straight.

Then Conrad had come along, badgering him with the tenacity of a hound dog, wanting to get to the bottom of the strange fire at his building, and the other petty vandalism he'd suffered. Another annoyance. Because, try as he might, he simply couldn't hate the guy.

It seemed his past was going to haunt him after all.

Old memories died hard. Actually, they didn't die at all, thanks to a town who enjoyed its gossip. And what, he wondered with some anticipation, would the gossip lines say after he reneged on the resort plans and they discovered what he'd done?

He waited for the swell of satisfaction to hit him, but it never did. Instead his stomach did a full roll in his chest. *Second thoughts*. Never once in all these years had he had a second thought. Not until he'd set his eyes on Chloe Walker.

Now he was full of them.

Frustrated, Thomas threw on a pair of shorts and made his way toward his gym, intending to abuse his body into exhaustion.

But halfway down the stairs he heard something, a sort of scuffle at the front door. It was so slight he might have imagined it, except for one thing – he didn't imagine anything.

Plenty of times Thomas had saved his own sorry hide only by his wits and a little luck, and since all he wore now was a flimsy pair of shorts, it looked as if he would have to do it again. With a lightning speed and stealthiness that only too many years alone on the streets had taught, he glided down the staircase and flattened himself against the wall.

Silence.

Then, after a few seconds, the scuffle came again.

Taking in the ten remaining feet to the front door, the wide open windows on either side of it, he hesitated. But since he was in a pitch-dark house, with no lights on in or out, he considered it safe enough.

Silently, he inched forward.

Eight feet, then five. Then came a muffled whisper that had his hair standing on end and goose bumps covering his exposed flesh. With a slight movement he stretched out his arm, keeping an eye on the front door. With a grim smile he found purchase in the coat rack, slid his fingers along it and snaked out an umbrella.

Moving closer, he gripped the heavy curved mahogany handle, but there was no more noise, not even a shift of wind.

When he heard the timid knock at the front door a minute later, he just couldn't believe it. What kind of a burglar knocked? And he knew it had to be a burglar, because certainly no self-respecting citizen of Heather Glen would be knocking so politely on his door past midnight.

No one in this town would knock on his door, period. They all hated him, had made that perfectly clear. Hadn't he just that afternoon gotten a nasty call from the president of the Ladies' Club, demanding that he go back to whatever unsavory hole he'd emerged from? Some lady, he remembered wryly.

A glance down at himself reminded Thomas he was very nearly nude, definitely not dressed for callers, whatever their intentions. But since he knew damn well he'd not locked the door, he wasn't about to leave it unattended now and run upstairs to grab his jeans.

When the front door handle turned quietly, carefully, adrenaline started flowing. Yeah, he was ready for a fight, and he couldn't help but almost hope it was his father. He was in the mood to deal with him now.

Raising the umbrella, he took another step forward, poised, waiting for the first move of this mysterious midnight visitor. Teeth bared, muscles tensed, he prepared for the fight, knowing that tonight, unlike all the nights of his childhood, the scales were balanced.

'Thomas?'

Shit. He knew that voice, that sweet, lovely voice which had been lately occupying more of his thoughts than he wanted to admit.

'Thomas?'

Maybe if he ignored her, she'd go away.

'*Thomas!*'

No, he thought with a sigh. No such luck. Chloe was the most persistent woman on earth.

Before he could so much as blink, he was flooded with light.

Chloe had flipped on the hall light with the switch by the front door, and now stood, clutching her coat closed, staring at him in mute fascination.

'Wow,' she whispered.

He could only imagine the picture he made, standing there in nothing but his shorts, umbrella raised high over his head, ready to swing.

'Thomas?' Chloe asked in a choked voice suspiciously filled with what he could only pray wasn't amusement. Her eyes ran down the length of him, stopping curiously in certain places of his anatomy that had him squirming.

This was the only woman alive, Thomas thought as his face heated, who could actually make him blush.

Finally she spoke again, and this time her voice was still choked, but all sounds of amusement were gone when she asked, 'Won't you catch your death of cold going out like that?'

CHAPTER 6

Closing his eyes, Thomas dropped his arms and leaned back against the wall. 'What the hell are *you* doing here?'

Chloe's mouth was still open and he sighed. Was he destined to play the fool for her, then? First falling on his ass in the snow outside her building, now this?

'I – Well, I just – ' With what looked like great effort, her gaze rose to his. Her eyes were lit with an avid curiosity. 'You're not dressed.'

'No shit?'

She bit her bottom lip and took another furtive sneak peek at that body which had her knees knocking together. Broad shoulders roped with surprisingly tough muscle, tapering to a hard, flat stomach –

'Chloe, was there something you wanted?' That low, impossibly sexy voice came with no little amount of impatience.

'Thomas, were you really going out like that? I mean, it's really cold and – '

'I know exactly how cold it is, Slim,' he said, in a voice more chilly then the frigid air blowing on him.

'Because you're standing there with the damn door wide open.'

'Oh!' With a silly little grin she couldn't possibly have contained, she stepped over the threshold, into his house, and shut the door.

'I was kind of hoping you'd shut it from the other side,' he suggested, putting the umbrella back in its place and crossing his arms.

So they were back to this, she thought. Formality. Sarcasm. Under all that dark beauty lay a darkness he protected well. She wanted in, darn him. She wanted to understand that tragic, tortured soul he only showed her glimpses of.

Why was it every time they took a step forward, toward friendship, he made them take three back? Before she came up with an answer for that one, she let her eyes run over him one last time.

'Amused?' he asked, staring at her in disapproval.

'No,' she answered truthfully. *Weak with lust, more like*. Wading through that thought, and no little amount of hostility from Thomas's side, she stepped further in.

But she got no further than one foot when, with one fluid motion, Thomas came forward, took her shoulders and backed her to the wall. All that impressive male nudeness came within a fraction of an inch, teasing her.

But there wasn't a speck of teasing in those opaque blue eyes. 'Let's get this over with, shall we?' he murmured, then abruptly took her mouth with his.

Surprise took her first, then a wicked sort of

delight as he pressed that hard torso to hers. Then he gave a startled gasp as he abruptly jerked back, narrowing his eyes on hers.

'What the hell – ?' he demanded, grabbing the front of her coat with two hands and ripping it open.

Nestled against her chest, Haroldina lifted her sleepy head. 'Meow.'

'Chloe,' he said in a dangerously quiet voice, his eyes never leaving the kitten's, 'explain this.'

'It's Haroldina.'

'I know that. Why is it here?'

She sighed. This was not going to go as smoothly as she'd hoped. 'Haroldina is a *she*, not an *it*,' she reminded him patiently, biting back her urge to giggle nervously as his furious gaze rose to hers. 'And she doesn't like storms. They scare her.'

'And this matters to me because . . .?'

He still had her trapped between his deliciously warm body and the cold, hard wall, she noticed. That had to be a good sign. But just as she thought it he backed away, plowing his hands through his dark, flowing hair. And with his taut arms raised, and all that wide expanse of chest stretched out, he looked so good she –

'*Chloe!*'

'The storm made her cry,' she said quickly, raising her eyes. 'And when she started crying, Thorton came pounding on the door, demanding I let him in – '

Now those eyes darkened with an emotion she couldn't name, but she was vividly reminded of her first impression of him. *Dangerous*. He took a step back toward her, his hands fisted tight at his side.

'Thorton *what*?'

'He banged on the door, insisting I let him in, and – '

'In the middle of the night, he came banging on your door, *making* you let him inside your apartment? While you were alone and unprotected?'

'Oh,' she said with a relieved smiled. He wasn't mad *at* her, he was mad *for* her. 'You don't have to worry. He's harmless, really he is.'

'No man is harmless,' he assured her. 'And I happen to know how you answer the door – just pulling it open without looking first. Were you dressed, at least?'

'Of course, because – '

'And, though you were alone, you just let him in?'

'But I wasn't alone. Conrad was there. And – '

'Conrad was with you,' he repeated softly, a murderous gleam in his eyes.

She had to sigh again. 'Thomas, this story is going to take me 'til dawn if you keep interrupting me.'

'Oh, please, by all means finish it.' With mock patience that didn't fool her for a second – his eyes were still shooting lethal darts – he backed to the bottom step of his curved oak staircase and sat.

'Okay,' she said with relief. He looked calmer – slightly. 'Anyway, Thorton came and discovered the kitten. He got mad, as I'm sure you can imagine. Threatened to throw me out into the night and all that.'

'Uh-huh.' Thomas nodded as if he understood perfectly. Congenially, he added, 'And Conrad was there too?'

'Right. It's our *Uno* night.'

'*Uno?*'

'A few us of get together every Friday night; we switch houses and play *Uno*. You should come next week; it's really fun and . . .' She trailed off at the look of absolute disbelief on his face. 'Well, maybe not,' she muttered.

'Tell me what happened next, Chloe.'

'Okay. Everyone but Conrad had left . . .' Again his eyes darkened to almost black.

'So you and Conrad were completely alone?'

'Not completely. We had Haroldina.'

'Of course. Haroldina.'

'So, when Thorton said I had to get out, Conrad told him that legally he couldn't do that. Not without a three-day notice to quit. Or something like that.' She smiled and shrugged. 'So I came up with something better.'

Thomas was still trying to adjust himself to the very real possibility of Conrad doing exactly with Chloe what he wanted to do with her right now – toss her down to the stairs and bury himself in deep. 'You came up with something better?'

Her smile was bright, and just a touch nervous, he noticed. 'Yes. Especially since you were with me when I found her that night. Remember, Thomas? How scared she was? How – '

'I remember,' he said tightly.

106

'Well, I thought *you* could take her.'

'*I* could take her?'

'Thomas,' she said with a little laugh as she stroked the kitten's head. 'You're beginning to sound like a parrot, here.'

He realized that, but it wasn't every day he got turned into a complete bumbling idiot by a woman he couldn't even decide if he liked.

No, he thought, watching as her shaky, jittery breathing had her chest rising and falling quickly. That was a lie. He liked her – far too much.

But then she was holding out that damn cat for his inspection and he stood, realizing what she'd just said. He backed up several steps. 'No way.'

'But, Thomas, she has nowhere else to go.'

For a flash second, he envisaged the little thing out in the snow, like the first night they'd found it. Huddled, pathetically hungry, abandoned.

Abused.

His stomach knotted. 'Dammit, that's not my problem. Make Conrad take it,' he said, brightening. 'Yeah, that's a great idea.' And perfect revenge for a man who was beginning to annoy the hell out of him. *Uno*, for God's sake. Couldn't Conrad come up with a better line than that?

'Conrad can't,' she said, stepping onto the first step. 'After prolonged contact, he's allergic.'

'Smart man,' he muttered, backing another step rather than come in contact with the furry little thing looking at him with wide eyes. 'What about your family?'

107

'I can't take Haroldina to them; they already think I'm irresponsible.'

'What does being responsible have to do with saving a cat?'

Her eyes shone brightly. 'I knew you'd understand. But they don't feel the same. They think I shouldn't have any animals until I have a place for them. They'd just . . .'

'They'd just what?' he asked, when she fell silent.

'Lecture. Remind me I'm not living up to my potential.' She took another step, and again he retreated.

'Nice family.' His voice was more than a little sarcastic, but instead of insulting her, it touched her the way he took her side without question.

'They *are* a nice family,' she insisted, not wanting him to get the wrong picture. They were nice, they just didn't always understand her. Okay, maybe they never understood her, but they did love her. That counted for something. 'They just don't understand my life.'

That gave him some surprisingly common ground with her family. 'And you let them go on misunderstanding?'

'Yeah. It's easier that way.' Suddenly Chloe stopped, tipping her head to the side to study him. 'Are you – ? *You are*. You're afraid of her.'

That stopped him, and good, as he realized he'd continued to back from her as she'd advanced. 'Of course not,' he denied. 'I'm not afraid of something as little and scrawny as that thing.'

'I think you are,' she said softly. 'I think you're afraid because you'll have to care for her, maybe even come to like her. And then, once you like her, your heart's involved . . . you could get hurt. Isn't that right?'

'I told you,' he said grimly, 'I don't have a heart.'

'Oh, but you're wrong there, Thomas.' She came up yet another step, stopping only when she stood directly beneath him. 'Very wrong.'

Thomas forced himself to hold his position, though he gripped the banister with white-knuckled fists. Christ, he wasn't afraid of that cat or of Chloe. And he'd just prove it. 'Fine,' he snapped. 'Leave it here. But only until you find another home for it.'

He was rewarded for his insanity with the biggest, sweetest, most singularly dazzling smile he'd ever seen. And it was all for him.

'Thank you, Thomas,' she whispered, her eyes bright. Slowly, carefully, deliberately, she rose that last step, to the one he stood so stiffly on. Holding the kitten close with one hand, eyes still on his, she laid her hand on his bare chest.

His skin leaped at the touch of her icy hand on his hot skin.

'Chloe,' he said on a gasp, 'where the hell are your gloves?'

'Shh,' she whispered, leaning close. 'Don't ruin this for me by getting all nasty. I'm having a very proud moment for the man I care about.'

The man she cared about? Him? His gut constricted. 'Don't, Slim.'

'Don't what? Don't care about you? Silly, silly

109

man. It's too late for that now.' Her lips – her *frozen* lips – glided over his cheekbone as she planted a kiss on him. 'And I won't forget this, Thomas.'

'Well, you'd better not,' he grumbled, relenting by taking her hand off him and rubbing it between his own. 'Because it's temporary. Understand?'

'Oh, I understand. Perfectly.'

Dammit, why was she staring at him like that? As if she was so proud of him she could burst? His insides twisted again, more painfully this time. 'It has nothing to do with fear,' he insisted. 'I just don't like cats.'

'What *do* you like?'

Unable to help himself, he let his gaze run over her face, lingering on those kissable lips. *You,* he found himself wanting to say. *I like you.* Instead, he dropped her hand and cleared his throat. 'Nothing. So, what the hell is *Uno* and how do you play?'

An hour later Thomas stood in the kitchen, staring down at *it*. 'Go to sleep,' he commanded.

It lifted its little head and gave him a sorrowful look. 'Mew.'

Thomas sighed. 'Look, I've already fed you. Twice. I know you can't be hungry anymore. It's nothing personal, but I'm beat. And I can't sleep with you wailing down here. Now cut it out.' Turning, he left the kitchen.

Halfway up the stairs, he heard the crying start again. Sighing heavily, he cursed Chloe beneath his breath as he turned around.

'Now what?' He flipped the light on. The kitten blinked up at him and fell silent. 'Is that it? You wanted the light on? Fine, it's on. Now *go to sleep!*'

The next time he didn't even make it to the stairs before the pitiful howling started. Nerves shot, he whirled, storming back into the kitchen, but the way the kitten cowered at him stopped him short.

'Hell!' He was a jerk, yelling at a stupid cat.

The way the thing backed from him had the heart he claimed not to have stuck in his throat. Dropping to his knees, he forced a smile on his face. 'I'm not going to hurt you,' he promised. 'I just want you to go to sleep. That's not such a hard thing to ask, really it's not. Could you try? For me? Please?' he added, feeling ridiculous. *Begging a cat.*

'Here,' he said, pulling open a drawer and yanking out several towels and arranging them to make a thick pallet. 'I'll make you a bed. How's that?'

Still those sad baby blue eyes just stared at him. 'Goodnight.'

He ran up the stairs quickly, so that he couldn't hear the thing cry. Diving into his bed, he pulled a pillow over his ears and squinted his eyes shut. Maybe if he just thought loud thoughts, he wouldn't be able to hear.

Coward.

But being under the blankets and pillows like that reminded him of earlier times. Of when he'd purposely hidden away from screaming voices and big, hurtful hands. Of when he'd needed to be invisible to escape from his harsh reality.

He fell asleep that way, and dreamed badly. Waking sweaty and gasping wasn't so unusual, he frequently had bad dreams, but the sun was shining brightly in his window and the radio alarm blared.

He'd overslept.

Because of Chloe.

Cursing her, and the general population of Heather Glen, he sat up. Then he realized that he couldn't feel his feet. They were numb, with good reason.

Haroldina was fast asleep on them.

Grumbling, Thomas made his way down to the kitchen. Haroldina followed him and he tried not to notice.

Coffee. He desperately needed coffee.

He was halfway across the living room when the phone rang, but when he yanked it off its rest and barked into the receiver, he heard only silence.

'Hello?' he demanded.

'I want you out of town.'

Recognizing the voice instantly, Thomas sneered. Oh, wasn't he just in the perfect mood to deal with this? 'Mr Mayor. How sweet of you to call and once again welcome me so nicely into Heather Glen. It's touching.'

'And stay away from my daughter.'

'If you insist, of course I'll let Chloe show me around, help me refamiliarize myself with the sights. How considerate.'

'I mean it, McGuirre. She's not like Deanna. People love her, care for her. If word gets out that

112

you two . . . Just make sure you stay far away. I won't see her hurt by vicious rumors.'

Neither would Thomas. 'What vicious rumors?'

'When people see you two together, they'll assume that – ' Thomas heard the mayor's teeth grind together. 'Just stay the hell away from her. Why are you back anyway?'

To make your life a living hell, just as you made mine. 'Because Heather Glen is such a wonderful place to live.'

Quickly Chloe's father tried another tactic. 'If you care about her at all, you'll stay clear. She's too giving, too open. Too trusting. You'll ruin her, Thomas. Is that what you want?'

He had no idea what he wanted. Other than the powerful urge he had to stuff the receiver into the mayor's mouth. Then he pictured Chloe, and wondered how hurt she'd be if she knew her father was making this phone call, if she knew how little faith he had in her to run her own life the way she saw fit.

'You're saying simply because she's associated with me her reputation will suffer?'

'Yes.'

Well, that burned. But he shouldn't have felt that quick spurt of hurt; he'd known it all along.

'I'm asking now, Thomas. Go away, please.'

'And if I don't?'

'I won't ask.'

Thomas gripped the phone. 'Is that a threat?'

But the line had gone dead. Slamming it down gave him little satisfaction. The urge to hurt something, smash anything, shocked him, even as he turned in the room looking for something to throw.

Even knowing he was acting like his father didn't stop him from searching for trouble. He needed a fight.

'Meow.'

Whirling toward the nuisance cat, he watched the poor thing freeze. Wide, wary eyes studied him, yet it remained still, resigned to its fate.

Thomas's heart drummed. His head pounded. Sweat pooled at the base of his spine. *No. God, no.* All his life he'd dodged his father's violent temper, only to find he had the same thing.

It sickened him.

'It's all right,' he whispered, talking to both himself and the cat. 'I'm okay.' He even managed a weak smile. 'Sorry I scared you.'

'Mew.'

With a sigh, he straightened. 'I need coffee and you need food. Let's go.' Resisting the urge to carry the thing, Thomas headed toward the kitchen, knowing the cat followed him.

Opening the kitchen door, he stopped so quickly that Haroldina plowed into the back of him.

At his table, waiting with a steaming coffee pot and two mugs, sat Chloe. Well, he thought, resigned, at least this time he had clothes on.

'Hi.' She smiled. 'It's not my morning to open *Homebaked* . . .' Her smile faded. 'What's the matter?'

Was he so transparent? Or had she overheard the conversation? 'Nothing.'

Setting down her cup, she stared at him. 'You look . . . upset.'

Furious, more like. Out of control, definitely. Losing his mind, possibly. And, while he couldn't completely get the disturbing phone call from his mind, he found something else occupied a good portion of his thinking capabilities this morning.

How damn fine she looked sitting in his kitchen.

'I thought I'd just come and check up on you two,' she said slowly. 'Make sure everything was going all right.'

She wore a man's tailored shirt that came to the tops of her thighs and a pair of leggings tucked into boots. Nothing even remotely sexy or revealing, yet his blood still surged at the sight of her.

What the hell was wrong with him?

'We're fine,' he said gruffly, his mouth watering at the sight of her and the coffee. 'But I can see I'm going to have to be more careful about locking my doors.'

She laughed and poured him a cup. 'Hope you don't mind, I brought you some muffins.'

God, he could smell them. If he wasn't careful, he was going to drool all over her. 'Great. You can go now.'

She ignored that. 'Is Haroldina okay?'

'Oh, sure. Dandy.' He shot the kitten a black look. 'You forgot to tell me cats don't sleep at night, Chloe.'

She stood as he came into the kitchen, then moved

115

toward the back door. 'Oh, that. Well, she'll learn to sleep the night through in no time.'

'Shame I won't have to worry about that, since in no time you'll have found another home. Right?'

'Uh . . . right.' Behind her she fumbled with the handle. 'See you later, Thomas.'

She had to turn to work the latch, and she still couldn't get it. 'Darn it,' she muttered, making him almost smile at her fierce tone.

Knowing the handle was a tricky, finicky thing, one that he fought every morning to go to work, he moved in close to help.

By the time he'd taken a second to inhale the sexy scent of her hair, she was getting worked up.

'Let me,' he murmured, straightening quickly, self-consciously, from where he'd been hunched with his nose practically in her hair. Get a grip, he told himself. She's just a woman. *A woman who was driving his hormones nuts*. 'Back up a little,' he said, more grumpily than he intended.

But she'd given up. 'I'll just go out the front door – the way I came in.'

'Wait a minute,' he said, reaching around her to help. Anything to get her out of here as quickly as possible.

It wasn't just her hair that smelled good. It was the entire woman. Having her caged in his arms like this put his body on full alert. 'Hold still,' he told her when she squirmed, her hip coming in close contact with the one part of him that always seemed exceedingly happy to see her. He gritted his teeth and said, 'Wait a second. I've just about got the thing – '

'Thomas?' she whispered, just as he too heard the strange ticking.

It couldn't be, he thought. *It just couldn't be.*

'Get out of here,' he said, very quietly. 'Back up and go.'

'But – '

'*Now.*' He reached for her to push her back behind him, so that he could follow her out. Easy movements were the key here, he told himself, even as his heart started to pump in anticipation.

But Chloe couldn't be quiet or easy, especially in the presence of a bomb. It just wasn't her nature.

Without warning, she whirled in his arms and shoved at him with the power of a star linebacker. 'Get down!' she screamed at the top of her lungs, flying at him.

She took him by such complete surprise that he only stood there as she landed on him, hard enough to propel them both into motion. He fell, with her right on top of him, and smacked his head with sickening impact on the tile, so that when the explosion came, for a minute he thought it was her.

But as fire and kitchen parts rained down on them his confusion cleared and he realized his mistake. He struggled to roll over to cover her, but dizziness prevailed. With unbelievable strength, Chloe held him down, dipping her head over him, *her* body protecting *his.*

CHAPTER 7

'Well,' Chloe said shakily two hours later, swinging her feet on the bed in the emergency department of Heather Glen's General Hospital. 'That was . . . exciting.'

'Are you sure you're all right?' demanded her father, eyeing the bandage on her arm.

'Yup. Just a small burn. That's it.'

'It's amazing,' her mother agreed, looking harassed. 'Conrad said the bomb was little, homemade, but that it had been rigged so that when Thomas went out that door he would be seriously burned, or worse.'

'I know.' It made Chloe sick that someone hated him that much. 'Thank God we're both fine.'

'Well, since you are so fine, maybe you can explain why you were in that man's house so early in the morning.'

'That's right,' her father chimed in sternly. 'I knew he'd be trouble, Chloe. I told you – '

'Mom, Dad . . . please.' Chloe lifted a weary hand to her head. She *was* fine, just tired. And she didn't need the third degree now, not when she wanted to make sure Thomas was okay. 'Surely you can't blame Thomas for what happened this morning?'

'You bet I can.' Her father crossed his arms. 'And I do.'

'Dad!'

'Who, then?' he demanded.

'Whoever wanted to hurt him,' Chloe said, trying, unsuccessfully, to chomp down on her temper. It didn't help that she knew her parents were just worried sick. 'That little explosion was set to go off when he opened his back door – something he does every morning without fail. If he had done so the way he would have if I hadn't been there, we wouldn't be having this discussion.'

'That's right,' her father added grimly. 'We'd be planning his funeral.'

Chloe's stomach turned; she knew it was true. Her urgent need to see Thomas tripled. 'I'm really fine,' she said gently. She hopped down from the bed and led them to the door. 'We're still having dinner tomorrow night? Good. I'll see you guys then. No, don't worry about me. Conrad's still here some- where. He can take me – ' She'd been about to say to her car, but thought better of that since her car presumably still sat at Thomas's. 'He'll make sure I get home,' she amended. With that she added her best smile.

Her father frowned, but let her push him out. 'Well, at least take the rest of the day off. You don't need to be cooking everyone's lunch now.'

'Yes, dear, he's right. Bring in someone to do that.'

How in the world had her parents, both hard-working, regular people, got to be such impossible snobs? 'I'll be sure to handle it. Thanks!'

When they were gone, she turned and sagged in relief. Finally . . . quiet.

'So, how are you really, Slim?'

Her heart stopped, then fluttered before shooting up to race speed. Slowly she turned back to face Thomas, who stood in the doorway, watching her intently. 'I'm fine.'

He nodded seriously. 'Good. So now I can tell you what you did this morning was a stupid fool move.'

No smile softened his words. Not one line on that rugged face eased. 'Which?' she asked shakily. 'Coming to your place or opening that door?'

The scowl on his face defied description. 'Saving my life,' he grated, clutching her shoulders and giving her a little shake. 'You could have been killed.'

'And you should have been.' The doctor had already told her he wasn't hurt, not a scratch on him, so she had no compunction about shoving a finger in his chest. 'Somebody went to a lot of trouble to try to scare you today, Thomas.'

'*Try to?*' His laugh was harsh, his eyes hard and unforgiving. 'They damn well did it. Christ, when I think of how you could have gone out that door before I even got downstairs. You would have – ' Stopping abruptly, he swallowed hard, dropped his hands from her and turned away. 'Well, obviously it doesn't bear thinking about. You'd better watch out, Chloe. Stay away from me. And don't come in without knocking first. It's dangerous to your health.'

That was guilt talking. She'd grown up with the masters of guilt-ladling, so she knew first-hand. And she couldn't let it continue, even when he stalked to the door, obviously finished with her. 'You're welcome,' she said softly.

He went still, his hand on the door. 'Why did you do it?' he asked. 'You put your life before mine, knowing what could have happened. Why?'

'You don't know me very well, Thomas, if you can ask that question.'

'You're right, and I'm not being fair, am I?' His broad shoulders sagged and he looked at her. 'Very well. Thank you,' he said quietly, surprisingly humble. 'But I really wish you hadn't.'

She knew he didn't mean he wished he were dead. But what he did mean tore at her heart just the same. She'd saved his life, and by doing so had taken the control right out of his hands. He hated that because it hurt. And what hurt even worse, in his eyes, was that she *still* held the upper hand – because now *he owed her*.

'Too late for that wish,' she quipped. 'Try another.'

He came back to her, and in a surprisingly tender gesture cupped her face, staring deeply into her eyes. 'All right. I wish that I'd been the stronger one, the quicker one. That *I* had protected *you*. Then I would have gotten hurt instead of you.' His free hand stroked her bandage in a move so light she hardly felt it. 'I'm very sorry for that, Slim. Sorrier than I can say.'

'So you're mad because I was macho and stupid and got hurt? You would rather have played that part?'

He smiled. *He actually smiled.* Chloe wondered if he even realized it. Or if he knew how beautiful his face was when he did. 'Something like that,' he said. Then he inhaled deeply. 'But I meant what I said before. Stay away from me; I'm trouble.'

She opened her mouth, but he laid a finger across it. 'I mean it, Slim. Don't defy me on this.'

Exhaling her frustration, she watched in riveted fascination as his eyes darkened. She couldn't help herself. She kissed his fingers, smiling when he yanked them away.

'And definitely stop doing that,' he told her, instantly grumpy again. Would the woman ever behave? And would his body ever stop reacting to every little thing she did?

'Stop kissing you?' she asked innocently, flashing him an impish grin. 'But why? You like it.'

With his fierce frown firmly back in place, he once again stalked to the door. 'You have no idea what I like, so stop it. And I mean it, Chloe. Keep away.' *Please, please.*

'I just don't understand – '

Because when I'm around you, I can't think. You unsettle me. 'You don't have to understand. Just do it.'

'What if I said you owe me?'

'Owe you?'

'Yeah. As in, now you have to do something for me?'

He hated that, knowing it was true. But he also knew by the sparkle in her eyes that she was up to something. 'Fine. Name it.'

'Ah,' she said, shaking her head, 'I don't think so, not yet. But when I figure it out, you'll be the first to know.'

Since he had no idea whether she was teasing him or not, for a minute he just stared at her. She stared right back, unwaveringly.

'I don't want to owe you,' he said.

A sad smile crossed her face. 'I know you don't.'

'I don't know what to do with you,' he said, quite honestly. 'I really don't.'

Again that irresistible smile. 'I know that, too.'

God, he had to get out of here – before he did something really dumb and kissed her again. And why the hell he even wanted to, when she was so obviously manipulating him, he had no idea. All he did know was that he needed distance. And quickly.

Chloe watched him go, feeling a bit discouraged. Ever since that man had come to town, wearing a chip the size of Mount Everest, her heart just hadn't been quite the same.

She'd started out wanting to get him to open up, enjoy life. So simple a goal. Just to learn to live, *really live*. That was what she wanted for him. That was all.

But she'd fallen into her own trap, because now that she'd gotten to know him she was hopelessly attracted. And now she still wanted him to enjoy himself, but with her.

She could look on the positive side. She had accomplished a lot in a very short time.

Oh, he wanted to dislike her. Wanted not to need her. But, most of all, he wanted to not be attracted. Luckily for her, he did like her, did need her and was greatly attracted.

Now all she had to do was get him to like it. If she could keep him safe long enough.

Thomas spent two long days repairing his back door and two longer nights trying to teach Haroldina to sleep somewhere, *anywhere*, besides on top of his feet.

On the third day, Conrad came by.

Thomas spared him a look before turning back to finish hammering in the doorjamb. 'What, no uniform today? What's the matter? Not enough crime in this one-horse town to keep you busy?'

'Nope. But with you in town it should only be a matter of time.'

Thomas stiffened.

'Relax, would you?' Conrad handed him up another handful of nails. 'I only meant that someone else is going to cause more trouble, not you. A person would think you have a guilt complex or something, the way you jump around.'

Guilt. In his life he'd never wasted a second on that emotion. Until recently. Which told him he was going soft.

Chloe's fault, dammit.

He couldn't afford soft.

He wouldn't give up.

He couldn't be scared off by a little vandalism. Okay, the kitchen bomb had been more than a little spray paint, but it hadn't hurt him, and thank God it hadn't really hurt Chloe. He wouldn't let it deter him.

'Could have recommended a contractor to do that door,' Conrad said lightly, running a hand down over it.

Exasperated, Thomas dropped his hammer and studied Conrad. 'Don't you have somewhere to be?'

Conrad grinned. 'Nope.'

'Great.' As if on cue, Haroldina carefully picked her way across the scattered tools, wobbling a bit at the glare she received from Thomas. Still, she came close and wrapped her body around his leg. Hair stuck to his jeans.

'Mew.'

Thomas closed his eyes and sighed. 'Fine,' he said to Conrad. 'If you're going to hang around and be useless, feed the damn cat, would ya?'

'Chloe's kitten?' Conrad bent down and held out his large hands for the kitten to crawl into. 'Haroldina? How come you have her?'

'Because you're allergic. Thanks a lot, by the way.'

But Conrad's good humor had faded, and he didn't smile as he studied Thomas – so seriously Thomas had to squelch the urge to squirm.

Carefully, Conrad set the cat down. 'She gave you her kitten?'

'No. She forced it on me.' Again Haroldina made her way to his legs and rubbed her head on him, staring up at him with adoring eyes, leaving him with the sudden ridiculous urge to bend and pet the thing.

'She gave you her cat,' Conrad repeated. 'Then saved your life.'

'Well . . .' He preferred not to think about it, but, quite truthfully, there was no way around it – she'd saved his sorry hide. And he still owed her. 'Yeah.'

Conrad shook his head. 'That woman's heart is too big, just way too big.' He straightened, staring at the kitten. 'She's going to give and give and give until there's nothing's left. Not one thing.'

'Give what?'

Conrad didn't even look at him, still spoke to himself. 'And the thing that drives me crazy is she can't even see what's happening. That soon there'll be nothing left.'

'What the hell are you talking about?'

Conrad gave him a long, measuring look. 'You figure it out.'

And then he was gone.

Thomas watched him for a minute, trying to decipher his words. He knew, even though he'd tried to push the fact away for several days, *he did owe Chloe*. Big time. So now what? How was he supposed to go on with his plans for Sierra Rivers knowing that?

It had been easy to crave revenge when he'd been the one wronged. The one betrayed by a town filled with selfish people who didn't care. But now, in order

126

to continue, he'd not only have to hurt a woman who didn't deserve it, but a woman he owed his life to.

He hated that.

She'd ripped the one thing that mattered from beneath him. *The only thing that mattered*. His control.

Because for some sick, unknown reason, he was falling for this sweet, open, caring woman who was so much the opposite of him in every way. *Fool. You're setting out to destroy everything she cares about. How would she feel about you if she knew?*

Shaking his head, he took a step toward his tools, knowing all that didn't matter. Not when between the two of them ran a white-hot sizzling sexual tension that made logical thinking impossible when he was around her. He'd kiss her again, regardless of all the secrets between them – he'd *have* to.

Even as he took the next step toward his tools he saw the flash of orange fur, felt Haroldina dash between his legs and get caught. Hopelessly tangled, amid the screech of the surprised kitten and his own oath, Thomas fell flat on his face.

As he lay there, tasting dirt and contemplating the way he'd let his life get so out of control, a warm nose pushed into his ear, accompanied by the loud, rumbling sound of a purr.

'Oh, yeah. Definitely going to kiss her,' he decided aloud. 'Right before I strangle her.' Good thing she'd actually listened for once, when he'd told her to stay away. She actually had, for two very long days.

He wondered, as he lay there in the dirt, how long

she was going to heed his advice. And if a very little tiny part of him hoped she'd disobey him, he could ignore it.

No Chloe was a *good* Chloe. An ant walked across his line of vision as he thought about this. A fly buzzed his ear. Haroldina watched him intently.

'I miss her, dammit,' he said to the cat. *He actually missed her.*

'Isn't this amusing? My son, right where the town thinks he should be. On his face.'

Every muscle in Thomas's body went rigid. Slowly he pushed to his feet. 'What are you doing here?'

'That's simple enough. Ran out of money.'

Thomas made a noise of disgust, and in a maneuver that purposely spoke of his lack of fear of the man who'd terrified him for more years than he could count, Thomas turned his back on his father and bent for his hammer. 'Why aren't I surprised?'

'Redecorating?'

Thomas whipped his head around at the sarcasm, searching James McGuirre's face for any sign of deceit. 'Yeah, just redecorating. I often do that using explosives. It hurries the entire process along so nicely.'

The grin that split James's face gave Thomas the shivers. He recognized it well, the pure maliciousness of it, since it had always preceded a particularly nasty beating. 'It looks like I'm not the only one that knows what you're up to.'

'Maybe you are.'

'You think I did this?' James scratched his head

and studied the damage that Thomas had nearly fully repaired. He shrugged massive shoulders that age hadn't diminished. 'Flattering, certainly. But sorry to disappoint you, son. I could have done better than this. Much better – and I would have, only I'm sure I'm not in the will.'

The only thing that Thomas was certain of was that his father *couldn't* have done better, that he knew nothing about explosives. That was what kept his hands off the man's neck this very minute.

Shaken, Thomas looked down at his own clenched fists, realizing for the second time how much violence he really had in him. Guess it really is hereditary, he thought grimly. 'Get out.'

James laughed. 'Not yet. I need more, son. More money.'

'No way.' He tossed the hammer into his toolbox, completely unable to concentrate on work. Not when the pounding savagery was coursing through his blood this way. He'd put a hole in the wall if he tried to hammer a nail. 'Get out. Now.'

The step James took wasn't toward the street but toward Thomas. His eyes were so dark they looked black. 'Just another ten thousand, that's all,' he said, his voice low, soft, and believably menacing.

Thomas remembered all too well what that voice meant: how he'd pushed too far. But he was no longer a scrawny kid, afraid of his own shadow. 'Go to hell.'

'You first, son. You first.'

They stood off, eyeing each other.

'Ran into Chloe today,' his father said casually

after a minute. 'And didn't she turn out to be something? Who would have thought – '

A red haze had settled over Thomas's vision as he took a step forward. 'Stay away from her.'

'Maybe. Maybe not.' He held out his hand. 'Ten grand.'

Christ. Thomas knew all too well how his father treated women. But he wouldn't dare do anything to Chloe. It would be plain stupid to mess with the mayor's daughter.

Even as he thought it, a slow, pure evil smile eased onto James's face.

'She gives great . . . hamburger.'

As he went inside to get a check, fury mottling his veins, Thomas fought within himself. *He didn't have to do this.* He could give it all up. Call off Sierra Rivers. Leave town. Forget the past fifteen years of plotting and planning the ruin of Heather Glen. Just let it all go.

But then he would be letting them win, James *and* the town. He couldn't do that.

Everyone thought him like his father.

Well, not everyone. Chloe didn't believe that, and neither, he was forced to admit, did Conrad.

He could tell them. With Conrad's connections with the law, they could probably have James put away again.

But Thomas shrank away from that, not wanting anyone's help, especially Conrad's. He'd have to explain, and that was something he couldn't bring himself to do. It'd be too humiliating to admit that he'd already actually paid the man.

In the face of that, another ten thousand didn't seem so bad.

Until he glanced around and saw his father's grinning, taunting face.

The check he'd just written was crushed beneath his fist. 'No.'

'No?' James cocked his head. 'Obviously I heard you wrong.'

'You heard nothing wrong. I'm not paying you. Not another cent. Get out.'

'You need to rethink this. Do it quickly and I'll forgive the rude way you're speaking.'

Outwardly calm, Thomas felt his heart race as he casually lifted his mobile phone from the step. 'I bet some people in Heather Glen would be fascinated by the news of your return. In fact, I bet there's plenty of people who'd love to see you. I'll just call – '

'This isn't over,' James said through his teeth, backing away. 'You'll give me more money. And the next time I ask you'll pay twice as much.'

As she had hundreds of mornings before, Chloe arrived early at *Homebaked*, already smiling in anticipation of cooking the day away. Nothing soothed nor pleased her as much as digging into the kitchen and whipping up something new.

Stomping the snow off her feet, she unlocked the door and entered, the anticipatory smile still on her face. The quiet dining room greeted her, and she knew it would only be a matter of time before the place was full and buzzing. To pick up business, she'd taken out an ad in the local paper, complete with a breakfast coupon. With any luck she'd have a full house by eight o'clock.

Despite what her parents and sister thought, Chloe knew she could work here for the rest of her life and never tire of it.

Knowing she needed to get started, she made her way directly into the kitchen. Idly, she studied her scuffed boots as she flipped on the light, thinking she'd be needing new ones soon. Then she lifted her head and nearly fell to her knees at the sight of her beautiful, clean, perfect kitchen – all but destroyed by vandals.

CHAPTER 8

Chloe heard the soft gasp of dismay and knew it was her own, but she just couldn't believe this was happening. Stepping into the kitchen, she could only gape at the disaster that lay in front of her.

The refrigerator stood open, its contents emptied out. Dozens of eggs had been thrown across the room. Ketchup, mayonnaise and mustard had all been squirted over the once spotless appliances and now stuck in a hard, caked mess to the steel. Flour and God knew what else coated the floor, inches deep in places.

In a final insult, someone had destroyed the new double-deckered chocolate cheesecake she'd planned for dessert. Using the fabulous frosting she'd already made, they'd dipped her basting brush and used it to paint across the white walls. IN THANKS TO MOUNTAIN MORTGAGE'S GREED.

Mountain Mortgage? Her loan company? *Thomas*?

A step into the kitchen had her feet crunching eggshells, grinding flour into the floor. She ignored that, standing ankle-deep in waste and stupefied silence.

What did Mountain Mortgage have to do with anything?

Thomas owned it. Knowing he couldn't have had anything to do with this was the easy part. Wondering why someone would do such a thing to her and then blame it on him was harder to accept.

Who hated her so much?

No, she thought, slowly revolving around the room, absorbing the disaster at her feet. Who hated Thomas so much?

It was that last thought that stuck with her for the balance of the next hour, even as she scrubbed egg whites off her tile, remade her chocolate frosting and attempted to go on as if nothing terrible had happened.

Outside her place, heart heavy, she put up a sign: CLOSED TODAY FOR SPRING CLEANING. Inside, she tried not to think about how expensive it would be to close while she stood in the center of the kitchen. Surveying the incredible mess, she struggled not to give in to the irresistible urge to cry. Never, in all the five years she'd owned the place, had she once had to close *Homebaked*. It had been a great source of pride – now shattered, like the drinking glasses that had been so thoughtlessly thrown onto the hard floor.

Refusing help, she turned away both a well-meaning Augustine and a startled Lana, preferring to deal with this in privacy. And, even though she knew it wasn't the smartest thing she could have done, she purposely neglected to call Conrad, or either of the other sheriffs.

Thomas was in trouble – big trouble. And somehow she just knew that if people found out what had happened at *Homebaked* it would only get worse.

From the very first, even back all those years ago, when they'd been just kids, she had somehow been able to sense Thomas and his feelings. Even feel them as her own. So it was no surprise when he showed up an hour later. She'd been expecting him.

When she heard the unmistakable roar of the Jag in her parking lot, she met him on the steps, shielding him from the mess she hadn't yet made a dent in.

'Hello,' she said, holding up a hand to block the bright early sunlight. 'What brings you here?'

Because of the bright day, she couldn't see his expression. 'What brings anyone here?' he asked, his face remaining in the shadows. 'Food? Coffee?' His breath crystallized in front of his mouth, drawing her attention there.

'We're closed today,' she whispered.

'I heard that,' he said solemnly, coming up another step to peer over her shoulder, but she blocked him. 'I also heard how strange that is. You never close this place. What's up, Slim?'

'The gossip line is more accurate than I've given it credit for,' she murmured. Would she ever get over that little thrill she got when he called her Slim in that low, intimate voice? It must be her imagination, she assured herself. He couldn't possibly mean to look at her like that. He couldn't possibly look as good as she thought.

He shifted on the step, the leather jacket he wore crinkling softly, seductively.

Nope, it hadn't been her imagination. He was as magnificent as ever, all tall, lean dangerous grace. Even his body heat reached her, and she longed to envelop herself in it. 'How's Haroldina?'

'You're changing the subject.' He folded his arms over his chest. 'But she's fine.'

'I didn't expect you.' Her voice seemed breathless, excited, even to her own ears. 'You made it clear in the hospital that you didn't want to see me.'

'I made it clear I was worried about you. I didn't want you to get hurt again.'

Too late for that.

His eyes narrowed, as if he'd read her mind. 'I want to know why you're closed.'

'Read the sign out front.'

A dark brow lifted so high it disappeared into his dark flowing hair. 'Sarcasm doesn't suit you.'

It would hurt him if she let him see the kitchen. Without question, she knew that. What she didn't know was why she protected him. Or why she wanted to. 'Is she growing on you yet?'

Wryly, he glanced down. Around his jeaned ankles were the unmistakable signs of orange fur. 'Shedding, more like. All right, Chloe Walker. I'll let you sidetrack me for a minute, because this is definitely a road I want to go down.' He glared at her. 'Have you found another home yet?'

'For what?'

'What do you think? The damn cat.'

'Ah,' she said with a small smile, lifting up on her toes as he craned his neck to look over her. 'At least she's no longer an *it*.'

He stopped trying to peek over her. 'I mean it, Slim. She's driving me nuts. Always whining. Never sleeps. I thought a cat was supposed to sleep a lot.'

'Love,' she whispered, startling him.

'What?' he asked, his voice suddenly a little hoarse. 'What did you say?'

She gave him an open gaze, her eyes deep and so soul-baringly honest he had to swallow hard. 'All she needs is love,' she repeated patiently. 'Too difficult, Thomas?'

'I – Yes, dammit.' He inhaled sharply. 'I've never had a cat. I don't have the foggiest idea how to – '

'Have you ever had a pet, Thomas?' she asked quietly. 'Any pet? No?' This time her sweet smile seemed sad. 'It's all right, it's much easier than you think. All you have to do is treat the animal as *you* want to be treated.

As he wanted to be treated. As if it were so easy.

'Can you do that?' she asked.

'You said this was only temporary. I never wanted a cat.'

'Then why did you take her?'

A laugh escaped him. 'Are you kidding? You barged into my house in the middle of the night and *made* me. Remember that, Chloe?'

'I remember. So you took her only because I made you? No other reason?'

Maybe because she'd looked so desperate, so

137

hauntingly vulnerable . . . so beautiful. Maybe because she'd asked him, and he hadn't known how to refuse her a thing. For the first time in too long he'd wanted to do something for someone else. Of course he hadn't slept a wink since he'd taken the tiny, noisy thing. 'Look, Chloe, I took it because you were in a bind. What other reason would there be?'

And why did he get the sudden suspicious feeling he hadn't given her the answer she'd been looking for?

'Fine,' she said, surprisingly and suddenly cool. 'I'll get another home for her and relieve you by the end of the week. Okay?'

'Okay,' he said uneasily. 'Enough of that. Now let me in.'

For a long minute she studied him, and he got the distinct impression she found him sorely lacking, but in what, he had no idea. Still, he shifted uncomfortably on the step while she stared at him.

'What?' he finally demanded. 'Did I grow a wart?'

'Of course not.' She turned, took the last stair slowly, as if she dreaded what was coming.

Just as suddenly, he did too.

The sight of her ravaged kitchen stunned him, and it was made all the more destroying because of her pathetic attempts to clean it up.

'Where you here when it happened?' he managed, his knees quaking with fear. He made himself look at her. 'Are you hurt?'

'No. It was this way when I opened up.'

The sweet scent of the ketchup and chocolate,

mixed in with the bitter mustard and the souring mayonnaise sickened him. Or maybe just the circumstances did that.

He couldn't read the words in chocolate she'd tried to wipe out. 'What did it say?'

'What?' she asked, coming up beside him, her profile weary and despondent as she hadn't allowed him to see before.

'What did the writing say?' he demanded, pointing out the smudged chocolate.

'Oh, that.' Moving past him, she kicked at an empty tin of flour. 'Nothing – '

Grabbing her as she passed, he whirled her around, holding her shoulders, his insides twisting. 'Chloe, tell me. What did it say?'

Shaking him off, she grabbed a sponge. 'Try Billy's gas station. He always has coffee in the mornings. Looks like you could use a nice, hot cup.'

Okay, he told himself, *bullying her would get him nowhere*. Besides, this vicious, all-consuming rage eating at him wasn't for her, but for whoever had done this to her.

Chloe stood ahead of him, scrubbing furiously at the wall. Her hair flew with each swipe of her arm; her entire body shook as she whipped her hand back and forth over the crusted stain. When he laid a gentle hand on her arm to stop her, she flinched.

'Go away, Thomas,' she said quietly, tiredly. Then she sniffed.

Oh, God. *Tears*.

His first instinct was to run, hard and fast. But this

was Chloe in front of him, fighting tears, and he found he couldn't leave. 'Hush,' he said, pulling her close, cupping her head against his chest. 'I'm not going anywhere. You're an awful wall-scrubber.'

She let out a muffled laugh against his shirt. 'I hope that's an offer for help because I've just about had it.'

'Where's your staff?'

'I sent them away.'

'Why?'

She snuggled closer, burying her face in his neck, wrapping her arms around his waist. Every single nerve-ending reacted to her touch, reminding him of exactly what happened to his body whenever she was near.

His voice was definitely a little strained when he asked, 'Why did you send everyone away, Chloe?'

Her lips, when she spoke, moved softly against his neck, driving him crazy. 'I thought I wanted to do this alone. *Homebaked* is like my baby, you know?' She sniffed again. 'I thought it would be better to be alone.'

'How is the dining room? The office? How much was taken?'

'Just the kitchen was wrecked. Nothing else was touched, and nothing that I can tell is missing.' Her fingers curled in his hair. A delicate thumb brushed against his earlobe, sending little shock waves of lust rolling through him.

'Did you call the sheriff?' he asked tightly.

She pulled closer. One of her hands slipped beneath his collar and laid against his bare neck.

Never had a woman so undone him without trying. He actually had to arch his back so that he could angle his hips away from hers, which were plastered to him. If he didn't, she'd find out exactly what her little caresses were doing to him, and he knew that would only egg her on more. 'Chloe?'

She sighed. 'No. I didn't call anyone.'

Already he had come to know her. Giving, caring, sensitive, and loyal to a fault. Which meant there was only one reason she hadn't asked for help and wouldn't answer him, and it scared him more than anything had so far. She was protecting someone, and he had the sick feeling he knew who.

'Please, tell me, Chloe. What did it say?'

With a sniff, she pulled away. 'It said, "IN THANKS TO MOUNTAIN MORTGAGE'S GREED."'

At first, he just stared at her. *His fault, all his fault.* 'I'm sorry,' he whispered, the words hopelessly inadequate.

'There's no major damage. Just an annoying amount of clean-up required.' From under the sink she pulled out a small bucket, then started to fill it with hot, soapy water.

'Let me call a service for you,' he said in protest. 'I'll find someone to clean all – '

'No.' Chloe picked up a sponge and dropped to her knees beside the bucket, attacking the stains on the floor with a vengeance that surprised him. 'I don't want strangers in here. Besides, it's my mess and I'll clean it up.'

'No, it's *my* mess.' With a sigh, he grabbed a sponge from the sink and sank to his knees beside her. When she lifted her head in surprise, he lifted a shoulder. 'I know how much this place means to you, Chloe. I'm so very, very sorry. I truly am.'

'I know you are.'

He wanted to kiss that weariness away. 'You should have called me.'

'I knew you'd come.'

She said it so confidently, with such absolute blind faith in him, that he was startled. No one had ever . . . He didn't deserve it, not one little bit. 'I don't like thinking about you opening this place up by yourself in the morning.'

A smile touched her lips. 'You do think of me, then.'

If she only knew how much. 'You know what I mean. Anything could happen to you.'

'I'm perfectly safe,' she said, dipping her sponge into the bucket, slowly wringing it out.

He did the same, then yowled at the hot water.

She smiled. 'Baby.'

'It's too hot!'

'It has to be. These stains are going to be tough.'

When he could feel his hand again, he started work on the floor. 'How can you know you're safe? What if you'd come earlier?'

'I still would have been safe.'

'Heather Glen isn't all that small or quaint,' he argued, taking her sponge when she wouldn't look at him. 'There is crime.'

'Not much.' Reaching for her sponge, she added, 'Until now.'

Without relinquishing his hold on the sponge, he said, 'I'm very sorry about this, Slim.'

'I meant,' she said softly, 'The crime against *you*, not me. I hate how you're treated here, Thomas. It tears me up. I love this town, I really do. It's lovely, small . . . cute.'

'Peculiar, more like.'

She ignored that. 'And until recently I thought it had the best people in the world living in it.' She dipped her head and studied the sponge they held between them. 'But now, lately, I feel so disappointed in them. They're letting past emotions and greed ruin them, and the town. There's so many changes, and not all good. Nothing's the same anymore. It scares me.'

'That's exactly why you shouldn't be here by yourself. Promise you won't open in the mornings alone anymore.'

She gestured at the mess littering the floor around them. 'You're wrong. I wasn't the target. Not really.' Her steady gaze met his. 'Was I?'

He had to admit the truth, that in all likelihood she was correct. She hadn't been the target; *he had*. But still, he hated the thought of her stumbling in on the act of someone tearing up her place. What had happened here took a lot of rage – uncontrollable rage. And it might turn on a person in a second if provoked.

Especially if it belonged to someone like James

143

McGuirre. He closed his eyes on bad memories and forced himself to concentrate. It could be any one of a thousand people in this town who hated him. He'd received many nasty calls and letters, not the least being that interesting call from the Ladies' Club of Heather Glen. For that matter, it could be the mayor, Chloe's father.

He glanced at her. 'Who have you told?'

'Told?'

He made a face. 'You must have let drop to someone that *I* am Mountain Mortgage.'

Biting her lip, she looked down.

'Slim?'

'Oh, Thomas, of course I can see why you're asking. Because whoever did this obviously had to find out through me, right?'

He managed a little laugh. 'Well, I sure didn't tell anyone.'

Her face reddened.

'Don't tell me,' he said dryly. 'You've told the entire town. Taken out an ad. Made a commercial. Hung a banner. Everyone, look, Thomas McGuirre owns Mountain Mortgage.'

'Worse.' She covered her mouth, muffling a nervous laugh. 'Remember our meeting?'

'How could I forget?' he asked wryly. 'You stormed out and nearly slammed the door on my nose.'

'You do remember,' she said a little guiltily, 'I apologized for that.'

'You had nothing to be sorry for,' he said grimly. 'I surprised you.'

'Yes, you did. Well, okay, I did storm out. And maybe I grumbled about it. Just a *little* bit,' she hastened to add, and he snorted.

'More than a little bit, Chloe.'

'And,' she continued, ignoring his interruption, 'Augustine and Lana *might* have heard me.'

'Might have?'

'Yeah.' Again she bit her lower lip, dragging it between her teeth. 'And maybe Lana can't seem to keep such things to herself.'

'What,' he said, suddenly tense, 'Are you telling me?'

Her eyes held apology, repressed humor and a lot of embarrassment. 'That maybe, just maybe . . .'

'Maybe what, Slim?'

Her gaze dropped. 'Maybe just about everyone knows.'

'Shit.' He sat back on his heels, his jeans hopelessly covered in muck. 'Double shit.'

'Also, my father knows.'

'Great.' But something in her expression made him take a closer look. 'Is this a problem for you? That he knows?'

'No, not really.' Again she blushed, tipping him off. 'Well, just a little tiny bit.'

'Why? Just out of curiosity here, what does it matter to your father who your loan is from?'

'It doesn't.' She inhaled deeply and looked at the ceiling, at the floor, just about anywhere but at him. 'It's just that . . . well, he blames me for not knowing ahead of time it was you.'

'Let me guess. He thinks that's irresponsible of you.' At her miserable nod, he swore again. 'Don't take this wrong, Chloe. But I don't like your family very much.'

'They worry about me.' She shrugged as if it didn't matter. 'My father's the mayor. My mother's the one and only orthodontist for miles and miles, and she's highly respected in the community. And my sister – '

'Doesn't bear talking about,' he said harshly. 'Look, they don't seem to give you very much credit. And you *are* a credit to them. Look how much you do in the community. That takes a lot of work and a lot of time. On top of that, you run a successful business. Doesn't all that count?'

'I'm a glorified cook.'

'Whoever put that idea in your head doesn't know you very well.' He peered at her, suddenly understanding. 'It's that they don't approve of what you do and you want them to.'

'Can we get off this subject?' she asked uncomfortably. 'I don't want to talk about it.'

'I bet you don't.' But he was willing to drop it because he understood better than most how unsettling discussing family could be. 'What a helluva mess we've got here.'

'You swear a lot.'

'You inspire me.' He sighed. 'That does it. You'll need a bodyguard.'

She laughed. 'You're kidding.' Her grin faded as she stared at him, wide-eyed. 'You're not kidding.'

'Absolutely not.'

146

'Don't be ridiculous. The point was made.' Her eyes were serious. Her weariness returned. 'We'll be fine now.'

'Are you forgetting the explosion in my kitchen? Or – ' He stopped himself from admitting that yet another of his properties had also been damaged. She didn't know how much he owned, and if she did, she'd figure out the rest.

'The point has been made,' she said stubbornly. 'I believe I'm safe.'

He'd drop that for now. But if Chloe wasn't worried or frightened for herself, then what explained the torment in her eyes? 'If you won't let me hire a cleaning service, at least let me reimburse you for your lost earnings for today.'

'No.'

Privy to her financial records as he was, he knew exactly her situation. He also knew exactly how generous she tended to be. The woman had next to nothing for herself. A day of no wages would hurt. 'Yes,' he said gently. 'It's the least I can do.'

When she would have protested, he stunned them both by placing his fingers over her mouth. 'If we hurry, you can be open by lunch.'

She took his wrist in her hand and lowered his fingers from her mouth, but didn't let go of him. 'Who did it, Thomas? Who wants to hurt you?'

She knelt on the floor beside him, with her huge eyes on him, and the mess around them faded. The nightmare that was his life disappeared.

All that existed was the two of them, and the deep,

147

undeniable thing that drew them together. He wanted her, quite desperately. It terrified him.

'Plenty of people would like to hurt me,' he said nonchalantly. 'You'd do a lot better to ask the question, who *doesn't*?'

'You're going to prove them all wrong,' she said. 'And then all this ugly, awful tension will be gone.'

'This isn't a fairy tale,' he said harshly. Oh, yeah, he was going to prove himself, all right. He would prove that he hadn't forgotten. That he could hurt them as they'd hurt him.

And when it was all over, and he'd triumphed, where would he stand with this woman looking at him with her heart on her sleeve?

She'd hate him.

'I know this isn't a fairy tale,' she said softly, tugging on his wrist that she still held, bringing his hand to her face so that it cupped her cheek. Unable to help himself, his fingers stroked her soft skin.

'But if we try real hard,' she said, 'we can still have the happy ending.'

'I don't – ' he started, but then she turned her face and kissed his palm. Her mouth brushed over his hand, and at the touch of her lips words failed him.

'You deserve the happy ending, Thomas,' she whispered. 'I promise you do.'

What the hell was she doing to him? His stomach knotted, all the blood dropped from his head to his lap and he couldn't think. All because she'd touched her lips to his skin.

It had to stop.

Surging to his feet, he ignored her startled eyes. 'I've . . . got to go.'

At his abrupt tone, she started to rise too, but he shook his head. 'Don't see me out. And what I told you in the hospital stands. Stay away from me. It's for the best.'

'You came to me,' she reminded him quietly.

Well, hell. She was right there. 'I was a fool today, Chloe. Forget I came.'

'You've never been a fool.'

That stopped him as he touched the back door. Turning, he forced himself to meet her eyes, where she still kneeled in the center of the floor next to the bucket. 'You're wrong there, Chloe.'

Slowly, she shook her head.

She'd hate him, he reminded himself. When this was all over and done, she would. And then those lovely eyes would be filled with contempt.

The thought tore at him.

Without another glance, he left.

Chloe watched Thomas go, her heart aching. The feelings between them were stronger than ever, so real and so vivid. It had been everything she could do not to fling herself in his arms and demand another kiss.

But that would have had him running, not walking, toward the door.

Why couldn't he give in to the wonderful, heady feelings between them? she wondered miserably. Why did they have to confuse him so? And what was it going to take for him to trust her with those feelings? For she wanted that, badly.

Was it because she had asked for his help with Haroldina? In truth, she could easily have found the kitten another home. But she'd given her to Thomas for one very important reason.

She'd wanted to show him what it felt like to have something to care for, and to have those feelings returned. He seemed loath to do that with a human, so she thought she'd start small and work her way up.

But now it seemed as if he hadn't yet developed an attachment for the darling little kitten. More time, she told herself. She couldn't rush these things, not when he'd gone his entire life caring only for himself.

Patience.

She groaned. Normally long on that virtue, she felt incredibly the opposite today.

So he wanted her to stay away. She knew darn well it was because he couldn't handle the closeness they were developing. Okay, he was genuinely worried about the danger he might put her in, but, while that was touching, she didn't want to stay away.

She didn't want him to get used to being without her. Not when her very presence unbalanced him so. And in her not so humble opinion, Mr Thomas McGuirre could use some unbalancing.

Less than twenty minutes later, while she still kneeled on the floor, scrubbing away, a van pulled into her lot. The sign on the side read, 'Betty's Cleaning Service'.

150

Chloe sighed. Thomas might have left her, but he hadn't forgotten. But he was getting more than a little annoying.

'Hello? Chloe?' An older couple, two people that Chloe just happened to know because they lived in a building right next to hers, alighted on the steps. Margaret and Bejamin Crown, sixty each if they were a day. Betty, a ninety-year-old herself, and too old to clean anymore, had years and years ago hired the Crowns. They were the only cleaning service in town.

'Hello.' Chloe sighed again and resigned herself. She would still turn away the cleaning service on principle, but with these two non-stop talkers, it would be an hour before she could be alone again.

Darn it, Thomas. Obviously he cared – very much. Spending money without a thought because he thought she needed help with the mess.

So if he cared so much, why he couldn't he admit it? And why did she have to stay away from him? She was going to have to do something about him.

Then she brightened. *Unbalancing.* That was what he needed. And she had just the thing to do it.

She'd seduce him.

CHAPTER 9

Chloe intended to do it, too. The fact that she'd never purposely set out to seduce a man didn't stop her. She'd read enough romance novels; she could figure it out.

And she truly meant to. Until she got back to her apartment building. Inside the lobby, where she picked up her mail, was a crew of men.

With ladders and buckets of paint at their feet, they were . . . painting.

'Hello,' one of them called, smiling down at her. 'Watch out for drops of falling paint.'

'Who are you?' she managed.

'Eddie's Painting Service,' another called. From six feet above on a ladder, he tipped his hat back. 'Chloe? I didn't know you lived here.'

Timothy Black was the son of one of her father's neighbors. 'And I didn't know you painted.'

A tall, thin, very fair boy, he blushed to his roots. 'I go to the junior college at night and paint for Eddie during the day.'

'But why are you painting *here*?'

152

'We've been commissioned by the new owner to paint the interior. We'll be back in spring to fix the exterior. After the new windows and fire escapes are installed.'

Thorton had owned this building since the beginning of time. Before that his dad had. Never, in Chloe's recollection, had there been any maintenance done. *Ever.*

'Are you sure you have the right building?' she asked, provoking laughter from the entire crew.

'No kidding.' Timothy removed his cap and scratched his head. 'I don't think these walls have been painted since the turn of the century.'

'Thorton would never – ' She stopped. 'What do you mean, *new owner?*'

Timothy shrugged. 'Someone bought the place. Ordered it cleaned up – though the building's still in escrow.'

A suspicion so terrible it made her head ache came over Chloe. 'This must have just happened.' Only last night Thorton had been hounding her for her rent, which was two days late.

'Yep. Just today. This guy works fast.'

Chloe grabbed her mail and headed for her apartment, planning on making a little phone call to confirm her fears. But halfway there, she fumbled. Topping her stack of mail was a plain envelope.

No return address.

Inside was a very generous check, drawn from Mountain Mortgage's local bank account. The note attached was short and to the point: *Sorry for the inconvenience at* Homebaked. *This should cover any lost income.*

Oh, it would, she thought a little dazed. It would cover her income for the entire week. That man! Bound and determined to keep her at bay, he actually thought by doing something like this, she'd be able to keep her distance.

Too bad she was just as bound and determined that they would maintain no distance between them at all. Then she froze as a new thought came to her. Thomas felt he now owed her, for saving his life. She'd even jokingly told him she would collect. Of course she had meant something far different than money, but the man who had never been shown love and affection couldn't know that. The first thing he thought of was probably money.

Maybe he was actually trying to buy her off, so he would no longer be 'indebted' to her.

'Chloe?'

Darn. Turning back, she sent Mr Thorton a little smile. 'Yes?'

Opening his door wider, he stepped out into the hallway. 'I want your rent check. By tomorrow.'

Because it was easier than telling the truth – which was that she wouldn't have the money until the end of the week, and then only if she was very lucky – she simply nodded. But curiosity got the better of her. 'You sold this place?'

'Looks that way.' He peered at her over his little bifocals. 'I mean it, Chloe. I want that money. You owe it to me, not the new owner.'

'Who did you sell to?'

'The mortgage company bought me out,' he said, with some surprise. 'I had no intentions of selling, but they offered me more than I could turn down. I couldn't believe it –' Abruptly, he cut himself off and glared at her. 'But even so, I still want that rent, young lady.'

Thomas had bought her building. *Why*? Another buy-off? Surely he didn't believe she would actually stay here rent-free. 'You'll have it,' she said weakly, turning away.

Blindly, she made her way into her apartment. There, she listened to her messages and sank her boneless body into the couch.

'Chloe.' She almost didn't recognize Conrad's voice on her machine, it sounded so strange, so strained. 'Why didn't you call me about *Homebaked* today? I want to hear you're all right. Is there anything I can do? And, dammit, call me!'

The next message was also Conrad. 'Don't be mad, honey,' came his gentle voice, 'but Lana told me that *Homebaked*'s loan got bought by Mountain Mortgage and that you're upset because supposedly that's Thomas.'

'I'll make her do dishes by hand for a week,' Chloe grumbled to no one in particular. 'Make that a month.'

'So I did some checking,' Conrad was saying. 'Now, now,' he said quickly, 'don't get in a snizzle. What are computers for if you can't snoop around a bit?'

Chloe sent her gaze heavenward and shook her head.

'Anyway,' he continued, 'guess what else Mountain Mortgage purchased?'

Every muscle went rigid. 'What?' she whispered as if he could hear her. 'God, what now?'

'The Teen Hood,' Conrad said. 'He purchased the lease, the land, the building . . . everything. What does that mean, Chloe?'

She hadn't the foggiest idea.

'Call me,' Conrad said. 'Soon.'

Chloe stared at the phone, knowing she shouldn't be surprised. First *Homebaked*, then her apartment, now this. Teen Hood – the place where she spent time helping rehabilitate troubled teens and tutor them in reading. The building they used was private, and they constantly had trouble making their lease payments.

She wanted to think it was a Godsend, but she wasn't sure. What would he do with it? For that matter, what would he do with *this* building?

Wearily, she covered her face. 'Thomas,' she whispered, 'what are you up to?'

For she had to face facts: he was up to *something*. First he'd reappeared in town after vowing never to return. Despite his obvious reluctance, he'd allowed her to befriend him. He'd purchased a lovely home for himself, making roots in a town that hadn't exactly made him welcome.

Then, even more curiously, he'd bought her *Homebaked* loan. Then her entire building. It now appeared he'd bought the Teen Hood as well. Crazy, but it didn't end there. Someone had placed an explosive device in his home and then had vandalized her restaurant.

What did it all mean?

Thomas would have given a lot of money to understand that as well. A simple check verified what he didn't want to know.

His father had left town and was this very minute in Reno, probably conning some poor sucker into letting him play for him.

So who had messed with *Homebaked*? And who had tried to blow him and Chloe to the moon?

Every time he thought about it he felt truly ill. He'd brought nothing but trouble to her. In return, she'd offered him unconditional friendship, she'd saved his life, and with every look, every touch she freely gave him, she reminded him what he could never have. Her heart.

He wasn't worthy of it – in fact, he had no idea why he even wanted it. Not only would he break that precious, giving organ of hers, but he'd disappoint it as well. Chloe would never understand what he planned for Heather Glen. It wasn't in her blood to hold grudges, to plan revenge.

The best, the kindest thing he could do would be to stick by his words to her. To make her stay as far away from him as possible. He couldn't hurt her that way. Yep, that was what he had to do. Keep miles away.

But then he thought about their last kiss and he knew he couldn't.

They were doomed.

It took her all day and she still had no idea if she'd been successful or not.

Exhausted, mentally and physically, Chloe climbed the steps to her apartment, head down, contemplating what she'd done.

What would Thomas say when he found out?

'You'd better be alone, Chloe.' Thorton poked his skinny head out his door and narrowed hairy eyebrows at her. 'No animals. I mean that.'

She lifted her empty – and bare – hands. 'I'm clean. I promise.'

Those piercing eyes didn't give. 'And I don't want *him* around here anymore either. He's trouble. No-good trouble.'

She assumed 'him' was Thomas. And while she was pretty sure it wouldn't be a problem, since Thomas had obviously no intention of bothering with her, it hurt her pride to admit it. 'My lease says nothing about regulating my visitors. And besides, doesn't he own the place now?'

'Humph. Not until escrow closes.' His door slammed.

The smile that crossed her face was short-lived. Feeling frozen, she let herself into her frigid apartment – no heat again – and slipped out of the heels that had been bothering her since she'd left this morning.

With a great big sigh, she plopped down on her couch, still in her coat. Would someone, any one of the financial institutions she'd seen today, give her a loan? She could only hope, because that was the one and only way she could think of to free herself of the strange and unreasonable hold Thomas McGuirre seemed to have over her.

She could pay him off. Then they'd be even.

The slate would be clean.

They could start completely over.

She hoped.

But in the meantime she needed a diversion. A cover for her sudden, inexplicable loneliness. Lonely? That was strange, she never got lonely. Never. There was always too much to do.

She could go to the Teen Hood. Or to Conrad's to play some *Uno*. She could even go to her parents' house for dinner.

None of those things appealed. It would be hard to give encouragement and help to the kids when she felt so discouraged and unable to help herself. Conrad, sweet as he was, wasn't who she wanted, and it was cruel to use him. And her parents . . . That didn't appeal at all.

The only thing that did was hopping in her car and going to see Thomas, and, since he'd made himself unavailable, that was no choice at all.

She'd cook.

Something fattening, she decided, and the heck with her diet. Yanking down her favorite cookbook, she flipped it open to desserts, determined not to quit until she'd consumed at least a thousand calories. Her mouth watered at the sight of the examples on the pages.

Running her finger down the long list of recipes, she stopped at something she'd never tried. Champagne cake. Interesting, she decided. Very interesting. She'd eat the entire thing by herself if she wanted.

She set off searching through her cupboards. 'I had one bottle of champagne; I know it's in here somewhere,' she muttered, shoving things aside in search. 'Can't have champagne cake without champagne.'

She found it, and with a loud pop opened the bottle, managing to crack the cork as well. Grimacing at her sloppiness, she promptly got ready to lose herself in the joy of cooking. She stopped to crank up some classical music – a must for cooking – and stoked up the fire since her fingers were still too cold to work fluidly.

It didn't help. But she couldn't very well cook with gloves on, so she cursed both Thorton and Thomas for the broken heater. Thorton just because he couldn't care less if she froze, and Thomas for spending money on paint when he should have replaced the darn heater!

Then her gaze rested on the opened bottle of champagne. Her recipe only required a quarter-cup. The rest of the bottle remained. Just sitting there innocuously on the counter. Hadn't she read somewhere that liquor warmed a person? Not a drinker, Chloe honestly didn't know. The next shiver caused her to spill the flour she'd just carefully measured and that decided her.

Grabbing the bottle about the neck, she took a long guzzle of the bubbly stuff, then set it down on the counter and sneezed three times. A shudder wracked her frame. *Yuck.*

To be fair, she thought a minute later as she shivered again, she should really give it one more try. Just an eensy-weensy one. She did, and it wasn't nearly so bad as the first one, she decided.

A few minutes later, as she buttered up the bottom of her pan, she realized something. The iciness in her limbs had started to dissipate. But her toes were still cold. Another swig should remedy that. This time she only sneezed twice.

Working with the flour and salt, she hesitated and glanced down at her teal business suit. She should change. Nah, she thought, shaking her head. Already made a mess of the thing. Besides, the suit reminded her of Thomas, and his incredible blue eyes.

He didn't want her. That deep, dark restlessness in him, the sense of desperateness she knew was just beneath his surface, wouldn't allow her to get close.

Her loud sigh echoed in the empty kitchen. *He didn't want her.* Looking down at herself, to assess the situation, she realized why. She was a mess. Flour decorated her skirt. Something that looked suspiciously like drops of champagne dotted her jacket. Wrinkles from shoulder to hem finished the picture.

She'd have to throw the suit away. On the way to

the oven, Chloe stopped for another drink of the now delicious-tasting champagne. Then she stumbled as she put in the cake, nearly spilling her efforts all over the floor.

She giggled at herself and took another drink. Time to clean up. Hazily, she looked around for the cork. But, while she found what looked like ten refrigerators and twenty-five ovens rotating through her vision, she couldn't find the cork.

Ah, she remembered. She'd broken it. And suddenly, she didn't feel much like cleaning up. Nope, she felt like celebrating.

Thomas didn't want her – which meant she was a free women. That was something to drink to, wasn't it? Besides, it would be a shame to waste the bottle.

Squinting, she held it up before her eyes. Only half an inch left. Wow. Had she really drunk that much? Well, it might explain why her eyes weren't working properly and her mouth had gone dry as cotton.

The phone rang, and for the life of her Chloe couldn't reach it in time. Things kept popping up in her way – the couch, the carpet, her own feet.

Tripping halfway there, she stumbled down to the floor, laughing at herself. Then Conrad's voice came over the machine.

'Chloe, where are you? Are you stressing over *Homebaked*? Or Thomas buying out the Teen Hood? Please, don't. We'll figure it out. *Call me.*'

Blinking the phone into focus, Chloe managed to crawl towards it. That's right, Conrad had just reminded her. *She was mad at Thomas.*

She'd just call him and tell him so.

It took her three tries to dial his number right, and even then she dropped the receiver so that she missed his first hello.

'Thomas?' She blinked and stared at the phone. 'That you?'

'Chloe?' His voice switched from irritated to worried. 'What's the matter? You sound funny.'

She giggled and slipped weightlessly from the couch to the floor, letting her head fall back on the cushion. 'I . . . feel funny.'

'Are you all right?'

'Oh, yeah. Thomas, how much champagne does it take to make one – she hiccuped and slapped a hand over her mouth – 'Drunk?'

Now the deep, sexy voice changed, leaped from mildly annoyed to disbelieving. 'Chloe, have you been drinking?'

'Silly. I don't drink. Liquor, that is.'

He sounded relieved. 'I didn't think so.'

Then the unthinkable happened. She burped. 'Oops. Excuse me.'

'You have been drinking,' he accused. 'Are you alone?'

'Nope. I'm here with my buddies. Flour, salt, water.' She laughed uproariously at her joke.

'What's going on, Slim?' he asked tightly.

'Making a cake. A champagne cake.'

'Champagne?' Now he sounded pained.

'I broke the cork.'

'I see.'

'Didn't want to waste it. How much, Thomas?'

'How much what?'

'How much to make one drunk?' she repeated in what she thought was a very patient voice. Was the man dense? Hadn't she already asked this question? Why couldn't he answer her? 'Never mind,' she said, exasperated. 'I called to tell you to . . . knock it off.' She listed to one side and dropped the phone again.

'Knock what off?' His voice came fast and a little desperate now as she fumbled with the phone. 'Chloe, *what the hell is going on over there?*'

'I'm gonna pay you off,' she promised. 'Just as soon as another loan comes through. I will.'

'We discussed this. The loan with Mountain Mortgage is fine. You don't have to – *What other loan?*'

'I'm gonna move out too. Can't be your bought woman, you know. I don't know whatever made you think I would. Tongues'll waggle all over town.' Again laughter overtook her, as she pictured the town's collective tongues, all hanging from their heads as they waggled back and forth.

'You're not all right. I'm coming over there.'

'No,' she said, shaking her head and making herself dizzy. 'Don't come. I'll smack you. I won't tolerate you buying all my stuff, you know. Even if I think it means you like me. You do like me, Thomas, don't you? A little?'

'Who told you I'm buying stuff, Chloe?'

'Ah-ah,' she said, slipping further down on the floor. Her head hit the carpet with a thud and she winced. 'Ouch. I'm not saying anymore until I know you like me.'

'Christ,' she heard him mumble. 'Chloe, I – '

'Yes or no.'

'*I like you*,' he said, quite succinctly. 'But you are driving me crazy here, Slim. How much did you – '

'It's cold here,' she complained, shivering. 'And it's your fault.'

'You're cold? And it's my fault? How's that?'

'Just is. Did you know that I don't have to measure when I bake a cake? That I can get it right every time by just . . . guessing?'

'I didn't know that. Look – '

'It's a special talent of mine.' For a minute, a melancholy feeling penetrated her fog. 'It's my only talent, you know.'

'Says who? Chloe, you're not making much sense here.'

'The mayor thinks I should get a new talent. So does his wife.'

'The mayor is an idiot.'

She giggled, then shivered. 'Brr.'

'Is that damn heater off again?' he asked suddenly. 'Is that why you're cold? I'll kill Thorton. He promised – '

Her stomach roiled. Her head pounded. 'I've gotta go,' she whispered, suddenly afraid she'd be sick.

'Wait – '

'Can't buy me,' she said stiffly, pushing herself to her knees.

'Do you have a fire going?'

165

'Can't buy me,' she repeated firmly, holding a hand to her spinning head. 'Stop trying. Either like me, or don't. But don't buy any more of my stuff.'

'Chloe – '

'Not that I have anything more for you to buy.' The timer in the kitchen went off and the buzzing made her wince.

'Dammit, Chloe – '

She dropped the phone back in its place and crawled into the kitchen. Couldn't burn the cake. Not when she'd gone to so much trouble. Ahh, she thought, slumping back against the counter. Much warmer in here, thanks to the oven. Much, much warmer . . .

CHAPTER 10

The woman was going to be the death of him. Thomas yanked on his coat and stomped out into the snow to the Jag. What the hell did she think she was doing, making accusations and calling him like that?

She'd been drinking. Yet Chloe hated alcohol, always had. Just the thought had him pressing the accelerator to dangerous, reckless levels on the slippery roads. What had driven her to this?

That was easy. *Him.* Self-recrimination hit hard and heavy.

Somehow she'd found out he'd bought her apartment and the Teen Hood, and she'd completely misinterpreted his reasons for it. She thought he was trying to own her, or something equally ridiculous. *She really thought that.*

Of course she did, he told himself with self-disgust. Because he had yet to tell her he'd set out to buy the entire town of Heather Glen under the cover of Sierra Rivers.

Then destroy it.

Chloe, in her infinite kindness, had automatically assumed he'd done what he had for altruistic reasons.

But he didn't have an altruistic bone in his cold, unforgiving body.

By the time he turned onto her street, he had convinced himself he would let her think what she wanted, as long as she didn't repeat it. He pulled into the dark, forbidding parking area of her apartment and noted that he needed to add lights. Taking the stairs two steps at a time, he felt the railing give under his weight. That would have to be fixed, too. As well as the dark, narrow hallway.

Add lights? Fix the stairwell? What the hell was wrong with him?

But he knew, and as always he was brutally honest – at least with himself – he couldn't stand the thought of Chloe living here, under these conditions. A bright, loving, caring creature like Chloe deserved far, far more. And that, at least, he could give her. The lights, the paint, the railing . . . they would be fixed – for her.

And so would the new heater he'd have installed tomorrow.

Insane, he thought as he knocked on her door. He'd gone insane. And all because of a sweet, giving smile that reminded him of things he'd never known, had only dreamed of.

It made him pound all the harder on the pathetically thin door. No answer. Dispensing with niceties, he let himself in, cursing her for leaving it unlocked.

Had she learned nothing?

'Chloe!' he called, squinting in the frigid darkness. Still no answer. With fear for her his major motivation, he moved in, flipping on lights, still calling her name.

On the floor of the living room a handful of tiny ripped pieces of paper was scattered. Bending, he picked one up and frowned.

She'd ripped up the check he'd sent her for the damage to *Homebaked*.

The insistent buzzing led him to the kitchen first, and the sight of her slumped on the floor had his heart in his throat.

His knees hit the floor beside her. 'Chloe.'

She stirred, lifted her head and gave him a huge smile. 'Made cake.'

Relief faded and anger bubbled hard and fast. 'You scared me to death.' Her skin was like ice. Cursing, he lifted her up against him. She promptly planted her face into his neck and he flinched. 'Christ, you're freezing.'

'Your fault,' she mumbled, snuggling closer. 'Mmm, you feel good.' She crawled into his lap, her skirt hitching up alarmingly high on a lean, bare thigh. 'Was mad at you,' she added, 'but you feel too good to stay mad at.'

'Chloe . . .' he started helplessly, forcing his gaze from her legs. It didn't matter. She was a boneless mass of soft, dewy skin that felt and smelled so incredible that even when he closed his eyes he still felt tortured. Just holding her did something to his insides. Something unaccustomed. Something mushy. 'I was mad at you too. Still am.' To prove it, he glared at her.

But she just giggled and pulled closer. Sighing, she

said, 'I like the feel of your arms around me. Even when you scowl so fiercely. They're sure nice, strong arms, Thomas.'

How was he supposed to stay furious at her? He couldn't even keep his distance. 'What am I going to do about you?' he wondered aloud, truly baffled.

'Keep me?' she asked hopefully, rubbing her cheek to his. Her champagne breath caressed him.

'I can't.' But for just a minute his arms tightened around her. He was sorely tempted. When he was with her, like this, he couldn't for the life of him remember why he fought her so hard. Revenge was the furthest thing from his mind, and so was the reason behind hurting Heather Glen. He simply couldn't remember.

Her lips met his jaw.

She made it so easy to forget.

But could he? Could he really just walk away from the carefully laid plans he'd spent his life perfecting?

'I'm dizzy,' she announced, hiccuping.

He eyed the tipped over empty bottle of champagne. 'No wonder.'

'I got bubbles up my nose.'

When she wiggled the mentioned appendage, he laughed.

She stared at him, amazed. 'You can,' she breathed.

'I can what?'

'You *can* laugh. Oh, Thomas. Do it again.'

In truth, he actually felt like it. And he'd never been a man to laugh easily. There'd been so few chances for it in his life. But Chloe made him laugh. Or at least made him want to want to. So startling was that revelation, he just stared at her.

'Never mind,' she said, smiling mischievously and cupping his face. 'It's enough to know I caused it. For now.' Still grinning impishly, she shifted her bottom, grinding it into his lap.

He bared his teeth and sucked in a deep breath. 'Chloe – '

'Want some champagne?' she offered, raising her eyebrows and wiggling her bottom again. 'Not that you need it, but – '

'You drank it all,' he reminded her, his voice rough and thick. God, he could use a glass of something much harder than bubbly. 'I think you'd better get up.'

'I'd say the same to you, but you're already "up." ' Then she grinned, a huge, face-splitting grin, and wriggled again. 'Aren't you?'

'Chloe – '

'Yeah,' she whispered, settling closer. 'Definitely up.'

'Stop it. You have some explaining to do.'

She laughed at that and tossed her arms around his neck. 'No explaining. Not now. Too dizzy.'

Then she tossed her head back over his arm and started singing. When she did, her teal suit jacket opened, revealing a cream silk blouse that dipped alarmingly low in front. 'Chloe – '

'You keep saying that,' she said, then flung back her head and resumed her God-awful singing.

He had to force himself to remain still, so that he didn't dip down and taste that tantalizing throat, that slim neck, that spot directly between her breasts that he was so aching to touch. *Control*, he reminded himself. But he'd never been so tempted to throw it all to the wind.

She bounced when she sang. Every time she did, her small, firm breasts bounced too, enticingly, only inches from his mouth. He licked his lips. As she moved against him she continually slid over the vee of his pants with her soft bottom. His hand curled into the fabric of the suit at her waist.

God, he wanted her.

As he sat there listening to her, with the cold from the kitchen floor seeping into him, he frowned at the insistent, annoying buzzing. Then he realized he smelled something burning as well. 'What is that?'

'Oh!'

She popped up, cracking the top of her head on his chin hard enough to make him see stars. 'Ow!'

Surging to her feet, she promptly lost her balance and teetered wildly. 'The cake!' she cried. 'Is it done?'

'More than done, I bet.' When he opened the oven, black smoke filled the room. Flicking off the heat and dumping the blackened cake in the sink, he turned and faced her, rubbing his sore chin. 'Explain this.'

She crossed her arms over her chest, or tried to. It took three tries. 'Nope. I don't think so. I don't have to explain anything to you.'

'Oh, yes, you do,' he assured her, reaching for her. Evading him, she flung her arms wild and spun

172

around the tiny kitchen, smacking him as she did with her hands. 'I don't,' she said in a sing-song, tipsy voice. 'Because I'm free. Free, free, free . . .'

Her next whirl landed her hard against his chest. For lack of anything else to do with her, he gripped her hips to hold her still, staring down into her flushed face. Unable to help it, he grinned. 'You're really quite smashed.'

His amusement faded immediately as she rocked her hips against his and closed her eyes. 'Mmm,' she murmured. And then did it again.

He was hard as stone in two seconds. 'Chloe,' he said a little hoarsely, 'don't.'

But she did, and this time she plastered her breasts to his chest too, flinging her arms around his neck.

There were rules about this, weren't there? he wondered a bit desperately. One couldn't take advantage of a drunk, right?

Then she yanked his head down and covered his lips with her sweet-tasting ones. 'Kiss me,' she demanded against them. 'I want you to kiss me.'

For one brief little fraction in time, he became a very weak man and did. Then he groaned and lifted his head. 'Chloe, wait.'

'I'm free,' she murmured, her eyes closed. 'Just remember that. You don't own me. You never will. I'm not a piece of property, you know. Kiss me again, Thomas.'

'Of course you're not a piece of property.' This explained everything. He wasn't the insane one; *she was.*

173

'But you keep trying to buy me.'

'The check I sent you was to repair the damage. Not to buy you.'

'You're trying to buy me,' she insisted, still wriggling in an impossible, erotic way that was getting to him. Her hips slid over his throbbing hardness.

Definitely getting to him.

'Mmm,' she said, her eyes still closed. 'Stop buying me.'

His hands closed over her hips to keep them still. 'What are you babbling about?'

'You bought this place. And my loan.' She opened eyes such a painfully clear green he could see himself reflected.

And he didn't like what he saw.

'Then you bought the Teen Hood,' she said, still staring at him very carefully, very still. 'You've purchased everything I ever cared about. Why?'

'You don't understand.' And she never would, he vowed. He couldn't handle what she would think about him, how she would hate him.

'I'm drunk,' she said, with the slow care only someone quite foxed can achieve. 'Not stupid.'

It was hard to think with her watching him like that, with her heart in her eyes. Then she hiccuped again and he had to smile, because she looked so damned cute with her hair tousled, her jacket askance, her stockinged feet bare. He wanted to scoop her up and never let her go. 'I never thought you were stupid,' he told her.

'Someone wants to hurt you.' Solemnly she

glanced down at the bandage on her wrist, and his gut tightened as he remembered how much worse it could have been. 'Someone almost did hurt you.'

'It's over.' He'd make sure of it, even though the only way to ensure her safety was to stay away from her.

'What does it all mean, Thomas?'

What could he tell her?

'I – ' She hiccuped again. 'I don't think you're going to tell me a thing, are you?'

'Would you remember tomorrow if I did? You're pretty trashed, Slim.'

With one finger she came at him, obviously intending to stick it in his chest. 'I resemble that remark, McGuirre. I mean I *resent* that.' Her finger poked him in the eye. 'Oh! I'm sorry!' Again she slung her arms around his neck and held tight. 'I'll remember every minute of this tomorrow. I think.' Her eyes closed and she mumbled, 'I should have my new loan by then. Then I'll show you. And them.'

'What loan?'

'Used my one and only business suit to try to impress the banks.' She slithered her body down his and waggled her eyebrows at him. 'Think it worked?'

Too much. He was, after all, only a man. A very weak, very bad man. Closing his eyes was a mistake, because he felt her all the more. 'I don't know. Who else are you trying to show besides me?'

'My family. They think I'm hopeless.'

Anger surged for this lovely, hurting creature in

his arms. 'Chloe, what they think doesn't matter.'

Her teeth sank into his earlobe and his damn knees went weak! Firmly he dislodged her hands from around his neck – no easy feat since she had the grip of a bulldog. Her fingers were icicles. Icicles that tried to drag him back against her.

'Come on, Thomas. Prove you like me.'

'I can't believe this,' he muttered, dodging her limbs, which suddenly seemed as if they'd multiplied. 'Chloe, come on – ' The breath halted in his throat when she rubbed a silken thigh against the part of him that never behaved near her. 'That does it,' he exploded, backing against the sink and warding her off. 'Stop it. Now.'

While she pouted, he made sure her oven was off. Then he went back for Chloe, who had sunk to the cold floor and wrapped her arms around her legs.

'C-c-cold,' she said.

'I know, Slim. I know.' He pulled her up.

'I love it when you call me that,' she murmured, closing her eyes. He tugged her to the front door.

'What – ?' She squinted. 'Where are we going?'

'I'm taking you someplace warmer.' He couldn't leave her alone here all night. She'd freeze.

'No. I don't want to go.' Stubbornly she crossed her arms, and gave him a look he was beginning to know all too well. 'Just try to make me.'

'Look,' he said, coming up with what he thought was a brilliant plan, 'you saved my life, right?'

'Right,' she said slowly, not trusting him.

'Well, then, I owe you.'

'Oh, no, McGuirre. You're not going to get off that easy. No way. You still owe me.'

He hadn't thought it would work, but it had been worth a try.

'I'll let you know when I want to collect.'

'Fine,' he ground out. He'd find a way to pay her back with money, so help him, he would. That way they'd be even for once and for all. No way was he going to do whatever it was she had in mind for him. 'You're still coming with me.' Grabbing her wrist, he started through the door.

'You're proposed – *supposed* to carry me,' she complained. 'I've seen it in all the movies. The hero carries the girl.'

'I'm no hero. Where's your coat and gloves?'

Those wide eyes filled with suspicion. 'Where are we going?'

'Where it's warm. Where the hell are your things?'

Finding the coat was easy. It lay crumpled on the floor, just where she'd dropped it. Getting her into it was another thing, since she was no better than a limp noodle. Bending over her, he tried to shove a hand through an armhole.

Laughing when he swore, she tipped her head back and gave him a smacking kiss on the cheek.

'Knock that off.'

With another laugh, she took his earlobe between her teeth.

Sucking in his breath, he glared at her while all sorts of interesting reactions charged through his body. 'I said, quit it.' And he resumed his efforts to dress her for the outside weather while she just gave him an innocent smile.

She didn't help the cause any by continuing to kiss whatever came close to her mouth; his face, his neck, his hands. By the time he'd finished, and belted the damn coat around her captivating body, he was sweating and horny as hell.

'Mmm. Nice and warm and toasty.' Again, she smiled at him. 'I feel good, Thomas.'

Yeah, she felt good all right. 'Great.' And he was sporting an erection that threatened to rip open his jeans. Her hands would have to stay cold, because he couldn't handle dressing her any further.

'Why won't you kiss me?' she asked, turning out a pretty lower lip.

'Because you're too drunk to kiss me back properly.' She had no idea what she was doing to him, or maybe she did and she enjoyed torturing him.

'No, I'm not. Come on, Thomas,' she wheedled, coming at him with those kissable lips all puckered and ready to go. 'Kiss me.'

Oh, he wanted to. With every fiber of his being and then some. But he found he just couldn't take advantage unless she knew exactly what she was doing.

Unless she knew exactly what she was doing? Since when did he worry about things like that?

Oh, he was losing it to even be considering . . . *No*. He would just pour her sexy little body into his car, take her to his warm house and lock her away in the guestroom.

That was absolutely all he would do.

She rubbed her breasts against his back when he turned to shut the door and he gritted his teeth. 'Great, just great,' he grumbled, frustrated beyond belief. 'Why couldn't you be a nice, quiet drunk?'

She laughed, a light, bubbly sound that only increased his discomfort. How was it possible for her to get more and more beautiful as the seconds went by?

Then his beautiful, sexy, very drunk Chloe sagged against him, still laughing a little. 'You're so wonderful, Thomas.'

'Gee, thanks.'

'No, I mean it.' She batted wide green eyes up at him. 'I really like you.'

'You just want to kiss me.'

She laughed again. And again his gut tightened.

He propped her up against the wall while he searched for the right key on her ring, then managed to keep her upright by putting an arm around her waist while he locked her door.

'Don't you dare pass out,' he told a yawning Chloe. 'I have a lot of questions for you.'

'Like what?' She walked beside him docilely enough, but Thomas wasn't fooled. Chloe was not a docile woman.

'Like what do you mean you're trying to get another loan?'

'Hmm?' Her head rolled against his shoulder; her body sagged against his.

'Dammit.' Cursing into the cold, dark night, he

scooped her up and carried her all the way down the steps. An elevator, he thought breathlessly. This place needed an elevator. Huffing a little, he made it to the car.

Her arms snaked around his neck and a little smile played about those kissable lips. 'You are my hero after all.'

'Don't bet on it,' he said gruffly, dropping her into the seat so that she bounced.

Her eyes flew open and he laughed when she gave him a dark look.

She held a hand up to her head. 'My world's spinning.'

'Wait until the morning.' But it was hard to remain amused when he knew what a long night lay ahead of him.

Chloe's fingers ran reverently over the leather interior. 'I love this car.'

He squirmed uncomfortably. In the past his car had always been a huge source of pride, a status symbol. A measure of how far toward his goal he'd gotten.

Now he wondered what he'd ever seen in such blatant luxury when others struggled just to live. He'd come from that world once, understood a poverty most couldn't possibly imagine. So how had he gotten so far removed from it as to have nearly forgotten his own roots?

Watching Chloe practically drool over what he'd bought without a thought to the price put things sharply into focus. And it made him feel like an ass.

'I never paid you for cleaning it,' she whispered,

running a finger over a stain on the leather seat she'd put there that first night, when he'd given her a ride home. 'I'm sorry.'

Damn her for making him feel small, petty. Decadent. 'I told you to forget it.'

'Why? Because I couldn't afford to have it cleaned?'

'Because it doesn't matter.'

'How can it not matter?'

'Because . . .' What could he say? 'Dammit, it just doesn't.'

She blinked those wide eyes at him. Then suddenly grinned from ear to ear. 'You're cute when you're mad. Know that?'

'I'm not mad,' he said through clenched teeth. 'And I'm definitely not cute.'

'Okay, maybe not. "Cute" isn't really the word I was looking for. Dashing. Handsome. Aesthetically pleasing – '

'Could you be quiet?'

'And so dark and tortured. As if just beneath the tough, dangerous surface you – '

'Quiet – '

'It's very attractive to women, you know. That dark hero type. I – '

'Chloe.' His voice was deceptively calm, very controlled. '*Zip it.*' He rubbed his temples. 'Just for three minutes.'

'Why three?'

Because then we'll be at our destination and I can put you to bed. Alone. 'You're giving me a headache.'

'And I didn't even share my champagne with you. Selfish of me. But then I didn't know you were coming, since you said you never wanted to see me again.'

'I never said that.'

'Yes, you did.'

He sighed, and if he'd known how he would have prayed for patience. 'Chloe, you're mistaken.'

Twisting in her seat, she tilted her head at him in that endearing way she had. 'You said I had to stay away from you.'

'That was for your safety.' *And his sanity.*

'Safety, smafety.' She smiled that sweet smile of hers, the one that never failed to wring a tug from what he was beginning to suspect was the heart he had after all. 'I don't want to stay away from you. You need me.'

He had to laugh because what else could he do? '*I need you*? How do you figure that, Slim?'

Closing her eyes, she leaned back, a secret smile touching her lips. 'You need me to teach you how to enjoy life. How to laugh, how to live . . . how to love.'

His gut tightened painfully. 'Obviously you're still drunk. I don't need anyone.'

'Humph.'

'Do you think you can let me drive? In peace?'

'No.'

'Why ever not?'

That grin of hers was going to be the end of him; he knew it. 'Because it's not in my nature to be peaceful. Call it a generic fault, if you will.'

He sighed, something he seemed to do a lot around her, and tried to concentrate on driving, telling himself that this unreasonable fear that had gripped him was stupid. She wasn't right. Not at all. He needed no one, not when he had himself. Besides, soon enough he'd be gone from here and she'd hate him. She'd go on with her own life, maybe even with Conrad.

His insides twisted again at the thought. And she just lay there, her eyes closed, as if she didn't have a care in the world.

'I don't need you,' he repeated, more for himself than her.

No answer. Not even a flicker to suggest she'd heard him.

'I mean it, Chloe. This is temporary. Tomorrow we go back to you staying away from me. *Far* away from me.' She wasn't listening. 'Do you hear me?'

She refused to look at him. Of their own will, his eyes feasted on her wild hair, her smooth pale skin, that long body which had toned and changed so much from their childhood days. Every part of him yearned to reach out and touch her, even if only once.

Impossible. He couldn't do it. Not knowing how he'd deceived her. It seemed, he thought wryly, even Thomas McGuirre had scruples.

Being this close to her tonight was murder. He knew he couldn't handle anything more. 'Chloe?'

'You never told me where you were taking me.' She peered into the black night, wrapping her coat further around herself and sinking into the seat.

He adjusted the heater and aimed it at her legs. 'My house.' He felt the full weight of her stare and couldn't help but return it.

'Your house?' Now her voice squeaked a little.

It looked as if some of his brave little warrior's alcohol was starting to wear off, taking her courage with it. He felt the corners of his mouth quirk. 'Yeah.' He let his voice purr seductively. 'That's what you want, isn't it?'

'I – Well, I – '

'Look at that – you're squirming. I never thought I'd see the day. What's the matter, Slim? Change your mind?'

She opened her mouth but nothing came out, so she closed it again, and suddenly he didn't feel like teasing her anymore. He just wanted her warm and safe. And, yes, dammit, with him.

'I'm kidding, so relax. I'm taking you to my house because I happen to have a heater that works and you're a frozen block of ice. But, since you're wide awake now, and gaining control of your faculties, you can start explaining things to me.'

'Like what?'

Oh, yeah, she was definitely coming to. Her eyes had filled with a guarded wariness, and she'd curled into a ball on the seat. 'Lots of things,' he said conversationally, hiding his surprising slash of pain over her reaction to him. Already it was happening. She was pulling away. And she knew only a fraction of what he'd done, what he planned. How much worse it would be when she learned the real truth about him. 'You could start with who told you I was buying,' he suggested. 'And why you're looking for another loan.'

He could see that she'd not been thinking clearly, but his questions had forced her to do so. She chewed her lip thoughtfully. 'How do you know that?'

'You told me, Slim. On the telephone.'

'I had been drinking. You should know better than to trust what an inebriated person says.'

'That's true,' he admitted, piercing her with a brief look. 'But since you don't have a lying, cheating bone in your body, I doubt you could manage to fib while sober, much less under the influence. Why, Chloe?' He had to know; it was killing him. 'Why does the idea of me owning the loan bother you so much?'

'It's not just that.'

'What, then?'

'It's everything. Is it true?' she asked quietly. 'Did you really buy the Teen Hood and the building where I live?'

He could see how important his answer was to her as she leaned forward, waiting for him to speak. Just the fact that she wanted to hear it from him, that she would actually believe whatever he told her, hit him harder than he'd thought possible.

She trusted him. She believed in him. In spite of the fact that he deserved her to do neither.

If he gave her a good, sound reason for doing what he'd done, she'd take it to heart, she'd trust him – simply because she really, truly believed in him.

Had he ever felt like a bigger jerk?

Doubts ran rampant through his head, for the first time since he'd started the wheels in motion against Heather Glen so many years before. *Doubts?* No, not possible. He couldn't afford them. This craziness had to stop. This unaccountable attraction for this woman had to stop. Right now.

'Are you ever going to answer me?'

'Yes.'

'Did you buy the buildings?'

'Yes,' he admitted to her, steeling himself for what lay ahead. This was the tricky part. She couldn't find out the rest of the truth, that he had intended on bringing down Heather Glen. She just couldn't. It would ruin everything. 'But not for the reasons you think.'

'For what, then?' Her face turned to him earnestly. 'Tell me, Thomas. Explain it to me.'

The sincerity in her eyes, the hope and expectation were too much. She had no idea what he was capable of. 'It's none of your business,' he said shortly. 'Why are you trying to get another loan?'

Her eyes searched his for one more minute before the light in them simply died out. Her shoulders slumped and she turned her head away to stare out the window. 'My head hurts,' she said dully. 'I don't feel like talking anymore now.'

Too bad, he thought, biding his time. Because they weren't finished with this. Not by a long shot.

CHAPTER 11

The pride in Chloe refused to allow her to speak to Thomas again for the remainder of the ride. Humiliation had her pretending sleep.

Had she really thrown herself at him?

Had he really turned her down? Repeatedly? It was too much. She felt the car slow, then stop. Felt, too, how he turned his gaze to her.

She forced her breathing even and kept her eyes closed. Not easy to do when she still felt the effects of her ridiculous binge with the champagne. Was it too much to hope that he'd just leave her alone and go away?

Yes, she discovered a minute later as he came around and opened her door, it was. Icy wind blew in and she shivered, despite her resolve to keep still and feign sleep.

'Chloe?'

No way would she answer, she promised herself. No way. He could just . . . She heard his long-suffering sigh when he lifted her against him, and she was torn between wanting to shove him away and the unbearable urge to cling tight and never let go.

The chill of the night far outweighed her pride, and she decided to give in gracefully, allowing him to shift her against his warm, securing body.

With her eyes closed, her head back, the air hitting her bare neck, Chloe's world spun violently so that she gasped and threw her arms around his neck.

His dark gaze met hers. 'You're back.'

'I never left,' she said breathlessly. God, he felt good, *too good*. With his strong arms banded around her, his dark head dipped so close she found she could forget he didn't want or need her, that she shouldn't trust him.

It all paled behind this unbelievable magnetic pull, the undeniable attraction that sizzled hot between them. And she knew, just knew deep within her, there was something happening that couldn't be ignored. She just had to show him.

If he'd only let her, there was so much she wanted to show him. Her gaze still on his, she slipped her bare hands inside his trench coat, over his chest.

His steps fumbled a little on the long row of steps that led to his front door. 'Chloe.'

Okay, maybe he didn't want her in his life. Maybe he didn't really need her, not the way she wanted him to. But he did *want* her, physically at least. She knew it by the way his heart beat hard and fast beneath her fingers. It was a start for what she knew was meant to be. Encouraged, feeling a little too brave, she slipped her hands inside his shirt as well.

His arms tightened on her.

Her fingers trailed over bunched muscle, a light

spattering of hair, then more bunched muscle. His breathing quickened. So did her pulse.

'Chloe. Don't.'

With a low, satisfied laugh, she moved her hands up around his neck, through his hair. Gripping the thick mane tight, she pulled his head to hers. 'Why? You like it.'

'You've been drinking,' he said, sounding breathless, looking pained.

'Not that much.'

They were at the front door now, and he hesitated. 'This is a damn fool idea. I can't believe I brought you here, not when I can't resist – Never mind. I'm taking you to a hotel.'

'No.' Dragging his mouth to hers, she gave him the steamiest kiss she could, pouring everything she had into it.

When he could come up for air, his eyes had gone dark and heavy with arousal. 'Do that again, Slim, and I'm not going to be able to remember why we shouldn't be doing this.'

'Good,' she whispered, and did it again.

His legs buckled so that he had to back her to the door to hold her steady. 'Christ.'

She only laughed, held him still with her fists in his thick hair and rubbed an open mouth over his throat. Every muscle in his body quivered in response, and unable to help himself he moaned when she kissed him again.

Passion tumbled from her, mixing joyously with his own. Letting her slide down his body to the floor, he barely managed to unlock the front door with fingers that violently trembled. She didn't move, didn't speak, just watched him with a shattering intensity.

Every nerve in his body was strung tight with desire. Crossing back to her, he kept his eyes on hers, saw the warring emotions there that mirrored his own: impossible, demanding need, surging excitement almost beyond bearing, and something even more dangerous, more terrifying. A basic affection that threatened the heart he didn't want to have.

'I want this,' she whispered. 'Don't make me go.'

Breathing became a near impossibility.

As he came close she tossed her head back so they didn't lose eye contact. Her hands flattened on the door behind her, making her look surprisingly open and vulnerable. 'You do want me back, don't you, Thomas?'

With a tenderness he hadn't realized he possessed, he smoothed back her hair. 'You can doubt it?' He kissed her jaw, pulled her close enough to prove his words with the hardness of his body. 'I want you, Chloe. I want you so much I'm shaking with it. I want to feel you, touch you, kiss every inch of your creamy skin, taste you until you're trembling and crying for me.'

Her mouth opened and she shuddered a little. 'I *am* trembling,' she whispered. 'And we haven't even started yet.'

He tugged her inside, slammed the door on the icy night and reached for her. His hands roamed her face, his thumbs rubbing across her lips, her cheekbones, before his fingers dug into her hair. He heard her breath catch, felt his own stop as his body sandwiched her between him and the door. Her hungry eyes met his and he realized something shocking.

Never in his sorry life had he needed anyone as he needed her in that moment. *Never.* All the pain, the misery, the bitterness faded at her first touch, his first taste of her. In his arms she was life, she was his happiness, she was everything he could ever want. Needing more of it, he moved closer, sank deeper into that sexy mouth, thrilling to the frantic beat of her heart pumping against his.

His hands had moved down to grip her hips, pulling her closer, closer, closer still. It wasn't enough. On a frustrated oath, he raised his hand to tear her coat from her, then the jacket of that damn business suit. Her clumsy hands yanked at his trench coat, and at her soft exclamation of frustration he stripped it off himself. Their hands tangled as she reached for the buttons on his shirt, their bodies entwined as they fought for a grip in a world that had tilted on its axis.

Finally, impatient beyond belief, he pinned her hands back, dragged her silky blouse out of her skirt and whipped it off over her head.

The sight of the lacy sheer camisole beneath nearly sent him over the edge, but before he could so much as draw another raspy breath, she'd kicked off her shoes, knocking them both off balance so that they rammed into the wall. A husky laugh escaped her, then a quiet sound of satisfaction as she ran her hands over his chest, his belly.

Her appreciation spurred him on. Dragging his mouth down her neck, over her shoulder, he filled his hands with her breasts. She made another sound, a low, grated whimper that drove him wild, but it turned into a moan when he bent down and suckled her through the thin material.

'Thomas.'

Her whispery voice sounded more like a prayer than a plea, but he understood. Streaking his hands under the short skirt that had been driving him mad for days, he hiked it high as he greedily cupped her bottom. Slowly, purposely, he slid himself over her, nestling his erection between her thighs. Arching back, she panted. 'Now. Thomas, now. Quick.'

'No.' He managed to get them as far as the living room, then sank with her to the soft, thick carpeting. 'Not quick.' Filling his mouth with the soft, hot flesh that spilled from the top of her camisole, he devoured whatever he could reach with the sudden insatiable hunger he had for her. 'This is going to take awhile,' he murmured against her skin. 'A long while.'

Impatiently he tugged off her skirt, then sucked in his breath at the sight of the lacy stockings and garter belt, topped by a tiny patch of matching lace that barely covered her mound. 'My God, Chloe. If I'd known what you had under here earlier – '

'Well, you know now . . .' Her laugh was shaky, and it turned into a needy moan when he pinned her body beneath his.

Sex had never been a priority in her life; she'd found it rarely lived up to all it was supposed to be. But, even knowing that, she wanted to try with Thomas, because she was beginning to understand that they belonged together, no matter how big a fight he put up.

And this was different, so different. So unexpectedly good.

His insatiable, eager mouth trailed over her heated skin, nipping at the curve of her shoulder, dipping beneath the strap of her camisole and licking at the skin beneath. And in that instant she knew. Making love with Thomas McGuirre was going to be like nothing she'd ever done before. The touch of his fingers drove her crazy, the stroke of his rough hands had her desperate for more.

Grasping at whatever she could, she felt the taut muscles of his shoulders, the hard, sleek lines of his back, before she ripped his shirt open and reared up to taste.

Quite simply, she couldn't get enough, but, thank God, he seemed to feel the same. The wild, greedy violence of his need staggered her at first, but the tender possessiveness of his mouth over hers, the way his hands shook on her body, the way his eyes ran over her with desperate, edgy need, all combined to have her drowning in desire. For him.

This burning she felt was all for him.

And if he didn't hurry up she was going to go up in flames right there on the floor of his living room.

'No hurry,' he murmured against her neck, reading

her mind. Flicking his tongue over her collarbone, he edged down the silky material between them with his teeth, then slid his tongue beneath it, teasing the curve of her breast. Grasping his head by the ears, she brought him closer, wanting him to take more, then gasped when he did.

When his mouth closed over a taut nipple, she bucked off the floor and right into his arms.

'You liked that?' he whispered huskily, doing it again just to feel her leap in his arms. This was exactly how he wanted her, deliriously frenzied and burning up for him. *For him*. No one had ever surrendered so fully as she did, and it moved him in ways he hadn't thought possible.

'What are you doing to me?' she asked on a bewildered breath when he slid the garment off her and took a pebbled nipple gently between his teeth.

'I'm doing what I've been dying to do since I first saw you again.' Slowly he undid her garter belt, peeled off the stockings, watching her as he did so. Then he crawled back up her body, dipping his head to spread kisses as he did. To test them both, he rolled his hips over hers, settling his hardness into her softness. Then he did it again, just to revel in that sound she made deep in her throat. The one that told him this was stunningly, startling different, that he'd taken her to a place no one else ever had.

That last little bit of silk on her was insubstantial, so easily torn away, but he didn't do it. Not yet. Teasing them both, he let one hand wander over her hip, toward her tummy, then played with the edging of her panties.

Chloe tensed, held her breath. 'Thomas,' she whispered, trying to push up.

'Shh.' He nibbled at her lips, teased the corners. 'Let me.' Beneath him, he could feel her building, knew she was ready to explode any minute, and she wasn't the only one. He was harder than he'd ever been in his life and he hadn't even removed his pants yet. Toying with her, with himself, he let his fingers slip under the silk, just a little, and ran them back and forth softly over her skin.

She shivered, grasped his hair in her fists and thrust her hips upward – a demand for more if he ever saw one. Keeping her mouth busy with his own, he let his fingers skim down, down, past crisp curls . . . and into heaven.

Wet, creamy heaven.

Moaning, she writhed beneath him, and he wanted nothing more than to rip those panties away and sink into her deep. Instead, he dragged her to her knees, letting his mouth wander over her neck, her face. When he rocked against her she ran restless hands over him, fumbling desperately at his waistband, but he held her off, knowing if she so much as touched him it'd be over before they'd even begun.

When he finally streaked fingers under silk, she went rigid in his arms, her every muscle poised on the edge, but he held back, just a little, just enough to prolong her pleasure. The mixture of rapture and torment in her expression nearly did him in. Stripping off that last silk barrier, he plunged eager fingers into her molten heat. With a surprised cry, she shattered in his arms with a series of shock waves that reached clear down to his troubled soul and mixed it irrevocably with hers.

Tensing against the unexpected surge of something much stronger than lust, he hesitated, unsure in a way he'd never been.

Opening startled eyes, still shuddering, she stared at him, right into him, and, as if she could read his thoughts, she smiled at him brilliantly.

The pure emotion he saw shimmering there was too much for a man starved of love. Ruthlessly he drove her over the edge again, hard and quick, then, before she could gulp in air, he unfastened his pants, pushed her back and drove in deep.

If he'd thought he'd been in heaven before, he'd never been so wrong. His own needs welled up, so frantic, so brutal he could hardly contain them. Even so he held still, afraid he'd hurt her.

His instincts were right, because her eyes widened and she stiffened in surprise. 'Oh,' she breathed. 'Oh, my goodness.'

Smiling a little against her neck, he pulled a patch of her skin against his teeth. 'Is that approval?'

'Oh, yes,' she purred, adjusting herself to accommodate him. Still, it took several thrusts before he was fully seated within her. Remaining motionless while she got used to him was a delicious sort of torture, but when she rocked against him, her hips pushing, circling, experimenting, he had no choice. He had to stroke.

'More,' she demanded, lifting up, clutching at him, tearing at him. 'Please, more.'

When he drove back in, she exhaled in relief. 'Again,' she urged. 'Again and again.'

He was lost. Completely lost. And all because she'd opened those incredible eyes and stabbed him with a look he'd thought never to see, such a pure, glorious gaze of love he couldn't breathe.

But if he couldn't breathe he *could* move, *had* to move.

Locking her legs around him, she threw back her head and sobbed for breath as her climax rocked them both to oblivion. Again, she touched deep, past his wounded heart and into his dark soul, and it triggered his own release.

All pretenses between them vanished; there were no secrets. In that moment all that existed was Chloe, the way she wrapped herself around him, how she quivered and cried out as he came, pouring far more into her than his seed.

The heart beneath his ear had just started to slow from its fierce thundering when Thomas surfaced.

Chloe's heart.

And he lay stretched over her as if he belonged there, his face nestled between her small, firm breasts, her arms cradling him close to her. He could have stayed there forever.

Eventually reality surfaced, as it always did. He *didn't* belong there. For the first time in his life he had to force himself to pull away, to evade the intimacy.

But God, she was sweet, all replete and damp beneath him, practically purring with satisfaction.

Get up, leave her. If he didn't, he'd drown in what she was offering. They'd make love again, and then he didn't think he'd be strong enough to ever stop. If he took her again he wouldn't be able to leave her. As he levered himself up he allowed his hand one last sweep down her willowy body. His own tightened in response and he knew he couldn't risk it. No, he thought as she arched into him, he couldn't take the chance.

Unable to bear to look at what he wouldn't allow himself to have, he didn't even glance at her as he rose and tossed her his discarded shirt. With some half-baked idea of shutting himself away in his bedroom until morning, he walked to the open doorway. But some part of him, some weak, needy part, had to see her one more time.

She lay there, just where he'd left her, though she'd dragged the shirt over her for modesty's sake. Her eyes, full and troubled, watched him while her hands worried at the material she clung to.

It killed him, the sight of her stretched out, so tantalizing yet demure. He wanted her again. Right now.

Not possible, he reminded himself. Not when he'd lost all semblance of control. She'd done that to him, stripped him bare.

But she was meant to be his, a little voice whispered. Look at her. She was his.

Should have been his. Except he'd destroyed any

198

hope of that when he'd plotted to ruin her and everyone she cared about.

Turning, he left her.

Chloe watched him go, hugging his shirt to her. It smelled like him and she inhaled deeply as she shrugged into it. From somewhere in the huge house, the central heater clicked on.

Thomas, of course.

Even now, when he was furious, he still cared. She'd hold that close and dear to her heart. Especially since it might be all she'd have to hold for some time to come.

'Mew.'

Smiling, she reached for the kitten, who'd just come into the room. Already Haroldina was growing, by leaps and bounds. 'Thomas taking good care of you, baby?'

Haroldina started to purr and rubbed her head under Chloe's chin. Chloe could only hope that meant yes, but she had a feeling it did. Despite his anger at her for leaving him the kitten, she knew he'd never abuse nor neglect Haroldina.

He couldn't, not after the life he'd led. Not when he knew exactly what it felt like to come from that world.

Yes, maybe he had a right to be mad at her for manipulating his emotions by forcing him to care for the cat. But she'd had no idea how else to show him that he could give love. That he could receive it.

Actually, she should be furious herself. He'd still not explained himself in regard to his purchases. But she couldn't retain the anger, not when she felt about him as she did.

For there was no question in her mind. She was falling in love with the dark, dangerous, daring Thomas McGuirre.

Haroldina left her, climbing up on a leather couch and curling into a ball. Immediately her eyes closed. Chloe watched her a minute, envying her ease in this house she herself wanted so badly to belong in.

Then, sitting with her arms wrapped around her legs, she gave herself a little hug.

And smiled, just a little.

Oh, she knew it looked bleak. After all, Thomas had just left her without so much as a word or a last touch. But close to her heart she held the real knowledge. The knowledge that no matter how much he fought her, she had indeed taken a piece of him with her.

They'd made love, shared souls, and she knew he knew it.

What had just happened between them was a once in a lifetime sort of sharing, and there was no mistaking it.

Certainly Thomas couldn't.

She'd seen the fear in his eyes when he'd lifted his head and met her gaze for that one brief second. Right before he'd stalked off, angry again.

Only this time his anger was directed at her. She'd made the unflappable Thomas McGuirre lose control. Until the end of time she'd savor that last moment, treasure the instant when he had come inside her. When for the first time he'd let himself go, trusting her, needing her, calling out for her.

'Chloe.'

She nearly leaped out of her skin at Thomas's soft voice He stood in the doorway.

'It's cold in here,' he said in a voice that wasn't quite his own deep, sure one.

She shifted to look at him and his gaze dipped to where she hadn't finished buttoning the shirt.

'I'll – ' He cut himself off and, swallowing hard, reached down with a warm, strong hand to pull her up, careful to maintain his distance.

When she made no move to cover herself, he gritted his teeth, yanked the edges of the shirt together and buttoned the top button. The backs of his fingers brushed over her skin, making them both jump. After a hesitation, in which he'd obviously hoped she'd finish the job, he sighed and quickly closed the other buttons. With each one his jaw locked tighter and tighter, and Chloe's legs got weaker and weaker.

She loved the feel of his hands on her.

'I'll show you where you can get some sleep.'

Okay, so their minds weren't on the same path. She could deal with that. But after what they'd just shared, she couldn't stop thinking sexually. Still shirtless, he stood before her in just his jeans. Her fingers longed to touch, to sweep over that chest, feel his hard stomach, grip his tight arms, hold onto those wide shoulders. What a picture he made, she thought, a little dazzled. The man was incredibly beautifully made, with his –

'Come on.' This time his voice came quicker, and not quite so soft. He sucked in a gulp of air when she continued to stare at him, and his jeans gaped away from him, leaving her with the most shocking urge to slip her hands down inside and –

'Chloe. *Please.*'

She bit back her secret smile and allowed him to lead her. At least he still wanted her, for there'd been no mistaking that hard bulge between his thighs just now. Nope. He could lie to himself all he wanted, but she wasn't buying it.

'Upstairs,' he said curtly, waiting for her to catch up.

Upstairs. Most likely as far from his own bedroom as he could get her. She couldn't really blame him. What had happened between the two of them wasn't something that happened every day. Or at least she hoped not. But she could see why he felt the need to run; it *was* a little scary. She just didn't appreciate it, especially since she wanted to be held.

She wanted him to make love to her again. 'Thomas – '

'No.' He didn't stop as he climbed the stairs.

Her lips curved. 'You don't even know what I was going to say.'

Now he did stop, and pressed at his eyelids. 'What, then?'

'Do you like Haroldina yet?'

He dropped his hands to his sides. For a minute he just stared at her. 'That's about the last thing I thought you'd say.'

'My mother says I'm a little unpredictable.'

'No kidding,' he muttered. 'I guess that's the one thing me and your mother might agree on.'

'Well?'

'Well, what?'

'Do you like her yet?'

He shook his head, inhaled deeply and looked everywhere but at her. 'The damn cat is fine.'

'That's not what I asked.'

'Haroldina and I are . . . coming to an understanding.'

She smiled, feeling love and pride overwhelm her. She understood that for Thomas that was tantamount to an admission of acceptance – one which he certainly didn't make lightly. 'That's the first time you've referred to her by name,' she said, her feelings for him welling up and over. 'Oh, Thomas.'

'Don't get all mushy on me now,' he said with mock disgust, backing up a step. But he didn't fool her, not for one second. 'I still want you to find her another home.'

'Oh.' Okay, maybe she still had a lot of work to do.

At the top of the stairs, he stopped. 'Here.' He opened a door and stayed on the threshold as she entered a lovely bedroom with a wide four-poster bed.

Her eyes sought his and she waited, forcing him to speak.

'Goodnight,' was all he said, gruffly. Then he turned away and disappeared before she could blink.

Oh, he was in for something if he thought she

would be so easily dismissed. She might be falling for him, but she still wasn't a complete idiot.

There were a lot of unanswered questions, and she intended to remedy that – while she had the chance. Because she knew darn well, especially now that she'd broken through his barriers, he would do everything in his power to stay away from her.

He needed to. To protect himself. If he could, he'd wipe her from his heart, erase her from his life and toss Haroldina out after her.

If he could, he would forget that their souls had collided.

And if she wasn't careful, he'd succeed, and all would be lost.

CHAPTER 12

'Are we ever going to talk about it?'

Thomas sloshed steaming hot coffee over the edge of his mug and swore before he turned to lean back against the sink. 'Do you always sneak up on unsuspecting sleepy people first thing in the morning?'

Chloe had the good grace to grin sheepishly as she came into the kitchen, looking better than anyone who'd consumed an entire bottle of champagne the night before had a right to look. 'You're my first. Well, not my first exactly. But – '

He watched her over the mug as she fumbled her words, amused in spite of himself. 'Oh, please, continue. It was just getting good.'

Her skin reddened. 'Stop it.' Moving into the kitchen with as much grace as she could muster, she tried to explain. 'I just meant you're my first sleepover. Since grade school, at least.'

Carefully, as if her answer hadn't so touched him, he took a sip and scalded his tongue. 'You aren't going to tell me you've never slept with a man, are you?' He held his breath as he waited for her answer, having no idea why that gave him such a thrill.

'Yes,' she whispered, stepping closer, silently daring him to laugh at her. 'I am. I've never actually *slept* all night at a man's house.' Another step brought her within arm's length. 'But for that matter I *still* haven't sleep all night long with a man. In his arms.'

Those eyes, he thought, carefully setting down his coffee. They'd be the death of him yet. 'Chloe – '

'No, wait.' With hands that noticeably trembled, she reached out and cupped his face. 'Don't say anything.'

Her light scent hit him. So did the soft touch of her fingers on his jaw. And she still wore his shirt. Nothing else but bare legs, tumbled hair and his shirt, which, to add to his agony, was missing the top button. Every move she made brought soft curves close to the surface as they threatened to spill out. He had to close his eyes against the unexpected wave of homesickness.

That was exactly what it was. *Homesickness*. He wanted her, but couldn't have her. And it was torture. 'God, Chloe. I'm so damn sorry about last night.'

Those fingers caressed, soothed. 'Shh.' She played with the sensitive skin behind his ear. 'It's such a thrill, Thomas, that you don't flinch away from my touch anymore.'

He sighed and opened his eyes, put his hands on her hips to make sure she kept her distance. Or that was what he'd meant to do, but somehow he ended up with her layered against him, his face buried in her hair. 'We can't do this.' Yet he pulled her closer, clung just a little, just for a minute. She fitted to him perfectly, as if she were made for his arms.

'We can do whatever we want to do.'

'No, you don't understand. *Christ*. The least you could do is have a hangover.'

She just smiled at him. Now he did set her aside, while his shirt gaped open on her, showing him exactly what he refused himself. Frustrated, he turned and looked through the garden window over the sink. Self-disgust filled him. He'd been selfish – unforgivably so. Now he'd have to hurt her.

During the night, more snow had fallen. The trees were heavy with it. White winter wonderland everywhere. Yet a deep frost filled his chest.

'Help me understand,' she said quietly from behind him. 'There's so many things I don't get, don't know. Maybe I can help you. If you would just tell me – '

'No.' God, he couldn't do that, couldn't explain the truth. But how else to get her to stay away from him? For he was far too weak to do it himself. 'I don't have to explain anything to you.'

'No,' she agreed, sounding more than a little hurt. 'But I was hoping you'd want to.'

Want to. What he wanted had nothing to do with this.

'Thomas, did you buy those buildings and my loan because you wanted to help me? It was a very sweet thought, if you did, but – '

'I didn't buy them for that reason.'

'Oh. Well – '

207

'I'm not going to explain myself here, Chloe.'
Couldn't.

'I see.' Her gaze met his. 'Well, what if I called in my marker?'

'Your marker?'

'What if I reminded you that . . .?'

'I owe you?' he asked softly. *Damn her.* 'Forget it – I'm paying you off. Now.' Stalking to the table, he yanked up his wallet and pulled out a check.

When he bent to fill it in, she cried, *'Don't.'* He lifted his gaze to her horrified one. 'I don't want you to pay me,' she said.

'Too bad. That's what I'm doing. Now you can pay your rent and I can stop worrying about owing you. We'll be even.'

'You'd like that.' Over her initial shock, she scoffed, making him feel small. 'Paying me off would be a great source of relief to you, wouldn't it?' She shook her head, eyes solemn and sad. 'I'll tell you a secret, Thomas. You don't owe me anything and you never have. Shame on you for ever thinking you could buy me, or that I would even let you. Friends don't do that. I pushed you out of the way that day because it was instinct. No more, no less. You would have done the same. And I'm sure you never would have let me pay you.'

He'd thought he'd sunk as low as he could go, but he was wrong. The way she looked at him, full of retribution and disappointment, crushed him into the ground.

'And,' she said, huffing a little, really on a roll, 'I

don't want to hear another word of it. We're through with that. Okay? Nobody owes anyone.'

'You have a way, Chloe,' he said quietly. 'A way of looking at me.'

'Of course I do. I see the *real* you.' She shot him one of her irresistible little smiles. 'That's why you don't like me.'

He thought of how he'd been reacting to her. 'I like you.'

'No. You lust for me. I don't think you really like me all that much.'

'You're wrong.'

'You're sorry about last night. You wouldn't be if you liked me.'

Inhaling deeply, he said, 'I said I was sorry about last night because we shouldn't have . . . I shouldn't have brought you here. It was a mistake.'

'You think what happened between us was a mistake?'

There was no disguising the hurt in her glorious eyes. And he felt like a jerk. 'It was . . . beautiful, Chloe.' In truth, he'd never experienced anything so mind-shattering and utterly perfect as making love with Chloe Walker. She'd been everything he'd dreamed of and far more. 'But, yes, it was a mistake.'

'No.' She shook her head, her hair flying. And now those eyes weren't filled with pleasure or laughter, but denial and the hot flash of temper. 'Making love like we did was not a mistake, Thomas.'

He managed not to move a muscle, not to flinch or change expression, but his stomach dropped. He wanted it to have been just sex. Just plain, good old-fashioned hot sex.

But it wasn't and he knew it. Yeah, it'd been plain, good and very old-fashioned hot. But it had been volumes more as well. He just didn't want her to know it too.

'That's what it was,' she repeated firmly. '*Love-making*. Not sex. We made love.' He did flinch then, and she tugged at him. 'Will you look at me? Please?'

He did, then nearly swore at what she offered him with her eyes. Herself. Her warmth. Her affection. And so much, much more.

It terrified him.

'It *was* a mistake,' he said carefully. '*My mistake*. Now I've led you to believe that there's something between us that there isn't.'

'You've led me to believe nothing. I'm a big girl, Thomas. I won't jump to any conclusions you're not ready to face.'

What he wasn't ready to face was the harsh reality that he'd done nothing to prevent her getting pregnant. It was horrifying, how completely lost in her he'd gotten. How lost in her he wanted to get again right now.

'Thomas? Why didn't you let me sleep with you last night?'

He slumped his weight back against the sink, his knees weak. She had to ask. *Because if I'd held you in my arms last night, I'd never be able to let you go. Never.* 'You're welcome to stay here as long as you want.' He swallowed hard on that one, because to see her would kill him, but he couldn't kick her out in the cold. 'But I'll make sure your heater is fixed as soon as possible.' *Today*.

She straightened, her hands falling limply to her sides. 'I see.'

The hurt dignity in her stance made him want to run away, like the coward he was, but he had to make sure he severed this now. To continue would just make it worse. Every moment he spent in her presence tore away at any tiny thread of control he'd managed to retain. 'Do you?' he asked. 'Do you understand what I'm telling you?'

'Oh, yes.' The deep breath she took threatened to lift the hem of his shirt to alarming heights, but she didn't notice. 'What I understand is that you are a silly, stubborn man who can't see past his own misery.' Hugging herself, she turned and moved gracefully to the door, where she stopped and gave him a frown. 'But I'm not giving up, Thomas McGuirre. I won't. Do you hear me?'

'Hard to miss it,' he said wryly. 'You're shouting.'

Lowering her voice was difficult, since she was shaking with fury. But she managed, knowing she had to make her point. 'What we have is different, special. A once in a lifetime sort of thing.'

He blanched.

'I know you don't want to hear that, that it's far too soon for you. But it's the truth, Thomas. So get used to it.'

She pushed open the swinging doors. 'But there's other things we have to get to first. Like what's going on with Mountain Mortgage. And why you've suddenly started making all these crazy purchases.'

He opened his mouth, but she went on. '*Crazy*,' she repeated firmly. 'I'm not the greatest businesswoman, but even I know you couldn't have bought either one of those buildings for investment. For that matter, if it was all legitimate, you should have turned me down for the loan for *Homebaked*, just like everyone else did, because that wasn't a sound investment either.'

'But you needed the loan.'

'Of course I did. And I'm grateful for it. But you're up to something, Thomas, and I'm going to find out what. Then I'm going to help you.'

His mouth fell open and she smiled, then laughed. 'Yeah, that's right. Because, no matter what, I'm on your side. Forever.'

She slammed the doors on his stunned expression, wishing she'd gotten a satisfactory bang out of them, but they just sort of whooshed shut.

Well, she thought, if she went by the look on his face, she could bet she'd definitely made her exit, even without the bang.

But then she realized, and had to laugh at herself.

She had no way home and no clothes except her crumpled suit, which still lay on the living room floor. *Some exit*.

'Would you like a ride?'

She froze at the deep, amused voice behind her. No, she wouldn't turn and give him the satisfaction. Absolutely not.

'It's the least I can do,' he said. 'After all, I made you come here. Remember?'

How could she forget? 'I wasn't that drunk, Thomas. You can absolve yourself of the guilt of seducing a drunk. That's not how it happened at all.'

'No,' he said in a surprisingly serious voice. 'It's not.'

She looked at him then. Saw the regret and a lingering sadness in his eyes that did give her hope. Yes, he was pushing her away, faster than she could dig her heels in. But he wasn't happy about it. 'You hate that you can't control what's between us, don't you?'

'Yes.'

'Why?'

'I can't give you what you want, Chloe. I'll never be able to do that.'

'And what is it you think I want?'

'What every normal person wants. A mate. A family. Security.'

Though he couldn't know it, or if he did he'd deny it, she could see the fear in his eyes. It brought sorrow and a fierce anger at how he'd been treated as a youth, was being treated even now by the town. For he knew a deep-rooted insecurity, no matter how he tried to hide it. From his feeling of worthlessness stemmed this inability to love and to let someone love him in return.

Right there and then she vowed to show him different. Even if it took the rest of her days, she would. She'd show him he deserved love as much as anyone. And that he could give it.

'I only want what you're willing to give me,' she said softly.

'You say that now. But you won't be happy like that for long. You'll want more. Then I'll make you unhappy.'

'No. Never,' she vowed.

'The town will never accept me,' he said unevenly, telling her for the first time how much that hurt him. 'Never. *Homebaked* will suffer.'

If he'd known her better, he'd know she would never hold that against him. That she'd never ask him for something he didn't want to give. She opened her mouth to tell him, to explain all the things she was feeling.

But he spoke first.

'Chloe, I want you to let me give you some money. I know your rent's past due and that you had a slow month at the restaurant.

For a minute she thought she hadn't heard him right. But she had. 'You want to give me money? For what?'

'Ah . . .'

A horrible suspicion came over her. 'You feel guilty and you want to give me money.' He didn't answer, and an even worse feeling hit her. 'Are you trying to pay me off for last night?'

'Not exactly. Not in the way you mean.'

Her heart cracked. 'I see.'

'I want to help you.'

'No, thank you. I'll be fine.' Keeping her chin high, Chloe made it to the staircase. Okay, she was a little behind on the rent. But she'd have it in another couple of days. And if *Homebaked* wasn't doing as well as it should, it was because she kept feeding people who couldn't afford to pay her. She knew she couldn't afford it either, but she hated to see anyone go hungry.

'Chloe, please.'

She couldn't look at him as she climbed the steps. 'It's my day off. I'm going to take a shower, if you don't mind.'

'You're – you're staying?' His voice cracked, telling her a lot.

'You said I could. Remember?' As if she would. No, she'd definitely leave. She had to, because if she stayed she'd very likely hit him over the head to bring some sense into it.

'Uh, yeah. I remember. But – '

'Don't worry, Thomas,' she said, having mercy on this man who had a hell of a lot more to learn about women than she'd thought. But that was all right. She was nothing if not very patient. 'I'll go. I just want to shower. Do you mind?'

By his silence, she surmised that he minded very much.

Too bad.

Out of desperation, Thomas locked himself away in the office in his house. He'd left his keys out on the kitchen table with a note telling Chloe she could take his car.

He could only hope she did.

The thought of her downstairs, in his shower, did things to him. So did the thought of her wearing the sweatsuit that he'd left outside her door, even just picturing her wandering through this house.

Oh, he was definitely lost.

The first thing he did was arrange to have the heater at her apartment fixed.

Then, to take his mind off her, he sat at his computer. There were a thousand things that required his attention. Ever since he'd come back to Heather Glen from where he'd based himself on the east coast, he'd been running Sierra Rivers by phone and fax. But he didn't feel like dealing with that at the moment, not when a particular sensuous brunette, one with a body to die for, was so strong on his mind. So he read his e-mail instead.

The first dozen messages were all business transactions. The last was not.

You may have forgotten who you are and where you came from, but Heather Glen has not. Any McGuirre is a no-good McGuirre. Take your rotten money and get out of this town. Do it now or, believe me, you'll regret it.

It came from City Hall, but wasn't signed. It didn't take a genius to figure out who it had come from. Chloe's father, the mayor. Hadn't he spoken of his disapproval often enough? He had a double motive to try to run Thomas out of town. His daughter and his precious town.

Thomas was just cynical enough to imagine the town meant marginally more than the daughter he had not an ounce of trust in.

Chloe. She'd once been his champion against her father. Against the entire town. And it seemed she still was.

'You're up to something, Thomas?' she'd said, 'and I'm going to find out what. Then I'm going to help you.'

His stomach did a full roll, then repeated the process. If she only knew . . . Would she still want to help him? He couldn't imagine she would.

Chloe didn't think like him, certainly wouldn't understand this need he had to pay back a hurt for a hurt. He'd hate to even see her face if she ever found out the truth about him.

Thomas rubbed his eyes and sighed. His e-mail message blinked at him incessantly. He erased it, not wanting the reminder of how unpopular he still was, and turned away from his computer.

Work, usually his only salvation, wouldn't help him today.

The hatred that was directed toward him shouldn't have mattered. It certainly shouldn't have bothered him. It should have just proved he was right in doing what he was doing to Heather Glen. After all, the bitter, petty, small-minded town deserved it.

But it did matter and it certainly did bother him. Because at some point, and he wasn't exactly sure when this had happened, he'd begun to doubt himself.

What right did he have to wipe the place out? Surely if he were a normal man he'd cut his losses and get on with life? After all, he still had everything.

But he'd lived for this, craved it. Wanted to revel in his power to give back as good as he'd gotten.

Yet he could no longer deny the fact – he wasn't enjoying it. And all satisfaction from his successes had long ago fled. So the question remained: why was he doing it?

And who was trying to stop him?

CHAPTER 13

To test Thomas, and maybe herself, Chloe took the Jag's keys and left the house. She had no intention of leaving him alone for long, but she did need to take care of some things. And she needed to think. No place better to do that than a dream car that was itching to drive as fast as she wanted.

Apparently Thomas had decided to be stubborn until the end. He wasn't ready to admit how he felt about her. Which was fine; she could wait.

But what if he didn't really feel for her at all? What if he was telling the truth when he said he wanted her to stay away from him? That they could never have a future?

No. Not possible. Not when he looked at her as he did, as if she were the only woman on earth. They belonged together. Her heart knew it, and so did his.

So what was the matter with him?

'Nothing a good kick wouldn't cure,' she said aloud as she pulled into *Homebaked*, trying not to worry about why he'd made those purchases he'd yet to explain.

Trust, she reminded herself. She had to fully trust

219

him. Otherwise how could she expect him to return the favor if she kept doubting him?

Augustine took one look at her as she walked into the kitchen and set down the sponge she was using. 'What the hell are you doing here? It's your day off. Go take it.'

'Nice way to talk to your boss.' Chloe tucked Thomas's keys into her pocket and headed straight for the refrigerator. This fear, this deep, unreasonable fear that Thomas didn't want her the way she wanted him, had her stomach growling. She needed food.

Augustine stood in her way. 'You look tired.'

'Again, thank you.' No, not just food. She needed to cook. Something without champagne this time. 'Tell me business has been hopping.'

'Without you giving away free food, we're doing just fine. Been busy all morning, as usual. Slow now, though.'

'Did you at least give Mellie a discount?' Bending low, she peered into the refrigerator. Hmm, it was full of all sorts of possibilities. Fattening possibilities. Something with apples, maybe. When Augustine didn't answer, she peeked up with a frown. 'Augustine. Did you?'

'No, if you must know. I didn't,' Augustine said, looking pained. 'Now before you go getting all panicky, she'd just received some money from her son.'

The son – who was supposedly a well-known surgeon in Sacramento – remembered his mother whenever a small thread of conscience hit him. The jerk. And Mellie should be saving as much of it as she could. 'Oh, Augustine,' Chloe started to say, filling her arms with ingredients, 'I wish – '

'She'll be fine. It's you I worry about.'

'Well, don't.' Simple apple pie. That was what she needed. And she'd serve it for dessert. 'I'll be fine too.' *If she could only get Thomas to open up.*

'Honey, your father's here. Wants to talk to you.'

Chloe turned from the refrigerator and looked at Augustine in dismay. 'Oh, rats.'

'Chloe!'

Why was she constantly inspiring people to say her name like that? *Chloe!* she mimicked silently. As if she were a three-year-old going through a bad phase. She sighed and dumped everything in her arms on the large wooden block. First the crust, she decided, before turning her attention back to the matter at hand. 'Well, I just don't feel like dealing with him now.'

'I've never heard you talk about him like that,' Augustine said, looking a little shocked. 'What's the matter?'

What was the matter? Oh, sure. She couldn't make her rent and was in danger of getting kicked out of her apartment. *Homebaked* was in a slump and she wasn't sure she could make it recover before it was too late. And the town she'd always loved suddenly didn't seem so cozy and comfortable.

But that wasn't what was getting to her. No, not by a long shot. What was getting to her was a *who*. A tall,

221

gorgeous who, with eyes that had seen too much and a heart that had been battered and abused. A who that in spite of it all was an intelligent, caring, passionate man – a man that she wanted in her life.

Chloe took a deep breath and looked at her friend. 'You won't believe it.'

Augustine put her small, tough hands to her skinny hips and scowled. 'I can see I won't like it much, whatever it is. But try me anyway.'

'I'm in love with a man who doesn't know the meaning of the word,' she blurted out miserably. None of the other stuff mattered, not her financial mess, her business, her town, nothing. Just Thomas.

'Oh, honey. You got your heart broke.' Immediately the spry, weathered old waitress snagged her in a bear hug that rivaled a woman three times her size.

'Not broke. Not yet anyway. Just a little cracked.'

'I'm so sorry. I'll go skin Conrad alive for this, I promise. What's the matter with that boy?'

'No,' Chloe said, laughing in spite of her heartache. 'Wait a minute. It's not Conrad.'

'What's not Conrad?' Lana came into the kitchen, her ears perking up, hoping for gossip. 'What did I miss? Darn it, you always start talking before I get in here.'

'It's not Conrad?' That stumped Augustine. 'Well, then, who the hell is it – ? Oh, no.' The older woman pulled Chloe back to stare into her eyes, her callused hands digging into her shoulders. 'Oh, Chloe. Tell me it's not true.'

'What's not true?' Lana demanded, coming closer.

222

'Tell me everything. Guys? *Hello?*' Impatiently she waved a hand in front of their faces, but both Augustine and Chloe ignored her as they faced off.

'Chloe?' Augustine waited. 'Tell me it's not true.'

Chloe squirmed under the sharp eye of the woman who cared more about the real Chloe than her own mother did. 'That depends on what you want me to tell you is not true.'

'You know damn well what.' But she sighed, giving Chloe a worried look. 'You did. I can see it all over your face. You've never been able to lie to me. You fell for that bad boy McGuirre.'

Lana gasped and covered her mouth. 'Ooooh.'

Chloe rolled her eyes. 'And would that be so awful?'

'Not on your eyes,' Augustine had to admit. 'That man is something mighty fine to look at, that's for sure.'

'True,' Lana agreed. 'Just yesterday Sally was at the bank when he came in and she said her knees went weak when he smiled at her.'

He'd smiled at Sally Robertson? That annoyed Chloe sufficiently out of the self-pity – and the hurry. She'd just keep his Jag as long as she felt like now. *Smiling.* Why, that was the same as flirting – and he *never* flirted with her.

'He may be incredible-looking,' Augustine said with certainty, 'but he's trouble, through and through.'

'Maybe,' Lana agreed. 'But trouble never looked so good.'

223

'Oh, for Pete's sake,' Chloe exploded. 'He's not trouble. *Troubled*, maybe. But he wouldn't bother a fly.'

Neither of her friends looked convinced. A tiny little seed of doubt planted itself in Chloe's mind. 'Does someone know something I should know?'

'My momma says he's dangerous.'

Chloe had to laugh. 'Lana, your momma says every male is dangerous.'

'Honey, I want to trust your judgement,' Augustine butted in, 'really, I do. But maybe Lana's momma is right this time. Everybody thinks so. Maybe that man – '

'That man what?' Chloe demanded, backing away to move to the apples. 'Maybe that man is just trying to make a go in a town he once belonged to? Is that a crime? No. The crime is gauging a man on something he has no control over, like his parentage.' Washing the apples vigorously, she tried to concentrate on letting the familiar motions of cooking soothe her. 'He's misjudged, guys. From day one he's been misjudged. And shame on both of you for jumping on the bandwagon and bad-mouthing a man who's done nothing to either of you. Or to anyone for that matter.' *Except to her heart.*

'She's in deep,' Lana whispered. 'Any time a woman defends a guy so fervently, it's gotta be bad.'

'Hmm,' Augustine agreed.

'Who's my lovely daughter defending now?' Mayor Walker walked into the kitchen and planted a kiss on his daughter's cheek.

Chloe bit her lip and forced herself to remain

224

silent. She'd actually forgotten her father was here.

'Don't tell me,' he joked into the sudden quiet. 'You're into a new project. What is it this time?'

With a dark look, Chloe dared her employees to say a word. Surprisingly they both remained dutifully silent.

'Come on, Chloe,' her father said, laughing a little. 'What's the new deal? Save the rats? Run off the pollution? Track the desert mongrel? What?'

'It's nothing.'

'It must be something to have you looking so down in the dumps. I know. Some down-on-his-luck stranger has convinced you to give all your money to the poor birds who perch on the top of the rectory of St Margaret's.'

'Dad, you know those poor birds all died when – ' Chloe stopped, and glared at Lana when she dared to giggle. Chloe had loved those birds, had fed them every day, despite the fact the general population had considered them a great nuisance. 'You know they died when the entire flock got struck by lightning last year because they wouldn't get off the flagpole during the big storm.'

'Exactly,' he said, crossing his arms and looking at her with amused triumph. 'My point exactly. You spent how much money trying to get them moved so they wouldn't perish? And they did anyway – which, by the way, the entire town was grateful for. No more bird poop gets tracked into church.'

'Oh, Dad, I'm not that bad.'

'No?' He didn't looked convinced. 'Okay, then

maybe you're starting a new committee to save the algae in the community pool. Wouldn't want to kill anything that's alive, would we? No matter how small.'

Again Chloe turned to Lana when a suspicious muffled sound escaped her. 'Everybody go away,' she said succinctly. 'I'm very busy.'

'We can see that,' Augustine said seriously, though her eyes twinkled.

Chloe looked down at what she'd done to the first apple and let out a harsh breath. She'd just about peeled the entire apple away. Tossing the core into the sink, she threw up her hands. 'I'm done here. Work hard, guys. See you.'

'Wait, honey,' Augustine said, coming after her looking contrite. 'We're sorry.'

'It's just fun to tease you sometimes,' her father chimed in, smiling easily. 'You're so gullible, Chloe. I worry about you. Tell me what you've fallen for this time. I'm sure it's not as bad as you think.'

Would it be so hard for him to believe she hadn't fallen for any scam? That she genuinely believed in her causes and that it hurt that he didn't? Would it be so hard for him to have a little faith in the daughter he thought of as a screw-up?

Obviously, yes, it would. Another apple bit the dust.

'Tell me,' he urged.

Why? So she could add to his belief that his daughter couldn't do anything right? That was the last thing she would do.

'Come on,' he cajoled. 'I won't laugh this time, I promise.'

Lana looked at her too. Augustine lifted her gray eyebrows, silently asking if Chloe needed to be rescued from the inquisition.

Did she ever.

Augustine stepped forward. 'Ah . . . it's not the big deal you think. She's fallen for the new line of vegetables we've been getting from the distributor.' She smiled brilliantly, revealing the gap between her teeth. 'You should see them, Mayor, they're spectacular. We should have an entire new menu by the end of the month.'

Chloe felt her eyes widen. She could have kicked herself for trusting Augustine to be able to pull the wool over her father's eyes.

Augustine bit her bottom lip while Chloe continued to look at her in horror behind her father's back. '*What are you doing?*' Chloe mouthed, lifting her shoulders. '*Vegetables?*'

Augustine shrugged helplessly. '*I'm sorry.*'

It didn't matter,' it was too late to correct it. The mayor wasn't fooled and Chloe knew it. And now his curiosity was tweaked. Risking a glance at him, she sighed deeply. Yep, his eyes were narrowed and leveled right on her.

Nope. Not fooled one little bit.

'Ladies,' he said quietly, still smiling. He was, if nothing else, correct to the end. Always had been. 'I'd like to speak to my daughter for a moment. Privately.' Turning, he placed a hand on Lana's back and led her to the door.

'Dad!' Chloe protested. 'Please. We're trying to

work here. You can't kick Lana out of the kitchen in the middle of the day. We're open. We've got customers – '

'Actually,' Augustine broke in, 'we don't have anyone out there right now – ' She coughed into her hand and moved back at Chloe's dark look. 'Okay, well . . .' Clapping her hands together once, before stuffing them in her apron pockets, she backed out of the kitchen, begging Chloe with her eyes to forgive her.

Keeping her hands busy with the apples, Chloe told herself it wasn't so bad. Her father couldn't possibly guess. Good thing, too, since he'd never quite forgiven Thomas for the way Deanna had turned out. As if it was Thomas's fault her sister seemed to be insatiable when it came to men.

'It's McGuirre, isn't it? There's been reports you've been seen with him.'

'Oh, really, Dad. You know better than to listen to idle gossip.'

'Haven't you been with him?'

If he knew exactly how much she'd *been with* Thomas, he would have a heart attack. 'We're friends.' *Friends who happened to have made wild, passionate love on the floor in his living room just last night.* 'Just friends.' That, at least for now, was true enough.

'Is that his Jag out there?'

'Yes. My car is . . . a little out of sorts.' Luckily it always was. But the need to continually hop around her father's questions annoyed her. Why couldn't she just come out with the truth?

Because she had no idea what the truth was.

'I know what's happening,' he said gently. 'Did you think you could keep it from me?'

Her heart leaped. 'What are you talking about?'

'He's preying on your naïveté, Chloe. I'm worried sick about you.'

'Dad – '

'Thomas McGuirre will stop at nothing until he gets what he wants,' he interrupted. 'And that includes you.'

'You're being ridiculous. The man moved back because – ' Because why? Even after all the time they'd spent together, she really knew next to nothing about him and his plans. 'Well, he's just back. And he has every right to be. It has nothing to do with me.' That much she was sure of.

'Please, Chloe. I want you to ask him to leave.'

Now Chloe carefully set down her knife. 'Leave?'

'As in leave town.'

Chloe didn't often go against her father's wishes. Not only was it easier not to, she rarely had need to. And in all her life she'd never openly defied him. 'I can't do that. I *won't* do that,' she amended. 'I'm sorry.'

'He's a powerful man, Chloe. Do you know how wealthy he is?'

'What does that matter?'

Her father looked uncharacteristically unsure. His confidence had all but disappeared. 'What if he decides he doesn't like how this town is run? That it needs new blood running it?' Restless, he walked the length of the kitchen. 'What if he decides the present mayor has been in charge too long?'

'That's ridiculous.'

'It could happen, Chloe. 'Maybe even by the next election. Maybe he'll even want to run the show around here. What would I do then?'

Having lost the taste for food, she moved away from the sink and the apples. Standing before her father, she shook her head. 'Thomas isn't interested in politics.'

'How do you know that?'

Well, he had her there. 'It's just a hunch. Besides, not many people even like him. You can't think he would be able to sway any election in this town.'

'People are fickle.'

'Not in Heather Glen.'

'Just ask him, Chloe. Maybe he'll listen to you. Just ask him what his plans are here.'

'He won't tell me.'

'Are you telling me you – Chloe Walker – would actually take no for an answer?'

'I'd have to.'

'That's very unlike you,' her father pointed out.

'I feel a little unlike myself today.'

'Ask yourself this, Chloe. Why would he come back? He didn't exactly get a warm welcome.'

Hadn't she wondered the same thing?

'Find out,' her father suggested. 'I think you'll discover, as I suspect, he's up to something. Something bad for all of us. Then maybe you can get him to leave.'

She snorted as she imagined trying to get Thomas to do anything he didn't want to do.

'I know you can do it.'

But she didn't want to. Couldn't imagine what it would feel like to watch Thomas walk away now.

'Consider it your next big project. Helping out your father.' Then he delivered the killing blow. 'You've never done that, and I've never asked you. It'd be nice if you helped me out this one time.'

Uneasily she stared at him. He was asking her to dig into Thomas's past, something Thomas didn't seem too eager to have her know about. Remembering how he'd grown up, she couldn't say she blamed him. 'He's not like his father. He wasn't when we were younger and he's not now.'

'James McGuirre was a no-good con man who would have gambled his mother away if given a chance. Thomas was a punk as a kid and he can't have changed all that much.'

It startled her to see her father like this. 'You have no idea what he's like. Not really. You don't even know him.'

'I know enough. Are you going to find out what's going on?'

'I don't know.'

'You will. And when you do, and if I'm right, will you see if you can convince him to leave?'

No matter what was going on, Chloe couldn't imagine it was bad enough for her to want Thomas to leave. Nothing would warrant that. Not to mention that if he did move from Heather Glen her heart would break. 'I'm sorry, Dad – '

'No, don't give me your answer now,' he broke in. 'Just think about it. That's all. Will you do that for me?'

Lana rushed back into the kitchen then, moving to the range. 'New orders,' she announced cheerfully, wobbling a little at the palatable tension shimmering between the two Walkers.

Chloe moved away from her father and scooped up her purse. 'I've got to go.'

'Chloe?'

Over Lana's head she met her father's gaze. 'What?'

'Are you going to help me?'

No, she wanted to cry. *Absolutely not. Don't ask me to.* But the truth was, he was right. He'd never asked her for a single thing. Not once.

It left her in the sorry position of having to choose between her father and her family and the one man she was beginning to want more than anything else.

'I don't know.'

Not until she was back in the Jag did Chloe come to the unsettling conclusion that she needed to know what Thomas was up to – for herself. Not her father. He hadn't just moved back; she knew that. Just as she also knew it had something to do with his business.

Was it really possible that his buying up her building, the Teen Hood and her loan had nothing to do with her? And why wouldn't he tell her?

Maybe because he was up to no good.

No, she didn't want to believe that. But this sudden fear deep in her belly told her she needed to know. Her father had never panicked, never worried about his job.

Until now.

Oh, Thomas, what are you up to?

She would find out, she vowed. But first she'd give him one more chance to tell her. Only if he refused would she try to find out without him. And only then, when she knew exactly what was going on, would she consider her father's request. Not a second before.

CHAPTER 14

Indecision plagued Chloe, not a common ailment for her. So many things to worry about, so many decisions to make. Too much for a woman not used to dwelling. Too much for a woman who wanted nothing more than to sit around starry-eyed over the night she'd just had with the man of her dreams. Okay, maybe not of her dreams, but close enough.

Without thinking, she drove to her apartment.

As she got out of her car she looked down at herself.

She still wore Thomas's sweatsuit. Had her father noticed? No, he definitely would have commented – right before he killed her.

'Chloe.'

Whirling around at that sexy voice she knew so well, she faced Thomas. He sat out in the weak midday sun, swinging his legs from his perch on the walkway wall.

'What are you doing here?'

Thrusting his chin toward the car she'd just parked, he hopped down. 'You've got my car, remember?'

Glancing around her, she saw no new or unexpected vehicles in the small lot. 'How did you get here?'

He stepped closer, the sun reflecting off his dark sunglasses. 'Taxi.'

His long coat whipped about his long legs, his dark, thick hair lifted away from his rugged face. His broad shoulders blocked the bright sun from her face. When he flipped up the glasses she saw that though his eyes remained serious his face wasn't tense, and his body seemed loose and relaxed enough. So he wasn't mad, as she'd at first thought.

'How did you know where I'd be?' she asked.

He'd stepped so close she had to tilt her head way back to see him. Those dark blue eyes slid slowly over her face, then over his clothes on her, all the way down to her feet and then back up. By the time his gaze met hers again, it had heated considerably.

'Where did you get those slippers?' he asked.

'From *Homebaked*. I had them in my office. I looked funny walking around in sweats and my heels from last night.'

At the mention of the previous night, his jaw tightened. Suddenly he didn't look nearly so relaxed.

'How did you know where I was?' she asked again.

'I got lucky.'

'Oh.' He hadn't shaved, she noticed. A dark shadow marred his already tough-looking face, making him look even more harrowed, more dangerous. More . . . stunning. God, she was breathless from just looking at him. 'Well, I – '

Unexpectedly, he hauled her up against him. 'I can't think until we get this out of the way.'

'What?'

His lips took hers in a startling, hot, deep kiss that rocked her world. Her body reacted immediately, her heart drumming hard and thick against her chest, her bones dissolving beneath his touch.

Just as suddenly he let her go. Staggering back a few steps in the melted snow, she could only stare at him. 'Wow.'

'Yeah,' he agreed, not looking nearly as thrilled as she felt. 'Pretty potent stuff.'

To still the heart she feared might leap right out of her chest, she placed her hands against it. 'What was that for?'

'I don't know.'

He sounded so confused, so miserable, she looked up at him again. And took instant pity. It was an easy thing for her to know and recognize what was happening between them. She'd grown up with love, with companionship, with easy affection and acceptance.

He had received none of those things.

Remembering now back to that last day when he'd left Heather Glen, her heart turned over. He'd had an ugly bruise on his face then, inflicted by his monster of a father. And enough bitterness in his eyes to choke them both. No, he'd never learned how easy love could be.

It had to be very difficult for him, and just a little scary, even if he felt only a fraction of what she was feeling. Patience, she reminded herself. And lots of love.

'Maybe we could do that again,' she suggested. 'Just another little kiss just to see where it leads us. Do you want to?'

'Just to see where it leads us?'

Though his voice was dry, she thought if she looked real deep she could see some humor swimming there.

'Yeah.' She licked her lips, watched his eyes follow the movement. 'Just to see.'

'You and I both know what happens whenever we stand within fifty feet of each other.' His low, sexy voice made her mouth dry.

'What happens?' But oh, how she already knew. Her insides tingled just at the thought. Yet she wanted to hear him say it.

'What happens?' Another unexpected touch from Thomas, his finger running over her cheek, had her stomach tightening, then fluttering. 'Our bodies crave each other, Slim.' Intently, he watched his finger skim over her skin. 'I see you and the temperature rises. It only gets worse the closer we get. Then we kiss and . . .' Again his jaw tightened as he fell silent, though his fingers continued to stroke her.

'And what?' she whispered.

'My body craves you, demands more of you, just like an addict needing a fix. I feel like I have to have you when it gets like that. Like I'll die if I can't. When I deny myself, I ache, I yearn, I – ' He broke off suddenly and swore, shoving his hands into his pockets. 'Hell, I just talk about it and I start burning up.'

'Burning can be good.'

Those eyes bored through her. 'I think I should go.'

'Then nothing's changed,' she muttered.

'What?' he asked, reaching for her when she started to turn away. 'I didn't hear you,' he said impatiently. 'What did you say?'

'Nothing.' After a kiss like that, how could he deny what was between them? How could he still want to keep his distance? 'Why did you come?'

He sighed and looked up at her building, frowning. 'I want to come up with you – just for a second,' he said stiffly, when he saw her hopes rise. 'I want to see how cold it is in there.'

'It's sweet of you to worry about me,' she said quietly, squaring her shoulders in that stance of pride that never failed to tug at something in his chest. 'But I can light a fire.' She wrapped her arms around her middle, reminding him that while he stood there in a coat, she wore just his sweatsuit. 'I'll be fine, so don't concern yourself.'

'Dammit, of course I'm going to concern myself. I don't want you to freeze to death.'

'I said I'll light a fire.'

'I want to come up,' he said through clenched teeth. He hadn't been able to get someone to agree to fix the heater today. The soonest would be tomorrow, maybe even the next day, which meant he'd have to worry about her for two more long days. And nights.

238

'And I said I'll be fine.'

There was no way he could go until he knew if her apartment was livable or if he would be forced to suffer through another sleepless night at his house, lying in bed, picturing her just down the hall. Last night he'd watched the clock the entire night while imagining all sorts of wicked, delicious things.

Things like that warm, giving, soft body, wrapped in nothing but his shirt, tangled in the sheets, her hair spread out on his pillow. Her scent filling the air.

Another night would kill him. 'I'm coming up.'

'I see,' she said quietly. Then she handed him the car keys. 'Sorry I didn't get back to you before you left the house. I didn't want you to be inconvenienced because of me.'

So formal, so distant. What had happened to the warm, laughing Chloe? The one who'd thrown her head back in abandon, crying out for him even as she wrapped her legs around him to pull him closer. The one who looked at him with sweet, caring eyes. The one who made him laugh.

Gone. Replaced by a Chloe he didn't recognize. Had he done that to her? 'You haven't inconvenienced me,' he said. If he kissed her again, would she melt back against him?

'Yes, I have.'

He bit back his frustration and annoyance. 'I'm the one that gave you the keys,' he said, surprising them both by taking her hand. 'Let's go.'

They hadn't set one foot on the landing of the first floor when Thorton's door started to open. Next to him, Chloe froze for a millisecond, then tugged him hard back around the corner. Flattening herself against the wall, she went utterly still.

'What are you doing?'

'Shh!' she commanded in a harsh whisper. 'Don't let him see you.'

Because it seemed so vitally important to her, he did as she asked.

Thorton's door opened all the way and he heard Chloe suck in her breath sharply. Clear green eyes pleaded for his silence. Standing as close to her as he was, with their arms touching, he felt her tension, her desperation. He also imagined that he could feel her skin, right through her clothes and his, though of course he couldn't. Unable to do anything else, he responded to her and remained silent, flattening himself against the wall as well.

When the door shut again, she let out a sigh of relief and relaxed.

Until she looked up at him. Then she seemed to hold her breath again. 'Um. Thanks.'

'What was that about?'

Before she could answer, Thorton's door whipped open again. Without hesitating, Chloe grabbed Thomas's hand and yanked him along, going the opposite way. 'Hurry,' she whispered, glancing at him over her shoulder as she tugged him along. 'Don't let him see us.'

Up the stairs they pounded, their steps echoing noisily. At Chloe's front door, she fumbled with her keys.

'Here,' Thomas said, pushing her gently aside. He opened the door easily, then just as quickly shut it behind them. Touching Chloe's heaving shoulders, he waited until she looked at him.

Her face was flushed, but somehow he knew it wasn't from exertion. 'Are you going to tell me what's going on?'

Turning away, she wrapped her arms around herself. 'No,' she said quietly, 'I don't think so.'

It was colder than a freezer in her apartment. His breath crystallized in front of his face as he spoke. 'You didn't pay your rent, did you?'

'I'm sorry you had to go out of your way, Thomas. But I'm fine now. Thanks. Try not to let Thorton see you as you leave. I don't want him to know I'm here just yet.'

She'd dismissed him. Just like that. *No one else would have dared*. If he hadn't been so shocked, he might have laughed at how politely she'd done it. 'In other words, There's the door. Please, use it?'

A sound escaped her, but since he couldn't see her face he had no idea if it was amusement or consternation she felt.

'We've settled nothing, Slim.'

'I wasn't under the impression there was anything to settle. You need your car and I've given you the keys. Thank you very much.'

'Another dismissal.' He crossed his arms, watching her. 'I'm not going anywhere.'

'Suit yourself. But it's pretty cold.' She moved to the fireplace and kneeled before it.

241

'I meant I'm not going anywhere without you.'
What the hell did he think he was doing? Having no
idea didn't stop him. 'Pack your stuff. You're not
coming back until the heater's fixed.'

'You might be used to giving orders, Thomas,' she
said calmly, crumpling paper for kindling, 'but I'm
not used to following them.'

'Fine. Come stay with me until the heater's fixed.'
She didn't budge, just struck a match. 'Please.'

Hesitating, she held still until the match burned so
low that she dropped it to the brick fireplace and
sucked on her finger. 'Darn it.'

A smile caught him off guard. 'Do you ever really
swear, Slim?'

He had to be quick, but he caught the flash of
smile. 'Not often,' she admitted. 'But you seem to
bring it out in me.'

'That bad, am I?'

Giving up on the fire, she rose. 'Worse.'

Unable to help himself, he moved closer. Lifting
her fingers, he kissed them softly where the match
had made them hot. Her eyes widened in pleasure
and surprise, making him realize how little he
touched her kindly.

Which slammed home the second realization – he
didn't deserve her.

Dropping her hand, he turned back to the door.
'Let's go.'

'I never said I'd go with you.'

'Are you saying you won't?'

He hadn't heard a sound, but knew she'd moved

242

up right behind him. When she wrapped her arms around his waist, hugging her face to his spine, he struggled to remain still.

'Is it so hard to admit that maybe you want me with you, Thomas? That maybe, just maybe, you're as lonely for me as I am for you?'

Her breasts pressed into his back, searing him. Taut thighs pressed against the backs of his. 'I just don't want you to freeze,' he said carefully.

'That's all?'

Despite the disappointment in her voice, he nodded, not quite trusting himself to speak. If he turned around, the bulge in his pants would prove him for the liar he was. 'Of course that's all.' He couldn't do it. He couldn't act completely indifferent when he wasn't. And he couldn't hurt her feelings on purpose. 'God, Chloe, please stop. I tried to explain to you this morning how I felt.'

'All I understand is that you keep saying I need to stay away from you. But then you keep showing up. No,' she said, holding tight when he would have pulled away, 'please don't stop doing it. It gives me hope.'

His eyes closed. 'There is no hope. The sooner you realize that the better.'

'And the sooner you realize you can trust me with all this other stuff the better.' Her cheek rested against him. 'You can tell me anything, you know.'

'No, I can't.'

'So you do admit there is something to tell me?'

Groaning, he pulled away and moved to the door. 'Get your stuff, Slim. Let's go.'

'Thomas – '

Looking at her was a mistake, a stupid one he just kept on making. Her gaze was on her feet, her hands folded together in front of her. Head bowed, she stared at her fingers, looking unbearably sad and . . . dejected, dammit.

'Chloe – '

'It's all right, Thomas. You've tried to tell me and I just won't listen because it's not what I want to hear. You don't want me.'

'It has nothing to do with – '

'I'll get my stuff. I won't bother you again about this, I promise.'

'Look at me,' he said tersely. Slowly her head raised. 'No, I mean *really* look at me, Slim.'

Curious, she cocked her head, her eyes on his. When he just stared at her, waiting with a light in his eyes she didn't understand, she ran her gaze over him quickly and impersonally – *at first*.

He saw the exact moment his problem registered on her, watched as her eyes widened first with shock, then embarrassment, then with such acute interest it only worsened his condition.

'Oh, my goodness,' she said, her eyes riveted to his crotch, continuing to stare at him with such intense interest he couldn't help but let out a laughing moan.

'Do I look like a man who's indifferent, Chloe? Like a man who's not attracted? Like a man who doesn't want you?'

Her eyes just widened a little more.

'Do I?' he demanded.

'Ah . . .' She bit her lower lip and kept staring. 'No. You don't.'

Her husky reply definitely caused a further reaction, but not exactly a comfortable one. 'Keep looking at me like that,' he said a little thickly, 'and I just might really embarrass the both of us.'

'I don't feel embarrassed,' she whispered, still watching the part of him that was leaping in response to nothing more than a look from her.

She licked her lips and he nearly moaned aloud. 'What do you feel?'

'I feel . . .' She tugged at the neckline of the sweatshirt she wore. 'I feel kind of hot.'

The laugh he let out was more a groan. 'So do I.'

Without stopping to think, he reached for her. At the same moment she came closer to him, and their arms got hopelessly tangled before he managed to get her against him, legs to legs, stomach to stomach, chest to chest. With her still smiling, he kissed her – a deep, hot, wet, questing kiss.

Her mouth was heaven. So was the feel of her against him. His will to keep her at bay voluntarily surrendered to the surge of primal need for her he hadn't even been aware of possessing. She must have felt the same need, for her fingers dug sharply into his shoulders as she clung. A little sound of yearning came from deep in her throat, and it was one of the sexiest sounds he'd ever heard.

He didn't hear the knock at the door, or if he did it didn't quite reach registering point in his brain. Not when he had this soft, delicious woman in his arms.

The one who was making those noises that drove him absolutely wild. No, he paid no attention to that door.

That was until it opened directly behind them and someone walked right in.

'Chloe – *Oh!*'

In his arms, Chloe jerked, then pulled back. 'Conrad.'

CHAPTER 15

'Well, isn't this awkward?' Conrad asked, stepping in uninvited.

'Ah . . . well.' Chloe bit her lip and met no one's gaze. 'A little.'

'Wouldn't have been if you'd knocked before you walked right in like you owed the place,' Thomas pointed out evenly.

'I did knock.' Conrad, looking more tense than Chloe had seen him in some time, leaned back against the doorjamb, his arms crossed over his chest. His computer, in its case, was slung over his shoulder. 'Next time I'll have to remember to pound.'

His expression carefully blank, Conrad turned to Chloe. 'I've been trying to reach you. I came by to see if you were all right.'

Now his gaze ran briefly down the length of her, and she became very aware of the picture she must make, in a sweatsuit obviously too big to be hers.

'Looks like you are,' he said, in a perfectly bland voice.

Suppressing the urge to touch her lips, which she knew were bright red and still wet from Thomas's mouth, she forced a light smile. 'I got your messages. I was going to call you back.'

'Were you?' His half-smile, when it lit on Thomas, didn't quite reach his eyes. 'I heard about the damage to *Homebaked*. I went by there this morning but everything looks good.'

'Yes.' With both men's eyes on her, it became difficult to talk. 'There was no real damage. Gossip always makes everything seem worse.'

'I didn't get this from an idle gossip. I got it from Lana.'

Chloe laughed. 'Same thing. Conrad, Lana runs the gossip train.'

'She was worried about you. So, it seems, is Augustine. She told me to make sure you're all right.'

'I just saw her. She knows I'm fine.'

'Lots of vandalism lately, it seems.' Again he looked at Thomas, who didn't blink an eye. 'Any more trouble, Thomas?'

'You asking as a sheriff or a friend?'

That gave Conrad pause. And he released his first genuine smile, though it was short-lasting. 'I didn't know you considered us friends.'

'Either way, I have no complaints.'

It seemed obvious to Chloe that Conrad didn't want to believe that. 'So, what happened?' he asked her. 'How did they get in?'

'Through the kitchen door.' She shrugged. 'You know how kids can be. Someone must have gone in on a dare. They dumped the ketchup and some other things. More a nuisance than anything.'

'You should have called me, Chloe. Or at least the station. It should have been reported.'

'It was no big deal,' she said. 'Really it wasn't.'

She felt Thomas's stare, felt, too, the way Conrad looked at her, not believing a word she said.

'I tried calling you all yesterday,' he said, frowning. 'Last night too.'

Now the two men were no longer just looking at each other, but were sizing each other up in a way that had Chloe nervous. 'I'm sorry. I didn't mean to worry you, but I've been busy.'

'Hmm.' Absently Conrad tapped the side of his computer, while seemingly having a silent conversation with Thomas.

Chloe wanted in on that conversation. 'Why do I get the feeling you two are discussing me and yet I'm standing right here not getting a single word?'

Thomas's mouth actually quirked, but he didn't speak.

Neither did Conrad.

The three of them stood in the frigid room staring at each other until Chloe let out a little laugh. 'This is dumb. One of you say something.'

'I plead the Fifth,' Thomas said.

'You're becoming predictable in your old age, buddy.' Conrad sighed and looked at Chloe. 'Okay, well, obviously you're still busy. I'm sorry I interrupted.'

He'd turned and stepped out before Chloe caught him. 'Wait, Conrad.' Pausing to glance over her shoulder at the still silent Thomas, Chloe leaned close, touched his computer and said quietly, 'Did you want to show me something?'

His eyes met hers, searching her face for a long moment. 'Are you really all right?' he asked in a low voice.

'Yes, of course.'

He nodded, but didn't look happy. 'What I wanted can wait.'

He *did* have something to show her. And why couldn't she shake the feeling she wasn't going to like it? 'But – ' She broke off, remembering exactly what she'd been doing when he'd opened the door. There, deep in his eyes, was the lingering hurt.

It had bothered him to see her kissing Thomas. He was just too polite to say it. Knowing that, she felt she had no right to hound him. Not now.

She'd save it for when they were alone.

'It's freezing, Chloe. Turn up your heater or you'll catch your death.'

'I can't.'

'What do you mean you can't?'

'She means she *can't*. Her heater is broken and Thorton's a greedy fool,' Thomas said.

'I'll talk to him,' Conrad said angrily. 'That's ridiculous – '

'I've already arranged for a new heater, but it won't come until tomorrow,' Thomas told him. 'For now, she's coming back with me to my house.'

Another long stare was exchanged between the two men.

'I guess that's where you were last night,' Conrad

said after a minute, shifting his computer to his other shoulder restlessly.

Tension filled the air.

It was very important to Chloe that these men, these two favorite people of hers, got over this awkward hump. She wanted them to like each other – very much. She and Conrad had been friends forever, and once, a very long time ago, had even entertained notions of being more than friends. Nothing had come of it – mainly because she really didn't feel that way toward him. But their friendship had grown even deeper after that.

She knew deep down that Conrad could easily have given it all up to try again. Just as she knew he truly wanted the best for her – even if that best was Thomas. Still, it couldn't be easy to take, watching his once close friend and his now best friend kiss.

And it hadn't been just a little kiss he'd interrupted. No, it had been the mother of all kisses.

Tugging a little on his arm, Chloe tried to pull him back further into the apartment, knowing they all had to face this right now. They were already on the verge of being friends again, she just had to help. If she could. 'Come in, Conrad. It is freezing in here. We'll start a fire and I'll make coffee.'

Thomas made no move to make him feel more welcome. In fact, Chloe thought a little irritatedly, if anything he seemed to be trying to intimidate Conrad, the way he stood there, silent and foreboding.

Conrad smiled down at her, an open smile reminiscent of the Conrad she knew. 'That's okay, but thanks. You're . . . busy.' His eyes went dark and serious. 'But I do need to speak to you when you get the chance. It's very important. Will you call me?'

For the first time she noticed he wore his badge. The urgency in his voice didn't escape her either. Something was up, and suddenly she thought she knew what. 'Have you seen my father?'

'This morning.'

That explained that. The mayor had involved Conrad, and by the looks of things Conrad and his trusty computer had found out something he thought she should know. 'All right,' she murmured, deep in thought, 'I'll call you.' What had he discovered? And why wasn't Thomas saying anything?

But then he did, and Chloe could only wonder why she'd wanted him to get into this conversation at all. 'I'll be happy to wait in the kitchen while the two of you have a little chat,' he offered in a kind voice that completely belied his intense gaze. 'If you have the need for privacy.'

'That's okay,' Conrad said. 'It'll wait.'

'Why do I have the feeling that it can wait only until I leave?' Thomas asked politely.

'Feeling a little sensitive, Thomas?'

'Any reason I should be?'

'Of course not,' Chloe jumped in. What was going on? She'd thought Conrad wanted to be Thomas's friend. Why did she suddenly feel as if they were drawing battle lines? 'Conrad, what's going on?'

No one spoke and she threw her hands up disgust. *Men.* She turned to Conrad first, because in her

252

experience he was the easier to manipulate. And much easier to make feel guilty enough to talk to her. 'Conrad. Talk to me.'

'It's nothing.'

Lifting her eyebrows, she just stared at him.

Shifting on his feet, he gave her a pleading look. She didn't buy it. 'Fine,' he said, shoving a hand through his hair. 'If you really must know, I don't think you should go to his house. I think you should go to your parents.'

'I see,' she said slowly. Was this jealousy or something else? Something worse – as in he didn't trust Thomas anymore. 'Why is that?'

He didn't answer that; Thomas did. 'Have I suddenly become a threat, Conrad?'

'Not a threat,' he conceded. 'But danger seems to follow you. I want her safe.'

'She'll be safe with me.'

'Like she was in your kitchen the day it blew up? Like she was in her restaurant after word got out you own the loan on it?'

'She'll be safe,' Thomas repeated. 'I'll make sure of it.'

'She'd be safer if you'd let me in. Maybe I can help.'

'No,' said Thomas. 'I don't need help.'

'I have plenty of room, Chloe,' Conrad said, dropping his gaze from Thomas to her and trying another angle. 'So does my mom, if you'd rather.'

So he'd accepted how she felt about Thomas, and he respected that. An unexpected lump blocked her throat and she knew he'd do anything for her. But she didn't want to leave Thomas, even if it meant putting herself in danger.

She wanted to make sure he stayed safe, and she couldn't do that if she wasn't with him. 'I'll be okay.'

'Chloe – '

'She's already made plans.' This from Thomas, and spoken with the attitude he reserved for the general population of Heather Glen.

Conrad's eyes stayed on Chloe. 'You know you can always call us.'

'I know.'

'It's okay to change your mind.'

'I'll keep that in mind,' she said carefully, willing him to understand.

With a nod of his head, Conrad left, without looking at Thomas again.

When the door shut, a heavy silence fell into the room.

Thomas broke it. 'I need to know,' he said in a strained voice, 'what exactly there is between the two of you.'

She'd known this was coming, could see the flash of suppressed anger and something that looked suspiciously like jealousy in his eyes. 'You *need* to know? Aren't you more concerned with the fact that Conrad seemed to know something we should know?'

'Not at the moment.' His deep eyes did indeed bore into hers, but he made no move to touch her. In fact, he stood still as a rock, his hands deep into his pockets. 'I think, after what transpired between us, that I *deserve* to know about you and Conrad. Don't you?'

She felt the blush creep up her face and cursed herself for that. No, she wasn't embarrassed – far from it. It was just that any mention of the previous night and what had happened in his house made her body separate itself from her mind. Every ounce of flesh, every single nerve-point reacted to him, even without a touch. And this unbearable yearning, this deep ache, was going to drive her bonkers.

'Slim?' Now he took a step closer, slipped a hand out of his pocket and lifted her chin. He must have mistaken her sudden flush of color, for his jaw tightened. 'You have something to tell me?'

'I can't believe you could wonder, especially after . . . after how I responded to you.'

'Well, I do wonder. So tell me.'

He could doubt her. That hurt. So did the way he was looking at her, as if he didn't trust her one little bit. All that deep desperateness, that dark restlessness that made up Thomas stared at her.

'Chloe?'

'It's not very flattering that you can question me like this,' she mumbled, turning away. Was it so hard for him to see there was no one else – that there never could be? That no one else had ever mixed her up so much? Maybe it was. Maybe what she wanted was impossible after all.

Before she could take another step, he'd whirled her around, held her arms while searching her face. 'Flattering or not, I need to know,' he said. 'I find I don't like to share. Especially with friends.'

Don't like to share? Suddenly everything brightened inside her, so that it was hard to contain her smile. He *did* consider Conrad a friend. He *did* like her more than he wanted to admit. '*I find I don't like to share.*' Oh, there was hope for this stubborn man yet!

'I don't know what the hell is so funny,' he snapped.

'Nothing's funny.' Unable to contain herself, she threw her arms around his neck and gave him a bear hug. 'The only thing between Conrad and me is a friendship that has withstood the test of time and . . .'

'And?' he said tersely. 'And what?'

'And the fact that we don't seem to agree about what to do with you.'

Thomas looked down at her. His hands had remained at his sides when she'd flung herself at him, but now they moved to her hips, squeezing gently before raising to her waist. 'I keep telling myself I can't do this,' he said unevenly, those clever hands glided upwards, skimming over her ribs, resting just beneath her tight, aching breasts. 'I can't be with you like this, I can't possibly want you like I do.'

'What happens when you tell yourself that?' she asked, suddenly breathless.

'Nothing.' He looked amazed, and more than a little disgruntled. 'Absolutely nothing. I still want you.'

Relieved laughter escaped her. 'Thank God.' With

her hands fisted in his hair, she tried to bring his face down to hers.

He wasn't having it. 'So tell me, Slim. Why are you running from Thorton?'

'Oh, that.'

'Yeah, *oh, that.*'

Pride kept her head high. It also refused to let her answer. 'I'll tell you just as soon as you tell me what you really do for a living.'

'You already know that. I'm a businessman.'

But in his arm she'd gone still. 'There's more to it than that; you've already told me that much.'

He had no intention of ever telling her the truth. How could he when she'd never be able to forgive him? His best bet at this point was to pull out of town and cut his losses. Just go and forget about the incredible amount of money he'd put into the town.

Walk away.

He was tempted.

If he did, Chloe would never come to hate him. And if he'd miss her until his dying day, he could at least remember the one night he'd had with her, could at least tell himself he'd left her in safe hands now that he controlled her loan and owned the building she lived in. No one could take away her business or home no matter how much money she didn't have. He'd see to it.

It was true that he'd miss seeing the ruin of Heather Glen. But it didn't matter.

Didn't matter?

Shocked at the thought, he dropped his hands

from Chloe and plowed them through his hair. But no matter how he ran it through his head, it remained true.

He no longer cared about destroying the town.

Not because he'd lost his nerve, or even his need for revenge. No, both his nerve and his anger were still firmly in place against the small-minded people and the hurts they'd inflicted on him.

'Thomas?'

God, that voice. That sweet, caring, sexy voice. He couldn't bring pain to her. That should have been his first clue. When he'd held the means in the palm of his hand to destroy her, he hadn't been able to do it.

'*Thomas?*'

Blinking a worried Chloe into focus, he took a deep breath. The best thing he could possibly do now was leave town. And fast. Before it was too late.

But her lips were blue and he saw her shiver. *Dammit.* 'Would you get a coat on? And do you ever wear gloves?'

Silently she moved to her coat rack. 'I can't seem to keep track of gloves. I'm forever losing them.'

Worrying about her had become a full-time job. One he wasn't sure he wanted to keep. 'You have gas in your car?'

Damn her, she smiled. 'Yes, Thomas. You do realize I've been handling that particular area for myself since I was sixteen? I'm a pretty big girl now.'

'If that were true, you wouldn't be running down hallways to avoid your landlord.'

She paled and he could have kicked himself. What

258

the hell had he said that for? 'I'm sorry,' he said, feeling horrified. He knew more than most how someone could do the best they could and still not make ends meet. 'I was way out of line on that one.'

'As a friend, maybe,' she conceded, still looking shaken. 'As a banker, you were right on. I guess that makes it pretty clear where we stand.'

'I didn't mean it like it sounded.'

'Yes, you did,' she said tolerantly. 'But that's all right. I needed the reminder.'

He couldn't think of what to say, but hated it that he'd hurt her when he'd vowed not to. For a long minute she simply looked at him. Thomas had the uncomfortable feeling she was looking right into the core of him.

Get out of Heather Glen, he told himself. Get out hard and fast, before you hurt her anymore.

'I have things to do,' she said, wrapping her arms tight around her.

'Not in here.'

'No. But the heater in my car works just fine.'

How they'd moved from that wild, mindless kiss to this quiet, polite, meaningless conversation, Thomas had no idea. 'I have things I have to do, too,' he said a little roughly. Guilt always made him abrupt. Yanking out his keys, he pulled the house key off. Slapping it into her hand, he moved to the door. 'Come to the house to sleep.' He'd nearly choked on that last word, knowing that with her in the house sleeping would be the last thing on his mind.

She didn't answer so he looked at her. 'Chloe?'

259

She nodded. 'Thank you.'

She would come, then. He hadn't driven her off. Relief threatened to make him giddy, but why, he hadn't a clue. Especially since he was going to leave here, go to his office and plan his departure from Heather Glen. Forever.

He slammed the door.

Less than five minutes later, he was revving his Jag on the road, thinking his mood couldn't get more foul.

But he was wrong, very wrong.

Two industrial buildings on the edge of town, buildings that he'd recently purchased through another subsidiary of Sierra Rivers, had been vandalized.

In twenty-five thousand square feet worth of buildings, there wasn't a single window left.

Chloe hadn't yet gotten onto the highway when the lights behind her signaled her to pull over.

If her heart hadn't been so impossibly heavy, she would have smiled as she pulled over to the side of the road and waited for Conrad to get out of his truck.

But the serious expression on his face matched hers, and her stomach dropped.

'What's the matter?' she asked him immediately, skipping their usual banter.

He wasn't in the mood either. 'I've been waiting for you. Will you follow me?'

'You bet. Where to?'

He smiled. 'I was afraid you'd say no.'

'Then shame on you,' she chided, reaching for his hand through her now opened window. 'You should know I'd follow you anywhere.'

'I wasn't sure that still applied,' he said solemnly, leaning down. 'Not after today.'

'Why? Because you saw me kissing Thomas?' There. Now it was out in the open.

'No, but speaking of that . . .' He tucked a piece of her hair behind her ear and smiled into her eyes. 'I want you to know something.'

'What?'

'I love you.'

'Oh, Conrad – '

'Like my sister,' he finished calmly, but his eyes were fierce. 'And as much as I want to like Thomas, want to think we could be friends again, I'm telling you I'll kick his ass if he hurts you.'

Love for him bubbled to the surface, making her throat burn, her eyes sting. 'Conrad – '

'No, don't do that,' he said softly, wiping at a tear as it fell. 'I know you love me too.'

'I do,' she whispered, feeling ridiculously weepy. 'You know I do.'

'Good,' he said firmly. 'Then listen to me and believe in me. I'm afraid you're going to get hurt.'

'He wouldn't,' she protested. 'Thomas wouldn't hurt me.'

'Chloe, this isn't a good place to talk. Will you come with me?' He straightened. 'Please? Just for a few minutes so I can show you something.'

She could see how much it meant to him, and knew

instinctively how much it was going to mean to her. When he pulled his truck in front of her, she followed.

They ended up in Grand Park, sitting on a bench surrounded by hungry birds. The cold, crisp air stirred Chloe's hair as she waited for Conrad to boot up his computer.

'Just tell me,' she urged, rubbing her hands on her pants.

'Where are your gloves?' He swore. 'Never mind, I can see you have no idea.' He jerked his own off and tossed them in her lap, and she gladly jammed her hands into the warm leather.

'Now tell me,' she said again, able to concentrate now that she was not so cold.

'I'd rather show you.' His fingers worked the keyboard.

The screen flickered beneath his touch. Chloe imagined all sorts of horrible grids and charts. Things she couldn't possibly understand. 'I'd rather you just tell me.'

'All right, then.' His hands stilled on the keys and his troubled eyes lifted to hers. 'You know the name of the company that's planning on building the resort here?'

As if she could forget. The newspapers wrote about it every day. At this point, with so many people – including her family and friends – so heavily invested in this supposed resort, she could only hope Sierra Rivers meant business.

But she was so afraid they didn't. That they would

for some reason decide not to build – after all, they'd never once been offered a guarantee. If that happened, she'd watch the ruin of a town she cared greatly about. Because she knew that many who'd invested would not be able to recover if their investments weren't bought out.

For that matter she didn't know how long *she* could survive in this market, and she hadn't invested. But when the resort came through, her business would increase. That was *if* the resort came through . . .

She tucked her gloved hands into her pockets and watched the birds scamper along the path, thinking if she could only get her hands on the man running Sierra Rivers, she had a mouthful for him.

She'd grab him by the collar and demand to know why he hasn't started buying up the property around town if he intended to build a resort. Why he wouldn't officially confirm or deny the rumors. And why he couldn't come forward and announce who he was.

The people of Heather Glen deserved the answers to all those questions and more.

'Do you know the name of the company?' Conrad asked patiently.

'Of course. It's Sierra Rivers.' She fairly spat out the name.

Conrad nodded solemnly. 'That's right. And do you know who owns Sierra Rivers?'

'No. But I'd like to.'

Something flickered in his eyes. Something like sympathy. 'Conrad? What's going on? What's this about?'

'What would you say if I told you that you do know him?'

'But I don't.'

'Yes, Chloe, you do,' he said gently, reaching out to squeeze her arm. 'You know him well.'

'I don't – ' Her stomach hurt; her mouth fell open. 'Tell me I don't.'

He said nothing.

'Oh, my God.'

'Do you know what I'm telling you?'

'No,' she whispered, suddenly understanding much more than she wanted to. 'Oh, no. Conrad, it can't be true.'

'It's Thomas.'

CHAPTER 16

She'd heard wrong, that was all. No reason for her stomach to drop away. 'Thomas?'

Conrad reached for Chloe's hand over his laptop computer. 'Thomas is Sierra Rivers.'

'I see.'

Silence fell over them. In the winter day, birds chirped, bare branches swayed in the chilly breeze. The sky was so painfully blue Chloe squinted as she studied nothing. Nothing at all.

Thomas owned Mountain Mortgage. Thomas owned Sierra Rivers. *Thomas owned her*. 'Are . . . you sure?'

But he would be. Chloe knew that Conrad would never have told her unless he was absolutely certain. His confirming nod was grim, unhappy.

'It's a fact. Thomas owns Sierra Rivers.' His bleak eyes met hers. 'What I don't know is why.'

Chloe could imagine, and what she imagined made her feel sick. 'He's been toying with us, Conrad. Playing a game.' She was going to throw up all over his expensive computer, not a question about it.

'No,' he said firmly, shaking his head. 'I don't

265

want to think that.' He looked at her. 'And you don't want to think that either.'

'No.'

Another long silence. More birds. In the distance, silver-lined clouds appeared on the horizon. A storm, she thought dully. More snow.

'You're thinking bad thoughts,' Conrad guessed. 'I can feel them.'

'I can't help it,' she admitted. 'What other reason is there for him not telling us?' Bringing her fingers to her suddenly aching temples, she closed her eyes. So many things had happened since Thomas had come back; so many of them had become happy memories in her mind.

It was all false now.

All of it – that first meeting, the buying of her loan, the buying of her buildings . . . making love – all of it had been part of some grand plan of Thomas's, some scheme that she didn't understand.

'Maybe he came here to help rebuild our dying town,' Conrad suggested, wrapping an arm around her quaking shoulders. 'Why couldn't that be it?'

'If that was all, wouldn't he have just told us? Just come right out in the beginning when I asked him what he did for a living? He could have just said, I am Sierra Rivers.'

'Maybe he wanted to be a silent benefactor. After all, some of the people here haven't been friendly to him.'

Including her own father. '*Most* of the people haven't been friendly.'

'Maybe that embarrasses him.'

266

'Conrad, nothing embarrasses Thomas.'

'The point is, he hasn't been made to feel welcome here. Maybe he feels uncomfortable.'

'Exactly. So why would he bother with us? He left this town in the first place because – ' Turning to Conrad, she grabbed his hands, nearly toppling the computer. 'Oh, Conrad.'

'What?' He managed to catch the computer and Chloe, who slumped against him. 'Chloe, what?'

'He didn't come here to save Heather Glen.' Her stomach roiled, her heart shattered. 'He came here to ruin it. And everyone fell right in with his plans.'

'Why would he do that?'

'Come on,' she said, disgust and fear and heart-break rolling together inside her. 'Think about this. You know how bitter he was when he left. How his father treated him. How my father practically ran him out of town. No one wanted him here; they treated him like an outcast. But he's not an outcast at all. I mean, look at him – the owner of the huge mega-corporation of Sierra Rivers – he must be a millionaire several times over.'

'Poor boy turns rich isn't that common, I admit. But what does that have to do with the fate of Heather Glen?'

'Revenge.' Just the word made her want to cry.

'You think he came back to destroy this town simply because some people were nasty to him?'

She was very afraid that was exactly what she thought.

'Look,' Conrad said gently, 'we don't know that he

doesn't intend to build that resort. We can't condemn him for anything until we know that.'

Maybe not. But he could have told her he was Sierra Rivers. She'd given him every opportunity to do so.

That he hadn't didn't bode well – for the town or Chloe and Thomas.

As had become habit, Thomas drove around checking his properties. The last vandalism would cost him a pretty penny. Replacing windows was damn expensive, and at the thought of the senseless crime, his blood boiled again.

Who was doing this to him? Who had found out what his plans were? *Were*, he emphasized. For he was no longer a threat to Heather Glen.

Thomas wanted to think it was James McGuirre trying to hurt him, wanted to believe he was the only person who hated him enough. But more checking had shown his father had gotten himself into hot water again and had spent the past week in Reno jail.

So who was after him?

After ensuring everything he owned seemed fine, Thomas drove back to his house. The late afternoon sun settled against the mountains, starting to drop. A chill hit the air.

He should march himself inside, open his office and make plans to leave this town. He should figure out what he would do with the properties he'd already acquired, for he had to do something. He owned more than half the town.

It was simply too much money to walk away from.

But he didn't want to think about it now, because if he did, he would be reminded that soon, very soon, he'd be long gone from Heather Glen. And from Chloe Walker, the one bright spot in his life.

His house was dark, still.

Chloe had not yet shown up, and he could only hope for her sake she did. If he had to go out and drag her back, his mood wasn't going to improve much.

Since he was so restless, serious work was out of the question. Yet energy chugged through his veins, a dangerous sort of energy he couldn't dissipate.

Exercise, he thought. Brutal, muscle-tearing, mind-numbing exercise was what he needed. Changing quickly, he made his way down to the basement, cranked up the stereo and proceeded to lose himself in weights.

An hour later he lay flat on his back on the mat, soaked and trembling, feeling marginally better. Though he was dying of thirst, he lay there, too weak to move, knowing tomorrow he'd be paying for this.

'Hello, son.'

Thomas jerked at the sound of his father's smooth drawl. Before he could so much as lift his head, a heavy booted foot settled on his stomach.

'How's things?' James asked, leaning down over his bent knee, which placed all his weight on Thomas's abdomen.

For a second Thomas couldn't breathe, but then his father lifted his boot slightly. 'I expect an answer when I talk to you, Thomas. Don't forget that.'

Rage flowed through Thomas, and he grabbed for the foot that held him down. But his quivering arms could do little more than hold the leg pinning him as his father bore down with amazing strength.

'Get out,' he said through his teeth.

James laughed. *Laughed.* 'You're a slow learner, boy.' More weight was applied and stars danced in Thomas's head. 'Listen up carefully, son. I need more money.'

'Thought . . . you were in jail,' he managed on the last of his breath.

James eased up again, slightly, and Thomas gulped in air, tugging to no avail on the foot that held him. 'Just got out. First person I wanted to see was you.'

'How lucky . . . for me.' Thomas fought with all his waning strength, but his father was wide, beefy, and had the extra advantage of height at the moment.

'Money, son. I want it now. Twenty-five grand this time.'

Thomas tried to laugh, but sucked in his breath instead when his father dropped down on him with all his weight, kicking at Thomas's ribs with his knees. James held Thomas's arms out, grinned and leaned close enough so that Thomas could see all the way into his empty eyes. 'No one laughs at me. Thought I taught you better than that.'

Throwing back his arm, he punched Thomas in the jaw with all his might.

With a grunt of surprise and pain, Thomas lifted his knee, slamming it into his father's crotch. James groaned and toppled over, his eyes rolling back in his head. Thomas followed, but before he could pin his father down James kept the momentum going, and they rolled and rolled across the matted floor, each struggling for the upper hand. They careened into a weight bench and the metal jabbed Thomas painfully in the back.

'You will pay me, Thomas,' his father gasped. 'I'm going to beat hell out of you until you say you will.'

Unreasonable fear welled up. How many times had he heard his father announce that he was going to beat him until he didn't know his own name? And how many times had he actually done it? Too many – too damn many.

He was grown now, Thomas reminded himself, even as his father's fists landed with unerring velocity. He could fight back. And he did – despite his already weakened condition. Shoving off the bench, he took his father down.

'I won't pay you squat,' he grated out, giving as good as he got.

'Yes . . . you will,' his father promised, squeezing Thomas tightly around the neck.

As Thomas's vision faded to gray he clawed at his father's hands. *No. He won't win.* With a renewed burst of strength, Thomas pushed him off, then dived on him as they scrambled for purchase over the floor, knocking into the weights scattered on the mat.

At the opposite wall, Thomas slammed his father into the corner. '*I am not going to give you a penny.*'

With a vicious snarl, James swung out with a fist

271

again, catching Thomas right in his already sore stomach muscles. Not willing to go down yet, Thomas struck back, his fist splitting against James's cheek.

With a bellow of rage, James flung himself away from the wall, knocking them both into the bench, which toppled at their weight. They hit the floor hard. For an immeasurable minute of time James kept the upper hand, taking punches at Thomas with incredible speed.

Thomas, who had taken more than his fair share of beatings from this man, fought back as he'd never dared as a child. Still, his father's strength and stamina took him off guard.

Pain edged into his conscious, sharp and glaring. But he couldn't let his father win, not again. With a strength born of pure will-power, he flattened James to the mat. Heaving himself up, he looked down into dark, furious eyes. 'Not only . . . am I not going to pay you,' he wheezed, dragging air through lungs that screamed in agony, 'but I'm going . . . to have you arrested for assault. And vandalism.'

'I've not vandalized anything,' he father panted. Blood ran from a cut in his lip. His left eye was beginning to swell. Thomas hoped he hurt like hell.

'No cop can hold me to Heather Glen.' With a feral snarl and a lunge, James rolled them over, landing on top of Thomas with painful results. 'Just as you can't hold me down now.'

With one last savage swing, James hit Thomas. 'I'll be back,' he warned as he staggered up.

While Thomas lay there, stunned and dazed, he heard his father tear up the stairs.

At least you didn't pay him, Thomas thought as his vision turned to black. *He hadn't let his father win.*

Chloe had no idea what she was going to do with her newfound knowledge, but she knew she wasn't ready to face Thomas. She'd become afraid, very afraid, that everything she'd hoped for between her and Thomas was a lie.

His lie.

After she left Conrad she headed back to her apartment, in spite of the cold. She had to be alone, if only for a few minutes. Had to sit and let it all sink in. Thomas owned Sierra Rivers. Thomas had come back to town knowing Heather Glen was expecting Sierra Rivers to build the resort – and he hadn't said one word. Not one word confirming the rumors or denying them. And certainly not one word about the fact he *was* Sierra Rivers.

Why? She had no idea.

Conrad hadn't wanted her to be alone, had wanted her to come with him to either his house or his parents'. Chloe had refused, knowing she was not going to be good company. Besides, she couldn't handle the pity in Conrad's gaze, the sympathy at how foolish she'd been to fall for Thomas McGuirre.

And she had fallen. Hard and fast. Stupidly.

With a loud screech, she pulled in at her apartment building. For a minute she just sat there, lost in thought.

Lost in memories, their first kiss, Thomas panicking over the thought of raising a kitten, the way he'd looked at her, his gaze shifting from vague suspicion to a hot yearning that stole her breath.

They could have had so much.

How dared Thomas not trust her? she thought, her insides aching a little at the loss. She knew there could be only one reason for that lack of trust – he was up to no good.

Short on luck and long on temper, Chloe forgot to tiptoe on the first floor. As a result, Thorton opened his door the minute she tried to pass.

'Chloe.'

'Oh, Mr Thorton.' Her heart sank. After what she'd learned about Thomas, she didn't have the strength to deal with this. 'Hello.'

'I slipped your receipt in under your door,' Thorton said, not exactly smiling, but not wearing his usual frown either. 'Thank you. No hard feelings, I hope?'

Receipt? Thank you? 'What are you talking about?'

'The rent,' he said with uncharacteristic patience. 'Thomas handed it to me this morning for you. Since I'll be leaving soon, I hope we'll part on good terms.'

'Thomas – He paid you?' Her voice cracked and squeaked, but she hardly noticed.

'Yep. Nice of you to add the late payment without me having to ask. I also appreciate the advance payment for the next six months. What happened, you hit the jackpot?'

Conflicting emotions seized her. Shock, anger, embarrassment . . . gratitude. Why had he done it?

Why would a man intent on seizing up a town bother paying one little nobody's rent?

Because he wasn't the monster she'd made him out to be in her head this last hour. Guilt flooded her.

She'd tried him without even talking to him – something she had no right to do.

'Goodnight,' Thorton said politely, shutting the door.

She stood there. Six months. He'd paid her rent for the next six months and he'd not said a single word. That was not the action of a person bent on destruction.

Yet he had to be up to something.

Should she go to him after all, tell him what she knew and let him explain? Or, better yet, should she keep this information to herself a little longer and trust in him to not only do the right thing but tell her about it?

Whirling, she ran back to her car and hopped in. She had no idea what exactly she intended, only knew she had to see him. Either this crazy attraction between them was nothing more than a distraction for him, a way for him to pass the time, or he'd become more attached to her than he wanted to let on.

Whichever it was, she was going to play it safe for now. At least until she was certain what he felt for her was real. And he happened to have the de luxe accommodation that had been promised to her. She was going to take him up on that – if only to see him again. But, she reminded herself firmly, she would absolutely play it safe.

She'd take that spare bedroom. Yes, she would. She wouldn't budge from it, no matter how sexy he looked, all rumpled and sleepy, with those bedroom eyes making her swoon.

No way would she get anywhere near him tonight. No way at all.

Safe.

The roads were slippery, but she drove carefully, anxious. Who was she kidding? She was going because she had to see him again. She was convinced, no matter what the evidence pointed to, that he had meant no harm to anyone. And she'd never doubt him again. Of course, she still had to deal with the little matter that he hadn't confided in her, But that was just a matter of time.

She just had to prove she was worthy of his confidence, his friendship . . . his love.

His house, when she drove up, was silent and dark.

Seeing the Jag in the driveway, she knew he was home, so she let herself in. But he wasn't anywhere on the main floor, or even upstairs. Curious, and getting worried, she called out as she wandered through the foyer.

Another peek into the living room proved she was still alone, though her eyes did falter on the soft, giving carpeting.

When she closed her eyes, just for a minute, she could see the two of them there all over again, making love. She could picture his fierce and tender expression as he braced himself above her, feel that taut, sleek body tremble as he pressed into her, hear their raspy breathing as they made their way to mutual ecstasy.

Her body tingled as if it were happening all over again. As if he were actually touching her, penetrating her. When she opened her eyes and found herself in the present she felt a keen disappointment. She wanted Thomas to look at her like that again, touch her like that again. But he couldn't until she found him.

Where was he? And where was Haroldina?

They weren't anywhere. Upstairs or down. A little seed of worry planted itself as she went through the entire house, calling for both him and the kitten. They had to be somewhere. A grown man and a kitten didn't just disappear.

On her second trip through the kitchen, she noticed the flight of stairs she'd missed on her earlier trek through. A basement?

More quickly now, her little seed of fear rooting into a full-blown unreasonable panic that goaded her on, she took the steep stairs.

Her heart pounded; her palms turned slick. Silly, she assured herself. Silly to be so terrified, so worried. Thomas was a very big man. A strong man. Nothing would have happened to him in his own house.

Nothing.

But she gasped as she entered the basement and saw him sprawled on the mat, unnaturally still and bleeding. In the crook of one arm Haroldina sat, calmly washing her face.

CHAPTER 17

'Thomas!' she cried, running to his side. Falling over his chest, she grabbed his shoulders. 'Thomas, can you hear me?'

One eye – the one that wasn't swollen and bleeding – slitted open. His mouth, his wide, sexy mouth, was bleeding from one corner when it opened. 'You're . . . hurting me.'

'Oh! I'm sorry.' She sat back on her heels, relief making her sigh deeply. 'I thought – Never mind what I thought. What happened?' Suddenly cautious, she looked over her shoulder at the equipment askew across the floor. 'Who attacked you?'

'Nobody.' Wincing, he sat up, holding onto his ribs, unable to contain his small groan as he moved. 'Shit.'

Fumbling through her purse, she found a pack of tissues. Wrapping one arm around his shoulder, she pressed a tissue to the side of his mouth and nose, where blood streamed freely.

'Oh, Thomas,' she breathed, wincing with him when he flinched at her touch. 'Wait. I'm going to call 9–1–1.'

With an amazing show of strength, considering how bad he looked, Thomas hooked her wrist and snagged her back down. 'No.'

'No? Thomas – ' She made an effort to lower her near hysterical voice when he jerked as she yelled in his ear. 'Thomas, please. You're badly hurt.'

'Not that badly.' He glared at her, then coughed, cautiously holding onto his ribs. 'Nothing that won't heal.'

'But – '

'No buts, dammit,' he said in a harsh whisper, closing his eyes as if it hurt to talk. 'Please, Chloe. Just . . . sit there for a minute. I'll be fine.'

'I – '

'Just for a minute,' he urged, letting go of her wrist to hold his head.

God, what else could she do? Forget playing it safe and keeping her distance. That had gone out the window the moment she'd seen him lying there, hurt and bleeding. She wanted to scream, cry, demand an explanation. She wanted to know what had happened to him, wanted to hold him. But he looked so desperately miserable, so full of anger and rage, she didn't dare do anything.

So she sat there. And waited.

He shifted, grimaced, remained silent. Chloe's eyes took in each and every injury she could see. Swollen eye, bruised jaw, cut mouth. The T-shirt he wore was torn at the side, revealing taut skin, bunched muscle . . . and another bruise. His gym shorts had blood on them – from his face, she

279

realized, her heart turning on its side.

Sweat trickled down his chest, glistening on his skin. His shoulders rose and fell as he breathed, and his dark hair fell over his face. Those long, defined legs stretched out, causing another grimace.

Haroldina rubbed her head against his arm, mewling softly, begging to be touched. Chloe held her breath, knowing how he felt about the kitten, cursing herself for ever forcing it upon him.

Thomas tipped his head down and the kitten received the same glare she had only moments before. Chloe bit her lip, fingers itching to intervene.

Haroldina, oblivious to her master's anger, continued to rub her head over his arm. Just as Chloe reached out to snatch the kitten back Thomas shocked her.

With a little sound of resignation, he curled an arm about the kitten and pulled her closer. 'Scared you, did he?' he murmured softly, his voice rough and scratchy.

To Chloe's shock and amazement, he stroked the kitten's head and back, closing his eyes when Haroldina purred with carefree utter abandon.

'Sorry, baby,' she heard him whisper. 'I'm so sorry.'

Chloe's throat closed around a lump the size of a fist, refusing to work no matter how she swallowed. Her eyes stung. The way he held that kitten, petting her, reassuring her, gave her such a surge of love and pride she didn't think she could contain it.

God, she loved this man. Loved him more than

she'd thought possible. Right there and then she vowed never to doubt him again, never to give him cause to doubt her. No matter what was going on, they'd get through it, because she believed with all her heart that he wasn't capable of hurting anyone. No matter what the evidence pointed to.

She must have made a sound as she struggled with the emotions he'd caused. Over the kitten's head, their eyes met. His were filled with an unbelievable amount of pain, and she didn't think it was all physical. Her chest tightened even more.

'What happened?' she whispered. 'Please, Thomas – please tell me.'

His gaze dropped.

'Who scared Haroldina?' she pressed. 'Can you tell me that?'

In answer he closed his eyes; his chin hit his chest. His large hands continued to soothe the kitten, even as he bled on the floor.

'Thomas – '

'Chloe, hush a minute. Haroldina's shaking.'

The kitten wasn't the only one. Thomas's hands, as they touched the cat, trembled.

Someone had hurt him. Chloe had never in all her life felt such rage, such fury for someone she hadn't even met. She knew in that moment that if whoever had attacked Thomas walked into that basement, she was angry enough to kill him.

It was important she remain calm. Thomas needed her. While she waited for him to make a move her eyes continued to run over him, still appraising, but suddenly seeing him in a different light. He made quite a picture, she realized, all lean, athletic grace. So much beauty, so much hurt.

'Let me in, Thomas,' she whispered, unable to remain silent any longer. *So much for distance.*

'You are in.'

She opened her mouth to say more, but he shook his head, his eyes beseeching her. She shut it again, having to bite her tongue to keep quiet.

He groaned when he struggled to his knees. That face she loved so dearly spasmed in pain as he rested on his hands and knees, his head dropped low.

The way he breathed scared her.

'I'll be right back.' She was going to call for an ambulance, no matter what he said.

Before she could move, he'd straightened and taken her shoulders in his hands. 'No.'

Unable to hold back any longer, she touched his mouth, ran her gaze over his hurt face. 'Oh, Thomas.' Slowly, carefully, she touched his shoulders, ran her hands down his arms as she looked at him.

He held himself rigid and said nothing.

'Who hurt you?'

He didn't answer, and she glided her hands to his waist. When he didn't object, she slid them around to his back, setting her face to his chest. Gently, she hugged him, and, most amazing of all, he allowed it.

'Careful,' he said in a strangled voice, pulling back slightly. 'My ribs.'

When she would have leaped away in remorse, his hands came up to hold her to him. She had to close her eyes against the powerful feelings of protection, of possessiveness. 'I hope the other guy looks like hell,' she whispered.

The sound that escaped his lips might have started out as a laugh, but it ended on a moan. 'God, Chloe. Don't say anything else. It hurts to talk, hurts to laugh, hurts to feel. You . . . make me do all those things.'

He let go of her to stand, and she could have cried at the agony on his face.

'Don't fret,' he murmured, looking down at her. 'It's not as bad as it looks.'

How could he say that? she wondered wildly. He looked so positively awful. But she held her tongue, sensing his humility, his broken pride.

'I hope half that blood is his,' she said fiercely, pointing to the blood spattered on his shirt.

'Me too,' he said feverently.

'Tell me you got him good.'

'I did.' Now, finally, his eyes lit with some of the old Thomas. The cocky, sure, cool Thomas. 'For the first time ever, I really got him good – Goddammit, Chloe.' His jaw tightened. 'What the hell is it about you that makes me tell you things I don't mean to?'

Her victory gave her no sense of satisfaction. 'Your father,' she breathed, horrified. 'He did this to you?'

Thomas turned away, and with a slow, painful gait made his way to the stairs.

'Wait.' She easily caught up with him, slipped an arm around his waist. 'Let me help you.'

Surprisingly, he did. And that, she worried, told

her he was hurting even more than she'd guessed.

Leaning into her a little, he sighed. 'He caught me off-guard,' he admitted. 'I'd already worked myself into exhaustion with the weights when he caught me.'

Her stomach clenched as she pictured Thomas suffering at the hands of his own father. 'I hoped you beat the crap out of him.'

'You mean more than he did to me?'

At least his voice had a tinge of humor in it now. 'Yeah. Give me all the details.'

'You're sick, Chloe. Real sick.'

'I know. Tell me.'

'I kneed him.'

'Good. I hope he hobbles for the rest of his life.'

'Me too.'

The steps were difficult. By the time they'd gotten to the kitchen Thomas's color had faded five shades. Since she'd plastered herself to his side, she could feel his muscles quiver. Slowly, with as much care as she could, she helped him lower himself into a chair.

Moaning a little, he bent at the waist, hugging his ribs.

She reached for the telephone. 'You've cracked a rib for sure. I'm calling for – '

'No.' The tension in his voice got her attention.

'Give me one good reason.'

'I'll give you two. I don't want you to and I'm going to be fine.'

She stood there, trying to stare him down, struggling to keep the pity and horror out of her face and voice. She wasn't succeeding. Thomas could see both those emotions and more, and it nearly unmanned him.

He hated pity, and if he hadn't hurt like hell, he'd have taken himself off into a corner to lick his own wounds and sent her packing.

'I think you should be seen at the hospital, Thomas.'

Torn between the desire to kiss her and strangle her, he sagged back in the chair and closed his eyes. 'I told you, I'm going – '

'Yeah, yeah. You're gonna be fine,' she mimicked, rolling her eyes. In two steps she was standing between his legs, challenging him with her eyes. 'If you're so fine, then stand up and kiss me like you mean it.'

If he could have, he might have laughed. She dared where no one else would have.

'Can't do it, huh?' Her voice cracked a little and she whirled from him so he couldn't see the face he suspected held more compassion than he could handle anyway.

'Don't move,' she ordered. 'I'm going to clean you up. Then I'll decide what to do with you.'

A minute later she came back, with the small first-aid kit he kept in his downstairs bathroom and a washcloth. He watched silently as she wet it in the sink. But as she moved toward him with a purposeful strut and an intense gleam in her eyes he had to smile.

Which only split his lip open further. He swore, and she touched him gently with the warm, wet cloth. When she'd stopped the bleeding, she rinsed it out and started over with his cheek. His eye got the same attention. Gentle, probing fingers touched his sore neck, ran down over his chest.

'Are your ribs cracked, do you think?' she whispered.

'Just bruised.' He could hope.

She shook her head and dabbed antiseptic on a cotton ball, which she pressed with annoying accuracy to every cut on him. Hissing through his teeth when she got to his eye, he forced himself to hold still.

Setting down the bottle and the cotton ball, she cupped his face in her hands and blew gently on the cut.

His gut leaped.

'Thanks.' Because his neck muscles were so sore from where his father had squeezed there, he had to clear his throat. Still, his voice sounded hoarse. 'I'm really fine now.'

'I don't think I believe you.' But she dropped her hands from him.

'I am.'

'Prove it.'

'Excuse me?'

Come on, McGuirre,' she taunted, lifting her chin with a saucy look that cracked him up. 'Prove you're fine and I'll leave you alone.'

He could barely lift his arms, they ached so badly, but he had something to prove now. Tugging her down, he just barely contained his wince when she landed on his thighs.

She gasped in protest and slid off him, kneeling between his spread legs. The ends of her shiny hair tickled his bare thighs. Her chin came to about his belly button; her mouth was intimately level with his instant erection.

Now every inch of him was in agony.

The air around them was so erotically charged, it crackled.

Softly, she said his name. When he looked into her eyes he felt the first sense of peace he'd had all day.

With light strokes she touched his face, everything she felt written all over her. It reached deep inside him, easing away the harsh reality of what had happened. Turning his head, he kissed her palm and whispered her name.

Her eyes filled. 'I'm so sorry,' she whispered. 'Are you really all right?'

'Yes.' Pity wasn't what he wanted or needed. 'Kiss me, Slim.'

But the beauty at his feet let out her next breath and it was a sob.

'Slim?' Again he had to clear his throat, but this time it wasn't because of any injury. 'What's this?'

Violently, she shook her head and stared at him. 'I just really hate what happened to you. I wish we could go back and change – '

'Shh.' Carefully, with the precision of a brain surgeon, he leaned forward and pulled her up a little, willing his body to follow his instructions.

Chloe sniffed.

His arms encircled her protectively, possessively,

and if her weight hurt he refused to admit it, because it felt so good to have her against him.

'I wish I'd come earlier,' she said fiercely.

Had anyone ever cared so much about him? Then what she'd said sank in. 'No, you don't.' What would he have done if she had? He hadn't even been able to help himself: how would he have kept her safe?

Beneath his hands, her shoulders shook. 'Slim, hush. Don't cry for me anymore. Everything is okay now. Almost as good as new.'

Sniffing, she lifted her head and gave him a watery smile. Gentle fingers ran over the column of his throat, where he imagined bruises were beginning to show. She frowned, but before she could comment he asked her the question he'd been wanting to ask.

'Are you ever going to kiss me?'

'I wasn't going to,' she whispered. 'I really wasn't going to.'

'Wasn't?'

'No. I – I can't remember why now.'

'So what's holding you back?'

Her lips met his halfway. Desperate to touch, to be touched, Thomas moved his hands over her, knowing he could hold her like this for the rest of his life and never get enough.

Too bad he'd never get the chance for that. *Take it now*, he told himself. *Take it now while you can get it. Soon you'll be far away and you'll never see her again.*

With a little sound in her throat, Chloe moved closer. When he felt her breasts press against his chest, a powerful hunger was unleashed. She must have felt it too, for she made another little sound and held his head to hers so he couldn't get away.

As if he wanted to stop kissing her.

He could kiss her forever. Shoving that soul-destroying thought aside, he claimed her mouth with a frantic, needful thrust of his tongue. She matched it.

Arching against him, she locked her arms around his neck. He yanked her blouse from the waistband of her jeans, impatiently ripped the buttons from their holes. He had to see her, feel her. Had to or he'd explode.

Reaching behind her, he undid her bra, then slid his hands forward to cup her breasts. She whispered his name thickly and he responded, lowering his head to take the tip of one of those perfect, rose-tipped nipples in his mouth.

Only he never got that far. Halfway he froze, and gasped as a razor-sharp pain ripped through him.

'Thomas?' Chloe touched his stiff shoulders. 'What is it?'

'Nothing.' But he fell back into the chair, a fine sheen of sweat popping out on his forehead. 'Nothing,' he said again, more weakly.

One glance at his strong, corded arms criss-crossed over his ribs and she knew. 'Come,' she said gently, reaching for him. 'I'm putting you to bed.'

Very slowly he let out the breath he'd been holding. 'I don't want you to put me to bed.'

She very nearly smiled at his petulant tone, but recognized that would be a very big mistake. 'Let's go.' She held out a hand.

Mouth tight, he held firm. 'I can't believe this. I can't even – '

'Thomas.' Bracing herself with a hand on each of the armrests of his chair, she kissed his ear, then licked beneath it until he closed his eyes, tilted his head toward her and let out a little moan. 'You'll be more comfortable upstairs, I promise you.'

Lifting her head a fraction, she met his gaze . . . and nearly gasped. He looked at her through incredibly long lashes, his eyes impossibly dark and deep. His expression was of such longing, such hunger, it took her breath.

Just the sight of him reduced her to nothing but a mass of nerve-endings waiting to blow. From the first, she'd sensed something hidden deep within him, something haunted. It touched her again now as he looked at her.

Strong as he was, as self-contained and controlled as he was, he looked almost vulnerable. Needy.

She wanted, more than anything, to take away his pain, to make him smile, make him burst with joy and happiness. But was making love the answer? Wouldn't it be better if they talked first? If she could get him to open up and tell her what was going on, then they could move from there.

But those eyes of his were on her, full of an awareness and a need she'd never been able to resist. When he looked at her like that, as if he needed her so badly he'd die if he couldn't have her, she couldn't refuse him a thing. Certainly not herself.

She knew she was crazy to get involved with him, especially now, when she knew he could be destroying one of the things she loved beyond reason – Heather Glen.

No doubt about it, Thomas McGuirre was a threat – the biggest one she'd ever faced. He was a danger to everything she loved. To everything she was.

Because not only could he take away her life as she knew it, he held her heart in the palm of his hand.

'Why are you looking at me like that?' he asked, with a little smile and a touching amount of self-consciousness.

Because I love you. 'How am I looking at you, Thomas?'

The little smile faded as he looked at her. He swallowed, hard. 'With . . . stars in your eyes. But there's fear there, too. Terror, actually.'

Now she was the one who had to take a deep breath, force her throat to work. 'Terror is the right word.'

His eyes stayed very deliberately on hers. His breathing seemed shallow, and suddenly he was the one who looked terrified. 'What's the matter?'

'Maybe it just hit me.'

He licked his lips. 'What maybe just hit you?'

They were both whispering now. 'How much I love you. Maybe.'

CHAPTER 18

Oh, yes, Thomas was a threat – the greatest Chloe had ever faced. She should run, hard and fast, but she'd just made the ultimate statement and she wouldn't, couldn't, take it back.

'Only maybe?' he murmured, the terror in her eyes now definitely mirrored in his. Most definitely. 'Well, thank God for that little maybe. You don't want to love me, Slim. I'm not a good bet.'

She wanted to argue, to admit that she didn't just *maybe* love him. She did. Wholly and completely. But then he touched her, stroked his fingers tenderly over her jaw, and she was hopelessly lost.

'You were going to take me upstairs,' he reminded her in a low, husky voice.

A sound slipped out of her, a sigh. She was going to give in; she couldn't help it. His gaze dropped hungrily to her lips, and something dark and thrilling flared in his expression.

It matched the dark and thrilling thing that was happening to her insides. Why, oh, why, did she have to feel this way for him? Why couldn't it have been easier? Why couldn't she have fallen for someone more open, someone better able to get involved, someone more willing to love?

Because this was what was meant to be.

With a light, sensuous caress, Thomas ran his fingers over her face, down the slim column of her neck, across her shoulder, slowly down her arm to her hand. Lifting it, he brought her fingers to his mouth. Watching her over their joined hands, he ran his silken lips over her knuckles.

His eyes held her, overflowing with lingering grief, passion, heat. Why was she so hopelessly attracted to him? she wondered as her pulse fluttered wildly.

Why?

Again his breath and lips fanned her skin, and she knew. It was because she was a sucker for the sensitive, wounded type. The confident, sure-footed man, who deep down was really just a hopeless, romantic fool.

She tugged her hand free, suddenly overwhelmingly shy, unsure. 'How about we, um, talk first?'

That brought a smile, then a wince as he held a finger to his split lip. 'I don't feel very much like talking.' But his gaze turned thoughtful. 'Having second thoughts, Slim?'

No, not second thoughts. But she wanted it to be real, didn't want any more secrets or lies hanging between them. 'I'm . . . a little confused,' she admitted. 'It's silly, I know, especially since we already . . . Since we've already . . .'

'Had sex on my living room carpet?' he suggested.

'Yeah, something like that,' she muttered. *Sex. Was that all it'd been?*

He watched her for another minute, even after she'd curled back into herself. 'I am not going to push you,' he said 'Does that help?'

The roughness in his voice made the underlying tenderness all the more irresistible to Chloe. Almost without her will, she responded. Her heart contracted. 'Yes,' she whispered. 'It helps. So would knowing you want me as much as I want you, and I don't mean just physically.'

'I want you more than I want my own life,' he said simply, so devastatingly that her throat closed.

'Sometimes,' she said, her voice catching, 'being with you really hurts.'

He nodded, his facial muscles beautifully taut. The hard, sensual lines of his mouth tightened. 'Being with you hurts, too. But *not* being with you hurts even more.'

Her heart tightened.

'The spare bedroom is still made up, if that's what you'd rather.'

In his whispered offer she heard volumes. Chivalry had made him offer, but it wasn't what he wanted. Far from it. She had only to look back into the deep eyes to know that. But she understood; the decision was hers.

He wouldn't press.

She almost wished he would, that he would take the decision out of her hands for her. But he was smarter than that. He wouldn't absolve her of anything. And he wanted her to make the first move.

He asked a lot.

If only she could ask as much of him. If only he could talk to her.

In the silence that followed she was excruciatingly aware of her shirt hanging open, of the way his hungry eyes dropped to feed on her. Her nipples hardened, as if he'd touched her. She wished he would, wished he would send her into oblivion so that she could stop thinking.

But he only continued to caress her with his eyes. It made her shake, made her legs feel wobbly to have him look at her like that. Heat burned through her, centering between her legs. Her mouth fell open, hot with yearning.

Still he didn't touch her.

'I want to understand you,' she whispered. Suddenly chilled, she gathered her shirt tight and hugged herself. 'I want to understand what's happening.'

The floor groaned softly as he rose, wincing a little. 'All that's happening,' he said, his voice heavy with regret, 'is that you've changed your mind about me. Is it too much to ask why?'

She shook her head, having no idea what she was saying no to. Over six feet of sleek, sinewy, hurting male stood before her, studying her quietly.

'I don't think I've changed my mind.'

'No?' he asked quietly. 'Are you sure?'

When she nodded, he bent, slowly, gently searing his lips over hers once, twice, lightly brushing fire over her sensitive mouth. The sweet, unexpected shock of it was startling, as was the incredible tenderness.

When he stopped and lifted his head again, she shuddered. Her throat, as she stared at him, thickened with a longing so fierce she couldn't control it.

She wanted more. Now. Forget everything else; she couldn't wait to have him. 'I definitely didn't change my mind,' she whispered, aching. 'Please, Thomas, more.'

'Be sure.' His voice shook. 'Because I can't go much further and turn back.'

'There is no turning back,' she promised, tilting her head up. 'Kiss me.'

Obediently his mouth brushed over hers in another light caress, while still nothing but their lips connected. It was erotically shattering, and the most wonderful kiss she'd ever had. It kindled her mind, set her ablaze with expectation.

His hand closed over her shoulder. His eyes, when they opened and focused on her, were filled with such naked longing, such searing pain, that she felt it as her own.

She felt it so strongly she cried out, and he stiffened, dropping his hand from her. 'What's the matter? Did I hurt you?'

'I feel your pain,' she gasped, placing her hands over her heart. 'That's never happened before.'

He closed his eyes on a groan. 'God, Chloe. I don't want you to hurt. Not like this. I don't want to be the one to bring you pain.'

It was far too late for that.

Then she saw him weave slightly, saw his color fade even more. It was a forcible reminder of what he'd suffered, of what he was still suffering. If he wouldn't go to the hospital, she'd have to care for him.

Not a tough chore.

But she needed to get him to rest.

As carefully as she could, she slipped an arm around his waist, tugged him gently out of the kitchen. No longer could she hold back, no longer could she concern herself about the outside world and what Sierra Rivers might do.

Right now, all that mattered was Thomas. Knowing that he didn't want to do anything to hurt her was more than enough. She wanted him, needed him, craved what only he could do to her.

The afternoon had faded away. It was the brief time that came each evening, when it was neither night nor day. Silently they made the climb up the steps. Outside the room where she'd slept once before, his steps faltered. Careful not to tighten her grip on him, she kept going, shaking her head at the questions in his eyes.

'Your room,' she whispered, sucking in her breath at the heat flaring in his expression.

The door opened beneath his hand and he backed to the bed, pulling her with him. Everything about him was shaking, even his breath, but he seemed determined to master the emotions, the pain, to prove that he didn't need anything. Not sex, not love, and certainly not her.

It broke her heart, but she followed, sensing he needed to do this, even though she burned to resist, wanted to fight for the answers she needed for her to give in totally.

She couldn't summon the strength, couldn't resist him. Too weak, she thought, but she didn't care.

'Be with me,' he said, his voice harsh, his hands on her waist soft and gentle.

Then he sat gingerly on the bed and pulled her between his thighs, nuzzling at her neck, his teeth nipping against her flesh. The roughness thrilled; the tenderness conquered. And her warrior didn't stop the battle, but went right on claiming her. His mouth took hers, the utter sweetness of it causing a sharp pain inside her chest that made her want to cry out.

Needing to tell him that this was just physical, that there was so much more they could have, she broke away. But he pulled her back, his hands easy on her but his eyes desperate. 'Don't leave me now,' he whispered. 'Stay.'

What a choice. To leave him now would kill her soul; to stay would just as surely kill her. For certainly, afterwards, *he* would leave *her*. Then her heart would break.

Even in the semi-darkness of the room, she could see his dark blue piercing gaze search her face. 'No one's ever done this to me, made me need so much,' he told her. 'No one but you. I've never met anyone like you, *ever*.'

He held her face and looked deep into her eyes. 'You make me see things, feel things . . . I think the woman you've become is someone to be proud of – just the way you are.' His thumb ran over her bottom lip. 'Do you understand me? You're perfect *the way you are*. I just want you to know that.'

Tears stung her eyes as he touched the part of her she kept deep and hidden inside. How many years had she kept this pain, these thoughts of unworthiness all to herself? Too many. For so long she'd harbored feelings of self-consciousness, given to her by her well-meaning family. *Chloe, do it like this. Chloe, you must be like this. Chloe, you've done it wrong*. The best meant intentions on their part had only hurt her, had only increased her feelings of insecurity. Now he was telling her she was perfect just the way she was?

When he slipped a hand between the flaps of her unbuttoned blouse, softly stroking the sensitive underside of her breast, her head fell back on her shoulder. He cupped that breast and slid his thumb over the tightened peak until she cried out.

And if she'd thought it had been painful to be with him downstairs, she'd felt nothing like this. It was agony, anguish, this waiting.

'I'm sweaty, Slim. And bloody.' As he spoke his thumb delivered glancing blows to her nipple so that she could hardly hear him speak past the blood pumping through her system.

'I don't care.' Sensing he was about to withdraw, she clutched his hand to her, far beyond shame or modesty now. She needed him to fill her.

'*I* care.' Though he didn't take his hand from her, he stood. Then moaned when she shrugged out of her shirt. His intent eyes watched his fingers move over her. 'Chloe, let me shower first.'

The image of his magnificent body standing beneath a spray of water decided her. Oh, yes, she'd let him shower. She'd join him.

Tugging on his hand, she led him into the bathroom, their eyes never losing contact. While he very cautiously tugged off his torn shirt and shrugged out of his shorts she started the water. When she turned back to face him he was standing there, startlingly, gloriously nude.

'You look a little startled,' he said quietly.

'Startled?' she breathed softly. 'No.' But her heart was pounding, threatening to burst out of her chest. When he came closer he spanned the fingers of one hand over her collarbone, so that she was sure he couldn't help but feel the wild fluttering of her heart. His gaze lifted to hers.

'If not startled, then what?'

'You're amazing,' she said without thinking, her eyes riveted to the part of him that made her tingle between her legs.

His short laugh brought a muffled groan, which had her automatically moving toward him, reaching out with hands as gentle as she could to touch the growing bruises on his sides. 'Oh, Thomas, how could he hurt you like this?'

'It's done,' he whispered, sinking his hands into her hair, tilting her head up to gaze at her with eyes that glittered like diamonds. 'It's done and you're here. That's all that matters right now.'

Right now. So it was to be temporary, then. It would have to be enough.

He kissed her then, holding her lips to his as his hands dropped low to undo her jeans. When he made a small, frustrated sound, she understood he couldn't bend to help her undress, so she did it for him, keeping her eyes on his. Slowly, holding onto the hand he held out, she stepped out of her clothes and then toward him.

'Jesus, you're beautiful,' he whispered in an aching voice. 'So beautiful, Chloe.'

He was the one who was beautiful, so much so that he should have been gracing the covers of magazines instead of whatever it was he did. With those bruises and cuts only adding to the warrior appeal, and his sculptured build sheened in perspiration, he could have made millions.

He looked at her and the muscles in his face bunched.

She could feel his frustration.

'I want to be able to lift you up and carry you into the water.'

Oh, he was a romantic, one who could probably talk her into anything, but at that moment it was a nice touch. Since he couldn't lift her up against that body she longed for, she stepped in the stall and under the hot spray. Following right behind her, he closed his eyes and gritted his teeth as the water hit him.

'Is it too hard?' she asked quickly, stepping between him and the spray. 'Thomas?'

'No, but it's hot enough to burn off certain . . . essentials.' His eyes opened, amazingly filled with humor. 'Are you, by any chance, trying to unman me? Because I think it might have worked.'

Laughing, she turned up the cold water and shook her head. 'I'm sorry.'

The amusement faded from his eyes as she moved close, and she was suddenly very aware of her body and how it must look, shimmering under the steady, steaming water, beaded with moisture.

In that moment, for the first time in her entire life, she felt beautiful.

Those blue eyes skimmed over her from head to toe, warming each and every square inch they touched. Slowly he shook his head back and forth. 'I hope to God I still work, Slim, because you are incredible.'

'You'll work,' she promised. 'Let me prove it to you.' Reaching for the soap, she sudsed up her hands and gave him a wicked glance that made him want to melt. 'Turn around,' she demanded, so sweetly that he did.

How could she do that, completely melt him with just a look? But he didn't have the time to wonder, not with her gentle, probing hands on him. All he could do was brace himself with his hands against the tile and feel.

Her palms curved themselves to his waist, then rose up and over the tensed, bunched muscles of his lower back, spreading soap upward in a motion that had him moaning and arching against her hands.

Then she bent and kissed the small of his back. When her lips met his skin, he stiffened in plea-

302

sure, shock. His heart – yes, dammit, it had to be his heart – leaped and goose bumps flanked his flesh. Still her hands and lips glided over him, mixing water and soap in seductive circles, causing wild, delicious sensations that completely took his pain away.

Painstakingly, with excruciating care, she covered every bit of him, from shoulders to feet, and by the time she'd finished he was so aroused he could hardly breathe.

'Turn around,' she whispered.

When he did, she was kneeling at his feet, her hands filled with a mountain of suds, her eyes filled with awe. Which quickly faded, to be replaced by concern. 'You're shaking,' she said in a rough whisper. 'I'll make this quick.'

It didn't matter how quick she made it, he thought, closing his eyes as her hands worked their magic on the front of his legs. He would die of pleasure far before she could finish.

When she got to his hips her gaze locked on his, but she didn't hesitate. Taking his erection into her hands, she ran the soap up and down him in a stroking gesture that had him staggering back a step and gratefully sinking to the tile bench.

He wanted to tell her not to do that, that it would all be over before they'd begun, but then she tossed the soap over her shoulder and replaced her hands with her mouth.

There were no words to describe what happened to him then. He'd been pleasured before, many times. But never by a woman who meant anything close to

303

what Chloe meant. And he couldn't take it. Lifting his hands to her head, he truly thought he could push her away. But the unthinkable happened – as it had happened only once before, also with her. *He lost control*. Totally and mindlessly. So that instead of pushing her away his fingers curled into her hair, holding her close. What made it even more devastating, even more thrilling, was her obvious inexperience, her sweet eagerness to please him.

Just when he was sure he couldn't take another second, she lifted her head and gave him a look of such pure, undiluted love that he yanked her close, ignoring his screaming ribs, his aching stomach muscles.

'God, Chloe, I don't understand what you do to me.'

'Why don't you think about it,' she whispered, rising and straddling his legs as the water pounded them, 'while I do some more?'

And she sank down on him, working him so beautifully, so masterfully that he leaned bonelessly back against the tile. Within a few more seconds she drove them both to a wild, shimmering, thundering implosion so agonizingly sweet it brought tears to his eyes.

Sleeping with Chloe nestled in his arms was an experience Thomas would never get tired of. Against his shoulder, her even, deep breath tickled his skin. She had one knee bent, tossed over his legs as she curled against him. Her hand, where it had fallen from his chest to his belly, hurt his sore muscles. But he wouldn't have moved it for the world.

He loved her.

Somehow, some way, he would have to find a way to make this work. He didn't want to leave her, couldn't imagine life without her. Maybe he could just tell her he was Sierra Rivers. Maybe he could right the wrongs. After all, he hadn't really committed any yet.

He could build that damn resort, and instead of being the bad guy he could be the hero. For once.

Not a bad idea – except for one little problem. He had to hope and pray she never found out his initial plan, because he wasn't sure what she felt for him was strong enough to withstand that particular knowledge.

In his arms, Chloe stirred, frowning, mumbling.

'What is it, Slim?' he whispered.

But she slept on and he started to drift off, imagining a little girl – his little girl – looking at him with Chloe's lovely eyes.

Then Chloe jerked and cried out.

'Shh,' he whispered, pulling her tight and ignoring the pain from his side. 'You're okay.'

'I have to make sure you don't,' she cried, holding him tight enough to make him cringe. 'I can't let you destroy Heather Glen.'

He froze. 'What?'

'I won't let you, Thomas. I won't.'

'You – ? Chloe?'

No answer.

Thomas's breath shuddered out when she suddenly relaxed, her breathing deepening. Against him, her body became a dead weight.

'*I can't let you destroy Heather Glen.*'

Seemed his little beauty had some secrets of her own. His heart hardened, then broke. So she was bound and determined not to see him succeed with what she *thought* his plans were, was she?

So determined that she would sleep with him to benefit the cause.

Too bad she didn't have a clue as to what that cause really was. And double too bad she thought she could scare him off with the vandalism, the threatening e-mail.

Oh, no, he thought grimly, he couldn't be scared off. Not this time. Not even by the woman he loved beyond reason.

CHAPTER 19

Chloe found Thomas in his study, standing at the window looking out into the dark night with an expression so pained and troubled she moved forward without thinking.

'Are you hurting?' she asked, automatically hurting right along with him. Images of what they'd done in the shower, then later in his bed, brought a healthy flush to her skin, but also worried her. She'd been careful, but, as always with him, she'd lost herself when he'd made love to her. Had she inadvertently brought him pain?

His head whipped toward her, and from the way he had to focus in on her she knew he'd been deep in thought. That gaze ran over her, from the tip of her head, past the thick midnight-blue robe of his she'd found on the back of his door, to her toes peeking out the bottom.

'I didn't see you,' he murmured.

'I didn't mean to startle you,' she said. 'I woke up and you were gone.' His pillow had been stone-cold, telling her she'd been alone for some time.

Why wasn't he saying anything? Why was he

307

looking at her like that, as if he couldn't trust her, as he had looked at her way back in the beginning, or at least until they'd made love?

'Couldn't sleep,' he offered finally, his voice even enough but icy, alarming her. *What had happened?*

'It's chilly in here,' she said inanely. He wore only a pair of sweat pants that clung to him in a way that made her swallow hard.

He just stared at her, as if he knew what the sight of his body did to her and it bored him. As if she were just one of a string of women.

'Are – are you all right?'

'Does it matter?'

How could he ask such a thing? 'Of course it matters. Thomas, what's wrong?'

His sigh, when it came, seemed harsh. His voice was bleak. 'Why did you come back here today, Chloe?'

'Well, ah . . .' Because she'd wanted him. But that seemed a funny thing to say when he was staring at her as if she were a possible enemy. 'Because you asked me to.'

'I practically demanded it,' he corrected. 'But you still could have refused. I didn't make you.'

'No.' She dared a step closer, felt the chill emanating from him. Chill – when only so recently he'd been so hot. For her. 'Thomas, please tell me what this is all about. What's the matter?'

He turned his head away, back toward the night, and didn't answer.

Fear gripped her, an unreasonable, boiling fear. Maybe everything she'd learned about him earlier was indeed true. Not only did he own Sierra Rivers, but he planned to ruin them all. That would mean he'd only been toying with her, biding his time until he could bring down the little town and everyone she knew.

Now that he'd decided to act, would he disappear?

'You still didn't answer my question,' he said quietly. 'About why you came here tonight.'

Honesty was her only pride now. 'I wanted to be with you.'

'That's it?'

If she had to, she could play this cool game too. She could be hard and distant. Cruel. 'What other reason would there be?'

He ignored that. 'Were you happy to see me, when I first came back into town?'

'You know that I was.'

Looking at her, the way she was so breathtakingly alluring, so damn seductive without trying, he knew that even now, when he knew her to be manipulating him, he wanted her. His robe covered every single inch of her delicious body, but it didn't matter. He could still feel her, taste her. It killed him.

'How about later? Were you happy to see me then?'

'Later?'

'Don't play stupid, Chloe,' he said cuttingly. 'It doesn't suit you.'

'I'm not playing anything.' But this time her voice wasn't nearly so calm, so even. 'I just have no idea what you're talking about.'

'Fine. Allow me to spell it out for you.' Turning to

face her fully, he tried to keep his devastation to himself. 'You claim to have been thrilled to see me again after so much time had gone by. How about after you found out who I was, what I was doing here? Were you still thrilled?'

She paled. 'What do you mean?'

Her obvious distress gave him no satisfaction, none at all. But it confirmed his worst fears. 'I was just wondering exactly how excited you were to see me. Enough to torch my largest warehouse? Ecstatic enough to blow my back door to Kingdom Come?'

'Oh, my God.'

He'd thought she'd gone pale a minute before, but it was nothing to the pure translucence of her skin now. He couldn't let it touch him. 'I admit,' he said harshly, 'messing with *Homebaked*'s kitchen was a stroke of genius. Knowing how you feel about that place, I never would have considered it was you.'

'Why do you think so now?' Her voice was so low, so utterly quiet, he had to bend closer to hear, which only aggravated his ribs and made him all the more deadly furious.

'Because, Chloe, you talk in your sleep.'

'Are you – ?' Her words wouldn't come out, not the way she wanted them to. Starting over, she said slowly, 'Are you accusing me of those horrible things? Of trying to hurt you?'

'You catch on quick.'

Without warning, she bolted, dashing out into the hall. For a minute he stood rooted in shock, but then he heard the front door slam shut.

She'd gone out into the snowy, stormy night in nothing but his robe. *No shoes, no gloves*. 'Christ,' he muttered, running after her.

At the front door, he had the presence of mind to grab two coats and jam his bare feet into his boots, which lay by the door. As he shrugged into one of the coats, grimacing as his ribs complained, he ran out onto the porch.

'Chloe!' he shouted, squinting into the dark.

Her car started.

'Goddammit!' he yelled, jumping down the stairs and streaking across the yard to where her car was parked.

Had been parked.

He watched the tail lights disappear for about two seconds before he was propelled into motion by a need for answers. He wanted to know how she could have done the things she had, and he wanted to see her face while she explained it to him.

How dare she run off? Swearing, he ran back into the house long enough to grab his keys, then tore out after her. Anger diluted the pain from the beating he'd taken, but the inner hurt had just started to spread.

He looked for her on the road, but even in his Jag he didn't catch up. Would she go home? Probably not, under any other circumstances, but all she had on was his robe.

What if she went to Conrad's?

Then he'd have to kill them both, he decided.

But there was no need for premeditated murder, not when he found her car at her apartment. Running out into the falling snow, taking care on her slippery, dark walkway, Thomas took the stairs three at a time and pounded on her locked door.

'Let me in, Chloe,' he demanded.

No answer. But then again, he hadn't expected one. 'I'll tear the door down,' he swore.

Quietly, it opened, surprising him into silence.

'Did you come here to press charges?' she asked evenly, crossing her arms over her chest. She still wore his robe, which was far too long. Her toes barely peeked out, but they looked blue.

Pushing his way in, he stormed directly to the fireplace. 'It's colder in here than it is outside.'

'Well, then, please feel free to go outside,' she said politely, but he heard something in her voice that time. Emotion. A trembly emotion that did something to him when all he wanted was to feel bitterness and pain.

In silence he started the fire, watched it carefully until it caught and started to send out a small measure of warmth. Without a word, he rose, grabbed her arm and jerked her close. 'Where are your slippers?'

She stared at him as if he'd lost him mind, and in truth he felt as if he had. He wanted to kill her and he was worried about the condition of her feet? 'Dammit, would you stop staring at me and tell me where the hell your slippers are?'

Not responding, she turned from him and disappeared into her bedroom. Five seconds, he promised himself. He'd give her five more seconds before he charged in there and –

'I can't find my slippers. I put on socks.' Chloe came close to the fire and held her hands out in front of her. 'I'm assuming that's okay with you.'

But she didn't look at him, and he knew she couldn't care less whether it was or not. When she shivered and moved closer to the fire, he bit down on his back teeth so hard he was surprised they didn't break. He hoped she warmed up soon, because he couldn't stand what knowing she was cold was doing to him.

'I asked you a question back at my house,' he said, 'And you didn't answer it. I expect you to now.'

'I see.'

No denials, no railings against what he'd accused her of. No nothing. She just continued to stand close to the fire and stare at it, as if it held the utmost importance for her.

'Are you going to tell me how you thought you could get away with it, or not?'

No answer. No movement. No emotion to even tell him she'd heard what he'd said. *She'd done it. She'd tried to kill him.* He felt sick. And so full of fury it scared him.

'I think you'd better leave,' she said, still not looking at him. 'I don't want you here.'

'Too bad,' he grated. 'You tried to kill me. I think I deserve an answer as to why.'

'You deserve nothing.'

Had he ever been this destructively livid? He wanted to hurl something, or, worse yet, like the McGuirre he was, he wanted to hurt someone. Who better than the woman before him, who had showed him he did indeed have a heart just before she slashed it into pieces?

Sicker yet, he wanted to kiss her senseless, until she begged and cried for forgiveness, until she told him that in spite of what she'd done she loved him.

Fool that he was, he would believe her.

But she said nothing, did nothing, just craned her neck and stared at him with those wide, vulnerable eyes, looking like a lost little princess in the robe that was miles too long for her.

'Did you think I would never figure it out?' he asked hoarsely.

'I was going to ask you the same thing,' she said in that same even voice, so filled with dignity and grace he had to close his eyes.

'I've done nothing wrong,' he said, trying to convince himself that he spoke the truth. He hadn't hurt anyone yet – had he?

'Haven't you?' She hugged the robe tighter, her eyes filled with things he couldn't face. 'Haven't you lied to me? Over and over again?'

'I never lied. *Never.*'

'Oh, please.' With an indelicate snort she moved past him, plopped down on the carpet before the fire, as if her legs wouldn't hold her, and stared grimly into the flames. 'How many times did I ask you what you were doing in town?' A helpless laugh came out. 'And how many times, Thomas, did you manage to evade that question? Even worse, I let you,' she added, with such obvious disgust he couldn't help but feel it too.

'So I run Mountain Mortgage.' Her eyebrows lifted when she turned her head to look at him. 'And, yes, I own Sierra Rivers,' he added, throwing up his hands. 'So what? Where's the crime in that?'

'You know the answer to that,' she said bitterly. 'You know you should have told me. I gave you plenty of opportunity to do so. And you're purposely leading this around to be my fault. All you had to do was be honest.'

If he'd been honest, they would never have gotten this far.

'Why couldn't you tell me what you planned?' she wanted to know.

But he was angry enough, perverse enough – hurt enough – to keep on the offensive. 'Which is what, Chloe? What is it you think I planned?' He had to know, suddenly, exactly what she thought of him. How little she thought of him. Knowing he deserved it didn't change his need to know.

Over her shoulder, she gave him an indecipherable look. 'I want to think you're going to build that resort.'

'But you're not sure?' Her doubt cut deep, had his heart bleeding. She didn't believe in him now; she never would.

'If you tell me you are, I'll believe you.'

'And this would be a done conversation? I'm Sierra Rivers, I'm building a resort, and everything's okay?' he asked in disbelief.

'No,' she whispered, turning her head away again so that he couldn't see her face.

315

Too late, he thought, his stomach tightening, because he'd seen the glint of tears. Tears he'd caused.

'Nothing will ever be okay again.' Her voice wobbled, caught at his heart. 'Because you think I tried to – ' Breaking off, she covered her mouth with a shaking hand. Her next breath was a visible shudder. 'You think I tried to kill you.'

Abruptly, she stood. 'I can't stay. I – '

He caught her as she walked by, held her apart from his aching body by her shoulders. 'Are you saying you didn't do those things? The explosion, the vandalism?'

In horror, she stared at him. The first tear fell from her drenched eyes. 'I can't believe that we just – ' She closed her eyes and another tear escaped. 'We just made love,' she whispered, 'Yet you can believe this of me.' Another broken sob tore at his gut. 'I can't believe it, Thomas. I just can't.' Struggling, she tried to break free. 'Let me go.'

Staring down at the beautiful creature he held captive, he knew his first inkling of doubt. 'Tell me it wasn't you.'

'I won't,' she cried, battling him so madly it took all his considerably drained strength just to hold her. 'I won't ease your conscience by telling you anything. You should just know!'

He did know, didn't he?

Images of her: how she'd shoved him with all her might out of the explosion's way, how she'd tried to hide *Homebaked*'s damage from him so the knowledge it was his fault wouldn't distress him, how she'd cried for him when his father had hurt him.

No. God, no. This woman wouldn't cause him harm – it wasn't in her blood. How could he have thought it, even for one second?

Looking down at her wild, ravaged face, he saw something else. Something far worse than the possibility of *her* hurting *him*.

He'd hurt her.

'I'm sorry,' he whispered, trying to draw her stiff body near. She wouldn't allow it. 'Please, Chloe, I'm sorry.'

She shook her head violently, smacking him in the face with her hair. 'You think I want you dead?'

'No,' he whispered agonizingly. 'I was a fool. A complete fool. I don't think it – not now.'

Again she pushed at him, her expression tormented. 'Why did you think it at all, Thomas? How could you?'

'You talked in your sleep.' He tried to explain and hold her at the same time. She was having neither.

Fighting him with every word, she ground out, 'Whatever could I have said that would make you think I'd hurt you?'

Grimly he held her, even when he got an elbow in an agonizing spot beneath his rib. 'You said, "I can't let you destroy Heather Glen. I won't let you"' Helplessly, he shrugged. 'What was I supposed to think?'

'How about that I only wanted to stop you? To help you see that hurting Heather Glen wasn't the answer?'

317

'I – Oh, hell, Chloe.' Closing his eyes, he let her struggle against him, even when it caused shooting pain through his every muscle. He deserved it. 'Trust doesn't come easy for me.'

Her head jerked up and she looked at him for a long time before saying, 'You believed the worst of me. The absolute worst.'

'I – '

I couldn't hurt my worst enemy,' she told him tearfully, still trying to free herself. 'Much less you. How am I supposed to get over that?'

'I don't know.'

The fight went out of her and he immediately released his hold, trying again to pull her close.

But as he loosened his grip she took advantage and wrenched away. 'I thought that we had something special, Thomas. Something different. I knew there were problems – mostly your inability to let go all the way, how you didn't want to trust me – but I really believed we could get over that.

Again his heart lurched. This time in fear. She was talking in the past tense, as if there were no future. Ever. She was leaving him. 'We can get over this.'

'No, Thomas,' she said quietly, shaking her head. 'I can't be with someone who doesn't believe in me.' She moved to the door of her bedroom, then stopped at the husky emotion in his voice.

'I need another chance.' He was searching her face with eyes that were as dark as night and filled with as many secrets. They'd narrowed with obvious con- cern, giving him the look of someone who cared.

But she had to be mistaken, she reminded himself. He couldn't care and think those things of her. No one could.

But she couldn't look at his expression without a tiny sliver of hope. If she wanted to, she could read a whole host of things in that face she loved. If she wanted to.

'Chloe – '

Don't you dare make me want you after what you thought of me, Thomas McGuirre. No one I've ever loved has really believed in me, so why should you?

He walked toward her, saying her name in a way that had her throat closing up. 'Please, Chloe. Be patient with me. Try to understand.'

Be firm. Stand up for yourself. Don't let another person take away any more of what little confidence you have left.

'I'll never understand how you could think I would hurt you. *Never.*' She took a shuddery breath that seemed to suck the very life out of her. Later, she could fall apart. Not now, not in front of him. 'I want you to leave, Thomas.'

By the time he reached her she was awkwardly blinking away tears she didn't want him to see, tugging the too large robe even closer.

'Please, Chloe, try to understand. Someone's been trying to hurt me. Then I find out you knew all along I was Sierra Rivers. That you knew,' he repeated, giving her a small shake when she turned her head away, 'and you didn't say a word. I just spoke without thinking.' When she would have broken

319

free, he held her by the shoulders. 'I'm confused, Slim. Confused as hell over the things I feel for you. And to be honest, maybe I was looking for a way out. If I could stop thinking about you the way I was and start blaming you . . . Hell, I don't know. You had the motive – no matter how flimsy – and I just reacted. I'm so sorry.'

Her sigh held as much sadness as it did regret, but instead of fighting more she sagged in his hands. 'You were so quick to believe that I would hurt you, Thomas. So unbelievably *able* to believe it.'

'Yes,' he admitted, catching one of her tears on his finger before it fell. 'But try to understand me,' he said softly. 'You came into my life and ever since then I haven't known what hit me.'

If he hadn't been so serious, so intent on making her understand, she might have smiled at the bewildered way he looked at her.

'You scare the hell out of me, Slim.'

How she wanted to turn into the warmth of his body and lose herself there, comforting both him and herself. But she couldn't afford to do that, not when she was so dangerously close to completely falling apart. 'Why do I get the feeling you prefer me in the role of attempted murderer rather than holding a part of your heart?'

'Because maybe it is – *was* – true.'

A disparaging sound drifted from her lips and she dropped her forehead to his chest. 'I need to think a minute.'

'Okay.' He didn't move, just held her arms.

She could smile after all. 'I can't do that with you touching me, Thomas. In fact, I can't think at all with you within sight.'

'Try hard,' he suggested. 'Because I'm not going anywhere – not until we work this out.'

'That sounds a little like a threat.'

'Just try to understand,' he whispered, feathering her cheek lightly. 'Just think about it from my angle.'

'No.' She couldn't, it would undo her. She yanked at the handle to her bedroom door, intending to get dressed this time before she rushed out into the cold, unforgiving night. But the door wouldn't budge so she stared down at her fumbling fingers, trying to figure out why. Above her, when she lifted her head, she saw his big hand holding it shut.

'No,' she cried again, dropping her forehead to the cold wood. If he said another word, if he touched her again, she'd cave. She'd give in, probably throw herself at him. But she refused to allow herself to be open to the kind of pain he'd caused when he'd unleashed his fury on her. It would kill her to continue to love him and then have him turn on her again.

But he was right there, forcing her around to face him. 'We need to work this out,' he urged in a rough, desperate voice that made her tingle, made her yearn even when she wanted to remain unmoved.

'Don't leave like this.'

'I have to,' she whispered. 'Let me go.'

'Nobody's ever felt for me like you do.' His hands dropped away. '*Nobody*. I've never had to be accountable for my actions to anyone but me, and I had myself convinced that was the best way. I couldn't get hurt that way, I told myself. No need to have someone care about me, love me. All it would bring is pain.' Now his voice deepened and became harsh. Thrillingly so. 'But I forgot something critical, Slim. Something I couldn't know, because I'd never let myself get involved like this before. I didn't count on the joy being with you could bring. The absolute glorious abandon. The simple exhilaration in life. I didn't count on that, but you brought it anyway.

The silence that fell between them was weighted – with hopes, with recriminations, with what might have been but could never be now. Or so Chloe made herself believe.

'It's too late, Thomas.'

'No.' The aching softness in his voice threatened the composure she barely held onto by a string. 'I'll never believe that. Neither do you.'

'You're wrong. I do believe that.' *Had to*. 'I could have forgiven just about anything, Thomas. Even if you had planned to destroy this town, I could have understood that better than you thinking what you did of me.'

Something flashed in his eyes. Guilt? It didn't matter to her, not now. Not when she'd been trying to live up to people's standards all her life. It had to stop. For her sanity, it would stop.

Even though giving up this man would likely kill her.

Forcing calm, she met his gaze evenly – had to or

she'd crumble. 'Please leave, Thomas. Get out of my life. Stop paying my payments. Stop trying to fix my life with paint and new heaters and stuff. Contrary to what you all believe about me, I will survive. And I want to do it without your help.'

'Okay.'

'Okay?' Suspiciously she squinted at him. Was that a gleam of admiration, of humor? No, darn it, it was tenderness. More than she could take. 'Define okay, Thomas.'

'Okay to not helping you make your payments anymore. You're not helpless, Chloe. I never meant to make you feel like you were.'

'Well, I'm not. I'm not a murderer either.'

'I know that too. But don't ask me to stay out of your life. I don't think I can do it.'

'Try.'

'Chloe – '

'Go, or you'll force me to call the sheriff.' Knowing how she would hurt him with her next words, she dug her nails into her palms. 'He'll come, you know. And he'll be more than happy to kick you out.'

'Chloe – '

'Thomas, please.'

He stared at her.

'I mean it,' she whispered, quickly losing both resolve and control.

When he hesitated, she walked to the phone, picked it up. The sleeve of his robe fell past her fingertips, covering the hand that trembled so violently she knew she'd never be able to actually dial. 'Go.'

'You're bluffing.'

'Try me.'

He was tempted, she could see that. But he wasn't willing to risk a night in jail, which was exactly what he would face if someone came out and thought that Thomas McGuirre was threatening or bothering Chloe Walker, the mayor's daughter.

He had no idea how much she hated to use his own weaknesses against him as she was, but, then again, he had no idea how desperate she felt right then either.

'This isn't over,' he vowed.

His eyes were on her with a piercing intensity that told her he meant it. He'd never give up. Well, neither would she. 'It *is* over.'

'I won't let it end like this.'

'You don't have much of a choice.' Her heart was breaking. There was no other reason for the knife that felt as if it was twisting in her insides. She was on the very edge, crumbling from the inside out, but she refused to let him see it. 'Go, Thomas.'

With one last, lingering look, he was gone.

Right where she was, she crumpled to the ground, wrapped her arms around her middle and let out a cry that came straight from the heart.

CHAPTER 20

Twenty minutes later, he was back. Chloe lifted her head from where she was still pooled on the floor, soaked in her own tears.

Thomas took one look at her, shifted the large package he held to one hip and swore luridly. Slamming the door behind him, he stalked to her. 'Christ, Chloe. It's two degrees in here and you're sitting there on the floor?'

'I thought I told you to go away.'

'Yeah, well, I don't listen very well, do I? Good thing too. *Shit*,' he added in an explosive whisper when he set down the big bag and took her hand. 'You're an icicle.'

'The f-f-fire went out, I guess.' The fire in her heart had gone out too.

With another particularly vulgar oath, he rose and fumbled in the bag. Then he disappeared out of her vision, but she didn't lift her head. Didn't have the energy.

Why couldn't he just go away as she'd asked him to do? If he stayed, she'd do something stupid. Like admit she loved him. Her vision misted as she fought the tears again.

She heard the sound of wood crackling and knew Thomas was stoking the fire she'd let die. Then another sound pierced her fog. A low, rumbling, motor sound.

He'd brought a small room heater and had plugged it in.

Hiding the enormous amount of emotion that caused – that he cared so much about her to make sure she was warm – she had to blink furiously and concentrate on her clenched hands.

'Chloe.' He hunkered down before her and took those hands now. 'Look at me. Please, Chloe.'

She didn't want to, but she looked up into his eyes anyway, bracing herself, knowing he'd be able to see everything she felt for him in her face. Bracing herself, too, to see everything he was trying to tell her in his.

Everything she feared was there, and more. She saw a need for her so strong and fierce it took her breath. Saw, too, the lingering traces of fury for whoever was trying to destroy him. But the soft light of tenderness and yearning made her ache beyond bearing.

'Oh, Thomas, I don't know what to do. You really hurt me.'

He pulled her up to her knees and held her waist, squeezing gently, possessively. 'I'm so sorry.'

'I know you are. But . . .' The desire he felt for her was strong in his gaze, so much so that it continued to steal her breath. But there was so much she didn't know, didn't understand. 'Why didn't you just tell me?'

'About Sierra Rivers?' At her nod, his eyes darkened even more, if that were possible. 'Does it matter now? I'm going to build that resort, going to stay. And I want you with me.'

'Just like that?' She wouldn't allow herself to think about how wonderful that sounded, not yet. 'Awhile ago you thought – '

'I was wrong,' he said quickly, harshly. 'Very wrong. Someone out there still needs to be caught. We'll deal with it. But now, just for now, let's just think about this. Us.'

'You want to build the resort?'

'Yes. But I want you more. Way more.'

Her breath caught. She was dazzled by the admission, by the bright, determined look in his eyes. 'You do?'

'Can I make love to you?'

She shivered, but not from the cold. 'Please.'

'You're so important to me,' he whispered, slowly tugging on the tie that held the robe together on her slender body. 'So damn important. I'll never hurt you again.'

'Promise?'

'That's an easy one,' he murmured, bending to taste her neck. With the tie undone, the robe loosened around her, billowed around that body he loved so much.

Gathering her hair in his hand, he drew her head

back until their eyes met. 'I need you, Chloe. You need me. I want to hear you say it. Please, won't you tell me?'

Reaching up, she framed his face in her hands. 'I need you, Thomas McGuirre. Only you.' Then she pulled his mouth to hers.

He knew, as he lost himself in that hot, sweet kiss, that he had to pull back. That now was the time to tell her the entire truth – that he had deliberately misled her earlier, that he had indeed originally come to Heather Glen to destroy it.

He could tell her that it had all changed, but he had to tell her. There was no excuse not to now. But she pressed her body to him, and, as always, when he was with her like this, he was lost.

Slipping his hands inside the robe, he found nothing but warm, bare, perfect woman. With a low sound of appreciation, he cupped her breasts in his palms, closing his eyes when she pressed up against his hands. Beneath his fingers, her nipples puckered and hardened.

'I dream of this,' he told her as he caressed warm, bare skin.

She let out a sweet moan that told him she felt the same way.

'I love this body,' he said, dipping his head to taste. 'It feels so good against mine.'

'Too many clothes,' she said in a husky voice, unzipping his jacket with fingers that fumbled a little nervously. For some reason that touched him. When she shoved the material aside and found him shirtless, she let out a breath of approval. 'New fashion?'

'No.' He cocked an eyebrow. 'I always chase after disappearing females in just a jacket and boots. No socks. Especially when it's below freezing outside.'

She bit her lower lip to bite back a little smile and reached for him, but he flinched at the touch of her icy fingers on his skin.

'I'm sorry,' she whispered, mistaking his involuntary movement. 'I'll be gentle. I won't hurt you. I'd never hurt you.'

'Chloe,' he said, sucking breath in through his teeth as her fingers ran lightly over his bruised and aching ribs. 'It has nothing to do with my injuries.' Though they were, in truth, killing him. 'You're hands are ice.'

She laughed, a lovely sound that warmed his heart. Then, with a saucy look, she pressed those icicles to his sides, making breathing difficult. 'So warm them up,' she challenged him.

'I'll warm you up, all right,' he promised. But he was unable, for a moment, to do anything but simply look at her, reveling in the shattering wonder of being with her. How he wished she would tell him she loved him again, with no 'maybe' attached.

But he couldn't rush her, not now. Not after what he'd put her through, how he'd hurt her. And he would have to hurt her one more time, he realized, when he told her the rest of the truth.

But that could wait – would have to wait. Because for now, with her exploring fingers and questing lips trailing over the chest she'd exposed, he could do nothing but feel.

Backing her closer to the heater and the fire, he let her drop his jacket to the floor before catching her lips in a long, lazy, drawn-out kiss that whirled and vibrated with something new, something different.

Love, he realized with a shock. He was truly making love for the first time in his life. Knowing that, he wanted to draw it out more, savor the moment. But Chloe had a different idea.

When she would have pulled him down to the couch, he gathered her close and began his assault, determined that he would not give up until she was trembling with the same emotion that had him in its grip.

He had to capture her roaming hands in his, drawing them to her sides, then behind her back, so she couldn't take him too close to the edge. Thomas couldn't remember ever having to do that with a woman before, but, then again, he'd never met one who could make him lose his control before she even touched him. This one could, but he didn't want that. No, he didn't want to lose control this time. He wanted to watch *her* lose it, wanted to revel in that. With his free hand he stroked her hair, caressed her face, touched her throat, while his mouth continued to seduce hers.

'I want you,' she said in a low, trembly voice, straining against him. 'Love me, Thomas.'

'I am.' He spread light, teasing kisses over her face, then sucked gently on her ear, and only when her head fell weakly back on her shoulder did he work his way down her neck, over her slim throat.

He could taste her raging pulse beneath his mouth, could feel how she trembled under his fingers. The noises she made were enough to have him hard and pulsing against her thigh. But he wanted more. He wanted her to be mindlessly, wildly out of control, wanted her to be completely lost to anything but what he was doing to her. He wanted to hear her scream for him.

Where the top of the robe met her throat he bent to nuzzle, his hand flirting with the opening. Low, needy whimpers came from her, and still he didn't rush. Oh, no, he wouldn't rush. He was going to claim her, but slowly, so slowly she could do nothing but feel the deep, intense thrill of being taken. Be helpless to the love that bound them.

He backed from her long enough to kick off his boots and shed his sweat pants. Her eyes flared, reflecting the heat, the fire, the arousal he'd ignited. Then he reached for her, easily sliding the robe off her shoulders to pool at their feet, so that there was nothing between them but hot, needy flesh.

Her eyes closed on a soft, helpless murmur and she lifted her arms to him. 'I need you now,' she whispered.

'Soon,' he promised, running his hands down her sides, around to cup her bottom against him. With light fingers he played, teased, caressed the back of her, until she shivered and moaned softly. Listening to the sounds that were sending him on his own collision course with an overwhelming climax, he devoured her neck and shoulders.

How he wanted to lift her up against him, lay her down on the couch and sink into her. Needed to.

But his ribs refused to allow that, so instead he began a trail of hot, open-mouthed kisses over her collarbone to the gentle swell of her breast. Bending her back over his arm, he captured a tightened nipple between his gentle teeth and rolled his tongue over it, again and again.

Her knees buckled but he held her up, moving lazily to the other side and repeating the process until her head rolled limply back and forth and she moaned his name on a sweet breath. Gently he pried her hands from where they'd fisted in his hair and held them to her sides.

'Let me touch you,' she begged.

'Not yet.' If she did, it'd be over. Nipping at her with his tongue and teeth, teasing her with little love nips, he felt her shiver and arch against him.

'Thomas,' she murmured, with a baffled, helpless sound, moving her hips restlessly against him in the ageless demand for more.

'Soon,' he promised again. 'Soon.' Then he sank to his knees before her, kissing his way to her belly button. Swirling it with his tongue, he worked his way down over a slim hip. Her skin glowed with anticipation; her every muscle clenched and quivered beneath him.

He kissed her inner thighs until she stiffened, so close to climax he could see the glistening of her own moisture at her opening. Then he kissed that precise spot.

Above him, she grasped his hair and gasped, trembled and gasped again. His tongue stabbed at her once, twice, and she shuddered, so close to the peak she was shaking.

With a small smile he backed off, and she cried out.

Helpless, just as he'd wanted her. Crying for him, shaking, lost to everything but what he was doing. He was so hot watching her, Thomas knew he'd come if she so much as brushed against him. Reaching up, he ran a finger over her, then slipped it in deep.

She panted, and thrust her hips at his eager mouth. When he glided his lips over the small, hard nub, she shattered instantly. She sobbed his name and her legs buckled again, and this time he let her fall, catching her and spreading her out on the carpet before the crackling fire.

Stretching his body over her, he met her lips, feeling more emotion than he could ever remember feeling. 'Look at me,' he whispered hoarsely, kneeling between her thighs.

He watched her blink and try to focus. The instant she did, he plunged into her.

Beneath him, she bucked and arched, but he held her close. God, it was beautiful. *She* was beautiful. He had to have more. But his ribs refused to allow him to move again. Carefully, he rolled to his back, taking her with him, Gripping her hips, he whispered, 'Now, Chloe.'

With a grateful gasp, Chloe rocked against him,

accepting him with a cry of pleasure. She couldn't get enough, couldn't seem to stop gasping, crying, begging for more. As he thrust into her he pulled her down, so that he could suckle and nip at her breasts, and it sent her spiraling into a second, even more dazzling climax.

A sound came from deep inside him, an anguished sound of such profound pleasure she shivered again. She was still shivering when he began to shudder and pulse within her. Grasping her face, he pulled her down for a kiss that seemed to come from his soul, then, in that final moment, he tossed his head back and moaned, long and deep.

Dark, deep, haunted beauty, she thought, with such love it choked her. Just watching him, watching as he voluntarily gave up his tightly held control with ravaging elegance, brought tears to her eyes.

Leaning over him, she cupped his face. He opened his eyes and gazed at her with such dazzling, brilliant emotion she couldn't breathe.

'I didn't mean to do that,' he whispered hoarsely. 'I didn't mean to lose myself like that. But you do something to me, Chloe.'

'Something good?' she said hopefully, smiling through her misty vision.

'Oh, yeah. Something good. Something real good.' Then he pulled her down into his arms and kissed her.

Wary of hurting him, she squirmed and tried to free herself.

'Going somewhere?' he wanted to know.

'I don't want to hurt you.'

He let out a laugh. 'You'll likely kill me, but what a way to go.'

'Shouldn't I get up?'

'Give me a minute,' he whispered hotly, cupping her breasts, 'and *I'll* get up.'

'I'll be waiting patiently,' she said with a giggle. And, in far less than a minute, she wasn't waiting at all.

Eventually, hours later, Thomas managed to rouse himself enough to watch Chloe as she slept in his arms in front of the sinking fire.

The need to wake her was strong. The need to make love to her again even stronger. In awe, he fingered her hair, lifted it from her face. She was beautiful, and she was his.

It had never been like this for him. He'd joked about her having never slept with a man before, but, in truth, *sleeping* with women wasn't a habit he'd developed either. The woman he'd been with had been nothing more than diversions, a quick sexual release.

He'd never wanted to lie around and hold them, just staring down into their sleeping faces, as he did with Chloe now.

She stirred, mumbled something, and he kissed her lightly, pulling her even closer in his arms. 'Sleep,' he whispered.

'Don't go,' she murmured, snuggling her face into his neck. 'Don't leave me alone.'

335

Closing his eyes against the onslaught of pure possessiveness, a surge of love so strong it took his breath, he could only hug her tight and shake his head, whispering, 'Never.'

To ease his aching conscience, he knew he needed to wake her up and tell her everything. Deal with her hurt and help her get over it. But he couldn't bring himself to break the mood, shatter the peace.

Tomorrow, he thought as he drifted off again. Tomorrow would bring plenty of time.

CHAPTER 21

The next morning Chloe hummed and sang as she worked. She couldn't help it; she just felt so good.

Turning from *Homebaked*'s refrigerator, she nearly danced directly into a frowning Augustine. 'What's the matter?' Chloe asked, tapping her foot to the rhythm in her head. 'Alarm go off too early?'

'No.' Augustine placed her hands on her bony hips and scowled deeper. 'You're singing.'

'Yes, I am.' She could sing all day. All night. In fact, she *had* been humming all night, in tune to Thomas's lovemaking.

'It's before seven. *In the morning*,' Augustine pointed out.

'You're right there. Can't get much past you, can I, Augie? Now, please move. I've got to get those muffins over there in the oven.'

'I want to know what you're up to, Miss Chloe Walker.'

Chloe laughed. The problem, she was beginning to realize, with a small town like Heather Glen was in hiring anyone older than herself. Since Augustine had known Chloe since she was a baby, she felt the need to be in charge. 'I'm up to running a business. Nothing else.'

'You've . . . been with him.' This was spoken in a low, horrified whisper, as if Chloe had committed a huge crime worthy of execution.

'Augustine!' Chloe struggled to clamp down on her ridiculous happiness and look serious. 'I'm your boss. Could you at least *pretend* to remember that?'

Augustine snorted, shook her head. Her arms went from her hips to cross very disapprovingly over her chest.

Chloe tried another approach. 'He's really a very sweet man, Augustine. And he makes me very happy.' Guilt always worked. Using it to its full advantage, Chloe lowered her voice and pouted a little. 'I would think you'd be thrilled for me.'

It worked like a charm. Immediately Augustine's face crumpled into a genuine, heartfelt – well, not a smile, exactly, but at least she no longer frowned. 'Of course I want you to be happy, honey. I just don't want to see you hurt. And Thomas – '

'Is never going to hurt me,' she insisted, impulsively throwing her arms around the older woman. 'So just relax and let me enjoy this. For once, I'm really, truly, happy. Okay?'

'Okay.' Augustine sniffed suspiciously, but when Chloe pulled back Augustine had already wiped the tell-tale moisture from her eyes. 'If he hurts you, I'll hurt him back,' she claimed ferociously. 'I mean that. I have a nasty right hook, you know.'

Chloe laughed, then spun around with her arms

outstretched. 'You'll have to stand in line. Conrad's already threatened the same thing. But you both have nothing to worry about. Thomas would never hurt me.'

Strong arms caught her from behind, surprising a gasp from her. A low voice murmured in her ear, 'Don't you look ravishing this morning, fair maiden?'

Another laugh bubbled, replacing her quick burst of fear. 'Conrad!' She slapped at the wide hands that held her against him. 'You scared me.'

He spun her around to face him. 'Why? Expecting someone else?'

She could hope, anyway. But Thomas had a life too, and lots of things to do. He couldn't spend every minute watching her, being near her. Nice as that would be . . .

'Chloe?' He shook her gently. 'Come back to earth, Chloe.'

'I'm trying. You're making me dizzy.'

'Sorry.' But he didn't look sorry as he grinned down at her. 'You look so pretty today.' He tweaked her nose. 'You're glowing. As if you'd – ' All amusement faded from his light eyes. He searched her face carefully. 'I get it,' he said, very quietly.

Chloe looked at Augustine, who, without a word, turned and walked out of the kitchen.

'You were with him.'

She sighed. A few steps took her to the counter, where she inspected the muffins, then bent to pop them into the oven. 'I seem to have it written all over my face, but, yes, if you must know, I was with him.'

'Did you ask him about Sierra Rivers?'

'We talked about it.' Carefully she started to prepare the meat she'd be using that morning, spreading out the bacon slices, separating the sausage links.

'Don't be coy, Chloe. What happened?'

The tenseness in his voice had her turning around. 'Why?' His eyes were grim. 'Something else has happened, hasn't it?'

He opened his mouth, but shut it again when Augustine came back in, slapping down two orders near Chloe. One look at their stressed faces and she lifted her eyebrows, then disappeared.

'Tell me, Conrad.'

'I spoke to your father yesterday, after I left you. We talked about it, then I dug back into the computer and – '

'Wait. Wait just a minute. You told my father about Thomas being Sierra Rivers?' Chloe slammed down the spatula and spun to stare at him accusingly. 'Whatever did you do that for?'

'He had to know, Chloe. Surely you can see that? The entire town is going to be affected by whatever Thomas does next.'

'I thought we had an understanding – that *I* was going to confront Thomas.'

'Did you?'

Chloe bit her lip and stared at the man she considered her best friend in the entire world. Stinging hurt rose up in her at the thought he would discuss this with her father. 'You didn't think I could handle this.'

340

'It's not that – ' he started, but she cut him off.

'It is that.' Suddenly chilled, she wrapped her arms around her middle, hugging her apron close. 'Did the mayor tell you he wanted me to get Thomas to leave town?' She could see by his expression he had. 'I see. What else did you two discuss? How hopeless I am?'

'Chloe, of course not.' Trying to soothe, Conrad moved close, took her shoulders and peered down into her hurt face. 'I'm just sick with worry that you'll get hurt. I told you that. You can't expect me just to back off and let that happen.'

'You're the one who told me to have a little faith in Thomas,' she reminded him. 'Have you forgotten?'

'That was before,' he said grimly. 'Before I learned the rest.'

'Which is what?' In Chloe's heart, her decision had been made. Thomas was Sierra Rivers, but it didn't matter. He had no intentions of hurting anyone and that was that. In his own way and time he'd tell her what she needed to know. She was as sure of that as her own name.

Conrad's mouth tightened; his fingers dug into her shoulders. 'I can't tell you yet.'

'Why not?' Suddenly she felt rather sick. 'What else is there?'

'I promised your father I wouldn't tell you until he could be here.'

She hated that – that they'd plotted behind her back. 'Well, where is he?'

Conrad had the good grace to look a little uncomfortable. 'He's busy this morning. We'll meet this

341

afternoon. In the park where we were yesterday. Okay?'

'No, not okay.' Grabbing fistfuls of his shirt, she shook him. 'Tell me now, darn you.'

'I can't,' he whispered, obviously torn. He held her arms. 'Please, Chloe, your father . . .'

'My father, what?' she demanded.

'He got me promoted,' Conrad said quietly, dropping his hands to her waist and squeezing. Unable to keep the pride out of his voice, he said, 'They added me to the force, Chloe. It's official. I'm a real deputy sheriff.'

'With pay and everything?' she asked, brightening. She'd always thought it was unfair how Conrad gave so much to the city as a volunteer and never got paid for it.

'Pay and all.'

'Oh, Conrad,' she said, hugging him. 'That's terrific. I'm happy for you – you know that I am.' She pulled back. 'But what does this have to do with Sierra Rivers?'

Again, he tensed. 'The mayor threatened to pull the promotion if I didn't wait until he was here to discuss this with you.'

'You've got to be kidding me.' But she could see by his expression he wasn't. 'Not only is that completely pathetic, it's the most unprofessional thing I've ever heard of. He can't do that!' Chloe backed away, stomped her foot – though she knew it was useless. 'I'm going to make sure that man stops manipulating us if it's the last thing I do!'

'He's just worried about you.'

'Don't you dare defend him.'

'It's the truth.'

'But to threaten you this way . . . it's so wrong, Conrad.'

With his old spirit he tugged on her hair, and the corner of his mouth lifted. 'This is like old times.'

'What is?'

'You protecting me. Remember, Chloe? How I was the last boy to grow? How small I was? Everyone picked on me except you. You'd hide in the woods and chuck rocks at anyone who dared to hurt me. You're doing it again.'

'Chucking rocks? I'm tempted.'

'Protecting me. I love it when you do that.'

She sighed, utterly incapable of staying mad with him for long. Besides, nothing he or her father could say would change her mind about Thomas. *Nothing*.

'So you'll be there?' he pressed, tucking her hair behind her ear. 'Today? At the park?'

'I'll be there for this pow-wow,' she confirmed. 'But my father is going to hear about this, believe me. It's going to stop, Conrad. Thomas is here to stay, and he's just going to have to accept that.'

Conrad looked at her solemnly. 'You haven't heard what we have to say yet, Chloe.'

'It doesn't matter,' she insisted, swallowing a little ball of dread at his pained, sympathetic expression. 'It just doesn't matter.'

And that was what she convinced herself over the next few hustle and bustle hours at *Homebaked*. She managed to believe it too. Especially when a knock at the back kitchen door revealed the local florist hidden behind a huge bouquet of red winter roses.

The card simply read, *'Can't stop thinking of you, Thomas.'*

She nearly melted, and for the life of her couldn't seem to catch her balance as she floated around, pretending to work.

'Are you in love?' Augustine demanded a little while later, with Lana looking over her shoulder, eagerly hanging on every word.

Oh, yeah, she was in love. Deep. 'Maybe.'

'Is he?'

She wanted to believe it – badly. But things with Thomas weren't that simple. Love wouldn't come easy to him. She knew that, respected that. Even understood it. But it didn't make it any easier while she waited for him to sort it all out for himself.

'I hope so,' she said finally.

'He'd better be,' Augustine warned, making Lana giggle.

'What are you going to do?' Lana asked, tipping her head to laugh at Augustine. 'Beat him over the head with your frying pan if he isn't?'

'That sounds like a fine idea,' the waitress muttered. 'And don't think I won't. That boy better stay scarce around here until he decides, or I will take that pan to his head, mark my words.' She moved to the door muttering, 'Better make that decision soon or I'm going McGuirre-hunting.'

Lana laughed hysterically, until she caught her

boss's hard eye. Whirling on one foot, she hightailed it for the dining room.

Chloe could only hope Thomas decided soon, too. Because she had no idea how long she could fend off Augustine for him.

Like Chloe, Thomas tried to work. He told himself he had to, for, in truth, he had a hell of a lot to do if he truly intended to build that resort.

And he did intend to do it.

But it was hard to concentrate on business when all he could think of was Chloe and how she'd looked this morning. He'd awakened to hear her radio alarm blaring. Feigning sleep, he'd had to smile when he'd felt Chloe's lips nuzzling his neck and throat.

'It's a sin to wake up this early,' he remembered telling her, his words turning into a low moan when those lips had inched down the covers to travel the length of his body.

Later, much later, she'd smiled up at him, all smug and satisfied, stretching sexily when he rose from the bed.

'Some people have work to do,' he'd told her, just as he realized that not only did he have no underwear, but he had no socks and no shirt. Just sweat pants and a jacket. 'Hell. And it looks like I have to get to it without my shorts.'

'You have a lot of work?'

'Hmm?' Distracted by the thought of going out into the cold without the proper clothing, he'd nearly missed her next words.

'Like a resort to build?' she'd asked, her trusting eyes going serious.

He'd turned to look at her. 'That's right.' *Tell her now. Just get it over with.*

But just the sight of her lying there, all sated and warm, *and his*, had had him walking back to the bed. Bracketing her hips with his arms, he'd bent, settling his lips over hers for a long, thorough kiss.

Remembering that now, and how they'd eventually each had to run from her house to their work, both far, far later than they usually would have, had him grinning ridiculously.

Thomas McGuirre, laughing out loud over the memory of a woman. It was unbelievable. It was great.

So great, in fact, that in the middle of the day he picked up the phone and dialed *Homebaked* just to hear her.

When Chloe answered, that stupid smile plastered itself to his face again. 'Hi,' he said inanely.

'Hi, back,' she said, sounding oddly breathless.

'I – ' Well, hell. He couldn't remember why he'd called her. 'What are you doing?' He winced and stared at the receiver. *What are you doing?* In his circles, he'd been known for his ease in seducing women. Was that the best he could come up with?

'I'm cooking, Thomas.' She laughed, still sounding out of breath. 'It's what I do for a living. Is that really what you called to ask me?'

'No.'

She laughed again, and the sound reminded him of a brilliant star, an unexpected summer shower. It reminded him of joy, hope, laughter. And how absolutely wonderful she was.

'I miss you, Thomas.'

His heart swelled so that it suddenly felt too big for his chest. He had to clear his throat. 'Can we establish for the record, here, whether we're talking about my body?'

'Of course,' she said, with another light laugh that had him soaring as high as the clouds.

'Well, then.'

'I'm kidding and you know it,' she said, suddenly soft and shy. 'I miss *you*, Thomas. You miss me too. Is that what you called to tell me?'

His pulse drummed so loud and hard he could feel the beat against every pulse-point. Having never said the words, he found himself strangely tongue-tied. Thirty-one years old and stuttering over such simple words. 'Yes, Slim, that's what I called to tell you.'

Now that pretty voice lowered to a conspiratorial whisper. 'I've been thinking about last night all day long, Thomas. Everyone wants to know why . . .' She laughed, and the sound had embarrassment in it.

'Everyone wants to know why what?' he pushed, finding himself whispering in that same tone.

'It's silly.'

'*Slim.*'

Her voice lowered even more. 'They think I look pretty today. They want to know what's different.'

'You look pretty every day,' he told her, feeling important. It was a thrill to know she needed him, too. Needed him to remind her how much she was worth. Vowing then and there to tell her every single day how much she meant to him, he asked, 'What did you tell them?'

'That making love is good for the complexion.'

'Chloe!' he said in laughing shock. 'Did you send Augustine into heart failure?'

'I didn't really have the nerve to say that,' she admitted. 'But she does want to know why I keep dancing around. She's muttering something about hitting you over the head with a frying pan.'

'Ouch.' He straightened and pushed all the work in front of him to one side. He couldn't think about fiscal charts, financial reports and long-term planning goals. Not now. All he could think about was her. 'Will you see me tonight?' he asked suddenly, unable to imagine being in his house without her.

'As in . . . a date?'

He smiled again at the pleasure and surprise in her voice, realizing with some regret that he hadn't spent any idle time with her. Taking her out to eat, going to a movie, just being together . . . those were all things they were going to have to try. 'Yeah. A date. What do you say?'

'Sounds lovely.'

He could hear the noise in the background, knew she was busy. 'I'll see you tonight, Slim.'

The smile on her face came right through the wire. 'Tonight.'

Sitting behind his desk in the office at his house, Thomas worked the keys of his computer, trying to come up with a viable solution for Heather Glen.

One orange paw came down on his fingers, messing him up.

Crooking an eye at the kitten, who was stretched out across his desk as if she owned the place, he warned, 'The sooner I get this done, the sooner we both get lunch. Scram.'

Haroldina yawned, obviously unfazed by such a mild threat. She knew as well as he did that he couldn't stand it when she was hungry.

Because of that very fact, she was already sporting a very unladylike belly, which she turned up now, obviously hoping he'd stroke it. 'You sure don't act like a poor neglected kitten.'

If a kitten could smile, this one did. But he didn't mind, not really, because he was more than just a little relieved that Haroldina no longer jumped at her own shadow. He'd hated watching her learn to relax, knowing from first-hand experience how difficult it was.

'Mew.'

'Fine.' Reaching out, he petted her soft belly once, then leaped in surprise when she turned her motor on and started purring. The rough sound startled a chuckle out of him.

'You ought to have to put on a warning light with that thing,' he told her.

She merely lifted her chin and stared haughtily at him.

Sighing, he turned his attention back to the computer and tried to concentrate. He'd spent a lot of money on Heather Glen, money that would be wasted by his decision to build the resort. On top of that, it would be damn expensive to buy the property he'd need now that he'd created greedy monsters out of the township.

But he didn't regret one penny of it. Not when it meant that he could keep Chloe forever.

Forever.

Instead of terrorizing him, the thought warmed him from the inside out. He'd no sooner lifted his fingers to the keyboard again than Haroldina sprang – again. This time she caused him to eject his disk.

'Dammit, cat.'

He lifted a hand to put the disk back in, but Haroldina, with a stuck-up grace only a cat can achieve, slammed a paw down on the keyboard again.

With a glare that didn't cower her one little bit, Thomas shoved her gently off the desk, then ignored her annoyed look. Before he could try to work she was back, pushing her nose in his ear.

'Mew.'

'You can't be hungry. Not yet.'

'Mew.'

Something speared through him, an instant understanding that had him puffing out air on a frustrated breath. 'Oh, all right,' he exclaimed loudly, exasperated. How had he got himself stuck in this predicament, *with a cat*, for God's sake? But looking at Haroldina, at her cute little expectant face, her deep baby blue eyes, he felt a strange twinge. A burst of affection. 'Let's go eat.'

'Isn't that sweet? My son, the softy.'

Thomas tensed, prepared. He'd been waiting, expecting, hoping his father would come back. He'd even left the doors unlocked, trying to make it easy.

This time he was ready. Slowly he turned to the door where his father lounged, leaning against the jamb, chewing on a stick. One eye had a colorful bruise around it and the corner of his mouth looked swollen.

Instead of filling Thomas with pride, it made him want to throw up.

'Ready for round two?' James McGuirre asked softly, his eyes dangerous and deadly flat.

CHAPTER 22

'I knew you'd be back,' Thomas said to his father with blunt contempt. With an easy, purposeful movement, he rose in his chair, scooped the rigid kitten close. In his arms she started to tremble, and rage washed through him. Every vein in his body pumped blood in triple time. His heart pounded dully, heavily, echoing in his head.

'Did you, now?' As if he didn't have a care in the world, James studied his fingertips.

'Yeah. I haven't given you any money, and you need money badly. Don't you?'

James had stiffened at Thomas's mocking tone. 'What I need is to teach you another lesson. You didn't learn well enough yesterday.' He cracked his knuckles and met Thomas's gaze.

Thomas swallowed the unwelcome burst of fear and let the adrenaline flow through his body. 'What I learned is you enjoy kicking a man when he's down. I'm not down and exhausted today. Not even close.'

James straightened in the doorway, his eyes coming alive with bitter hatred. 'I can still take you, son. Make no mistake about that.'

'I doubt it,' Thomas said coolly, challenging. He didn't even wince when the kitten clung to him by her needle-sharp claws. 'But either way you won't get any money.'

'You'll pay up if it's the last thing you do,' James corrected with a small shake of his head. Those cold eyes landed on him, showing not a trace of emotion. 'And it just might *be* the last thing you do, Thomas.'

Once, those words would have sent him spiraling into a deep, unreasoning terror that nothing or no one could protect him from.

No longer.

With a calm that he didn't feel, Thomas carefully pried Haroldina's claws out of his chest. With care, he put the tiny, quaking kitten on his desk chair, taking a quick moment to stroke her fur down and try to reassure her with his eyes. It didn't work. Her orange fur immediately sprang up again, and her tail puffed up to three times its normal size.

With the same slow precision, he turned to his father, forcing himself to stay loose and relaxed. 'Get out.'

James laughed, a low, ugly sound. 'We keep having this conversation.'

'Then stop coming.' His mouth curved. 'Better yet, go out and do something stupid. Get yourself locked up again – this time for a good long time.'

'That'll cost you.'

'It won't cost me anything.' He'd had enough. 'Get out.'

'You want me out?' Something greedy shifted in his father eyes. 'Then pay up.'

'I don't think so.' With an air of confidence, he moved around his desk, facing the man who had terrorized him for too many years to count. 'If I'm right, you've already cost me. Enough that if I brought in the authorities you'd be locked away but good.'

'You have nothing on me.' For a minute his father actually looked vulnerable, unsure. 'If you're talking about the explosion you had, and the other vandalism, I told you, I had nothing to do with that.'

'Right.'

'I didn't. You've got lots of enemies, son. Plenty of people around here are eager to hate you as they once hated me.' This last was spoken with a pride that made Thomas feel sick.

'You expect me to believe you didn't have anything to do with the vandalism?'

'I don't expect you do anything but give me money.' James crossed his arms. 'And this time the price has gone up. Fifty grand.'

A root of unease planted itself. As Thomas had already thought, he couldn't be sure James was smart enough to wire that bomb. He also couldn't figure out how his father would have had access to the kind of files he'd have needed to discover which properties Thomas owned.

It had been so easy to convince himself that his father had been at the bottom of all this hatred directed toward him, and the very real possibility that there were others who hated him as much as this man hurt unexpectedly.

Thomas lifted the telephone, and as his father watched in obvious growing trepidation he dialed nine. He lifted a brow at his father, baiting, bluffing. 'Two more numbers is all it'll take to get the police here. You want that?'

'You won't do it,' he taunted. 'I know you, son. You've got the McGuirre pride. No way will you call and admit you can't handle your own father. That, in fact, I can and will beat the shit out of you again. You'd be the laughing stock of the entire town.'

Without another word, Thomas punched in a one.

James stepped forward and put his finger down on the phone, cutting it off. Every muscle inside Thomas coiled. He was ready to defend himself.

He wouldn't lose again.

But surprisingly James backed up a step, well out of range. 'Not this time.' Surreptitiously he rubbed at his own ribs, and Thomas hoped they hurt like hell. His sure did.

'Then leave.'

'Are you saying you won't give me money?'

Thomas smiled, suddenly empowered. 'That's what I'm saying.'

James took a few steps back when Thomas advanced, but he shrugged casually. 'You're a damn hard-headed fool, then, Thomas. A real fool. Because, believe me, I will get what I want from you.'

'You've threatened me before,' Thomas said mildly, pausing to pick up the poor, terrified, huddled kitten once more. He held her close and stroked her. Thankfully she relaxed a couple of degrees, but still kept her narrowed eyes on his father. 'And I've lived through the worst you can do.' *Barely*.

'I told you I didn't have anything to do with the vandalism.'

Thomas just shrugged. And, in a move that cost him every bit of control he had, he walked right by his father and out the door, turning his back on the man who could no longer hurt him.

James followed, and Thomas had never been so aware of anyone in his life. His every sense shot to overdrive as he walked with taut suspense, wondering when his father would make a move.

Thomas went into the kitchen, and with Haroldina in the crook of one arm he pulled out a bowl. She mewled appreciatively.

'You're ignoring me,' James said roughly. 'I taught you better than that.'

'Oh, get out already, would you?' Thomas set Haroldina down right on the counter and reached for a can of kitten food. '*Beefy Stew*,' the can proclaimed. '*Give your kitten muscles while feeding it the nutrition he deserves*.' Well, his poor kitten could use more muscles – less belly, maybe – he'd try it.

Beside him James's fists clenched, and Thomas went still.

But James didn't swing. Instead, he let out a breath and stalked to the back door. 'There's only one thing to do,' he said, his voice spewing maliciousness. 'And you're going to be so sorry you've driven me to this.'

Thomas calmly forked meat into the bowl.

'Actually,' James said cryptically as he let himself out, 'you won't be the one to be sorry. *She will*. But you'll blame yourself just the same.'

She will? 'What are you talking about?'

'I'll tell you when I come back for the money. I'll want cash this time, and, believe me, this time you'll pay willingly. *Very willingly*.'

Thomas's eyes narrowed. His stomach tightened. 'Wait – '

But the door had slammed and James was gone.

Thomas stared at it, hoping he was mistaken, hoping to God he was jumping to conclusions.

Because if he wasn't, and this deep, sinking feeling he'd just gotten was correct, then James had just slyly threatened Chloe.

Dropping Haroldina, Thomas ran to his car.

That afternoon, Chloe found herself in her tiny office with her books spread out before her. Utterly incapable of concentrating, she leaned over the papers with her elbows and stared dreamily into space.

Tonight, she thought with a wicked gleam, tonight she and Thomas would –

'Did you forget about our meeting?' Conrad smiled indulgently at her before squeezing into the small space not taken up by Chloe's desk.

'No, I didn't – ' When she glanced at her still watch, she let out a deep breath. 'Darn it, the thing's stopped. I'm sorry, Conrad. How late am I?'

'Nothing to worry about, since your father didn't show up either,' he assured her, perching a lean hip on the corner of her ancient wood desk. He was in full deputy sheriff's attire, and the leather of his holster squeaked, reminding her that he was fully armed now. 'I thought I'd come to you, that's all. Kind of slow today – there's no one in your dining room. Maybe you should come up with some early-bird special, or a late lunch special. It'd draw more people.'

'It's exactly halfway between lunch and dinner. I'm rarely full with customers at this time of day,' she reminded him, wondering why she'd never noticed until now that he tended to treat her as her father did. As if she were a child who constantly needed help and advice. 'We'll pick up in a little while; we always do.'

'I'm sure you will,' he murmured easily.

Chloe gritted her teeth, unsure as to what was the matter with her. Conrad didn't meant to sound so placating, so . . . vaguely patronizing. 'You said earlier you had something to share with me?'

'Yes, I did. I wanted to wait for your father – '

'Forget it, Conrad,' she said, losing her patience. 'Either tell me now or move out of my way. I'm busy.'

She'd taken him aback; she could see the hurt and surprise in his eyes. Sighing, she rubbed her temples. 'I'm sorry. That was out of line.'

'No,' he said, studying her with worried eyes, 'you say what you mean. It's one of the things I admire so much about you. Don't stop doing that now.' He lifted his laptop from his shoulder, slipped it out of the case and flipped it open on his lap. 'I brought proof. I had a feeling I'd need it.'

'Proof?'

'Of Thomas's intentions, Chloe.' His gaze landed on her, sympathetic and full of understanding. 'He doesn't plan to build that resort, I'm afraid.'

'Says who?'

'Says lots of things. Namely, the fact that one thing Sierra Rivers doesn't have is a construction company. Which means he'd need an outside source to build this resort. Nowhere, at any time, has he put out a request for bids. In fact there are no plans registered, either, with any architectural firm or any engineer.'

'So?'

'So,' he said patiently, 'it's my belief that no plans have been drawn up.'

She could only stare at him. 'Maybe he hasn't gotten that far yet.'

'Think about this, Chloe,' he said gently. 'If you were going to need to buy up a bunch of land, would you really let out rumors announcing that? Let everyone else buy up what you need? Drive up the price of the very land you intend to buy?'

She had to admit that part didn't make much sense, but she hadn't wanted to discredit Thomas. Her eyes closed in pain as she thought about it now. Not once had he confirmed or denied to her his plans about the resort. In fact he'd been alarmingly general. 'It doesn't matter. I'm sure there's an explanation.'

'There's not,' he assured her. 'In fact we have a witness who'll testify that Thomas intended to take down this town.'

'What? Who?'

'James McGuirre. We just brought him in on charges of conspiracy, but we'll let him cop a plea if he co-operates. He says Thomas did it all for revenge, including . . .'

'Including what?' she demanded.

'Including getting close to the mayor's daughter.' It was obviously difficult for him to say. 'It was the final revenge.'

Oh, Thomas, she thought, sagging a little in her chair. Can it be true? Could you really have been playing with me this entire time? 'No,' she whispered aloud. 'I don't believe it.'

'Chloe.' Conrad's face was leaden with regret. 'It's true.'

'Maybe it was in the beginning, but he's changed his mind. I know it. He – ' He what? He'd never claimed to love her, and he'd misled her at least twice. First when he'd bought up her loan without telling her, then again when he'd deliberately hidden the fact he was Sierra Rivers. Of course he could have done it.

When Conrad's large, hot hand settled on her face, she jumped in surprise. 'I'm sorry,' he whispered, bending closer. His thigh on her desk brushed her limp hand, and she jerked it away. 'He's hurt you and now I'll have to hurt him.'

'Conrad!' She leaped to her feet. 'You don't know for sure. Why – '

He kicked out with his foot and her office door shut. A quick flick of his wrist and the door was locked. 'I do know for sure, dammit. And you gave yourself to him without a backward glance for me. Didn't you have a clue as to how I felt, watching you fall all over him?'

Shock kept her still when he rose swiftly and pulled her up by her wrists. 'Didn't you?' he asked again.

'I – No.' Horrified, she looked into the face she'd loved so long she felt as if he were her own family. His grip, gentle yet unbreakable as steel, had her tugging back in automatic response.

'Don't,' he whispered harshly, his face contorting. 'Don't make me hurt you, Chloe. That would kill me, but I'd do it. To keep this a secret, I'd do it. Don't push me.'

'To keep what a secret?' she cried, but he made a hard noise in his throat and transferred both her wrists to one hand so the other could cover her mouth.

'Quiet.' He went still as stone, listening, holding her close.

No one came.

No one would, Chloe thought, becoming frightened of this man she'd trusted with her life. Lana was off this afternoon, which left only Augustine. Not only was her hearing rotten, she'd never think about coming down the long hall from the kitchen to check on Chloe. Not when she alone was running the dining room and the kitchen.

Not when she knew Chloe was with Conrad, her trusted and best friend.

'I'm going to take my hand away, Chloe,' he said, in that calm, quiet voice which in the past had soothed her. 'And I expect you to be a good girl and listen to my every word.'

Over the hand that held her silent, she could only stare at him. Had the entire world gone mad? Thomas was using her. Conrad had lost his marbles. Her father – No, she thought. Not him too.

Conrad's hands on her wrists tightened a little, and he shook her gently. 'Do you understand? Answer me, Chloe. I hate it when you don't.'

Helpless, she nodded, and he slowly removed his hand. Her sigh of relief was cut off in her throat when he drew her close against his body and held her there, again in a grip she couldn't budge from.

He smiled in satisfaction. 'This is nice – real nice.' Then he frowned, and Chloe nearly didn't recognize him, he looked so . . . dangerous. 'But I shouldn't have had to force this issue, Chloe. Not when I've waited so long.'

'I – I have no idea what this is all about,' she whispered. She could feel his heartbeat against her, fast and furious, and knew he was not nearly as calm as he seemed.

Somehow that terrified her more than anything else so far.

'Don't you?' His smile was soft as he gave her

another gentle squeeze. 'I love you, Chloe. I always have.'

'But you never said – ' She gasped when he easily turned her to face him fully, and snuggling her unbearably close to his body. He was very hard.

'I waited for you to feel it back,' he murmured, rolling his hips against hers, settling his hardness to her softness in a way that made her want to be sick. 'I've been waiting so long.'

'Conrad, no.' With all her might, she squirmed, but he restrained her with pathetic ease.

'Yes,' he whispered in her ear. But then he sighed and straightened. 'But this part – ' briefly he ran one hand down the length of her, cupping her to him with a sigh before releasing her – 'will have to wait. We have other things to deal with first. Your father, for one.'

Freed suddenly, Chloe fell back against the desk and gripped the wood hard. Conrad still blocked the door. 'I want you to let me out,' she whispered. 'If you don't, I'll scream.'

'Scream,' he said calmly, his eyes never leaving hers, 'and I'll have to hurt Augustine. You don't want that, Chloe, so be quiet and good. I have things to explain to you.' He waited a beat while Chloe just stared at him. Satisfied, he went on, 'I thought you would listen to your father when he asked you to get Thomas to leave town. You didn't.'

'I never promised I'd do it.'

'Now that you haven't,' he continued mildly, as if she hadn't spoken, 'I'll have to force you to. He just doesn't fit into this picture, Chloe.'

'I won't.'

'If you don't, of course, I'll be forced to get rid of him.'

Now he watched her carefully, but Chloe had steeled herself, convinced she mustn't react to anything. It was impossible to believe that this was Conrad talking to her – her best friend. He'd completely lost it.

'Your father doesn't have a good grip on this town anymore,' he said sadly. 'He's not kept a tight enough rein and now he's gotten Heather Glen in a hell of a mess. I'll have to replace him. You'll convince him of that. The people will love it, once he endorses me. I've always been very popular. Then,' he went on, ignoring her disbelieving wide-eyed stare, 'you'll marry me, of course. It's my greatest dream.' He smiled while Chloe gripped the desk in horror. 'Together, with both Thomas and your father out of the picture, we'll put this town back on the map. We'll be heroes.'

'Oh, my God. You're mad.'

'I'm sorry. I wanted to give you time, to make sure you loved me as much as I love you, but then Thomas came back and ruined everything. You stopped looking at me with stars in your eyes – '

'I never looked at you that way! *Never*. Conrad, I'm sorry, but you must know I never felt that way about you. I love Thomas. Just let me out,' she said beseechingly, 'and then – '

'No.' He took her shoulders, tightened his fingers on her until she winced. 'We'll go out together. I can no longer trust you to get rid of Thomas; I can see that now. Dammit. I'll have to keep you somewhere while I do it myself.'

Even with nothing in the tiny office but her desk and a closet by the door, Chloe didn't have enough room to maneuver, or fight her way out. Besides, she thought with welling panic, Conrad was so much bigger than she. And armed.

'Wait,' she said quickly, her eyes burning at the thought of Conrad going after an unsuspecting Thomas with his gun, 'let's talk this out some more. I'm sure we can come up with something.'

'Do you really think so?' he asked.

'Yes, I know it.' Eagerly she grabbed his shirt, having no idea how she was going to get out of this, only knowing she had to stall. 'Conrad – '

Then a voice called her name through the office door, that deep, low, husky voice she'd come to know so well. 'Are you in there?' he asked softly, knocking once.

She opened her mouth to scream a warning, but Conrad moved so fast her head spun. In less than a blink he had her in a stronghold grip with a hard hand over her mouth. 'Quiet, honey,' he whispered in her ear. 'I'm sorry, but you're going to have to send him away. I can't do anything to him in here, and risk a customer or Augustine coming in.'

'Chloe?' Thomas called again.

'Tell him – *Shit*.' The doorknob had started to turn. Conrad's voice turned harsh and ugly as it rasped in her ear. 'Get rid of him. If you don't . . .'

He gestured to his gun. Then he backed into the closet, leaving the door open a crack.

The lock snapped as Thomas opened the door to her office wide, momentarily covering the door to the closet.

'Hi,' he said. 'Sorry about the lock. I think I broke it.'

But she didn't smile back, didn't budge from where she stood in front of her desk, wide-eyed, her mouth a little open. She couldn't, not with the corner of her eye on the sight of Conrad's hand hovering over his gun. He'd shoot Thomas without a regret. The horror of it had her making a little strangled noise.

'Chloe?'

Her lips moved, barely. Her voice cracked. 'Go away.'

At first Thomas thought he didn't hear her right. But then he saw that her eyes were flat, her color pale. She looked, he noted with sickening clarity, very unhappy to see him.

Okay, so it was a fluke. The whole thing: her falling for him, her thinking she was in love with him. He should have known it was too good to be true. 'I'm sorry,' he said, very quietly. 'Are you busy?'

She nodded emphatically. 'Very. Go.'

Did he have a choice? Quietly and heavily, his heart – the very same one she'd just recently brought back from the dead – dropped to the floor. He started to turn back to the door, then stopped. 'No,' he said.

'No?'

God, she looked panicked. Terrorized. Horrified at the thought of having to spend another second with him. 'I've been without warmth and affection in my life for too long, Chloe. Too damn long.' The office was so small it only took one step to bring him within touching distance of the only woman he'd ever love. 'You brought those things back to me. Gave me hope. Gave me joy. Don't you dare change your mind about me now.'

Because he couldn't help himself, he cupped her face, felt her tremble, and he found himself doing something he never would have believed a month ago. *Begging*. 'Please.'

Those eyes he loved so much filled. Her luscious mouth quivered. 'Thomas,' she whispered brokenly; 'You have to go. Please, I – '

'I don't want to go,' he said in a voice filled with aching emotion. 'Look at me. Look at what you've done for me. You've brought me so much, Slim. So much. You've made me feel things I thought I'd never feel. Thought I couldn't. But I do now. Because of you.'

'No. Don't feel. Not because of me.' She shuddered and clung to him for a brief second when he reached for her waist. 'You have to go, Thomas,' she said, with an urgency he didn't understand. 'You *have to*. Please, just do it.'

'I can't,' he whispered, slipping his arms around her and burying his face in her neck. 'And don't ask me not to feel. Because I do – so much. I love you, Chloe.'

With a sob, she straightened and shoved at his chest. Lifting her drenched face, she opened her mouth, but she never said a word. She didn't have to.

The unmistakable click of a gun being cocked, directly behind him, spoke for her.

CHAPTER 23

At the soft but deadly sound of a gun being cocked behind him, Thomas stiffened. Chloe's frightened gaze met his, and in that instant he knew.

Chloe hadn't changed her mind about him. Far from it. Instead, the brave, petrified woman had been trying to get him out of the office and out of danger. God, she loved him enough to risk her own life for his safety, and he'd doubted her.

Relief made him giddy, but not weak. With his eyes he tried to convey all that he felt: reassurance, hope, love. Then he gave her a last, quick squeeze and mouthed, 'Quiet. Don't move.'

As if he had all the time in the world, he slowly dropped his hands from her, prepared himself for what lay ahead and turned. Still, it was a shock.

Conrad smiled. 'Expecting someone else?'

'Actually, yes.' His father, maybe. Or even Chloe's father. Anyone but the quiet, mild-tempered Conrad.

'If you would have just done what you were supposed to do, Thomas, we wouldn't be in this predicament.' Conrad stepped the rest of the way

369

out of the closet, the gun in plain sight and leveled right on him.

Thomas reached behind his back and felt for Chloe, gripping her waist. He held her there, directly behind him, so that she couldn't be in range of the gun Conrad seemed to enjoy waving. 'Really? What predicament is that?'

'Like you don't know.' With his foot, Conrad shut the office door, then backed to it.

With the little space they had, with one lunge Thomas could have reached out and touched the gun. But he knew it would go off long before he got to it, most likely ripping him in two in the process. It would go right through him to Chloe.

Somehow, miserable and as painful as it had been, he would rather have faced his hot-headed father one on one again than deal with this cool, distant and obviously crazy Conrad. Thomas had been in many difficult situations in his life, most of them dangerous, yet this was a new one – facing the front of a loaded barrel. What could he do, other than try to talk their way out? 'I really don't know what you're talking about,' he said conversationally. 'Tell me.'

'You were supposed to leave. Better yet, you should never have come back.'

'Supposed to leave –' *Christ*. Now he finally got it. 'It was *you*. You set the bomb. You blew out the windows on my building. Destroyed that other office, too. You – ' Stunned, he went still. Fury mottled his veins, pumped his heart. 'You were the one who got into *Homebaked*'s kitchen that morning, made that mess.'

Conrad nodded, and, though he didn't look happy or even pleased with himself, Chloe made a noise behind him in reaction.

Thomas pressed back gently against her, trying to warn her to remain silent. Obviously they were dealing with a man on the edge, and it scared him that she would try to do something heroic.

'I needed you out,' Conrad admitted. 'But that was before I realized who you really were.'

'You mean before you found out that I ran Sierra Rivers?'

Again Conrad nodded. 'Things were going just fine for me before Sierra Rivers burst in on the scene. You nearly ruined everything for me.'

'Things always went fine for you.'

'No. Without you here I would have been mayor. Married Chloe.'

Behind him Chloe fidgeted, obviously unnerved. Thomas couldn't blame her much for that. He was pretty damned unnerved himself. 'There was never anything between you and Chloe.'

'You're wrong there.' For the first time Conrad's disturbing calm faltered. 'From the time we were little we had something. Inseparable. We only got closer as time went on. What was between us would have only grown even more special with more time, but you interfered.' In his hand the gun wavered, then rattled.

'Put that thing away before you hurt someone,'

Thomas said, swallowing his quick burst of fear. Maybe talking wasn't the right plan. If he made Conrad too nervous too quickly, it'd all be over.

'So confident,' Conrad mocked. 'So sure of yourself. What's it like, Thomas, to always know you're right? To always be in charge? To be able throw your money around like royalty?'

Thomas let out a bark of laughter. 'You're kidding.' But he could see Conrad wasn't, and he sobered quickly. 'Conrad, you know where I came from. What I lived with.'

Conrad's jaw tightened. His shoulders rolled back. 'And you still came out on top.'

And got the girl, Thomas thought, knowing Conrad thought it too. 'I thought we were friends.'

Now Conrad laughed. 'You never wanted a friend. You were always a loner.' He smiled. 'In a way, I'm doing you a favor. You like to be alone; you got it. I've put away your father, you know. Ah, I can see you *didn't* know that yet. Yes, he's behind bars again. Seems he's going to try to cop a plea by giving us the scoop on you, but alas . . .' Conrad blinked sympathetically '. . . it won't be enough. He's going to stay there, just because he reminds me of you. If that doesn't make you feel nice and alone, just the way you like it, then remember this. I'm going to keep Chloe for myself, too. We belong together.'

Frowning suddenly, Conrad tried to look around Thomas to see her, but she'd put her head against Thomas's back. 'Chloe, come here.'

'NO.' Thomas held her behind him, his stomach in knots. 'She stays with me.'

Conrad lifted the gun higher, aimed it directly at his chest. 'Think again.'

'She stays with me,' he said again firmly.

'I don't think you understand – Ah, Chloe. Good girl.' Conrad smiled approvingly as Chloe stepped around Thomas.

Thomas grabbed for her, but she side-stepped him. 'He'll shoot you,' she said softly, beseechingly, her eyes brilliant with unshed tears. 'Please, Thomas. Don't make me watch you die.'

'Touching as this is,' Conrad noted dryly, waving the gun a little, 'it doesn't really matter what either of you want. Chloe. *Now.*'

Thomas watched in suspended disbelief as Chloe stepped up to Conrad, her head raised high. 'Don't hurt him,' he heard her say in a low, shaky voice. 'Please, Conrad, if nothing else, listen to this. If you hurt him, you hurt me too.'

Hearing her beg for his life did something to Thomas. Something deep, something very frightening. 'No,' he whispered hoarsely, 'it's not going to end like this.'

But Conrad reached for Chloe with one hand, just as his other shifted, moving his first finger from the handle of the gun to the trigger. Conrad looked at Thomas, and for a split second no one moved, nothing happened – except the small, clear flash of victory that lit Conrad's eyes.

Thomas was going down. He knew it, could feel it

in every goose bump that had raised on his flesh. Conrad had no choice now but to finish this off, and quickly, before he drew anyone else's attention. And that made him more than a danger just to Thomas.

Chloe's life hung in the balance too.

Not without a fight, Thomas promised himself, as rage flared hot and quick, and he lunged forward.

Chloe screamed and leaped too, also for Conrad, clearly intending to make sure Conrad didn't shoot.

But behind them all the office door opened, and a flash of something whooshed through the air, accompanying a heavy sort of 'thunk' Thomas couldn't place.

In that split second, time stalled. Thomas, already in the air, died a thousand deaths watching Chloe throw herself at Conrad. The explosion of the gunshot was like a light switch inside Thomas, clicking everything back onto double time. Filled with more terror than the darkest of his nightmares, he burst to life again with a furious vengeance.

Not Chloe. Please, God, not Chloe. He hit his knees hard on the concrete floor beside the heap of limbs that made up Chloe and Conrad and tried to separate them. *Don't let that bullet have ripped through her precious body*.

His heart in his throat, he shoved a limp and unresisting Conrad away from her. With a gentle care that completely belied the heart-stopping panic pounding through him, he stretched her out, running his hands over her, desperately searching for where the bullet had entered.

'Oh, God, is she hurt?'

For the first time he realized Augustine stood there in the office doorway. 'I don't know,' he said grimly, blinking back the stinging hotness of tears which threatened to blind him.

But then Chloe opened her glorious eyes and blinked him into focus. 'Thomas?' she whispered, before flinging herself against his chest.

'You're – ' He had to stop and clear his throat before he could even speak, an action made all the more difficult because the woman he loved beyond reason was slowly choking him to death. 'You're not hurt.'

'No. And neither are you, thank God.' Then she burst into tears.

Over Chloe's shaking shoulders he caught sight of a still unmoving Conrad, and a sense of dread and understanding took him. But then a cackle of laughter caught Thomas's attention.

He lifted his gaze to Augustine, who smiled wickedly and lifted a heavy steel-lined frying pan. 'He was so busy planning his life out, and taunting the two of you, he never knew what hit him,' she exclaimed triumphantly. 'And, believe me, I hit him hard.'

Chloe pulled back and stared at Augustine in amazement. 'Good aim,' she managed. 'But next time do it sooner.' She looked at Thomas and her mouth quivered as it smiled. 'A lot sooner.'

Yanking her close, he squeezed her so hard he knew he was probably hurting her, but he couldn't let go. Not now, not ever.

'I'm calling the sheriff,' Augustine said, frowning at Conrad. 'A real one.' Fumbling the phone, she barked out orders while Thomas just held Chloe as tight as he could, trying to reassure himself that she was indeed all right, that the horror was over.

Above him, Augustine sniffed and shook her head, looking down at Chloe. 'I liked Conrad. I really did. Ever since he was only a boy. But when I came to talk to you, and I heard him saying those things to you – honey, I went a little wild. I went running back to the kitchen for something to whack him with and all I could find was a frying pan – though it seems kinda fitting, now that I think about it. I'm just sorry it took me so long.'

'It doesn't matter,' Chloe said with a little laugh that sounded like a sob. 'You came, and I'm so grateful you did. Thank you, Augustine.' Letting go of Thomas long enough to reach up with a hand for the other woman's, she smiled through dazzling eyes.

'Don't you *dare* thank me,' Augustine scolded, bending to kiss Chloe. 'I love you, honey.' Then she glared once at Thomas. 'Make that a lesson, boy. Hurt her and I'll smack you, twice as hard as I did him.' Then she ruined the entire effect by crying and kissing him too.

A siren sounded in the background, and Conrad, still crumpled in a heap at their feet, moaned.

Thomas nudged him with his toe, prepared to jump him if necessary, but he didn't budge. 'She got him good,' he muttered, then sent up more thanks that the guy's aim had been off.

Chloe jerked in his arms when feet pounded down the hall, and a sheriff, followed by the city's two paramedics, pushed their way in. In less time than Thomas would have thought possible for a small town with more bureaucracy than New York City, Conrad was loaded on a gurney.

When Chloe, who had stood up to watch, gave a whispered statement to the sheriff, Conrad was strapped down and read his rights.

Thomas looked at Chloe as she solemnly watched Conrad taken from the room. In her weary profile he read exhaustion, hurt, anger . . . regret. She looked as if she'd lost her best friend, and he knew she felt as if she had.

'Chloe – ' he started, reaching for her.

But she backed from his touch, wouldn't meet his gaze and fumbled for the door. 'Augustine needs me. The dining room is standing room only, filled to the brim with curious customers. I've got to see to them.'

'You should relax. Close the restaurant,' he protested. 'You've had a shock – '

'Please, don't tell me what to do,' she said quietly, straightening her clothes and meeting his worried gaze with her steely one. 'I've had enough of that for a lifetime.'

'I'm not trying to tell you what to do,' he said gently. 'But I know this is very difficult for you.'

'I'm fine.' But she hesitated, gave him a look of longing that had his heart stuttering. 'I need to do this,' she whispered. 'I need to be busy right now. It'll help me move on.'

'Chloe . . .' God, the tortured look in her eyes was going to kill him. 'I'm so sorry. So damned sorry. Please, let me help. We need to talk – '

'Not now. Not . . .' She hesitated and he tensed, waiting for her to say not ever. 'Not yet,' she finished softly. 'Just not yet.'

Then she was gone.

Kicking the desk didn't dissipate one little bit of the bottled fear and frustration inside him. He'd nearly watched her die before his very eyes. It had shaved years off his life. He knew he'd never forget how he'd felt, watching Chloe walk toward Conrad, who held a loaded gun.

He loved her, dammit. He'd even told her so and she hadn't said a word about it.

Maybe he should just go tell her again.

Whoa, cowboy. She's got a room full of people just waiting to soak up all the juicy stuff that has happened to her. The last thing they needed was more fodder to eat up.

Well, too bad. It was time the people in this town learned what he was up to. What he planned to do. More than time for them to learn to accept him. *And for him to learn to accept them.*

That was how he found himself storming into the crowded, noisy dining room, craning his neck for Chloe. People noticed him all right, and whispered behind his back, but Chloe was nowhere to be found.

He tried the kitchen next, but she wasn't there either. No one was.

She'd left him, he thought, panic welling yet again.

Then he heard voices on the back porch and went running out there, skidding to a halt before Chloe, who stood, leaning against the rail.

'Hello,' he said stupidly.

She just blinked at him.

'I want to talk to you.'

Again she just looked at him.

'I told you I love you before, there in your office,' he blurted out without stopping to think. 'And you never said a word. No response, no nothing. Maybe you didn't hear me.'

She said nothing, but she did swallow. Hard.

'Maybe I should say it again.' *Why wasn't she saying anything?* But his mouth was on a roll so he shouted, 'I love you, Chloe Walker.'

Now her mouth fell open. Her face reddened.

Behind him, clapping and hollering sounded, and by the pitch level he knew it had to be more than one person. Closing his eyes on the mortification, he tried to tell himself it didn't matter he had an audience, that Chloe wasn't alone on the porch.

Turning to face his punishment, he found Lana and Augustine, grinning broadly. '*Shit.*'

Obviously in desperate need of comic relief, they laughed uproariously. Thomas didn't think he liked being the one to make them feel better.

But then Chloe cleared her throat, and they straightened, gave him one last idiotic grin and disappeared back inside.

'Well, I'm getting real good at making an ass of myself,' he muttered, turning back to face the beautiful woman who was still just staring at him.

'Are you?' she asked softly.

'Looks like.'

'I thought maybe you were just getting real good at sharing your feelings.'

Hope flared. 'That too,' he told her, not daring to touch her but wanting so very badly to.

Pushing away from the railing, she came close, tipped up her head. 'You did plan to ruin this town,' she said very quietly. 'From the very beginning. With very little effort, you still could.'

His heart stilled and went cold. What was she saying? That she hadn't believed him when he'd said he wouldn't? 'Yes, yes and no.'

He expected her to rant and rail and denounce him for the fraud he felt he was. It didn't help to know he deserved her anger. He should have told her, dammit. He should have done this long ago.

But she wasn't into ranting, railing, or anything of the sort. This was Chloe, the trusting, sensitive, compassionate woman he loved above all else. She just stood there quietly, dignified and so full of graceful suffering it made him wince.

'What do you mean, no?' she asked.

'I mean I wouldn't.' Taking a chance, he ran his arms up and down her arms, trying to soothe away her shocked chill. 'Slim, I am not going to take down Heather Glen. I told you that and I meant it.'

She just stared at him. At least she hadn't backed away, he told himself. This was a good thing. 'I think it's time I told you everything. Every last little thing.'

Chloe still didn't move, just stood there before him, watching him. Her skin felt hot and cold to the touch at the same time and he wondered if she needed medical attention. Her pupils were so huge and black he could hardly see a speck of color around them.

It was an effort to remain calm when all he could think about was what would have happened if he hadn't shown up at her office to surprise her. 'I'd really like to have a shot at Conrad.' He tried to warm her with his hands, but her skin retained a chill no matter what he did.

'He's not going to hurt me again,' she said clearly, not sounding shocked at all. 'And if he does, I plan to hit him myself, so stop changing the subject. You were saying about Heather Glen?'

So formal. So very annoyed. 'I was saying that – Yes, dammit. All right. I did come here to destroy this town and everyone in it.' She stiffened under his hands, but she'd asked for this. 'God, Slim, for years it was all I thought about. During those lean times, when I first left, I dreamed about it every night.' How many nights had he gone to bed hungry – if he'd even had a bed? How many nights had he planned how he'd come back and show up each and every person who had ever treated him badly?

'Oh, Thomas.'

Thinking he heard disapproval, he dropped his hands from her and turned away. 'Then I made my first deal. Made what I thought then was a ton of money. It got easier after that, and in no time I had more money than I knew what to do with. I never went hungry or wanted for another thing again, but I still wasn't satisfied. So . . .' He hesitated, very unsure of this part, very unproud of what he'd wanted to do.

'So you came here to hurt us like we'd hurt you,' she finished for him.

'Only I never did.' Now he faced her, because he had to. 'Because I met you. I took one look into your warm, loving eyes and got lost, Chloe. Lost and found all at the same time.' Grimacing, he shoved his fingers through his hair. 'God, that sounds like an excuse.' Reaching for her hands, he ran a thumb over her knuckles, then brought them up to his mouth to kiss them. Watching her over their joined hands, he said, 'But it's the truth, Slim. You did something to me, opened me up. Showed me what I was missing. I knew I couldn't do it, I couldn't hurt you, and I never looked back.'

'I know,' she said softly.

'You have to believe me – ' he started, then stopped abruptly, dropping her hands and grabbing her hips. 'You know?'

She nodded. 'I know you couldn't hurt *anyone*, not just me.'

He thought about the violence that streaked through him whenever he dealt with his father, and knew he wasn't worthy of her trust. 'No,' he corrected. 'It's *you*. You keep me on track.'

'You couldn't hurt *anyone*,' she said again firmly, reaching up and taking his shoulders to shake him. '*Anyone*. I know you; I understand you. Do you think

I don't know how you fell for a little kitten named Haroldina, just because you couldn't stand for her to be hurt or hungry? Oh, Thomas, don't you see?' she asked him, shaking him gently again. 'It's not me who has changed you, but *you*. You, Thomas. And I do love you, by the way. More than anything.'

Thomas's throat seized painfully as he was struck by the sudden fierce love that took him by surprise. Drawing her possessively close, he kissed her long and hard. Finally he lifted his head. 'I'll never disappoint or hurt you again, Chloe.'

'I know.' She grinned through a veil of shimmering tears. 'Because if you do, Augustine will come looking for you!'

EPILOGUE

Thomas frowned at his computer and tried again. Nope. Still couldn't find the file he needed. Damn. Where could the fourth year's annual reports for the resort have gone?

'Mew.'

An orange paw slammed down on his fingers and he sighed. 'Harold,' he said sternly, 'I just fed you five minutes ago. Go away, I have work. Heather Glen's business committee elected me Man Of The Year, and today Mayor Walker is making the announcement at the meeting, and I can't find my reports. Some Man Of The Year,' he muttered, his fingers racing over the keyboard as he searched.

He could hear Chloe's father now, teasing him mercilessly about letting Chloe wear the pants in the family. He sighed, but there was pleasure there in the torment too, at knowing he'd been fully accepted. And was loved.

A second cat, this one much bigger than the tiny, wobbly kitten, hopped up and stared at him. 'Meow.'

'No way,' Thomas said, shaking his head, keeping his eyes on the screen. 'I'm not giving in to this. Go away.' But he reached over to stroke both cats.

Then a third cat hopped up, this one much older and much more graceful. She leveled Thomas with a long, hard stare. Then she started to purr. Thomas, helpless to resist, scooped her close. 'Listen, Grandma Haroldina, I swear I just fed your child and grandchild five minutes ago.' He scratched behind her ears, just the way she loved it. 'You believe me, don't you?'

In answer, the cat rubbed her head to his chest, spreading gray and orange hair across the front of his dark gray suit.

The door to his office slammed open, and at the sight of the two and four-year-old girls standing there, smiling from ear to ear, all three cats went running for cover.

Thomas hid his grin and faced his beautiful brunette-headed, green-eyed children. 'Hi, girls – ' He yelped when they threw themselves all over him, spreading hugs and kisses, clambering up his body. Four arms flung themselves around his shoulders and four icy hands encircled his neck – 'Yikes!' he cried, pulling back, trying to reach for those hands. 'It's twenty degrees outside. *Where are your gloves?*'

'Lost,' they both cried, snuggling close. Thomas had to laugh. Just like their mother, he thought, who couldn't have found a glove to save her life. But then he sucked in his breath, suffering as they pressed those icicles to his warm skin.

At a sound in the doorway, his gaze rose to the beautiful woman leaning there, watching from behind a veil of misty tears.

'I love you,' Chloe whispered, pride and joy spilling from her eyes.

Thomas smiled, knowing he had everything he could ever want – minus a few gloves.

THE EXCITING NEW NAME
IN WOMEN'S FICTION!

PLEASE HELP ME TO HELP YOU!

Dear *Scarlet* Reader,

As Editor of *Scarlet* Books I want to make sure that the books I offer you every month are up to the high standards *Scarlet* readers expect. And to do that I need to know a little more about you and your reading likes and dislikes. So please spare a few minutes to fill in the short questionnaire on the following pages and send it to me.

Looking forward to hearing from you,

Sally Cooper

Editor-in-Chief, *Scarlet*

QUESTIONNAIRE

Please tick the appropriate boxes to indicate your answers

1 Where did you get this Scarlet title?

Bought in supermarket ☐

Bought at my local bookstore ☐ Bought at chain bookstore ☐

Bought at book exchange or used bookstore ☐

Borrowed from a friend ☐

Other (please indicate) _____

2 Did you enjoy reading it?

A lot ☐ A little ☐ Not at all ☐

3 What did you particularly like about this book?

Believable characters ☐ Easy to read ☐

Good value for money ☐ Enjoyable locations ☐

Interesting story ☐ Modern setting ☐

Other _____

4 What did you particularly dislike about this book?

_____

5 Would you buy another Scarlet book?

Yes ☐ No ☐

6 What other kinds of book do you enjoy reading?

Horror ☐ Puzzle books ☐ Historical fiction ☐

General fiction ☐ Crime/Detective ☐ Cookery ☐

Other (please indicate) _____

7 Which magazines do you enjoy reading?

1. _____

2. _____

3. _____

And now a little about you –

8 How old are you?

Under 25 ☐ 25–34 ☐ 35–44 ☐

45–54 ☐ 55–64 ☐ over 65 ☐

cont.

9 What is your marital status?

Single ☐   Married/living with partner ☐

Widowed ☐   Separated/divorced ☐

10 What is your current occupation?

Employed full-time ☐   Employed part-time ☐

Student ☐   Housewife full-time ☐

Unemployed ☐   Retired ☐

11 Do you have children? If so, how many and how old are they?

_____

_____

12 What is your annual household income?

under $15,000	☐	or	£10,000	☐
$15–25,000	☐	or	£10–20,000	☐
$25–35,000	☐	or	£20–30,000	☐
$35–50,000	☐	or	£30–40,000	☐
over $50,000	☐	or	£40,000	☐

Miss/Mrs/Ms _____

Address _____

_____

_____

Thank you for completing this questionnaire. Now tear it out – put it in an envelope and send it before 31 December 1997, to:

Sally Cooper, Editor-in-Chief

USA/Can. address
SCARLET c/o London Bridge
85 River Rock Drive
Suite 202
Buffalo
NY 14207
USA

UK address/No stamp required
SCARLET
FREEPOST LON 3335
LONDON W8 4BR
Please use block capitals for address

RESWE/6/97

Scarlet **titles coming next month:**

SWEET SEDUCTION Stella Whitelaw

Giles Earl believes that Kira Reed is an important executive. She isn't! She's been involved in a serious road traffic accident and is in Barbados to recover. While she's there she decides to seek out the grandfather who's never shown the slightest interest in her. Trouble is – he's Giles's sworn enemy!

HIS FATHER'S WIFE Kay Gregory

Phaedra Pendelly has always loved Iain. But Iain hasn't been home for years. Last time he quarrelled with his father, Iain married unwisely. Now he's back to discover not only has Phaedra turned into a beauty . . . she's also his father's wife.

BETRAYED Angela Drake

Business woman Jocasta Shand is travelling with her rebellious niece. Sightseeing, Jocasta meets famous soap star Maxwell Swift – just the man to help her get even with Alexander Rivers. But Maxwell already has a connection with Alexander . . . and now Jocasta is in love with Maxwell.

OUT OF CONTROL Judy Jackson

Zara Lindsey stands to inherit a million dollars for the charity of her choice, *if* she is prepared to work with Randall Tremayne for three months. Zara can't turn down the chance to help others, but she thinks Randall's a control freak, just like the grandfather who drove her away from home ten years ago. So *how* can she have fallen in love with Randall?